Murder at Church Lodge

GREG MOSSE is a 'writer and encourager of writers' and husband of internationally bestselling author, Kate Mosse. He has lived and worked in Paris, New York, Los Angeles and Madrid as an interpreter and translator, but grew up in rural south-west Sussex. In 2014, he founded the Criterion New Writing playwriting programme in the heart of the West End and, since then, has produced more than 25 of his own plays and musicals. His creative writing workshops are highly sought after at festivals at home and abroad. His first novel, *The Coming Darkness*, was published by Moonflower in 2022. *Murder at Church Lodge* is the first in a new cosy crime series featuring amateur sleuth Maisie Cooper.

Murder at Church Lodge

Greg Mosse

HODDER

First published in Great Britain in 2023 by Hodder & Stoughton
An Hachette UK company

1

Copyright © Mosse Futures Ltd 2023

A CIP catalogue record for this title is available from the British Library

Paperback ISBN 978 1 399 71513 3
eBook ISBN 978 1 399 71514 0

Typeset in Monotype Plantin by Manipal Technologies Limited

Printed and bound in Great Britain by Clays Ltd, Elcograf S.p.A.

Hodder & Stoughton policy is to use papers that are natural, renewable and recyclable products and made from wood grown in sustainable forests. The logging and manufacturing processes are expected to conform to the environmental regulations of the country of origin.

Hodder & Stoughton Ltd
Carmelite House
50 Victoria Embankment
London EC4Y 0DZ

www.hodder.co.uk

For Finn

Cast of Characters

Maisie Cooper
Stephen Cooper, Maisie's brother
Gerald Gleeson, landlord of the Fox-in-Flight
Alicia Knight, village shopkeeper
Beatrice Otterway, Alicia's partner at the village shop
Hilary & Malcom Casemore, elderly neighbours
Sergeant Jack Wingard of the Chichester police
Inspector Barden & Detective Constable Hands, Scotland Yard
Jon Wilkes, blacksmith
Reverend Millns, vicar of Framlington
Mr Chitty, owner of Chitty's Cycles
Nicholas Chitty, his grandson
Florence Wingard, Jack Wingard's grandmother
Maurice Ryan, Stephen's solicitor
June Strickland, barmaid of the Fox-in-Flight
Mr Strickland, June's father
Police Constable Barry Goodbody of the Chichester police
Charity Clement, Maurice Ryan's assistant
Nigel Bacon, a wealthy neighbour
Mohammed As-Sabah, Stephen's old friend and army colleague
Bert Close, stable hand
Derek & Daphne Fieldhouse, landowners

PROLOGUE

It was early, soon after dawn, and the kitchen at Church Lodge was bitter. The flagstones were so cold that Stephen could feel the ache through the worn soles of his threadbare slippers. He couldn't face another cup of black tea so he was drinking cold water, fresh from the iron tap over the enormous butler sink, using a dimpled pint pot he had 'borrowed' from the pub. There was nothing to eat but a rather dreadful dehydrated ready meal.

Perhaps, he thought, a pint of water every morning will put me right.

He pulled his notebook towards him – actually a cheap school exercise book bought at Woolworths in town. He opened it in the middle and pulled out two folded sheets, eight lined pages, wondering where to begin.

The letter wouldn't take long but it wouldn't write itself.

Perhaps the best place to start would be June, the young woman he had left sleeping, upstairs in his bed, but that seemed indecorous.

If not June, then, should he begin with a sort of general apology? That, inevitably, might be appropriate, but would it get them anywhere?

How about a list of the people he had offended or tricked? No, that would take too long and, if this morning was indeed to be the first step on his journey to becoming a new and better man with an early swim in his neighbour's heated pool . . .

He sighed. It wasn't fair. Here he was, in his prime – well, thirty-seven couldn't be too far from a man's prime, surely – a man of business with stacks and stacks of ideas but no capital to put them into practice, a fair military record, a fine shot, a reasonable horseman and swordsman, a competent swimmer, a moderate runner.

Actually, he wondered, was that all still true? Were his achievements as a modern pentathlete really worth reminiscing about?

Yes, he decided. If nothing else, he was still a fine shot. In the more athletic disciplines he was not bad, perhaps, for his age. And his weight.

He frowned and squirmed on the hard kitchen chair. Under his dressing gown, his swimming trunks were much tighter than he remembered them. But, of course, it wasn't the swimming trunks that had shrunk. It was his backside that had expanded.

Stephen pulled his dressing gown tighter around his chest and told himself to focus. He had an envelope and a stamp, kindly provided by his friend Beatrice in the village shop.

'I'll put it on the tab,' she'd told him, with a wink.

Yes, everything was about to change. Today was the first day of a new regime – honesty, hard work and physical fitness. It was unfortunate that, for any of this to take effect, he would need to disappear.

He picked up his pen. It was a cheap ballpoint, also from Woolworths. He had sold the valuable fountain pen his father had saved up to buy him as a coming-of-age present.

Taking a good deep breath, sitting up a little straighter, he began. Once he had started, the words came quite easily.

Well, you won't be surprised to hear that I am writing to you because I am in trouble. I'm sorry I've waited until now to be in touch and I don't doubt you would be correct in thinking badly of me.

I could go on with the apologies but it's more useful to come to the facts. Bear with me. There's a lot to tell . . .

In the end, he filled almost all of the eight lined pages. He folded his letter and squeezed the thickish paper into his envelope. Then he crept upstairs and hid the exercise book in the bottom drawer of his wardrobe, taking care not to wake June, thinking to return for it – but not for her – before he left for good.

Back downstairs, he slipped quietly out of the front door, down the drive to a letter box, set in the stone of Church Lodge's gatepost. He dropped the envelope in the slot.

To his surprise, he could hear the sit-upon mower at the other end of the garden, in the orchard bit. Wasn't it still pretty early? How long had he hesitated over his letter?

He couldn't tell, of course. The good-quality wristwatch his mother had saved up to give him, also on his eighteenth birthday, had been sold as well.

Never mind.

It was a couple more minutes before he went back inside, just long enough for a quick chat with someone who needed putting in their place. By the time that was done, the cold dew had soaked into his tired slippers so he popped in through the kitchen door and put them on the back ledge of the Aga. It was warm from the previous evening so they would soon dry out.

He padded out barefoot across the cold damp grass, past the locked outhouse, beneath the bare branches of the winter trees to the narrow gate in the high flint wall and hesitated for a moment, feeling oddly out of breath.

Or was it dizziness brought on by lack of food?

Perhaps this wasn't such a good idea, a plunge into a chilly pool – albeit heated just enough to take the edge off – on a February morning?

Stephen looked up at the sky, grey and dispiriting, then stepped through into a private garden, enclosed by more walls and hedges and tall trees. He removed his dressing gown and approached the water. A few wraiths of steam rose from the surface. He prepared to dive. A small smile stretched his generous lips.

Soon Paris, he thought, and Casablanca – sunshine and blue skies forever.

But he was wrong. He was not alone and, in a flurry of argument and bitter recriminations he went too far. Strong arms wrapped around him, thick cloth was wrapped about his head and forced into his mouth, choking him until he was dead.

I
LUST

ONE

It was a cold Wednesday in the last week of February, towards the end of the afternoon. In the West Sussex village of Framlington, a Norman church sat squat and, if truth be told, a little neglected, at the end of a narrow lane. It had no special architectural features, no historical oddities, but it had served sixty generations of local people in their weekly devotions and important life-changing ceremonies. Their births, marriages and deaths – hatch, match and despatch.

Today was despatch.

The service of commemoration was ended, the modest congregation making their way outside in their decent black for mourning, adjusting their scarves and gloves, preparing their words of condolence. The grass between the gravestones was wet, the overnight frost having melted to unhealthy damp.

Maisie Cooper went ahead and took up a position by the lychgate. At five-foot-eight, she had a slim figure, short curly hair, good complexion, large brown eyes, and was dressed in her light-blue travelling clothes because her brother's death had come as a surprise.

The first mourner approached, a fat man in grey flannel trousers, his eyes full of sympathy. It was the man who ran the pub. As he spoke, his face assumed a quizzical expression. Maisie knew what he wanted to know. She wanted to know herself.

How had it happened?

The publican gave her a sad smile.

'Everything will be ready when you're ready, Miss Cooper,' he said. 'I'll go and put out the sandwiches and that.'

Halfway along the path, the two ladies who ran the village shop were talking to anyone who would listen about what a lovely man Stephen had been. They were an unusual couple, not old themselves but dressed in old-fashioned clothes. Could Stephen possibly have been friends with them, one with grey hair pulled back in a ponytail from her narrow face, the other smiley and hearty-looking? What might they have had in common?

Another two mourners approached, the Casemores, an elderly woman with arthritis twisting her fingers and her vague husband. Maisie did her conversational duty with her mind elsewhere. In reality, she was thinking about the uniformed police officer standing in the shadows beneath the yew tree, his helmet under his arm, an expression of bland interest on his face. He looked about her age, thirty-four or thirty-five. He hadn't come close, hadn't spoken to her. Even now, he kept his distance, and she only caught glimpses of him between the gravestones, between the people, solitary and watchful.

She trusted him about as much as she trusted the two men in gaberdine mackintoshes, standing a little to one side, watching everyone with undisguised interest. They were representatives of Special Branch and would be pleased, they'd told her before the service, 'to have a word'.

Maisie had no idea if their interest was protective or suspicious, wary or benign.

The Casemores moved on and there, behind them, was Jon Wilkes, the blacksmith, a heavily built man whose fingernails looked as though they were probably never quite clean. His hands were scarred with scorches and burns and his 'best suit' bore marks of the forge – smuts of soot and holes made by sparks. He wore it with the air of a man who wasn't sure why he had bothered, given he would very soon take it off again. Maisie remembered him from when she was a girl – a much younger man in a heavy leather apron, taking no mischief from the horses or their owners. He had a loud voice, as if he was hard of hearing.

'I liked your brother,' said Jon. 'He took an interest in things but he weren't inquisitive. I'm sorry he's left you to clear up after him.'

Maisie was about to say 'thank you' or 'you're very kind' or 'he would be glad to hear you say so' or one of the other commonplace replies that came jostling into her mind. He stopped her by putting a second calloused hand over hers.

'Nay, you needn't say anything back. Keep your peace.'

She smiled gratefully and he walked away. There was a lull. She saw the Special Branch men were discussing something in whispers.

Maisie didn't think she could cope with their questions right now. She didn't believe she had to. She wasn't under arrest, was she? She certainly hadn't done anything wrong. As far as she knew, Stephen had done nothing wrong. But that was the problem. She couldn't be entirely sure.

Half a dozen more mourners filed past, then the two shopkeepers were approaching, almost the last.

'My dear Miss Cooper,' said the hearty-looking one. 'My name is Beatrice—'

'Thank you so much for coming,' Maisie said.

The woman would have replied had Maisie given her the chance, but she needed solitude and quiet, walking away up the path, between the mossy gravestones, past the yew tree and the uniformed officer and in through the south door of the church.

Inside, the low light of the February sun was casting beautiful patterns through the stained-glass windows. The pale pillars of limestone provided the perfect medium to receive their organic pigments of green and blue and red. Even the darker flagstones beneath her feet were coloured with smudges of the old Christian stories, told by the coloured glass.

There was the Good Samaritan, someone whose generosity Stephen might very well have been happy to take advantage of. Next to it was the wedding at Cana, a 'holy estate' that her brother had steadfastly avoided. And turning water into wine? No, despite his easy confidence and charisma, he was much more likely to mess things up and turn the wine into water . . .

Had been more likely. Not any more. He was gone.

Maisie stood for a moment at the bottom of the aisle by the font. This was the church in which she and her brother had been confirmed, where they had sung, quite reluctantly, in the village choir, edging out of the stalls to take communion in company with the rest of the devout.

Up by the altar was the trestle table, covered with a white tablecloth. Maisie approached the display. There was no coffin because the post-mortem wasn't yet complete. The vicar, Reverend Millns, had led a simple ceremony of commemoration, with the cremation set for three days' time on Saturday. But there seemed to have been some kind of competition between the neighbours to provide the most impressive show: carnations, chrysanthemums and lilies, some hybridised into unlikely, unnatural colours. Someone had offered half a dozen yellow roses.

Almost smothered by the shop-bought blooms was a posy of wild flowers – no easy task in February. Maisie had been brought up in the country and she recognised daphne, a sweet-smelling flower with pink petals and dark-green waxy leaves. There were also a few cyclamens and snowdrops. The effect was charming and unobtrusive, a note of honest emotion in the midst of ostentatious display.

The wild-flower posy made her think about the coffin she had chosen for Saturday, the wood stained a dark red, in imitation of mahogany. She had asked the undertaker if it were possible to leave the wood untreated.

'Oh no, Miss Cooper.'

'Why not?' she had asked, wondering if it might be for some technical reason.

'We don't have any items in untreated wood,' the undertaker had told her. 'It wouldn't look proper. Why, it would seem as if no trouble had been taken. Not to put too fine a point on it, like a pauper's burial, and he wasn't a poor man, was he, your brother?'

Maisie had felt the undertaker's eye appraising her, as he had doubtless appraised many previous customers. She'd found the experience uncomfortable.

'Fine, the red-stained deal.'

'Very good,' he had replied, as if she had passed a test.

The memory faded as Maisie walked up the aisle and rested her fingertips on a corner of the trestle table.

'Goodbye, Stephen,' she murmured.

The was a noise from behind her and Maisie withdrew her hand as if scalded.

'The verger will set the floral tributes aside for Saturday.'

Maisie turned to look. It was Reverend Millns, a bland, uninspiring man with an unfortunate moustache and nicotine stains on his fingers. Did he want her to leave? Was he preparing another service?

'Thank you.'

'Come along then,' he said to someone lurking outside the door.

The verger bustled in and began removing the flowers, taking them away to the vestry. Last of all, the posy of winter flowers fell from the table, landing on the flagstones with a soft sound. They were wrapped what looked like writing paper.

'Just a minute.'

Maisie darted forward and saved the posy from the verger's heavy feet. The vicar gave her a doubtful glance and the two men went outside.

But for her, the church was now empty and, for the first time in her life, Maisie realised she was alone. She had no surviving parent, no sibling, no husband and no child, just an aunt who she hadn't seen since she was tiny. There was nothing and no one to whom she was tethered or beholden.

She sat down in the front pew. She could walk away from the church and churchyard, out into a new life, and who could stop her? She could emigrate to Australia like the 'ten-pound Poms', or find a whitewashed villa on the Costa Brava. Wasn't that what people did these days? Hadn't she fled her own life once before, packed up her things and started again, not long after her parents' deaths ten years ago?

But, of course, she wouldn't do anything like that. At least, not yet. There was probate and solicitors and all the rest of it. There was the local policeman, whoever he was, and Special Branch. And, before all that could be resolved, there was the wake at the local pub, the Fox-in-Flight – more condolences, more sympathy, the inevitable glances of curiosity, the leading questions.

'Had you heard from him lately, Miss Cooper?'

'Was he not a strong swimmer?'

'What do the police want?'

Maisie supposed she would be told, in the fullness of time, how it was that Stephen had managed to drown, if it was a heart attack or a stroke or something. She supposed a post-mortem examination was being carried out, that its results would soon be available.

Maisie raised the posy to her face, smelling the fresh scent of the modest blooms. There was a fragrance of damp soil, too; the paper it was wrapped in a little moist.

Yes, definitely writing paper, she thought. From a pad of Basildon Bond, perhaps? It seemed to have some writing on the inside.

She unwrapped the posy and the flowers stayed bunched together, tied with a piece of string. She held the paper at an angle to catch the light. Written upon it were six lines of poetry in a swirly, flowing hand. Did she recognise them? She thought she did, though she couldn't remember where from.

> *The secret things of the grave are there,*
> *Where all but this frame must surely be,*
> *Though the fine-wrought eye and the wondrous ear*
> *No longer will live to hear or to see*
> *All that is great and all that is strange*
> *In the boundless realm of unending change.*

For a few seconds, Maisie held her breath. The church was very quiet. The low February sun dipped beyond the yew tree and left the stained-glass windows. The light became flat and grey.

She read the lines a second time and then, without thinking what she was doing, she screwed the scrap of paper into a ball inside her fist.

Yes, she wondered, but what were the 'secret things of the grave'?

Two

Sergeant Jack Wingard of the Chichester police left the cold churchyard while the bereaved sister was in the church, driving away in his up-to-date white Ford Zephyr, his mind busy.

There was no need for the intervention of the men from Special Branch. Everything was in hand, whatever the bishop might think. Important as it might be to identify the culprit – and Jack had already solved that riddle – the crucial thing was the recovery of the stolen items. It wasn't just a question of their monetary value, but also their historical importance – in particular, a sumptuously illuminated and illustrated devotional book. Created in the early sixteenth century, it was an ecclesiastical commentary on the 'seven deadly sins' and the 'seven holy virtues'.

Of course, as a policeman, Jack was more often called upon to address sin rather than virtue.

He had never held the book in his hands but he knew it well from its position in the crypt of the cathedral, under glass, resting on a cushion, open at a double-page racily entitled 'Lust', gorgeously decorated with ancient inks and gold leaf, illustrating carnal desire.

Which, in a way, brought him on to a separate strand of reflections, this time an issue not exactly related to police business and a question, he would argue, of love, not lust.

Maisie Cooper.

Might he have approached and spoken to her? He wished he had. But at a commemoration service for her disreputable brother?

No, of course not.

He slowed as he arrived in Chichester and waited, his indicator noisily blinking, for the Framlington bus – a single-decker Southdown service in bottle green with cream trim – to pass in the other direction. He took the right turn into Parklands, a suburban street of pleasant bungalows on the edge of town. He parked in front of a low pink house with a well-tended front garden of woody shrubs. His grandmother, with whom he lived, was doing some pruning, wearing thick gloves to protect her from the spines of the pyracantha, the 'firethorn'. Her white hair made her look older than her sixty-eight years.

He got out, went to meet her and picked up her trug.

'I think we're back in charge,' she said, appraising her work.

'Good. At least someone is.'

'What do you mean?' she asked.

'Nothing.'

'Don't be sullen. What happened?'

'Like a fool, I stood under the yew tree and watched.'

'You didn't approach her?'

'How could I? It wouldn't have been right.'

'Did she see you there? Did she recognise you?'

Sergeant Jack Wingard frowned and shook his handsome head.

'She didn't know me from Adam.'

THREE

Maisie walked quickly back to Church Lodge, the ugly, baggy house where Stephen had lived. It was on the way to the pub in any case.

She crunched up the gravel drive, unlocked the front door, skipped across the chequerboard hallway and along the dark corridor under the sweeping staircase to the kitchen. She put the posy and screwed-up verse of poetry on the kitchen table, wondering once more what the lines might mean. She drank half a pint of water from a dimpled pint pot at the sink, asking herself what had possessed Stephen to choose to live here. Had he liked the frigid rooms, the antiquated plumbing?

She went back out. The pub was only a hundred yards away, past the little cottages where the arthritic Mrs Casemore and her vague husband lived, past the shop owned by the hearty-looking Beatrice and her friend with the grey ponytail, but on the opposite side of the road. Reverend Millns was on his way in, having changed out of his ecclesiastical robes, smoking a crafty cigarette. For want of anything better to say, Maisie asked him if the owners of the big house, Framlington Manor, had been present in the churchyard.

'He was not in attendance.'

'Is it still the Fieldhouse family?'

'Oh yes.'

'Is there a Mrs Fieldhouse?'

'Yes, his wife, the power behind the throne,' he replied with a rather acid tone.

'And she wasn't there either?'

'You wouldn't expect to see her in the graveyard, would you? Very difficult.'

Maisie was about to enquire why it would be 'very difficult' when he trod on his cigarette stub, held open the door and she was caught up in another round of sympathy and condolences.

***

Maisie did her best but the reception turned out to be at least as depressing as she had feared. After enduring it for an hour, she felt she couldn't take it any longer, but also knew she was obliged to be the last to leave.

She took a break, standing to one side, watching Jon Wilkes, the blacksmith. He had a paper plate in his hand and was piling it up with one of everything from the buffet – egg and salad cream sandwiches, cheese-and-pineapple toothpicks, a slice of bacon flan, a piece of McVitie's ginger cake and an overcooked sausage. Perhaps he felt her gaze upon him, for he looked up and gave her a conspiratorial grin.

'I prefer to eat on my own,' he told her, his voice – as usual – unnecessarily loud. 'Because of my denture. You don't mind if I take my plate with me?' He waved his spare hand at six dispiriting feet of cold cuts, sandwiches and cakes. 'Gerald Gleeson's done you proud, though.'

I suppose so, thought Maisie.

'There's no need to stay,' she told him.

Jon looked round the room, appraisingly.

'There's no one here I would call friends of yours, though you were local. Course I'm an old man now but I remember you as a bonny child who loved the horses. Paris, is it?'

He put a piece of ginger cake in his mouth, an inquisitive look in his eye. Maisie turned the question back at him.

'Did you see Stephen often?' she asked.

'He was friendly enough, passing the time of day. Old Nige Bacon, his neighbour, reckoned to be his bosom pal, but you can't be friendly with a man who mistreats his own horse, can you? Now then, you should come to the forge and we'll have a chat.'

Maisie smiled. It would be pleasant to see the inside of the forge after so many years.

'I think we're winding down, Jon. The pub will have to set up for the evening soon. Don't feel you have to stay to the bitter end.'

She watched him move the ginger cake from side to side in his mouth with his tongue, his lips not quite closed. He put a sooty finger in his mouth to unstick it from between his denture.

'If the mood takes you, you know where to find me,' he told her. 'He knew horses. That would be the army and his pentathlon, would it?'

Maisie smiled, unhappily. Here was someone who, in a way, knew Stephen better than she did – at least, knew the person her brother had become, the man she had seldom seen since she abandoned her life in England and fled to Paris, leaving everything behind.

'Thank you, Jon. Yes, he loved horses,' she said politely, and moved away.

As she neared the bar, the publican offered her a glass of warm white wine. She refused and watched him serve Jon Wilkes a pint of Harvey's Sussex stout. The blacksmith had evidently changed his mind about leaving and sat down, taking a good swig, swishing it like mouthwash, a look of contentment in his dark eyes.

What had he meant, that these people weren't her friends?

Well, she reflected, just that. Her friends were in Paris, where she lived. It was a miracle, she thought, the coincidence of Stephen suddenly being in touch with her just before his untimely death. She hadn't set foot in England for years.

The idea made her uneasy. There was more to it than that, wasn't there? Some kind of police investigation, for a start, involving Special Branch. What did they want? She didn't dare imagine.

But if Stephen's phone call to her Paris apartment hadn't been a coincidence, what had it been?

A cry for help?

A warning?

Maisie sighed. She hadn't even heard his voice. Her flat-mate, Sophie, had taken a message. Otherwise, she would have pressed him for more details.

She did another circuit of the Fox-in-Flight. Everyone seemed happy – at least, as happy as one is allowed to be at a wake. They weren't just there for the free food and drink. She drifted in and out of conversations about, well, the same as every other day: the weather, gossip, politics, holidays, all the rest of it.

The rather frail elderly Casemores with matching white hair – one arthritic, one vague – were gently arguing about whether they needed a new stair carpet. They had moved into the village after she had left. Maisie felt she rather liked them.

'It is quite worn through,' Mrs Casemore said to her husband, shaking her head. 'What will people think?'

'It will see us out, dear,' he replied.

'In any case, it's really the responsibility of the landlord, wouldn't you say?'

He shook his head sadly. 'I don't think that's a fight we are likely to win.'

A boy of about twelve was eating his sandwiches in front of the fire, his face red. He had that slight air of undernourishment proper to his age. He would fill out in time, Maisie supposed, with muscle or with fat.

An older man with steel-grey hair held flat with Brylcreem advised the boy to move away from the flames. It gave Maisie a jolt to realise that she recognised the man from when she had been twelve herself – Mr Chitty, from the bike shop on North Street in Chichester.

'Yes, Grandpa,' the boy begrudgingly replied.

She was about to speak to Mr Chitty when she heard Reverend Millns talking about Stephen. She turned to see him smoothing his unfortunate moustache and hoped he was saying something charitable, out of duty if nothing else. But no, he was discussing the redevelopment of Stephen's house, Church Lodge, and the possibility of it being divided into flats.

'The location is exceptional, the grounds extensive. Further construction might be undertaken. There is no need for someone to live in a park, is there?'

The vicar gave a spiteful emphasis to the word 'park', as a class warrior might refer with contempt to 'the opera'. Then he saw her out of the corner of his eye and Maisie stood in silence as he delivered a tepid wave of professional condolences. She let it wash over her, wishing she felt more able to engage with these mostly friendly strangers.

She couldn't. She was alienated by grief.

She did two more circuits and watched Jon reverse out of the front door, careful not to dislodge any of the booty from his paper plate. Through the window she saw him weave between the parked cars – two Rovers, an Austin and a Triumph Herald – and disappear. With his departure, there were only six people left, two of whom were working and another two of whom were the Special Branch officers.

She followed Jon outside and sat down on a damp bench underneath the saloon bar window, grateful for the fresh air, glad to be alone – if only for a moment.

FOUR

It was a chilly evening. The sun had gone and there was already a cold sheen of condensation forming on the windscreens of the cars. A tractor went past, pulling a cartload of straw bales, probably delivering to the stables on the edge of the village. The exhaust sent up clouds of vapour and that particular sooty smoke typical of burning agricultural red diesel.

Then, as the air cleared and the sound faded, there was a moment of stillness and quiet, as if some higher power had organised a lull, a period of reflection and contemplation. No cars, no vans, no voices, no passing pedestrians. Even the light went off in the window behind her.

Mistake, mistake, mistake, thought Maisie. Allowing a public service. Holding a reception. But, above all, leaving all her friends in Paris – her lovely flatmate Sophie, and the rather foppish man who lived downstairs who hadn't yet plucked up the courage to ask Maisie out. And for why? Because Stephen had, almost posthumously as it turned out, asked her to come and see him. And why should this simple request have been so, well, un-refusable?

That was easy. Because that was just how it was. He was her brother – her older brother – and she had been in the habit of doing his bidding since, well, forever.

When would that have started? Probably around three or four years old. The fact she was now thirty-four years old did not change all that.

She had a brief, vivid flashback to the previous Sunday morning, the moment when, arriving at the railway station in

Chichester, instead of Stephen she had been met by a heavily built man with a rich voice and expressive hands.

'Good morning, Miss Cooper. My name is Ryan, Maurice Ryan. I'm Stephen's solicitor. He asked me to meet you . . .'

At that point, neither of them had known that Stephen was dead.

She shivered and wondered what her French friends were doing just then. Were the first signs of 'Paris in springtime' about to reveal themselves – blossom on the cherry trees, daffodils in the public gardens? Were people still mourning the death of Jim Morrison? Would she ever drive the new Renault 5 that she had been lusting after ever since she saw it announced in the press? Was it true that President Pompidou would soon approve the UK joining the Common Market?

'Excuse me, miss. Would now be a convenient time for us to have a word? I think all your guests are gone.'

It was the older of the two Special Branch officers. She knew they were called Hands and Barden, but she couldn't remember which was which. They loomed over her in the gloom.

Why was it so dark? Were there no street lamps?

'Yes, of course.'

'It's a raw night. Could we go back to your brother's mansion?'

'Mansion?' said Maisie, surprised. 'I don't think that's what it is.'

'To Church Lodge, then.'

'Of course. If you wish.'

Maisie led them across the road and along the narrow pavement to the top of Church Lane. They crunched up the untidy gravel drive to the front door. The enormous key turned easily in the lock. She pushed it open and stepped back to let the two officers enter.

'After you,' murmured the older one. 'Ladies first.'

'Let me just put on the lights.'

She crossed the chequerboard hallway and flicked the switch. Nothing.

'Power cut,' he said, matter-of-factly.

'Didn't you notice the lights went out at the pub?' asked the younger one.

'No, I didn't. Has that started already?' She had read about the United Kingdom's strikes and shortages in the French newspapers. 'Wait here. There are candles in the kitchen.'

She went along down the dark corridor beneath the sweep of the staircase. The kitchen was a frigid room in the north-east corner of the house with a stone floor and a wooden drying rack on a pulley in the ceiling. The post and the scrunched-up poem were in the middle of the enormous rustic table. In the drawer she found string, used paper bags, cutlery and old-fashioned utensils, but no candles. Where had she seen them?

Her eyes began to adjust to the gloom. There they were, next to a pair of threadbare slippers on the ledge at the back of the cold Aga. It was a box of six from Messam's hardware shop on East Street, alongside a packet of Swan Vesta matches. She went back to the hall and, to her surprise, found it partly lit by a friendly blaze burning in the grate.

'The fire was all laid in. I just put my lighter to it,' said the senior man, the inspector. 'Now, might I ask, are you aware of this?'

He unfolded a front page torn from the local paper, the *Chichester Observer*. Had he found it in the kindling basket? The headline was a robbery. Someone had stolen some historic jewellery and an extremely valuable illuminated devotional book from the crypt of Chichester Cathedral.

'Very shocking,' he said, 'to steal from the house of God. I wish I had a photograph to show you the little book. I'm told it's calf leather and, of course, all the pigments and dyes are natural and found locally – even the gold leaf from some-where in Hampshire.'

'Why are you telling me this?'

'Perhaps someone mentioned it at the wake this after-noon? There's not a great deal of crime in this part of the world. You know how people like to gossip.'

'No, no one has,' she said shortly. She didn't like gossip.

'It's from two weeks ago. You would have still been in France?'

'That's right.'

He left a pause, inviting her to elaborate. Maisie waited him out.

'Shall we perhaps fetch ourselves some chairs?' he sug-gested, looking annoyed. 'You might be more comfortable sitting down.'

'No,' said Maisie, 'I think you can ask me your questions as we are. This will do very well.'

She watched the two policemen exchange a glance, the younger one asking the older a question with his eyes. Instead of putting the page of the newspaper in the basket with the kindling, the older man folded it carefully and slipped it into his jacket pocket.

Maisie found herself becoming irritated. What had this to do with Stephen? What were they fishing for?

'In fact,' she insisted, 'will you tell me your names again, please? I would like to write them down.'

'I'm Inspector Barden, miss, and this is Detective Constable Hands.'

The inspector was taller and older, with dark hair slicked back from his forehead with Brylcreem, like Mr Chitty. The younger man, Hands, had a short back and sides and oily skin, disfigured with acne. Maisie took her diary out of her handbag and made a show of writing down their names.

'And you are from . . . ?'

'Do you mean which division, miss?' asked Barden.

'Yes, I mean, I know you are Special Branch and I have a vague idea what that means – organised crime and international things, I suppose – but what police station? And do you have serial numbers or are you just known by your ranks?'

'Now why would you want to know all that?' asked Detective Constable Hands condescendingly.

Maisie fought back. 'I will thank you not to talk down to me. I don't believe I have done anything wrong.'

The detective constable blushed. Even by firelight she could see.

'No, Miss Cooper,' he said. 'I beg your pardon.'

'This is a very unsatisfactory situation, Miss Cooper,' interrupted Inspector Barden, sadly shaking his head. 'You must see that.'

'Must I?'

'Here's your brother who, I suppose you must be beginning to suspect, may have been involved in something I'm not at liberty to disclose. He dies suddenly, poor man. Was there an accident or illness behind it? We're not yet certain.'

'The post-mortem examination will tell us?'

'It will,' he agreed. 'But here's the thing. Mr Cooper died on the Saturday morning and, not long after this tragic event, at almost precisely the same time, in fact, his sister arrives in Chichester from Paris, abandoning her job, her friends, and who knows, her pets and houseplants.' He smiled. Maisie thought he was trying to defuse the tension. 'And all this is apparently a coincidence, despite you and Mr Cooper having not met for, as far as we can ascertain . . . How many years, Hands?'

The younger man's acned face was still red from being told off.

'Seven years, sir.'

'Ascertain how?' said Maisie.

'From customs and passport control, Miss Cooper.'
Barden beamed.

Of course, thought Maisie.

'Stephen rang me,' she told them, 'and left a message saying he would like to see me. I was owed some holiday, so I came.'

'Like it in Paris, do you?'

'I do, but shall we keep to the point?'

'Just as you wish, Miss Cooper,' said Barden. 'So, yes, seven years. But you arrived just an hour or two too late, as it were. Now, that seems to us a peculiar sequence of events and I'm sure you will agree that it is quite normal for us to wish to ask one or two innocent questions about how these circumstances all fit together?'

Maisie waited a moment, wondering to herself what it was that Stephen could have done to excite the interest of Special Branch. Something big, surely? Could it be to do with his military background or his connections in the Arab world? That would explain why Special Branch were interested.

'I will answer your questions, Inspector Barden, if you answer mine.'

'Now then, Miss Cooper,' said Barden, shaking his head, 'that isn't how these sorts of things work at all.'

Maisie had lost all patience with Barden's avuncular approach. She wasn't sure he was an enemy, but he certainly wasn't a friend either. 'I suppose it isn't.'

'So, to begin—'

'No, Inspector. I mean I understand that this isn't how you expect "these sorts of things" to work. In this case, though, you'll have to make an exception.'

FIVE

In the end, Maisie allowed Hands – the junior officer – to go and fetch three upright chairs.

'Be careful,' she called after him into the gloomy dining room. 'There's a racing bike just inside the door.'

Hands retuned without mishap and arranged the chairs facing the fire while Inspector Barden expertly stoked it, creating a wigwam out of some mossy logs. Maisie thought they were probably well-seasoned prunings from the mature fruit trees in the large garden of Church Lodge. They burnt up well.

The inspector sat down and glanced around the hallway. By the light of the candles, she saw his practised eye taking in the chandelier with only three bulbs out of a dozen sockets, the lack of curtains on the double-height windows, the spiders' webs on the cornices and the dust and fluff where the chequerboard tiles met the tall skirting boards.

'Was your brother short of money?' said Barden abruptly.

'I wouldn't know,' Maisie replied.

'And you?' Barden mused. 'Would you call yourself well off?'

'I have another question of my own,' said Maisie. She thought she had an idea why Special Branch would be so interested in Stephen's death. Surely they wouldn't have come all the way to Sussex to investigate a petty theft – albeit one from the cathedral. 'Is it international? Is it about oil?'

'Now, why would you ask that?'

'Because he served in the Gulf. Because he could speak Arabic.'

'You are a very intelligent woman,' said the inspector, nodding.

'That's where the major oil producers are these days, aren't they?'

'And how would your brother be able to make a contribution to all that?'

'I don't know – diplomacy, business negotiations? I suppose it must be useful for someone to be able to converse as an equal.'

'And he could converse as an equal, could he?'

'Oh, yes.'

'And why was that?'

Maisie considered for a moment. Was she under any compulsion to tell him? She decided that there was no reason why she shouldn't.

'Stephen joined the army in 1952, straight from school. His regiment was involved in British mandate operations in the Middle East. He was three years older than me and already spoke French. That was where he began to pick up Arabic. He became friends with another junior officer who was originally from Kuwait, a member of the ruling family, I believe. Later on, Stephen was posted to Kuwait just before independence. That helped him a lot.'

'Can you give us the name of his friend?'

'It may come back to me,' Maisie prevaricated. 'It was a long time ago.'

'I see.' Barden and Hands exchanged a glance. 'Would you tell us a little more?'

'About Stephen?'

'If you wouldn't mind. It helps to have a complete picture of the man and you are his closest relative.'

Yes, thought Maisie. *I realise that.*

28

'Well,' she said, 'it is incomprehensible to me that he should drown without being taken ill, in some way. As well as being a gifted linguist, he was an accomplished athlete.'

'He competed at the Melbourne Olympic Games of 1956,' said Hands, 'in the modern pentathlon?'

'If you know, why do you ask?'

Inspector Barden did his best to smile. 'The detective constable was just letting you know that we haven't been allowing the grass to grow under our feet. Now, I did wonder – if you will forgive the digression – why would it be called modern?'

'To distinguish it from the classical pentathlon.'

'That would be the Greek version?'

'The ancient Greek version, yes – long jump, javelin, discus, running and wrestling.'

'Whereas the modern pentathlon comprises . . . ?'

'Fencing, swimming, horse riding, shooting, running.'

'The attributes of the perfect soldier, wouldn't you say – cunning, daring, decisive?'

'A kind of old-fashioned view of the perfect soldier, but yes, that is the idea.'

Maisie thought again of a few of the things that some of the villagers had said to her in the hours leading up to the church service – about how exciting it was to have someone like Stephen in their midst. Old Mrs Casemore had compared him to James Bond 'on the television'. Someone else, the publican she thought, said he was 'like a character out of a film'. She wondered if Stephen had deliberately nurtured the idea that he was a kind of playboy-spy. She wouldn't put it past him.

She realised she had stopped listening and that Barden was asking her something else.

'What was that?'

'I was saying, they sound like expensive hobbies, fencing and horse riding. Officer-class hobbies, if I might say so.'

'If you like.'

'How would he have been able to afford that?'

'Well, we both attended a small private school with stables and an old-fashioned curriculum. Then, he was in the army and competed in his regiment's colours.'

'Yes, I see that. But today? Did he keep up the horse riding, for example?'

'I don't know.'

Maisie stood up, annoyed at being asked questions she couldn't answer, wishing she had known her brother better. She was feeling stiff from standing around in the cold in the churchyard, sitting outside the pub. She pulled her chair a little closer to the hearth and added two more logs.

'You attended what you call a "small private school", but you're not from money, either of you – as a family, I mean.'

Maisie sighed.

'Our parents were working people. But our aunt, our mother's sister, married into money. She took an interest in our upbringings.'

'Would you tell Sergeant Hands her name and address?'

'I can't. She and my mother became estranged when I was very little. I don't even know her married name.'

Saying it, Maisie realised how odd it sounded, but that was what her parents had told her.

'How mysterious,' said Barden, lightly. 'And she provided the funds to send you away to school, and all that.'

'We were weekly boarders just a few miles away from our small red-brick council house in this very village. We weren't Empire children sent home from colonial offices in the antipodes, so—'

Maisie stopped herself, wondering why she was always so defensive of their parents' decision to send them to Westbrook College. She was aware that Barden was looking at her appraisingly once more. By pulling closer to the fire, she had lit herself more brightly, while he remained in shadow.

'Sir?'

'Yes, what is it, Hands?' said the inspector shortly.

'You remember there was a reduced service on the train, sir? We don't have very much time if we're to make the last connection.'

Barden frowned and checked his watch.

'No, I don't suppose we do.' He stood up. 'That will be all for today, Miss Cooper. It is "miss", isn't it? You have never married?'

'Answer me this, first, and I'll tell you. Do you have suspicions against Stephen? Criminal suspicions? Is that what this is all about?'

'I can't discuss suspicions, only facts.'

'That doesn't answer my question.'

'Among the things I don't know, miss, is this: I haven't discovered why you seem unwilling to co-operate with our inquiries.'

'Because you have given no justification for your questions. Perhaps you would prefer me to engage a lawyer to attend our next meeting, if there is to be a next meeting?'

'Oh, yes, there will be. You can be quite sure of that.'

Frustrated with herself for beginning to lose her temper, Maisie stood up and went to the door, pulling it wide. The power cut was still in progress. There was no glow of electric light in the inky-blue sky. The stars were bright pinpricks of white. A wave of cold air came rolling into the hallway, undoing all the good work done by their small fire.

The two policemen left without another word and she watched them walk away in step, down the overgrown gravel drive and back towards the pub where, she supposed, they must have a taxi waiting to take them to the station.

She heard a rustle in the undergrowth beneath a large rho-dodendron bush. What was it? A fox or a hedgehog?

She felt a frisson of anxiety, as if she was being watched. She went back inside, shut the door and locked it, giving it a little push. It still moved slightly within its frame, allowing a cold draught from either edge.

She abandoned the hallway and returned to the kitchen. She took off her shoes and put on the slippers she had seen on the back ledge of the Aga. They were much too big and they made her think of playing dress-up with Stephen when they were little in the red-brick council house on the edge of the village. Inevitably, the memories saddened her.

Despite this, she was glad, finally, to be alone. Until, that is, she heard another noise from the garden – the call of a vixen, harsh and unpleasant, uncannily like that of a fright-ened child.

SIX

On the night of Wednesday into Thursday, Maisie slept badly – in the spare bedroom, not Stephen's own – in sheets that felt damp, though she didn't think they really were. Or perhaps it was because of the elderly feather-filled mattress that must have been there when Stephen bought the place? Before getting into bed, she had tried to even out the stuffing, but it was too heavy for one person alone, so she ended up sleeping in the same dent that strangers had used before her.

How many bodies had lain there over the years, leaving behind a miasma of their sweat and stress and dreams?

As often happens when one sleeps badly, the hours just before Maisie woke were coloured by extraordinary nightmares – of running and hiding, chasing and fighting and a wild animal emerging from the rhododendron bushes. At the end of one of these subconscious adventures, she emerged sufficiently from sleep to take herself in hand and get out of bed.

The sun had been up for a little while and shone brightly through the uncurtained windows. The air was chilly and she was glad she had the threadbare slippers to wear on her way to the bathroom.

Despite the cold of the house and the power cut, the water from the tap was warm. She supposed there was a back boiler behind the fireplace in the hall, and it had retained some of its heat overnight.

She washed thoroughly, standing at the basin, and put on clean clothes from her small travel suitcase before going downstairs. She was very hungry, having eaten nothing at the wake and or after the Special Branch officers had left. She doubled back along the corridor, under the sweeping staircase, to the kitchen, taking the basket of kindling with her from the hall.

Mentally crossing her fingers, she flicked the light switch. To her relief, the power cut was over and the meagre sixty-watt bulb over the rustic table came on. Her eye alighted on the hand-made posy of wild flowers and the scrunched-up ball of writing paper.

I'll think about that later, she decided, and hid both things away in the drawer with a miscellany of old-fashioned utensils.

She put the whistling kettle onto one of the electric stove rings with just enough water for a single cup. From a rectangular tea caddy with an oriental design – an aristocratic man in traditional dress, sitting beneath the spreading branches of an ornamental cherry tree – she shook two generous spoonfuls of loose tea into a small teapot. The kettle whistled and she poured the hot water onto the leaves and left them to steep.

Feeling a need for fresh air, she opened the back door – the key was in the lock – being careful not to rub up against the coal scuttle. She looked out at the lawn and the orchard beyond. The fruit trees – apples, pears and cherries – looked skeletal without their leaves. The grass was covered with a light frost, just beginning to melt. The world smelt clean and alive. Beyond the orchard wall, a faint mist was rising.

Maisie strained her tea and drank it black, without sugar, on the doorstep. She watched a robin turning over dead leaves, its quick eyes and beak searching for insects. The sight reminded her of how hungry she was.

She finished her tea and went to look in the food pantry, a cupboard set in the north wall to keeps things cool. She found a Vesta dehydrated ready meal whose packaging appeared sound. Beef curry. She read the instructions, how to combine the two sachets, one of rice, the other of dried meat and vegetables.

What time was it? She checked her watch. Could she really eat a beef curry at eight-thirty in the morning?

At the back of the Aga, where the previous evening she had found the candles, was a bottle of sunflower oil. A large frying pan was lying on the draining board. Nothing else was needed, only water.

She rinsed the frying pan, put it on the ring and gently fried the packet of rice. As it changed colour, she added three-quarters of a pint of water and the contents of the other sachet – grey, unappetising lumps of dried beef, spices, herbs, finely diced vegetables – and brought it all to a simmer.

Against all expectations, within five minutes it began to smell quite appetising. The grey pallor left it and the curry began to look, if not *cordon bleu*, at least something like the image on the packet.

She felt herself becoming impatient. Finally, all the water had been absorbed and it was – what was the word? – reconstituted. She ate it from the frying pan itself, sitting on a tea towel on the back step.

The curry was both cloying and delicious, warming her from within. She felt her hunger abate and decided it might be fun to go to the supermarket and buy half a dozen packets to take back with her to Paris as tongue-in-cheek gifts for her friends. Perhaps they would organise an ironic dehydrated-dinner party?

But what would they drink? Red wine? White?

No, lager, that would be better. Perhaps she would ask her flatmate Sophie to invite their languid neighbour from downstairs.

Just as she was scraping up the final spoonful, she heard a banging on the front door – urgent, insistent. Perhaps even angry.

She put the pan in the sink and followed the noise along the kitchen corridor to the hall. Where had she left the keys? Oh, yes, there on the stone mantelpiece. She put the heavy iron one in the lock and hesitated. Through the semi-obscured glass, she could see the figure outside.

It was a woman with bleached-blond hair sculpted in unbecoming curls, like a teenager aping her mother's or even her grandmother's style. She wore a minidress in a colour somewhere between orange and pink. Over the top, she had pulled on a man's cardigan in chocolate brown wool. She seemed tall, but that was because of the high heels on her knee-length, white plastic boots.

Maisie turned the key and opened the door just enough not to appear suspicious or rude.

'So,' said the woman, truculently.

'Yes?' said Maisie.

'That's what you look like. I hope you're pleased with yourself.'

The woman's voice was simultaneously aggressive and hurt, like a child denied something they had been promised. How old was she – twenty-five, twenty-six?

'I don't understand,' said Maisie, with an attempt at lightness. 'Why should I be pleased with myself? What is it I'm supposed to have done?'

'How long have you been here? Where did he used to see you? In Chichester, was it?'

'When you say "he"?' asked Maisie, confused.

'Who do you think?' she blurted.

Reluctant to ask the angry young woman in, Maisie stepped outside and pulled the door almost closed behind her. She realised she was holding the bunch of keys clenched in her fist like a weapon and made an effort to relax.

'Perhaps I should introduce myself. My name's Maisie.'

'Don't we sound posh? You think that makes it all right?'

In the army, Maisie had been in the habit of saying: 'I'm not posh, I just went to a posh school.' But she just asked: 'Makes what all right?'

'Him carrying on. I suppose people like you don't have to have morals. You're that well off, it doesn't matter how you go on.'

Maisie tried to see through the bluster to the genuine upset beneath. 'I think there's been—'

The woman interrupted, looking like she was about to cry. 'How do you think I feel, not invited – not to the church, not to the wake?'

'Is that all?' said Maisie, apologetically. 'I'm sorry, I didn't know who to invite. I just mentioned to the vicar and the publican and hoped everyone who knew him would find out that the two things were happening and those who wanted to come would do so.'

'Well, we don't live in the village, do we? We live over in Chichester since old Canon Dander turned us out. How would it have been if I just waltzed in without being asked?'

'I sympathise, I really do, but quite a few people came who weren't directly asked.'

'I'm not lots of people, though, am I? I expect you was glad not to have to . . .' The woman's voice faded to nothing. She bit her lip and kicked a white plastic toe at the gravel. 'Not to have to face me,' she said, without raising her eyes.

'Look, I'm sure this is a misunderstanding,' said Maisie, uncertain what that might mean. 'Perhaps you could tell me your name?'

'Cooper.'

'Yes, that's right. I'm Maisie Cooper.'

'No, not you.'

'Do you mean Stephen, Stephen Cooper? I'm sorry if I'm being slow, but I'm not following you. I'm his sister.'

The woman gaped. 'What did you say?'

37

'I'm Stephen's sister, Maisie.'

The woman took a moment to think about this, looking Maisie up and down. 'But you're so young and pretty.'

'I'm thirty-four but yes, Stephen was three years older than me. I live abroad and I got a message from him to come over and I came and, when I got here, I found out that he'd had an accident. And I'm sorry that I don't know who you are and you didn't feel you were invited to the ceremony or the reception.' She made an effort to smile. There really was something deeply hurt in the woman's eyes. 'You would have been very welcome, you know.'

'I thought you were his bit on the side.'

'Did you?' said Maisie astonished.

'I thought you looked like his type.'

'Please, let's not talk about whether or not I was my brother's type. So, I'm Maisie Cooper and you are . . . ?'

'I told you, Cooper. Not Steve, me. Well, him and me.'

'Stephen and you,' said Maisie, the truth beginning to dawn.

'Yes, him and me. He was Steve Cooper and I was – I mean I am – June Cooper.'

Maisie took a breath, then cut through the Gordian knot of confusion in a phrase.

'You're Stephen's wife.'

'That's right. I'm his wife.'

'I see,' said Maisie, wearily. 'Perhaps you should come in.'

SEVEN

They sat in the frigid kitchen. Maisie went to close the back door, giving herself a moment. What other surprises might Stephen have left her? No pleasant ones, that seemed certain. Meanwhile, June sat at the table, pulling her cardigan close across her chest.

'I know it's cold,' said Maisie. 'There's a boiler in the basement, but it doesn't work. Did you move in here? Do you know anything about that?'

'No, I just stayed over sometimes because of my pa,' said June enigmatically. 'Steve lived in this room in winter. It was the only one he could keep warm. Why don't you light the Aga?'

'Can you show me how?' asked Maisie, encouragingly. Maisie knew very well, but she thought the conversation might go better if June had something to do. 'Please?'

'All right.' June knelt down on the cold flagstones, her plastic boots creaking. She pulled the basket of kindling towards her. 'I suppose you want to know a bit about me?'

Maisie thought she detected a need in June to talk, to be paid attention to, like a child once more.

'That would be lovely. How about you tell me how you met?'

'At the pub, of course,' said June, looking a little more cheerful.

'The Fox-in-Flight?'

'That's right. I help out.'

'Behind the bar?'

'I do earlies for Gerald Gleeson when he goes upstairs to have his tea and a sit-down. Then he comes back at nine o'clock when the news is on. Steve noticed me and we got talking.'

Maisie considered the scene with curvaceous June behind the bar and Stephen – never Steve, surely? – with his roving eye.

'Go on,' she suggested with a smile.

'He stayed till closing and offered to take me home. That Nigel Bacon lent him his car. Usually, I got a lift with my pa, but I put tuppence in the payphone and put him off.'

'Yes, you said you and your father don't live in the village?'

'Out here in this dump? You're joking,' said June, dismissing one of the Sussex Downs' most desirable addresses. She twisted up a couple of spills of newspaper from the kindling basket and pushed them into the sticks. 'Matches?'

Maisie passed them and June struck one on the cement between two flagstones, leaving an ugly mark. She put the flame to the paper and the fire began to draw. Maisie passed the coal scuttle from by the back door and June began positioning the lumps of grey coke with her fingers.

'It burns without smoke. Isn't that what they say?' asked June, truculently. 'How can anything burn without smoke?'

'I don't know,' said Maisie. 'Shall we sit at the table and have a chat? I could make us some tea.'

'Don't suppose you have any milk or sugar?'

'No, I'm afraid not.'

'I thought as much. He was just the same,' said June. 'I'll go without then.'

'I could run to the shop?'

'Never mind,' said June, standing up and running her fingers under the cold tap.

Looking at June's outsized man's cardigan, Maisie felt an unexpected wave of deeper emotion. Here was someone who was genuinely, deeply hurt by Stephen's death.

'I suppose he was all you've got,' said June, mirroring her thoughts. 'Why didn't you ever visit him?'

'I came as soon as I was asked. He rang, but I wasn't there so he left a message with my flatmate.'

June sat down at the table. 'He didn't have the telephone. He said he didn't like it, but I know better.'

'He was cut off?' Maisie guessed.

'Exactly.'

June had left the heavy cast-iron door of the firebox a couple of inches ajar and the Aga was drawing nicely. Somehow, the warming room caused June to thaw and she told Maisie the whole tale – essentially of her attempts to preserve her 'honour' in the face of 'Steve's charm'. Then, with a certain number of odd euphemisms based on the behaviour of farmyard animals, it became clear that she had, with a tinge of regret but also a carnal satisfaction, 'given in' and 'allowed him his way'.

'I understand,' said Maisie.

June went on, describing surreptitious meetings and days out to Bognor Regis and Portsmouth. Now and then, she smiled at a particular reminiscence. Then she stopped and an expression of cunning settled on her lovely face with its clumsy make-up.

'Do go on,' said Maisie. 'It's so nice to hear about him. It seems as though you made one another happy.'

'Well, then we came to it. I told him he wouldn't get any more unless we were married.'

'Any more?' said Maisie.

June gave her a look. 'You know . . .'

Maisie smiled, despite herself. Lust would be a powerful enough motivation.

'Oh, yes, of course.'

'So, he got it organised for us.'

'Organised what?'

'Marriage, what do you think?'

It was odd that no one had mentioned a marriage – not Reverend Millns, not any of the neighbours.

'In the village church or at the registry office?'

'Neither.'

'Is that right?' said Maisie, wondering what she might mean.

June leant down and pushed two fingers into the top of one of her boots. She drew out a piece of official-looking parchment, folded into a square. She put it on the table as if it was some kind of religious relic. For the first time, Maisie took in June's rings, several on each hand, a clean circle of skin around her grimy wedding finger, suggesting she had recently taken one off.

'Do you want a look?'

June unfolded it, revealing a convincing-looking document that asserted in Latinate legalese that Stephen Cooper and June Cooper, née Strickland, had duly and in accordance with the law been consecrated husband and wife.

'But there was no special service?' asked Maisie lightly.

'Didn't need one.'

'No?'

'Stephen knew people,' said June with rather touching – though misplaced – pride.

Maisie looked at the document. It really was beautifully done. The penmanship was so regular that it might almost be taken for Gothic print. But, here and there, a flourish gave it away as manuscript. And she could just see the remnants of faint pencil lines that had been rubbed out once they had served their purpose. The folds in the paper were deeply marked, as if it had been handled many times.

Poor June, thought Maisie. Stephen had cooked up a sham certificate so she would think herself married and continue to have sex with him – and she had been completely taken in.

'I didn't move in,' said June. 'We were waiting for the right moment to break it to my pa. He knows we were together but I've only been staying over some nights. I suppose it meant Steve really loved me.'

'Is that the date?' asked Maisie. 'Just ten days ago?'

'That's right,' said June. 'He gave me a ring as well, but I don't know if I should show you.'

So that was the reason for the cleaner band of skin on her wedding finger, thought Maisie.

Just then, the kitchen clock began its ten o'clock chime.

'Oh, I must go,' said Maisie. 'I have to see the solicitor in Chichester at eleven. There's a bus at ten past ten, isn't there?'

'We can take you,' June offered brightly.

'Who's that?'

'My pa and me. He brought me up from town. I expect he'll want to get a look at you, too.' Maisie hesitated, feeling a little like an exhibit and June took it as a refusal. 'Well, if you don't want to—'

'No, please, that's very kind of you. Let me just get my coat and a scarf.'

Maisie ran upstairs for her things, putting on a smear of lipstick and pushing her fingers through her hair. It was short and naturally curly so, unless it was plastered flat against her skull, it generally looked presentable.

But the face that looked back at her in the bathroom mirror was drawn and frowning, unhappy and disappointed.

'Oh, Stephen,' she sighed.

EIGHT

The journey into Chichester was uncomfortable. It turned out Mr Strickland was a second-hand dealer with premises on the northern edge of the city, outside the Roman walls.

'You'll not be right up to the solicitor's door,' he warned.

'That doesn't matter,' Maisie told him. 'I can walk the rest of the way.'

Mr Strickland was a short man with an outdoor complexion. Under his many layers of clothing – shirt, jumper, waistcoat, jacket – she thought he was probably wiry and strong. The transport he offered was a lorry, loaded up behind with scrap metal, including a bicycle, missing one wheel and a saddle.

Now that's an idea for getting about, thought Maisie.

She sat up front on a bench seat, wedged between the two Stricklands. Her knees knocked against theirs as the lorry swung through the tight S-bend into East Bitling. The noise of the engine made conversation difficult, as did the rattling of the scrap. All the same, she did her best.

'This is very kind of you. I understand the bus isn't completely reliable.'

Neither June nor her father replied directly. Mr Strickland made a non-committal sound in his throat and June shook her head, as if it was just one more thing in her litany of misfortunes. Maisie decided to try again.

'So, you used to live in Framlington, June mentioned?'

'She never should have,' replied Mr Strickland. 'That's no one's business but ours.'

Maisie realised that there was something else going on, some kind of argument or disagreement between June and her father.

'But you're local?' Maisie persisted. 'I think I know the name Strickland. Could I have been at school with someone from your family?'

'Where would that have been?' asked June's father.

'She went to Westbrook College,' said June with an air of pulling a conversational rabbit out of a hat. 'She was a weekly boarder, like Steve, with the posh kids. He told me.'

'Steve,' said Mr Strickland under his breath, shaking his head.

Maisie gave up and tried to relax, watching the trees go by through the dirty windscreen. When they reached Chichester, Mr Strickland pulled up on a scrubby bit of land beside a dilapidated warehouse, opposite a telephone box. Outside was a heap of scrap metal, slowly rusting itself into oblivion, and a large brazier in a pool of cold ash. Above the double doors was a hand-painted sign: *'Strickland & Sons, quality goods, bought & sold.'* Maisie wondered if there actually were any sons.

Strickland jumped out, unexpectedly nimble, holding the door open for her. Maisie shuffled across, sliding out between the steering wheel and pedals. As she climbed down, Mr Strickland put a hand on her lower back and ran it down onto her behind. She felt herself flinch.

'I'll be quite all right,' she said quickly, in a voice pitched rather higher than she meant.

Mr Strickland removed his hand and walked away. June, still sitting on the bench seat in the cab, caught her eye.

'He's a dirty old man,' she said. 'Don't think you're special.'

For a second, Maisie could think of nothing to reply. Then she felt a wave of sympathy for June.

'Is he unkind to you?' she asked.

'You what?'

'Your father?'

'You don't choose your family, do you?'

Maisie contemplated poor bruised June. She had an idea she'd had much more to cope with than just Stephen's unkind deception.

'I expect we'll see one another again, June,' she said. 'I'm very sorry I didn't know to invite you, but—'

'That's as may be,' June interrupted, 'but I've got my rights. Don't think I don't know what's what. I should have what's coming to me.'

'What's coming to you?'

'I've got my marriage lines and I've got this.' She took a gaudy ring out of the pocket of her cardigan and put it on her wedding finger. 'Just so you know.'

'Did Stephen give you that?'

'That's for me to know and no one else to find out. You should go or he'll be back out trying to touch you up again.'

'All right. Thanks again for the lift,' said Maisie brightly, but June's face was closed off, like a hurt child. 'Let's speak again soon. Goodbye.'

★★★

Maisie walked briskly away between pleasant flint-faced houses, towards the town centre. It had become a lovely day, crisp and bright. Although she knew it wouldn't last, Maisie enjoyed the warmth of the sun on her face. Yesterday's biting wind had quite disappeared.

She passed St Paul's church and crossed the road at Northgate, noticing the George and Dragon pub. A lorry was pulled up from Harvey's brewery and barrels were being rolled down a timber ramp through a pavement trapdoor into the cellar. There was a sour smell of spilt ale.

A little further on she approached Chitty's Cycles. Maisie remembered seeing Mr Chitty at the wake and, sure enough, there he was in a light-brown warehouse coat, helping his grandson adjust the brakes on a rather splendid Raleigh Chiltern ladies' bicycle with a wicker basket and a comfortable leather saddle. He looked up and smiled.

'Good morning, Miss Cooper.'

'What a lovely day,' she replied, holding out her hand for the boy to shake. 'What's your name?'

'Nicholas, miss.'

'Pleased to meet you. Do you like getting your hands all oily?'

'I love it,' said Nicholas.

A customer arrived and Mr Chitty and his grandson disappeared into the shop.

Because the Stricklands had given her a lift, she was early for her eleven o'clock appointment. The solicitor's office was near Chichester Cathedral, on West Street. To pass the time, she went in through the magnificent west door and was delighted to hear the boys' choir from the Prebendal School practising a stately plainsong. Their treble voices floated through the enormous space, reverberating from the Norman pillars, fading up into the clerestory.

She took a seat on a narrow chair, three rows from the altar rail. Nearby, a verger was busy with Brasso polish and a pair of rags, one to apply and one to buff off. There was a faint odour of incense.

She thought again about the stolen devotional book with its enumeration of holy sins and holy virtues. That, of course, brought her back to June and to her brother. What had Stephen seen in her? He had tricked her into a sham marriage. Could it have been anything beyond the obvious carnal infatuation? Had he, in fact, truly fallen in love with poor, deceived June Strickland?

NINE

Sergeant Jack Wingard was at the police station, busy with a group of eleven-year-old children, first years on a trip from the local high school. They were in a prefab unit to the rear of the main building and he was talking them through the dangers posed by traffic. The session was one he had delivered before. Normally, he made a point of learning every child's name before the hour was up, but today he was distracted.

He took some questions. They were good kids and wanted to join in. He made them laugh and then shocked them with some graphic descriptions of the kind of injuries suffered by pedestrians struck by cars. He told them, to squeals of delight, that it was better to be thrown in the air than crushed under the wheels. Then, he handed out big sheets of paper for them to divide into groups and design posters to advise on road safety. As they argued and sketched, he sat on the corner of his desk and looked out of the window.

Jack liked the outreach part of his job, being a part of the community. He thought he was good at it, managing to combine authority with approachability.

Police Constable Barry Goodbody, on the other hand . . .

Barry was outside, washing the windscreen of one of the cars, in shirtsleeves. He was a work in progress, not the worst recruit Jack had been required to mould into a serviceable copper, but not the best either.

Jack's eyes drifted to the tight buds on the cherry tree, just waiting for a few days of warm sun before unfurling their brand-new leaves. It reminded him of the blossom walk in the grounds of Westbrook College and, in a natural chain of connections, the end of his last summer term when he, seventeen years old and knowing nothing of life, had first seen Maisie Cooper.

He had only met her because of the school play, bringing the classes of boys and girls together for once. He could still feel the unexpected, inexplicable depth of emotion, the sense of longing and, at the same time, the sense of being found.

He sighed. How brief it had been. Just a moment of connection and a kiss, brief and perfect, at the end-of-term party. Was it any wonder she didn't remember? Then, the very next day, everyone went their separate ways for the summer, Maisie following her brother into the armed services, the Women's Royal Army Corps. She would be away for 'a tour', three years at least, without a backwards glance.

He thought, perhaps, it was that disappointment that had made him enlist in the police force, to have something worthwhile and purposeful to do with his life. Had he not had his grandmother to think about, keeping him in Chichester, he might have gone into the armed forces, too. In any case, despite the interest of several eligible young women in the town, he had never forgotten Maisie.

Having chosen the police force, looking after his grandmother had held him back. Major promotions were only available to officers who moved about, accepting the challenges of different stations and different environments. He had stayed in Chichester and hit a glass ceiling at the rank of sergeant.

'Please, sir?' said one of the children.

Jack swung his attention back into the room. 'Go on.'

'How's this?'

He went over to look. There were three children in this group and they had designed a poster with a sad-looking girl

49

sitting at the side of the road with her arm in a sling. An out-sized and anatomically inventive skeleton loomed over her. In the distance, they had tried to draw a car with its front end crushed by a collision with a wall. At the top, in block capitals, they had written: '*THINK ONCE, THINK TWICE.*'

'That's very good,' said Jack. 'Can you colour it in?'

The other groups all wanted him to look at what they had drawn. He went round the room, congratulating them, suggesting additions, telling them he was proud of them, that they were 'real bright sparks'. But, inside, he was thinking about a sparky girl of just eighteen with curly hair and a beautiful smile who had come back into his life, quite unexpectedly, as a grown woman, someone who perhaps might mean something to him again but, as he had told his grandmother, didn't know him 'from Adam'.

All those years ago, he mused, it might have been better to 'think once, think twice'.

TEN

Sitting on the hard cathedral chair, listening to the high, clear voices of the choir, Maisie began to piece together the jigsaw of Stephen's life. He had lived hand to mouth – that was clear – without a telephone or proper heating or a car. He had deceived June – poor, sweet, gullible June – in order to continue having sex with her, promising her . . .

Well, what had he promised her? Not material wealth, that was certain. Or might he have had some project about to be fulfilled, that would imminently make them rich?

Oh. The robbery. Could that be it?

Annoyingly, Inspector Barden had refused to be drawn. She got up and went to look for the entrance to the underground crypt, finding it in the north transept at the bottom of a flight of ten steps where a small man in a dusty shapeless suit emerged from behind a broken door, carrying a leather-bound ledger.

'Excuse me,' she called down to him, 'is this where the robbery happened?'

He looked up, a doleful expression on his pale face.

'Awful business.'

'Do you know the circumstances?'

'One moment.' He fastened a padlock and chain across the broken door, then climbed the stairs to meet her. 'I don't believe I've had the pleasure . . .'

'I was just passing. I read about it in the *Chichester Observer*.'

He nodded. 'I'm confirming the inventory for the bishop. The losses are historically significant,' he said with sad eyes.

'The book, above all?' she asked.

'The book, the rings, the salver . . .' He glanced at his watch. 'I must go. Good day to you.'

He bustled away. The choir practice came to an end and the boys processed out. She followed them at a polite distance, through the west doors, into the sun. They disappeared through a narrow gate in a tall flint wall, moving in silence – boarders with no family home to go to in half-term, kept on by the school so their parents could preserve their freedom.

Maisie felt suddenly sad for them, in their tiny red cassocks and white surplices, strange miniature versions of the cathedral priests.

Who had chosen this life for them? Those same parents, she supposed. But they ought to be out on their bikes somewhere, in the woods or down at the seaside, getting up to mischief.

A line from a poem, *The Waste Land* by T S Eliot, came into her mind.

'What you get married for if you don't want children?'

It made her think of June Strickland and her bogus marriage certificate and whether June had wanted children with Maisie's brother. From there, she remembered the stanza on the paper that wrapped the damp posy, now stashed away in a drawer.

Was there was a connection with Eliot? She thought perhaps there was.

For the second time that morning, she was surprised by the chiming of a bell – an impressive booming sound from the top of the stone bell tower. It was eleven o'clock on the dot.

The solicitor's office was just two doors down. By the time the chimes had ended, she was asking to be admitted into Mr Maurice Ryan's dusty lair.

II
SLOTH

ELEVEN

At least, Maisie expected the solicitor's office to be a dusty lair. She was, as yet, only in the antechamber.

The appearance of Maurice Ryan's professional secretary was surprising – a sleek, middle-aged woman of African heritage with curly hair that had been chemically relaxed then smoothly styled. She wore a lemon-yellow twin set accessorised with artificial pearls.

'I'm Miss Clement. Mr Ryan won't be long,' she assured her. She had a faint accent. 'Your brother was a charming man, an interesting client. I'm very sorry for your loss. Do take a seat.'

'Thank you.'

The waiting area was a bland, neutral space with three mixed dining chairs positioned along the apple-green wall. Above the dado rail were smudges of hair oil on the paintwork. Miss Clement sat opposite at a modern desk with a typewriter that had been pushed to one side. On the walls were four small prints. One of them she recognised as Constable's celebrated landscape with Chichester Cathedral in the distance, seen from the canal. The prints were framed but weren't under glass. One of them was badly faded from being hung in direct sunlight.

Maisie felt the time tick on. Two minutes, three minutes – not long really. Miss Clement occasionally turned a page of the local newspaper, the *Chichester Observer*. From Mr Maurice Ryan's room she could hear nothing at all. She wondered if he was keeping her waiting as a matter of form, playing a kind of game.

Four minutes.

'He's just on the phone. I'm sure he won't be long,' said Miss Clement, making a note on an A4 pad. 'Can I get you a cup of tea?'

'Thank you. I would like that very much.'

With a smile of great charm, Miss Clement went through into a small kitchen. Through the narrow doorway, Maisie saw her fill a stainless-steel kettle at a tap encrusted with limescale and lean her two hands on the draining board as she waited for it to boil. The kitchen door swung shut. Maisie thought it was just gravity rather than a desire for privacy.

Left alone, she tried to visualise Mr Ryan. He had kindly met her at the railway station because Stephen had no car to get about. When was that? Last Saturday, four, no five days ago. He had been rather florid and over-exuberant, much more her image of a house agent than a trained legal mind. But he knew she was travelling overnight and would be weary, kindly coming to offer her a lift in his bottle-green Rover.

They had driven to Framlington and discovered Stephen's death and a police investigation in full swing. She had been forced to return to Chichester and put up at the Bedford Hotel – a grimy two-star and all she could afford – for three nights before she was allowed the keys to Stephen's home. The next day, the Wednesday, Ryan had surprised her by attending the commemorative service and asking to see her again.

Maisie sighed. It was all so different from what she had imagined as her train had swept through the Sussex Downs, past the airport at Gatwick, then Arundel with its cathedral and castle on the hill. She had expected Stephen to be doing well, at last, emerging from the shadow cast by their parents' deaths.

It was ten years, after all.

And she had wanted his solicitor to be different, someone more old-fashioned, a small man with beady eyes and, perhaps, a high collar. Yes, she wanted an elderly lawyer, surrounded by yellowing paperwork, occupied in managing the affairs of equally elderly customers and rather excited to be dealing with Stephen's more up-to-date needs. She wanted an office lined with waxed-oak shelves, comfortably stuffed with ledgers and legal precedents. She had a romanticised picture in her mind of Stephen's file, wrapped in dusty manilla card, tied with red string, adrift on a sea of competing documents on a huge kneehole desk inlaid with walnut or rosewood.

'Here you are,' said Miss Clement.

'Thank you.'

She took a sip of her tea. The water had properly boiled and it had the flavour of loose, not bags. It was good and strong.

'Is it all right?' Miss Clement asked. 'You never know what people prefer, do you?'

'Lovely,' said Maisie. 'Just what I needed.'

The door to the inner office swung open and Mr Ryan appeared.

'Miss Cooper, thank you so much for coming. I'm sorry to keep you. What a pleasure to see you again. Aren't I the lucky one?'

Given the circumstances, Maisie thought the sentiment was a little inappropriate. Miss Clement seemed to see it, too.

'Really, Maurice.'

'Sorry. Put my foot in it again.'

He held out a big fleshy right hand for her to shake, smoothing his hair with the other. Maisie put down her tea and stood up.

'Good morning, Mr Ryan.'

'Yes, a lovely morning.' He beamed, waving a hand at the large sash window. 'Will you come through?'

The inner office was a little more what Maisie had imagined, but not much. The desk and low bookcases were dark wood, perhaps mahogany. Apart from a heavy beige rotary telephone and a leather blotter with a little-used piece of absorbent paper, Ryan's desk was empty.

'Please, take a seat,' he told her.

Her only options were two low club armchairs in tan leather. Maisie chose the one on the left as Ryan strode round to his wooden swivel chair.

'Well, this is a pretty state of affairs, isn't it?'

'I beg your pardon?'

'Your brother's circumstances. The police.'

'Absolutely,' said Maisie, hoping he would answer her many questions. 'Yes. What can you tell me about that?'

'First things first.' Ryan pulled out a desk drawer and took out a folder full of official papers in various dimensions – bank statements, invoices, requests for payment, demands for payment. Ryan took her through them methodically. It was more or less what she had expected, but depressing all the same.

Stephen's outgoings had consistently exceeded his income and things were approaching a crisis. He had received a large sum of money five months before, the previous September, from a limited company. Almost all of that sum had been immediately drawn out in cash. Since that point, he had received a regular monthly deposit from 'B Otterway'. Otherwise, it was all expenditures and a steadily increasing overdraft.

'Do you recognise the company name for this large deposit last September, Miss Cooper, BFI Limited?'

'No, I don't.'

'Or this other name, "B Otterway"?'

Maisie considered. She had an idea the name did mean something to her. 'It rings a bell, but a very faint and distant one. Is it important?'

'Well, they're both a source of income.' He jabbed at the numbers with the forefinger of his right hand. 'If whoever they are still owes him money, either the company or this Otterway chap, that might be to your advantage.'

'I see.'

There was a pause. Maisie waited.

'Your brother wasn't an industrious man,' said Ryan. 'Not a self-starter.'

'No,' said Maisie. 'He generally followed the path of least resistance. He was . . .' There was another pause. She didn't want to say he was lazy.

'There is one other thing,' Ryan told her. 'I am afraid that this will not come as good news, though I imagine it won't be a complete bolt from the blue.'

'Go on.'

'You have seen that your brother did not work, that his estate is comprised mostly of debts.'

'Yes.' Maisie nodded. 'His phone was cut off. There are final demands for payment of electricity and water bills on the hall table, unopened. What about Church Lodge? Is there a mortgage?' she enquired.

'The house your brother lived in? Did you imagine it was his?'

Maisie sighed. 'I suppose I did.'

'How would that be, if he was idle?'

'Mortgaged to the hilt but his, all the same?'

'It was rented.' He gave her a meaningful look. 'The owners have asked that I retrieve the keys – forthwith.'

'Today?' she asked. 'You can't be serious?'

'That was their request. I'm terribly sorry.'

'But where will I go?' asked Maisie, sadly. 'I can't go back to Paris before the cremation and I have spent almost all my money.'

'I don't know, I'm afraid.' He seemed genuinely pained. 'You have no relatives in the area?'

'None,' said Maisie, astonished at how bereft all this was making her feel. 'It's been years . . .'

She stopped and contemplated her hands, twisting them together in her lap. There was a short pause, then Ryan appeared to take pity on her.

'I can prevaricate, perhaps, put them off. What do you think? I could try and get you to the weekend?'

'Who is the owner? Someone in the village?'

'It's a company,' said Ryan carefully. 'Yes, that will give you a chance to . . . do whatever you decide to do. We open the office Saturday morning. Shall we say midday?'

Maisie took stock. 'That's the day of the cremation.'

'Of course, it is. Charity and I will be there. What time?'

'Eleven.'

'In that case, let's say I'll come to you at stumps, at close of play.' He sketched a forward defensive shot over the desk. 'Say five-thirty, to give you the whole day?'

'You'll come to Church Lodge.'

'That's the ticket.'

Maisie stood up. The cushions of the leather club chair made a noise like an inhalation. Politely, Ryan stood as well.

'I'll be there,' she told him.

'I'm delighted to help. I'm sorry I did not have better news. Did you have expectations?'

Maisie laughed at the quaintly Victorian expression.

'Of Stephen? Well,' she said lightly, 'he was never what you might call driven. But I wish I had brought more traveller's cheques with me.'

TWELVE

To Maisie's surprise, Maurice Ryan didn't precede her to the door.

'There's something else, isn't there,' she guessed.

'There is.'

She sat back down in the tan club armchair. 'I suppose I'd better hear the worst,' she joked, but Ryan's face was grave.

'So, about the police,' said the solicitor. 'Have they spoken to you?'

'They are playing their cards very close to their chests,' she complained.

'Apart from the obvious, I mean.'

'The obvious?'

'That your brother was . . .' He stopped and she saw he felt he was on the verge of an indiscretion. 'You don't know, do you?'

'Know what?'

He shook his head and sat down.

'This is very irregular. If there were not the pressure of time, I wouldn't broach the subject.' He tapped his fingers on the desk. 'Let's come back to that,' he said, waving a hand as if to dismiss the question. 'Tell me, how close were you?'

'I really know very little of Stephen's life. I wouldn't be surprised if you knew him much better than I. Was he . . . ?' Maisie wasn't sure what the correct phrase would be. She thought back to Inspector Barden's hints and questions. Then she decided that, as Stephen was dead, it didn't really matter very much. 'Was he a scoundrel?'

'I wouldn't know about that,' said Ryan guardedly.

He leant back and his chair creaked. Maisie felt that they were at cross purposes, but couldn't quite see how.

'Do you know,' she asked, 'what their focus might be? The police, I mean?'

Maisie waited. Ryan drummed his fingers on the desk.

'With the post-mortem, it seems there is no doubt. I'm very sorry to have to be the person to tell you. Chichester is not such a big town after all and small-town life is . . . I was talking to a doctor friend from the golf club yesterday afternoon and he let it slip. I am, after all, responsible for probate and would have been notified in any case.'

He stopped and sat back, placing the palms of his hands flat on the desk either side of the blotter, organising his thoughts.

'The autopsy has been completed,' Maisie guessed, with a sinking feeling in her stomach. 'It wasn't simply that he drowned.'

'It was not,' said Maurice Ryan.

'And?'

'The police have reached the unequivocal conclusion that your brother must have been a victim of foul play.'

'Of foul play,' Maisie repeated, her stomach lurching for a second time.

'Of murder.'

***

Despite her repeated requests for more details, Maisie found Ryan impossible to draw out.

'You must understand that I can't possibly go further on the matter,' said Ryan.

'Why not?'

'It's a question of professional etiquette.'

'In what way?'

'Between myself and the police. You can see that, can't you?'

'We aren't talking about an engagement announcement. This is . . .' Maisie stopped. What was it exactly?

'It's very shocking,' said Ryan.

'You can say that again. All this time I've been here and no one has intimated . . .'

Or had they, though? Arriving at Church Lodge on the Tuesday, she had kept herself to herself but for just a few times when she had spoken to a neighbour, the shock of bereavement meaning she didn't notice their leading questions, their quizzical glances.

'Perhaps you would like another cup of tea, with plenty of sugar. That might help.'

Without waiting for her answer, Ryan went out, leaving Maisie to think.

Yes, there had been an undercurrent that she had been too rushed, too surprised by the suddenness of Stephen's death, to understand. Her years in the army and then away in Paris had made her, on her return to Sussex, a stranger in a strange land, despite having been brought up here. She had become stand-offish and antagonistic.

And why was that? It wasn't their fault, any of them. They were who they were. Their behaviour was independent of her presence. If she had never come back, they would have gone on just the same, going about their business, wondering about Stephen's death, gossiping, making assumptions.

It all came back to her brother, what he had done and what had happened to him. And now, it seemed, he had been killed. It didn't seem possible. It didn't seem real.

'Damn,' she said out loud. 'Damn.'

All these strangers – every one of them connected and somehow wary of her, suspicious of her. But that was a legacy of what Stephen had done, how he had lived, how he had died. It wasn't her fault.

The door opened and Ryan came in, holding it open for Miss Clement.

'After you, my dear,' he told her.

'Thank you, Maurice.'

There were two cups of tea this time, on a tray with an open packet of Bourbon biscuits. Ryan ate one as Miss Clement passed Maisie her cup. Watching their easy co-operation, Maisie felt lonely. She pulled herself together and tried another tack.

'I apologise,' said Maisie. 'I quite see that you cannot divulge the circumstances of Stephen's death. Who should I approach?'

'The police station should be your first port of call. The sergeant was at the church. He's a good sort. Did he speak to you?'

She remembered him as not much more than a uniform, standing in the shade of the yew tree.

'No, he kept his distance.'

'You might ask for him there. You would be within your rights,' said Ryan.

'Now, then,' interrupted Miss Clement, 'you drink your tea. You could do with it.'

'Look at you,' Ryan told Miss Clement. 'Taking care of everyone, as always.'

A look of warmth passed between them. Were they married? Was his secretary using her maiden name for professional reasons?

Miss Clement hovered until Maisie had finished, providing a kind of professional emotional support, talking with her faint accent about this and that and nothing – the planned restoration of the cathedral whose buttresses they could see out of the window, the robbery from the crypt, the preparation of floats for the gala, the planned pedestrianisation of the city centre. Maisie drank the over-sweetened tea but could not manage the Bourbon finger biscuits.

'I didn't expect this,' she said quietly.

THIRTEEN

Maisie left the solicitor's office feeling lost. Outside, it was still a lovely day. The sun was pretty much as high in the sky as it would get, perhaps just tipping over into the afternoon. She walked up West Street to the old Market Cross, turning things over in her mind.

It was shocking, yes, but the news hadn't made her feel differently about Stephen. She had been under no illusions about his morals or his behaviour. He had become almost a figure of fun in her conversation – a lazy, charming chancer. Perhaps she had been looking forward to his misadventures providing darkly comic stories with which to entertain her Paris friends at dinner parties?

Certainly not now.

It gave her a chill, however, to think of him as a victim of . . . Well, she didn't know what. Poison? A gun or a knife?

She turned onto South Street, intending to follow Ryan's advice and see if she might be able to speak to the sergeant at the police station. Surely he would be there on duty? It was, after all, the middle of a working day. She went past the fishmonger and the grocer, both open onto the pavement with marble slabs to keep their produce cool. Even their staff looked hand-picked for the rosiness of their cheeks, the regularity of their smiles.

At the bottom of South Street, the wooden railway gates were closed to traffic so she climbed over the pedestrian bridge. Just as she reached the middle of the span, an incoming British Rail train thundered beneath her and she felt a brief desire to shout her frustration at the sky under cover of the noise. But she climbed back down and continued round the canal basin, walking along the unfenced embankment, her eyes on the stagnant depths.

Murky, she thought to herself with a shudder. Then she had a horrible premonition of being shown Stephen's bloated, drowned face.

They wouldn't, would they?

The police station was a large red-brick building, built at an angle to the road, with a busy car park full of official vehicles. As she approached the main entrance, a party of schoolchildren on some kind of educational visit came trooping out, laughing and chatting. A teacher followed and called them to order. By chance, the sergeant was with them too.

Maisie stopped and watched him. He was kind and attentive. The children clearly liked him. He dismissed them one at a time, teaching them to stand to attention and salute, addressing them by name. Then the teacher and her class crocodiled away and Maisie approached.

'Excuse me. Perhaps you won't remember me, but I would be grateful for a few minutes of your time.'

'I remember, Miss Cooper,' he replied. 'Of course.'

A lorry went past, rattling and bumping, followed by a double-decker Southdown bus.

'Could we go somewhere private, perhaps?'

'I can give you only a few minutes. Please follow me.'

'It's about Stephen's murder,' she said.

The policeman paused to look at her. There were competing emotions reflected in his face. Yes, there was sympathy, but also a kind of . . .

What was it? Disappointment? Pity?

'I have another school group but I will see what I can do. My name is Wingard.' For Maisie, the name rang a bell. She told him so. 'It's a pretty widespread Sussex family,' he replied.

They passed through the public lobby into a narrow corridor, lit with unpleasant fluorescent strip lighting. It gave Maisie the uncomfortable feeling that she was being taken into custody. The feeling was reinforced when he showed her into a spartan interview room.

'Would you like to take a seat?' said Sergeant Wingard. 'I will only be a moment.'

He didn't wait for her to sit down. Left alone, Maisie was at least encouraged by the fact that he left the door open. She popped her head out into the corridor, wondering what else was going on in the bowels of the station. No hardened criminals, she thought, being browbeaten for confessions. Chichester was a place where even minor crimes were enough of a surprise for them to become news. Hadn't there been something about gravel pits on page one of Charity Clement's *Chichester Observer*?

Thinking of the newspaper made her think of the page Barden had shown her. It hadn't actually come from the kindling basket in the hall at Church Lodge, had it? No, it was too smooth and, at the same time, too deeply creased, as if it had been living in the pocket to which Barden returned it, folded.

Had he shown it to her as a kind of provocation, to test her reaction? What precisely was the connection between Stephen and a robbery from the crypt of Chichester Cathedral? She didn't dare contemplate.

She went to the window that gave onto the rear of the station and saw a second group of schoolchildren, with a different teacher, lined up politely outside a prefabricated building. Sergeant Wingard approached with another officer, a uniformed constable with a sullen, narrow face. She couldn't hear what was being said, but she got the impression that Wingard was apologising for not being able to take the session and was delegating it to a junior colleague who looked displeased.

68

The teacher led the group of children into the prefab. A brief, unhappy altercation between Wingard and the constable played out in dumbshow. Then, the constable nodded and turned on his heel, following the children indoors.

Wingard, left alone, shook his head. Maisie ducked out of sight, hoping he hadn't seen her spying on him, and sat down calmly at the table. Very soon, she heard his footsteps in the corridor and he came and sat opposite her.

'How can I help you, Miss Cooper?' he asked.

'Thank you for making time to see me.'

'It's not a problem.'

'You were otherwise engaged?'

He glanced up at the window. He had seen her. 'It doesn't matter. So, this is to do with your brother?'

'Yes.'

'And the ongoing investigations?'

'Investigations, plural?'

'Our own and Scotland Yard – or Special Branch or however we have to refer to them.'

Maisie was surprised at his tone. He seemed frustrated, but not with her – with the investigating officers from London.

'I would be very grateful to know the details of my brother's death. I believe I have the right to ask? I haven't been able to ascertain exactly what happened. More recently, it has been put to me that he was . . .'

She found she didn't like to say the word.

Wingard frowned. 'Was it June Strickland?'

'I beg your pardon?'

'June made the formal identification of his body. Did she put two and two together?'

'She didn't mention it.'

'But you've spoken to her? Did she show you her "marriage lines"?' He used air quotes to show he didn't believe they were real.

69

'She did,' said Maisie, uncomfortably.

'I'm afraid, Miss Cooper, your brother was what some people call a character,' said Wingard. 'I would call him a wretch.'

Maisie felt her hackles rise. 'Is that so?'

'I'm sorry, I know we shouldn't speak ill of the dead. But the way he deceived that young woman was disgraceful.'

'Yes, but—'

'And the way he went about the town, claiming credit in one place, then another. Oh, he made a plausible enough show, that's certain. But, not to put too fine a point on it, he robbed his barber and his butcher and the rest of them and he's left them all whistling.'

'By being killed, by being murdered,' said Maisie, more loudly than she meant.

There was an awkward silence, broken only by the clock on the wall. Maisie looked down at her shoes. If Sergeant Wingard wouldn't help her, she thought desperately, what could she do? Might she still make the two o'clock bus? But then what? Go back to Stephen's cold rented house and wait for the cremation on Saturday, then slink away to Paris none the wiser?

No, that would be a betrayal.

Unexpectedly, Wingard surprised her with a complete change of tone. 'Excuse me, Miss Cooper. I apologise. I spoke out of turn.'

'Yes, you did.'

'I hope you will forgive this lapse. It is not a habit of mine.'

'No. I mean, yes.'

He gave her a brief smile and she felt reassured.

'The post-mortem,' he told her, 'was completed yesterday. In the normal course of events, I would have come out to inform you this morning but, as you've seen, we have a programme of school visits. Please accept my apology.' He became formal. 'I am sorry to have to confirm, Miss Cooper, that our initial investigation has determined that your brother was murdered.'

'It was his solicitor who told me – Maurice Ryan. He knew from his own professional contacts.'

Wingard nodded. 'Of course.'

'But he wouldn't tell me anything else. He said I would have to come and speak to you. But perhaps you can't help me either?' Maisie heard her voice waver and almost break.

'As next of kin,' said Wingard, slowly, 'you do have certain rights.' He seemed to be weighing something up. 'I believe it would be in order to show you the initial report of the investigation into his death. You'll not be allowed to take it out of the station. You'll have to read it here, in this room.'

'Thank you. That would be very kind.'

'It won't be pleasant reading, Miss Cooper.' Wingard looked grave. 'Would you like me to find a WPC to sit with you?'

Maisie swallowed. 'No thank you. That won't be necessary.'

'As you wish.'

Sergeant Wingard left the room for a second time but was back in less than a minute with a manilla folder tied with red string, rather like the one she had imagined she would see on the solicitor's desk.

'I'll leave you to it,' he said.

'Thank you,' Maisie repeated, keen to get on, but he lingered. 'Was there something else?'

'You and your brother went to Westbrook College, didn't you?'

'That's right.'

'So did I – as a scholarship boy.'

And, with that, he was gone.

FOURTEEN

Maisie opened the folder, revealing a title page: 'Initial Report of the Investigation into the Death of Stephen Cooper of Church Lodge, Framlington.' There were two official stamps and two signatures accompanied by what she supposed were police badge numbers. She turned the page and looked inside.

The report proper was, of course, written in a leaden style, enumerating facts with wearying precision. Now and then, there were unanswered questions or balanced probabilities, but speculation and interpretation were absent. Even the witness statements were infected by what the French call the '*langue de bois*' – the wooden tongue. She supposed they were transcribed by the investigating officers, all personality removed, then merely signed by the witnesses themselves.

In any case, the facts were these. Maisie had left her Paris apartment in one of the lovely Dutch-style houses on the Place des Vosges on the Friday evening, heading for the Gare du Nord and the overnight boat train. The following morning as she trundled up to London Victoria through Kent, Stephen had got up with the intention of taking a swim in a neighbour's pool. This was a known fact and part, it seemed, of a new fitness regime.

At nine-thirty that same day, the police received a call from Stephen's neighbour, Nigel Bacon, a semi-retired financier. He was ringing about a man in his swimming pool. At first, the police officer who took the call was uncertain as to the precise nature of the complaint.

'What might be the problem, Mr Bacon, if the man in your swimming pool is known to you, if it isn't a question of trespass?'

'No, not trespass, for God's sake. The man's dead,' quoted the report.

Maisie didn't think Nigel Bacon had been at the wake, but she had seen him in the church and graveyard. He was one of those blustering red-faced men whose sense of personal entitlement far exceeded any honest assessment of their contribution to the progress of civilisation. Jon Wilkes, the blacksmith, had complained that the man mistreated his horse.

The next page of the report was on a different size and quality of paper. It was a plan of the village, traced she supposed from an Ordnance Survey map. It showed how the ugly house where Stephen lived shared a boundary with Nigel Bacon's property with a mark that indicated a gate in the wall. Maisie tried to visualise the location.

Of course, that was why she had seen mist rising over the eastern wall of the orchard garden. It was rising from the neighbour's heated swimming pool in the chill of the morning.

She turned another page.

On receipt of Nigel Bacon's information, the police sent a team to the property and retrieved the body from the water. Bacon maintained that he had expected his neighbour to use his pool. He, Bacon, was a habitual early riser and Mr Cooper's presence would not disturb him. The report went on to describe attempts to revive the victim, immediately seen to be vain. The corpse was formally identified at the scene by June Strickland who was listed as 'a close friend of the deceased'.

Maisie went to turn another page but found that she was moving into the details of the physical examination. She put her hands in her lap, taking a few steadying breaths. This was her brother they were talking about with such clinical precision.

Steeling herself, she went on, finding herself confronted by a dozen eight-by-ten black-and-white photographs. The top one was a wide view of the pool, taken from quite a distance, but still with an unmistakable shape floating turtle-like, just beneath the surface of the water. Unable to contemplate what the other photographs might reveal, she put them to one side, face down on the Formica table.

Much of what followed was irrelevant to her understanding of events – medical and forensic information, seemingly leading nowhere. Or perhaps she was missing the point? In any case, what she felt she needed to know most of all was why the police had formed the opinion that Stephen had been murdered, rather than having simply had a heart attack or a stroke and drowned.

Maisie's eyes glazed over, lost in memory, picturing a summer holiday at a hotel in the New Forest a couple of years after the Second World War had ended. Stephen had taught her to swim. She must have been seven or eight years old and he ten or eleven. The swimming pool had been perhaps twenty yards in length and shockingly chilly compared to the warmth of the sun. He had waded up and down beside her as she paddled, giving her just enough support to keep her chin above the water, encouraging her, berating her, congratulating her, challenging her.

Yes, thought Maisie, that had been the nature of their partnership. He leading the way, she following, but doing what felt like 'great things' because of it.

'Great things, indeed,' she murmured.

She realised her eyes were wet and felt glad there was no one else in the room to see her. In any case, it was, as everyone knew, different for girls.

Not for their parents, of course. They had lavished love and opportunity equally. But, in the wider world of clubs and teams and competitions, Stephen had flourished and she had been sidelined. It had been true from the age of seven when they both joined the local Dolphins swimming club, right up to the pinnacle of athletic endeavour, when Stephen went to the Melbourne Olympics to compete in the modern pentathlon and she stayed at home.

When Maisie had joined the Women's Royal Army Corps straight from school, she knew she was the better horsewoman, the better runner – possibly the better fencer. But there was no women's competition for what the founder of the modern Olympics, Pierre de Coubertin, hoped would 'test a man's moral qualities as much as his physical resources and skills'. Coubertin modelled the event around the 'adventures' of a cavalry officer behind enemy lines.

'His horse is brought down in enemy territory; having defended himself with his pistol and sword he swims across a raging river and delivers his message on foot.'

'He', never 'she'.

Maisie gave herself a shake and returned to the document.

The post-mortem examination, conducted in the morgue at St Richard's Hospital in Chichester, found the condition of the internal organs to be consistent with Stephen's age and 'sedentary habits'. There was no evidence of stroke. As the pool was heated, the idea of a heart attack brought on by the shock of cold water was discounted. He had been weighed, tipping the scales at fourteen stone and eight pounds. That was considerably heavier than when Maisie had last seen him. She supposed that was normal for a man approaching forty. A certain amount of dissipation was inevitable, wasn't it?

That made her think about June Strickland – she couldn't bring herself to think of her as June Cooper, even though that's who June believed she was.

Then she remembered Sergeant Wingard's unexpected reaction. What had he called Stephen?

75

'A wretch.'

That was quite odd, wasn't it? Why was he so exercised by Stephen's deception of June? It was unkind and cruel of her brother, yes, but was there more to it? Did Sergeant Wingard nurture his own attachment to Stephen's 'wife'?

Maisie forced herself to return to the document. There was a two-page inventory of the contents of Church Lodge, conducted by a Constable Goodbody. It listed all the indoor rooms and an outhouse referred to as a 'produce store'.

Finally, she found what she was looking for – the post-mortem description. The document made reference to three numbered close-up photographs and she felt relieved that she had not looked at them. It was enough that he was gone. To contemplate his wounds and puckered, drowned skin would be too much.

She discovered Stephen's eyes were red with broken capillaries and that no chlorinated swimming-pool water was found in his lungs. A complicated testing procedure revealed a high level of carbon dioxide in his blood. Close physical examination identified bruising around the nose and mouth and along his arms. The scene-of-crime team had retrieved a certain number of fibres, as yet unidentified, that had adhered to Stephen's unshaven face, despite his plunge into Nigel Bacon's pool.

In summary, Stephen had been dead, asphyxiated, before he hit the water.

FIFTEEN

The door swung open and Sergeant Wingard stood looking down at her.

'Have you finished, Miss Cooper?' he asked.

Maisie returned his gaze. He had mentioned Westbrook College. Ought she to remember him?

Perhaps, but they would have been in separate boys and girls classes and might not have been in the same year group, of course. How was it, though, that with the benefit of a private education he had not yet progressed beyond the lowly rank of police sergeant?

'Miss Cooper?'

He was frowning and she realised she hadn't answered.

'Yes, I've finished. I don't suppose I can ask you any questions?'

'I will try to help.'

'Do you have any idea who did it?'

'Forgive me, I can't answer that.'

'The report doesn't touch on the Special Branch investigation.'

'No.'

'Can you tell me why?'

'They aren't connected.' Maisie pressed him to go further, but he refused. 'I'm sorry I can't say more.'

'You know his phone was disconnected? Do you know where he called me from?'

'Perhaps from the pub, the Fox-in-Flight?'

'Yes, of course.' Maisie tried another tack. 'Did you know my brother well?'

Wingard hesitated. 'Not very well.'

'Were you investigating him for other reasons?'

He looked wary but the tone of his voice did not change. 'I can't answer that, either.'

Maisie glanced up at the wall clock. It was gone two. She had missed her bus. She went on, not troubling to mask her frustration.

'Who owns the house he lived in? Maurice Ryan said it was someone local.'

'For information on that, you should speak to Derek Fieldhouse.'

'At Framlington Manor?'

'Yes.'

Maisie paused a moment, then said: 'I suppose I will, eventually, be grateful for your assistance. At this point . . .' She made a disappointed face, hoping to encourage him into being more forthcoming. 'I really do feel that I am completely in the dark.' She smiled hopefully, but he waited her out in silence. 'Never mind,' she told him, defeated.

He led her out of the interview room, down the corridor with its unpleasant fluorescent lights, past a desk sergeant who looked at her with frank curiosity, then out of the front door.

Outside, she shivered. The sun already seemed less warm as it had begun to fall down the sky. She turned, intending to press him further but, without another word, Wingard had gone back inside.

★★★

Just in case she was mistaken about the bus timetable, Maisie walked to the station. She met a driver, lounging against a

78

barrier, lighting a cigarette from a packet of twenty Roth-mans.

Yes, the after-lunch bus had gone. The next was the 'after-school bus, the sixteen-oh-two'. Until then, Maisie was stranded in Chichester.

For want of anything better to do, she walked slowly back up South Street and bought a single Granny Smith apple at the greengrocer's. It was a little soft, being out of season, but still sharp and juicy. When she reached the old Market Cross, at the junction of the four cardinal streets, she sat down and tilted her face to catch a little of the fading sun. Over in the west, it would soon dip down into a bank of grey cloud – grey like her mood.

Oh, Stephen, she thought. *Why didn't you get in touch sooner?*

Sixteen

Through the window of the open-plan office, Segreant Jack Wingard could see just a sliver of blue sky above the low grey cloud. He sat becalmed at his desk, silently berating himself, his hands absently tidying several untidy files.

What was he trying to do? To alienate her even further? It was enough, wasn't it, that she didn't remember him? Was it really necessary to make himself . . .

Well, difficult?

He was frustrated, of course, at the awkwardness of juggling several competing objectives: following up the clues to Stephen Cooper's murder; finding the stolen cathedral property and proving himself the equal of Special Branch; protecting June; and, after years of trying, finally putting Strickland behind bars.

Also, he felt hurt that Maisie Cooper didn't recognise him. Had he changed so much?

Actually, yes. His blond hair had darkened to brown. His complexion, too, with beat duty, out in all weathers. And he had put on muscle, making him quite different from the willowy blond boy she had briefly known at school.

Angry with himself, when his phone rang he snatched it up and barked: 'Wingard.'

It was Inspector Barden of Special Branch.

'I just thought I'd give you a call and fill you in, Sergeant, regarding our little chat with Miss Cooper.'

'Thank you, sir,' said Jack, glad of the senior man's courtesy. 'I've just spoken to her myself.'

'You've told her it's murder?'

'Yes, sir, although the solicitor had already done so.'

'Small-town life, eh?' said Barden. 'Well, there's no way she was involved. She hadn't yet arrived.'

'No, sir.'

Barden gave him a neat résumé of everything Maisie had said.

'It's very clear that she knew nothing of what her brother was up to, either, but we will have to speak to her again. You know, I'm sorry to have to be treading on your toes like this, Wingard. It isn't my doing or how we normally go about our business. The bishop insisted.'

'I understand, sir.'

'She gave us another lead, though I'm not sure what it's worth.' Barden shared what Maisie had said about a possible connection to the international oil trade. 'What do you think?'

'Sounds pretty unlikely, sir.'

'We'll have to follow it up. It might have made him an enemy. Any progress your end?'

'The post-mortem result wasn't a surprise, obviously. Now we have confirmation we can go through his papers and so on. There may be something there.'

'And the girlfriend's father, Mr Strickland? Might he lead us to the goods?'

'It's possible,' said Jack, 'but I don't think he knows where they are.'

In his London office, Barden was called away.

'Thank you, Sergeant. You'll keep me informed?'

'Of course. Thank you, sir.'

Jack put the phone down and leant back in his chair. He would ask Police Constable Barry Goodbody to get on to the solicitor, Maurice Ryan. If the man was difficult, they would have to get a warrant. He checked his calendar. Thursday. It might have to wait until after the weekend.

His eyes drifted round the untidy open-plan office to which he had devoted most of his adult life. But he was thinking about a girl he had briefly known at school, with quick wits, curly brown hair and a lovely smile, who had unexpectedly reappeared and . . .

Oh, well, he thought. I've come this far on my own. What difference does it make?

But, deep down, he knew. All the difference in the world.

SEVENTEEN

Sitting on the cold stone bench, Maisie felt confused. He had been frankly rude, hadn't he? Yes, he had apologised but . . .

It was odd. There was something unspoken between them, between her and Sergeant Wingard, something she couldn't yet define.

She pulled herself together, focusing instead on the things she did know, and it struck her that she should make a list. To start with, there was the cremation, planned for Saturday, the day she was to become homeless.

What was she thinking? She wouldn't become homeless on Saturday, even though she would be handing back Stephen's keys. Her real home was a shared apartment on the top floor of a Dutch-style house on the Place des Vosges, not the ugly rented rooms of Church Lodge.

How she wished she could be home right now, sitting at the open French windows in the afternoon sun with her flat-mate Sophie, eating a fresh-prepared meal from the *traiteur* – the local delicatessen – on their knees.

What if, by Saturday, the puzzle of Stephen's death had not been solved? Would Special Branch even allow her to leave?

She tried to change the pattern of her thoughts, but it was hard. She couldn't escape a sense of guilt. She should have written and called. She should have found ways to be in touch more frequently. They had been so close as children and teenagers: mucking out the stables on the edge of the village in return for time in the saddle; working for a pittance in the fields gleaning potatoes that the farm machinery had left behind; beating for the pheasant shoots; naughtily drinking cider by the mill pond in West Bitling. Surely, with all that shared history, she might have helped him somehow. But no, she had been too busy living her own life.

And now he was dead.

No, not just dead. He had been murdered and he had called her and asked her to visit just before it happened, just before someone had smothered him with . . .

What had he been smothered with? The police report didn't pronounce, just referenced the fibres found on his face. A towel? His own dressing gown? Maybe she ought to go and talk to the neighbour, Nigel Bacon. He seemed pretty central.

Anyway, a few days before it happened, Stephen had called her and she hadn't been there to hear his voice.

She wondered about that moment. What might he have said to her, if she herself had answered the telephone?

'I miss you, Maisie . . .'

'I'm in trouble, can you come and help . . .'

'I've got myself mixed up with some bad men and I need . . .'

But what would he have needed from her, if he was in trouble, if he knew his life was in danger?

She had been out with a party of Americans at a smart restaurant near the Bastille. All she had seen was a bland message, written on the back of an envelope by her flatmate, Sophie.

'*Ton frère a appelé. Il veut absolument te voir. Il t'expliquera.*'

Yes, he had called. He urgently wanted to see her. He would explain. There was a Chichester telephone number.

84

If she could ring back, Maurice Ryan – Stephen's solicitor – would take a message.

So, yes, she had come to listen to Stephen's explanations. But she had been too late.

Wingard had mentioned the payphone at the Fox-in-Flight. Might someone have overheard him? But overheard what? And, obviously, he would have been speaking French since Sophie didn't speak English. Would anyone in the village pub have understood that? He must have had to push a good handful of coins into the slot for an international connection.

Thinking of money, Maisie considered the fact that Stephen had managed to whisk June Strickland away to Bognor Regis and Portsmouth for days out. He had a small regular source of income from 'B Otterway' and a large sum of money added to his account late last year from a limited company, albeit one he had immediately withdrawn. Would that have been enough to put food on the table and pay his rent?

No, Maurice Ryan had shown her that he was in arrears, that the landlord wanted the property back, that Stephen was 'idle'. He had turned into the sort of person people thought the worst of, even her.

What a disaster.

She shivered slightly, the cold of the stone bench beginning to seep into her bones. What was she to do? What choices did she have? Attend the cremation. Hand back the keys. But before then?

Discover, if she could, why he had been . . .

Again, the word wouldn't come, not even in the silent voice inside her own head. She knew what the word was. She had just read it in the 'initial report' at the cheap desk in Sergeant Wingard's interview room. But her brain refused to acknowledge it.

Stephen hadn't always been what Wingard called 'a wretch'. What had made him change? She knew he had seen death – many deaths – in the Middle East. He had told her some gruesome stories. She knew that the scars had stayed with him. And on top of fighting for his country, their parents had died, Eric and Irene Cooper. It had affected them both deeply but, perhaps, Stephen had found it harder to move on from than she had.

It happened one Saturday in December 1962, ten years before, in the heart of London. Stephen was twenty-seven years old and still in Kuwait. Maisie was twenty-five, had left the Women's Royal Army Corps after her second three-year tour and was working in a west-country hotel as a junior manager, her first real experience of independent adult responsibility.

Their parents had gone up to London for their wedding anniversary to attend a musical in the West End. The cast came on stage but, right from the opening bars, a London 'pea-souper' fog began to infiltrate the auditorium. People at the rear of the stalls and up in the gods complained to the ushers that they could no longer properly see. Audience members and actors couldn't help themselves coughing. Finally, at the interval, it was decided to call a halt.

The fog was the result of particularly damp and heavy weather conditions and several million London hearths burning dirty, sulphurous coal, creating a blanket of noxious, particle-laden smoke over the capital. Despite the smog, Eric and Irene decided to walk back to their hotel near the British Museum.

They wrapped their scarves around their mouths and noses – Maisie knew this because it had figured in the police report – and rather lost their way. At the junction of Southampton Row and Vernon Place, they waited at the icy kerb as a bus driver poked his head out of his window because he was unable to see though his windscreen to steer. The double-decker drifted into the middle of the road. Eric and Irene assumed the bus was turning right and stepped out. Just at that moment, the driver saw the road sign he was looking for and lurched left. Their parents were crushed under his wheels. They might have survived their injuries had it been possible to get them quickly to a hospital, but no ambulances were available and response times in the pea-souper fog were catastrophically slow.

An accident, that was all.

Maisie thought that was something to hold on to, so as not to become bitter. Stephen hadn't been able to take the same attitude. He seemed to take it as a personal slight. He had been granted leave and they had briefly lived together, for the first time as adults.

'Two more deaths,' he had told her, his voice hoarse with emotion. 'I mean, it wasn't so long ago the whole world was bombing itself to hell. And that's my job, by the way, using violence to "keep the peace". You'd think that would make it easier, wouldn't you, to accept that death is so meaningless, so commonplace?'

What a terrible experience that had been, Stephen drinking too much and taking his pain out on her. In retrospect, she believed that was the moment when Stephen lost his 'eye', his moral bearings. And it was not long after that she took advantage of their tiny shared inheritance to move to Paris, taking a job with a small tour company looking after English-speaking tourists in the French capital, leaving Stephen alone.

***

Sitting on the cold stone of the Market Cross, Maisie shivered. A milk float went rattling past. Time was ticking on and the sun had disappeared behind the cathedral bell tower, but she felt paralysed by all she had to think about and do – and the awkward question of how she would pay for it all.

In her handbag were traveller's cheques to the value of just a few pounds, plus just enough ready money to get about for a few days and buy a bit of shopping. And there was, quite literally, less than nothing in Stephen's bank account.

Ryan, the solicitor, had been right. She had had 'expectations' – that Stephen would, at the very least, have been solvent, that there might have been a little equity in his home, something in his bank account, enough to pay for the 'cakes and ale' at the wake.

And there would be a bill for the cremation. Or could she avoid it? Wasn't it possible for Stephen's body to be disposed of as a . . . ?

Oh God, that was what the undertaker had advised her to avoid – the 'pauper's funeral'. And that was another unsettled bill, the red-stained deal coffin. What was she going to do about that?

EIGHTEEN

With no answers to any of these questions, Maisie turned her mind to the other mysteries she felt she had to resolve, vaguely aware she was deliberately avoiding the central question of Stephen's murder.

Who was the author of the cryptic poetry wrapped around the posy of wild flowers with its reference to the 'secret things of the grave'?

She had a sudden flash of inspiration. The Romantic poet Percy Bysshe Shelley. Not a contemporary of T S Eliot, but she had read them both in English classes at school. That was why thinking about *The Waste Land* in the cathedral had given her a hint.

But did that really get her anywhere?

What else should she be thinking about? The unspoken disagreement between June Strickland and her repellent father? The fact that Nigel Bacon – the man who discovered Stephen's body, after all – was cruel to his horse? Perhaps she should visit the stables?

That brought her back to her main and most immediate problem – transport. She hadn't bought enough traveller's cheques from the Thomas Cook office in Paris to use taxis. Everything was dependent on the unhelpfully sparse bus timetable.

Then it came to her.

The bicycle shop, Chitty's, on North Street, with the friendly older man with his steel-grey hair and light-brown warehouse coat. She could hire a ladies' bike – not like Stephen's racer in the dining room at Church Lodge, which had far too large a frame – and be independent. She could get one with a dynamo for lights and she could go out and about and ask everyone who was prepared to speak to her about how Stephen had lived. Then, surely, she would uncover the secret of why and how he had died.

She stood up, brushing the seat of her skirt. She felt stronger, more determined, no longer directionless and idle. She had a plan.

★★★

Pleased with herself, Maisie went first to Chichester Library, a round modernist building in concrete and glass, designed like a wheel with the bookshelves as its spokes. She found the poetry section and, as luck would have it, there was a *Complete Works of Shelley*.

Because she didn't know either the title of the poem or its first line, it took her a little while to track down what she wanted. Eventually she found it, with a dedication from Ecclesiastes: 'There is no work, nor device, nor knowledge, nor wisdom, in the grave, whither thou goest.' The poem was actually called 'On Death', which Masie found gloomily appropriate. Maisie found an empty page in her diary and copied out all thirty lines, but she supposed only the quoted verse was important.

> *The secret things of the grave are there,*
> *Where all but this frame must surely be,*
> *Though the fine-wrought eye and the wondrous ear*
> *No longer will live to hear or to see*
> *All that is great and all that is strange*
> *In the boundless realm of unending change.*

What was it about? The fact that death is the end. But why the reference to 'secret things'? Was that a kind of hint? And who, in the village of Framlington, was both a lover of poetry and a friend of Stephen, dear enough to leave such a heartfelt – but cryptic – tribute?

Her mind buzzing, she put the book back on the shelf and returned to North Street via Sainsbury's where she bought a loaf of bread, half a pound of butter and some strong cheddar cheese, counting out the unaccustomed coins on the counter. At Chitty's bike shop, a bell on a loop of bent metal announced her entrance. Inside, she smelt the distinctive odours of rubber, three-in-one oil and saddle leather.

'Good afternoon, Miss Cooper,' said the smiling older man. 'How can I help you?'

'I wonder if you rent bicycles?' she blurted.

'Not as a matter of course,' Mr Chitty told her with a slight frown, 'but we will always do what we can to help a customer.'

The transaction took very little time. It appeared that Mr Chitty had recently acquired a second-hand ladies' Raleigh Chiltern that would suit, the one she had seen earlier that morning, outside in the street. He had refurbished it himself and it was in good condition. The price – by the day or by the week – was so very reasonable that Maisie wondered if he was doing her a special favour. To complete the transaction, she filled in a form and gave Stephen's address as her own.

'Yes, of course,' said Mr Chitty, his expression serious. 'But we have another matter to discuss.'

'We do?'

He put a finger alongside her name on the form then looked up at her.

'Yes. I wonder—'

'I saw you at the church and reception with your grandson,' she interrupted. 'You knew my brother. Is that it?'

'You have a look of him, about the eyes, I think. Now, this is perhaps a delicate matter . . .'

He pulled the form towards him, as if taking it out of her reach. Maisie thought he was about to change his mind and refuse to help.

'He was murdered,' she said, abruptly. 'I need to find out why. I need the bicycle to get about.'

'Indeed, but—'

'Please help me. Please don't turn me down. I don't know what else to do.'

Nineteen

Mortifyingly, Maisie felt tears begin to prick at the corners of her eyes. She squeezed them back and groped and struggled with the clasp of her handbag, trying to locate her handkerchief. Without a word, Mr Chitty went to the front door, shot the bolt and turned the card to 'Closed'. He invited her to sit down on a chair, leading her to it by the hand.

'Oh, my dear, you are very cold. Have you been sitting outside? The sun is nowhere near as warm as it appears.'

'No, I mean, yes.'

'I will bring you a nice cup of Ovaltine.'

He toddled away and, despite her embarrassment, Maisie felt herself smiling.

Ovaltine. At least it made a change from the ubiquitous healing properties of tea.

She dabbed her eyes, glad she was not in the habit of using mascara or shadow. While she was waiting and regaining her composure, she saw Mr Chitty's grandson peering round the doorjamb of the workshop at the back. He smiled at her, then slipped away.

Mr Chitty returned with the mug of Ovaltine. He had mixed it well and there were no lumps of malt floating in the warm milk. Against her chilled fingers it was almost too hot, but oh, so welcome. When she had drunk half of it, Chitty spoke again.

'Now, it is not a question of refusing your request. I merely ask for information. As you have no doubt surmised, we already have a cycle out at that address. A men's racer, a

93

Gazelle Champion. Mr Cooper was very keen on it. He was paying for it in instalments.' He gave her a sad smile.

'He failed to keep up the payments,' said Maisie.

'He did. He assured me he was only temporarily embarrassed, however . . .'

'You know from other shopkeepers around the town that you were not alone.'

'Indeed. I would like to retrieve it, if possible. He promised he would keep it indoors. Did he do so? Or is there perhaps a shed or an outhouse?'

'There is an outhouse but the bike is in the dining room.'

'Ah, that is good news. He at least looked after it, do you think?'

'I haven't looked closely. I'm afraid I have no way of transporting it.' She finished her drink. 'You are welcome to come and pick it up.'

He gestured to her mug. 'Would you care for some more?'

'No, thank you. I feel much better.'

In the end, it was decided that Mr Chitty would drive to Framlington in his van after closing his shop at five-thirty. In the meantime, he would allow Maisie to take the ladies' bike.

'Unless you would like to wait and have a lift?' he asked, politely.

'You are very, very kind,' she told him, 'but I'm looking forward to it.'

'The wind is brisk. You will need . . .'

He went behind the counter and took a pair of windproof cycling gloves from a drawer. Maisie looked in her handbag.

'I'm not sure I can afford anything else.'

He put them in the basket and, as an afterthought, added a combination lock and a pair of cycle clips. 'Shall we call them a part of the deal?' said Mr Chitty, generously.

***

Maisie loved the bike. Cycling north out of town, she played with the gear lever to make sure she got the hang of the changes – the reverse of her journey into town with the Stricklands and so much more pleasant.

At least, she enjoyed it while she was in the wooded sections, sheltered between the trees. After the S-bend in East Bitling, she came out onto a straight road between bare arable fields and discovered that the south-west wind was in her teeth. The cold breeze scoured her face and she was very grateful for the gloves. She changed down to the easiest gear. Once she was back at Church Lodge, she felt a sense of achievement. She was no longer a victim of circumstances. She had a certain amount of autonomy.

She brought the ladies' bicycle indoors and checked on the men's racer – the Gazelle Champion – in the dining room. It was very muddy and it made her think about Stephen's 'idleness' and another 'deadly sin' – sloth.

She took the racing bike into the kitchen and carefully cleaned it with warm water from the kettle using a box of 'Man-size' tissues she found on a shelf of the dresser, alongside several cookery books and, surprisingly, a copy of the Qur'an.

'What an interesting person you were, Stephen,' she said aloud.

She relit the Aga, putting on a few lumps of coke from the scuttle, then sat down at the table. She wanted to turn her vague musings at the Market Cross into a comprehensive list of things that she must do and find out, intending to do this while feasting on her frugal meal of bread and cheese.

She unwrapped the loaf but, before she had time to find a bread knife and cut herself a slice, she heard a soft rattle at the locked kitchen door and she froze.

Shockingly, the handle was being quietly turned, as if to test whether it would open – someone surreptitious, attempting to gain entrance unobserved.

There were a few seconds of silence, then she almost jumped out of her chair when, through the dirty glass of the window, she saw a blurred face, peering in.

III

ENVY

TWENTY

The banging on the kitchen door rattled the key in the lock. In fact, there were two of them, tied together on a piece of binder twine. She unlocked and opened up to find a red-faced, anxious-looking man, breathing heavily and clenching his fists at his sides. He wore a waxed jacket over an Arran jumper and heavy corduroy trousers.

'What's going on?' he asked her.

She recognised him from the churchyard.

'It's Mr Bacon, isn't it?'

'I mean, what's been found out?' His eyes glanced past her round the kitchen. What was he looking for? 'I mean, what the hell was he doing in my swimming pool? I mean, I know what he was doing in my swimming pool. He was swimming. I mean, he asked to. He wanted to get back in shape. No one likes to be called a fat man. We were pals, you see, as well as neighbours? But what was he doing there, dead?'

Maisie stepped aside and gestured for him to come indoors. 'You were pals, you say?'

'You know, we both lived alone – well mostly. He was a dog, if you know what I mean, pardon my French.'

Maisie wondered why it was that a certain sort of Englishman believed that any kind of risqué remark should be classified as 'French'.

'Do you mean June?'

'Yes, the luscious June. I had my eye on her myself but never seemed to get any encouragement . . .' His voice faded away on an unpleasant tone of self-pity. He shrugged his shoulders and shook his head, like someone trying to dispel an unpleasant memory. 'So, what news? Have you discovered anything?'

Maisie hesitated before answering. Events seemed to be happening out of their proper order. What was he asking, exactly? Did he know that she had been to see the solicitor and the police? Is that what he meant? Should she be wary of him? Could it have been Nigel Bacon she heard skulking in the rhododendrons?

'I don't expect I know any more than you do.'

'Want to see where it happened?' he asked, looking oddly excited.

Maisie had a momentary flashback to the police file and the wide photographic shot of the swimming pool, the unmistakable shape, floating turtle-like just beneath the surface of the water. She steeled herself.

'Yes, I would.'

'Good girl,' said Bacon. 'Call me Nigel, by the way. I expect Stephen spoke about me. Pals, we were.'

He held out a hand. Because of his manner and his heavy, country-squire clothes, he gave an impression of fleshy indulgence, but he was actually quite wiry and his handshake was firm.

'Yes, I saw you in the churchyard. Thank you for coming.'

'Couldn't face the wake. Sorry.'

'It went well,' said Maisie. There was a pause and she felt obliged to make further conversation. 'I suppose the idea is to make sure everyone is left with a happy memory of the deceased.'

'Good luck with that,' said Nigel and laughed heartily. 'No offence, but he wasn't everyone's cup of tea, our Stephen. Dear me, no.' He wiped his eyes. Was he pretending to cry? The air wasn't cold enough to make them watery, surely?

'I'll fetch a coat,' said Maisie.

'No need. It's just across the lawn.'

'Let me lock the door.'

'Oh, no need to do that round here.'

'All the same.' She ushered him outside and Maisie turned the key. 'Which way?'

Nigel set off across the damp grass beneath the bare fruit trees. Maisie was glad she hadn't taken off her outdoor shoes. Here and there were clumps of cuttings where a mower had left them behind. They came to the flint wall that divided the two gardens. Nigel pointed out a section that had been mended, new biscuit-coloured mortar alongside the older grey.

'We did that together one Saturday. Got the materials from the building suppliers, mixed up the cement and the sand like a couple of pros, made the repair. How does the expression go? "Good fences make good neighbours." I think he enjoyed it. He liked working with his hands. But you know that, of course.'

'Of course,' said Maisie, but the Stephen of her memory didn't like to get his hands dirty. He didn't even like cooking, because of the mess it made.

Perhaps he had been trying to get on Nigel's good side? Or perhaps he did it in lieu of the rent he owed?

'He would have come this way,' said Nigel. 'Didn't expect him that early, though.'

Maisie frowned. Was that important?

They walked a little way along the wall to a wooden gate with an iron handle. There was a muddy scar on the ground where it dragged across the grass.

'Would he have needed a key for the gate?'

'He had one, but it was never locked. We were pals. Through here.'

Remembering Strickland's unwanted hand on her bottom, Maisie found she didn't want to walk in front of him.

'You first.'

'Ladies first, surely?'

Just for a second, Maisie noticed a glimmer of calculation in Nigel's pale-blue eyes. She wondered if this was his usual manner or if he was putting on a performance of some kind. She thought back to the church, trying to visualise his behaviour, but that didn't help. People were different in church, on best behaviour.

'Please, show me the way.'

'If you prefer.'

Nigel stepped through the gate and Maisie followed into a manicured, formal garden. Everything was clipped and shaped. Pathways were laid out with lines of low box hedges. Rosemary bushes were constrained in carefully defined borders. Bay trees were topiarised into recognisable forms – an elephant, a cockerel and, incongruously, a space rocket. Was it all a little bit lax, however, lacking in recent attention?

He waved a hand. 'Not my work. I don't have time for all this. I get a man in.'

'It's very creative.'

The swimming pool was between the flint wall and a brick patio, no more than three or four strokes for a good swimmer.

'Well, this is it,' said Nigel. 'Poor old Stephen.'

Maisie glanced at him. He was bowing his head, determined that she should notice how sad he was.

'Did you see Stephen on that morning?' she asked.

'No.' He pointed to an upper window, the only one that overlooked the pool. 'But I'm not often in that part of the house. Only because the gun cupboard's up there.'

'The gun cupboard?'

'Locked, armoured, quite safe. Just a pair of shotguns. I used to lend one to Stephen now and then. What an eye he had – a proper Dead-Eye Dick.'

Maisie could imagine that – Stephen being charming and affable in a gang of sportsmen, the life and soul, then irritating everyone by never missing.

'I have some old photographs of the village. They show my house and his.'

'It wasn't his. He only rented.'

'You don't say,' said Nigel, sounding surprised. 'Well, I never did.'

You were pals, Maisie thought, *but you didn't know that? Or are you pretending not to know that? Or was it a secret Stephen found embarrassing and tried to conceal?*

'I could show them to you,' he said. 'The photographs?'

'Another time.'

'Poor old Stephen,' he said again, as if to himself. 'You did your best, old man, didn't you?'

TWENTY-ONE

As Nigel stepped back from the pool edge to give her a moment alone, Maisie thought about how he seemed to want her to believe that he was Stephen's friend when, in reality, the impression he gave was of someone jealous – someone who envied her brother's success with June, his accurate aim with a shotgun, his easy charm. But she forced herself to concentrate on what was in front of her. This was the place where he died.

The photograph at the police station had been taken from the far side, from the brick terrace, with the water in the foreground and the flint wall in the background. He weighed fourteen and a half stone, a significant weight to transport if he had been killed somewhere else.

Dead weight, in fact.

Nigel came closer, on the verge of further speech, but Maisie moved away. She could see a steel wheelbarrow leaning against the side of the house that might have served to move her brother. She wondered if the police had thought to examine it. She supposed they knew their business. Perhaps she would ask Sergeant Wingard.

'How are we, then?' asked Nigel, abruptly. 'Bearing up?'

'Yes, thank you.'

'It must be an unpleasant experience to stand here and . . .' He stopped. Maisie half-expected him to offer her a cup of tea with plenty of sugar. Mercifully, he maintained his silence and she was able to examine the layout. It was true that only one window overlooked the pool. The neighbours were all too far away and, in any case, behind a screen of evergreen trees. The murderer had taken advantage of a very private space.

'Have a drink with me,' said Nigel with a sort of guffaw. 'It's cocktail time. Nearly, anyway.'

'No, thank you. I should go,' she said. 'I'm expecting somebody.'

'Later then. You could come to me or I could meet you at the Fox-in-Flight when it opens?'

'I appreciate you showing me the garden and the pool.'

The truth was, she felt almost faint from hunger. She had eaten nothing but a single Granny Smith apple since her breakfast curry and it was now well after four o'clock. She pulled herself together and looked him in the eye. He returned her gaze and she once more saw the glimmer of calculation.

'What was it you wanted when you came to the kitchen door?'

'Ah, yes, fair question. He has – had – something of mine.'

'What was it? I can look for you.'

'Rather you didn't,' he said shiftily. 'If you don't mind. I left it for him. Brown-paper parcel, private things, just between the two of us. No need to open it up.'

'I wouldn't dream of doing so. Do you know where it might be?'

'How could I know?' he asked airily. Then added, reddening: 'Under his bed?'

Maisie felt queasy. Something in his manner had given her a clue as to what the brown-paper package might be.

'I'll look and tell you if I find anything.'

'Bring it round, would you? Don't open it, but come in for a drink.' Again, the sharpening of his gaze. 'Spoken to the police, have we?'

'Briefly.'

'Must be unsettling.'

What was he probing for? Maisie wasn't sure how to bring the conversation to a close, then she heard a vehicle crunching the gravel on the far side of the shared flint wall.

'That's my appointment,' she improvised. 'I must leave you. Thank you again for showing me the place. Goodbye, Mr Bacon.'

'Nigel,' he insisted and held out his hand.

She shook it and he held on for a few seconds too long.

As she stepped through into the orchard garden of Church Lodge, she had an uncomfortable feeling that he was watching her still. She turned to shut the gate and, sure enough, he held up a hand and waved.

'So glad to meet you properly, Miss Cooper,' he called.

She nodded, dragging the gate across the wet dirt, then walked away, quickly crossing the fresh-mown lawn under the bare fruit trees.

The vehicle she had heard on the gravel wasn't Mr Chitty from the bike shop. It was far too early. No, her saviour was the coal lorry. She was just in time to see the coalman drop two grimy sacks by the kitchen door and stomp away, back to his round. For a split second, Maisie thought about calling out to him and asking him how well he had known her brother, but she changed her mind. Almost inevitably, if they spoke, it would be to discover yet another unpaid bill and she already had far too many of those to think about.

She went indoors and returned the two back-door keys to the lock. Then, after a moment's thought, she undid the short length of binder twine to separate them, adding one to the collection in her handbag and using the other to lock herself in. If Nigel Bacon came snooping round again, she didn't want him – or anyone else – to be able to 'gain entry', as she thought the police would say.

She thought about his brown-paper package. What was it he had loaned to Stephen? She reckoned she had a pretty good idea and did not like it one bit.

The Aga was warm. She added some knobs of coke from the scuttle, then washed her hands in cold water with a bar of hard soap at the enormous kitchen sink.

She sat down at the table and pulled open the drawer, finding the posy and scrunched-up poem. She put the posy in water, using a 'decimalisation mug' she found in a cupboard – white china with a UK flag and conversion rates between old shillings and new pence. Then she found a bread knife among the old-fashioned utensils and cut herself a generous slice, using the same serrated blade on the butter and the cheese. She took a mouthful and leant blissfully back on the hard wooden chair.

***

In her job as a high-class tour guide for wealthy foreign visitors to Paris, Maisie was often invited to lunch or dine with them in the finest restaurants. Sometimes she would choose their dishes, often explaining their ingredients. For herself, she liked plain cuisine, but she understood how hard the chefs worked to make something palatable out of snails-in-their-shells and frog's legs. She knew about the ritual cruelty imposed on defenceless geese and ducks to produce *foie gras*. She was practised in the application of tabasco and pickles to disguise the unabashed raw beef in *steak tartare*. She had joyously overindulged at both the Crillon and Maxim's, just off Place de la Concorde. She knew all the oyster-and-sauerkraut establishments on the Grands Boulevards.

Yes, she had been lucky. Her friends envied her this easy access to the finest in Parisian cuisine, 'at no cost to herself'.

She had never, though, enjoyed any of those meals quite as much as she savoured two thick rounds of sandwiches, fresh white bread, salted butter and mousetrap cheese, one cold afternoon in February, using greaseproof paper as a plate in the flagstoned kitchen at Church Lodge.

Twenty-Two

A little later, Maisie was surprised by the chime of the kitchen clock. She had almost dozed off at the table in the warm room, for the first time in a couple of days full of food. She rolled her neck and shoulders, feeling she would rather enjoy a cocktail, just not with Nigel Bacon.

It took her a few moments to regain mental sharpness. She contemplated the sky outside the window. It was five o'clock but she could only just make out the tracery of bare tree branches as a network of something slightly blacker against the blue of the night. When she got up to flick the light switch there was no reaction.

Oh, she thought, another power cut. Were they regularly scheduled? It was the same time as yesterday, wasn't it? She must remember and organise her activities accordingly.

She found the matches and the box of candles at the back of the Aga almost by touch, lit one and dripped liquid wax onto a saucer to make it stand up. The cheese had made her thirsty, so she poured herself a glass of cold water from the tap over the big kitchen sink, drinking it down in three long draughts. The glass was the dimpled beer mug that she now supposed Stephen had 'borrowed' from the Fox-in-Flight. When she had finished, she rinsed it out and left it upside-down on the wooden draining board.

What next?

Mr Chitty was due in a little more than half an hour. It would only take ten minutes for him to drive the four or five miles out through the trees and fields to Framlington. Mean-while, there was an ache in her thighs that it took a while to remember was due to the unaccustomed exercise of cycling.

Plus, the cold. It had been chilly, especially in the teeth of the south-west wind. She wished she had packed a pair of trousers as well as her two workaday skirts.

She left the warm kitchen, walked along the corridor beneath the sweep of the staircase and out into the chilly hallway, shielding the flame of her candle with her hand. She stood for a moment in the centre of the chequerboard floor tiles, listening to the house.

It was very quiet. Not a creak came from window frames, floorboards or rafters. Of course, houses normally spoke to their owners because they were expanding or contract-ing with the movement of heat and cold. But the boiler at Church Lodge wasn't working. The only warmth came from open hearths.

She had a worrying thought. If she didn't light the hallway fire, perhaps she would have no hot water this evening? No, surely the Aga would be connected somehow? It would make sense if it was.

She went upstairs, looking in briefly at the bedroom she had chosen to sleep in. There was a draught like a knife, gut-tering her candle flame. A lover of fresh air, she had left the sash window open a crack overnight. She put down her can-dle and tried to close it. The window was sticky and it was a struggle to pull it down.

She tidied the bed that she had, shamefully, left unmade and went along the landing to Stephen's room, feeling the unevenness of the floorboards beneath her feet, the sag in the centre. His room was a mess, too, with clothes strewn across two low chairs and onto the floor.

Was it her brother's slackness or the aftermath of the police search? Who had been responsible? She had seen the name in the report. Constable Goodbody, that was it. Maisie wondered if Goodbody was the same constable with whom she had seen Sergeant Wingard arguing out of the rear window of the interview room at the police station.

Against the left-hand wall, the dark doors of an enormous wardrobe hung open. Maisie approached, holding her candle out in front of her.

The wardrobe was full to bursting with all kinds of male garments on wooden hangers – two dress suits, a tweed suit, three or four lounge suits, five or six smart shirts, three patterned flannel shirts. Her flame twinkled on a bright cufflink left in a white cuff. On the floor of the wardrobe were several folded jumpers and a few towels.

She turned round, holding her candle high to illuminate the room. Stephen had tacked a grey woollen blanket to the window frame, in lieu of a curtain, tied back with a broken shoelace. There was a small electric bar heater, one of whose two elements had shorted out with a black stain where the incandescent wire had melted. She bent down to look under the bed.

Here, as Nigel Bacon had predicted, was a package wrapped in brown paper and tied with string. For a moment she wondered if it had anything to do with the cathedral robbery but, when she slid it out, it felt like a stack of magazines.

She put it on the bed, vaguely listening to the traffic from the road through the village. A tractor, she thought, on its way back to a barn somewhere, perhaps one of the villages in the Downs, Harden or Bunting. Could it be from the Fieldhouses' land, the most important landowners hereabouts?

Thinking of the Fieldhouses, was it strange that neither Derek Fieldhouse nor his wife had attended either the church or the reception? Sergeant Wingard had suggested they owned Church Lodge. Theirs was perhaps the only Framlington name Maisie remembered from when Stephen had last written to her. When was that? Eighteen months ago, at least. What had he written?

> *There's a crowd of clowns living here but then there always were, you remember? Rife with social division. Derek Fieldhouse does his best to "cross the social divide" but it isn't easy when you own the place and no one much likes you.*

Something like that – acid, sarcastic.

No, that wasn't fair. It had been warm enough to her, just not very interesting, not very engaged. The sort of message one might send out of duty to an aged relative who had despatched a postal order as a gift. It really was very sad to recognise how they had grown apart. Then, that sadness was overtaken by the extraordinary fact that he was dead, that someone had hated him enough to kill him, and that his death would be forever.

She wanted to go back downstairs but discovered, to her surprise, that she could no longer move. This was the room her brother had called home and she was overwhelmed with the unbearable waste, the remainder of life unlived, the joys that would never be experienced, the wrongs that could never be put right.

For the first time in she couldn't remember how many years, she sat down on the ruffled eiderdown and properly wept.

TWENTY-THREE

Jack Wingard had been at the police station from six o'clock that morning and was now off duty. As was his habit, he walked home, stopping briefly at the fish-and-chip shop on St Paul's Road – two pieces of cod and a portion of chips to share. In the pink bungalow on Parklands Road, his grandmother, Florence, had already laid the table and they ate in companionable silence with the mundane chatter of the *Nationwide* magazine programme on the television in the background.

Eventually, Jack cleared away and washed up in the small square kitchen. When he came back to the living room, his grandmother looked up, expectantly, from her knitting.

'I know,' he said. 'I'm brooding.'

'It's fine to brood if, in the end, it helps you work out what you need to do.'

There was a pause. Jack sat next to her, watching the TV screen, thinking about turning up the volume.

'She came in,' he told her, abruptly.

'Oh, good.'

'Not really.'

'Did you not remind her – tell her who you are?'

'I wanted to. I got distracted.'

'What by?'

'I don't know.'

'I see,' said Florence. She picked up her knitting. 'Do you think perhaps you didn't tell her because you first want proof that she remembers you as well as you remember her?'

'Maybe,' said Jack, grudgingly.

'And you're jealous of the life she's been living,' said Florence with a twinkle, 'foreign parts, glamorous, never a thought for poor old you, trapped back home with an aged grandmother.'

'Not that aged.' Jack laughed. Then he said, more sombrely: 'I think I snubbed her.'

'You didn't.'

'Yes.' Jack brushed non-existent dust from his trousers. 'I don't know . . .' he said again.

Florence smiled, sympathetically. 'It's difficult, but you have to speak up, my boy.'

'Perhaps I should go for a walk.'

Florence nodded and resumed her knitting. 'Good idea.'

'No more advice?' Jack asked.

'Honesty is the best policy. If she's forgotten you, what harm can it do to remind her?'

'That would make sense if I wasn't also investigating . . .' He stopped. 'Never mind.'

'I know. You mustn't tell me what terrible crimes are going on in Chichester.'

He laughed. 'You'd be surprised.'

She put down her needles.

'What's happening with the cathedral robbery? I read that the little book is almost priceless – unique.'

'A book of sins and virtues,' said Jack. 'There's a connection . . .'

He didn't finish his sentence. Florence reached out and touched his arm. 'Go, walk until you're tired, otherwise you won't sleep.'

Jack nodded. 'Sound advice but I think I might just go back to the station.' He leant over and kissed his grandmother's pink cheek. 'Don't wait up.'

He went out into the narrow hallway and put on an overcoat because the evening was cold.

Of course, he thought, wandering out along Parklands Road, there was indeed a connection. It seemed clear that Stephen Cooper was on the verge of 'doing a runner' and had fixed upon the most likely source of local portable value to take with him. The precious cathedral artefacts could easily be packed away in a suitcase and, if he was intending to go and join his sister in Paris, for example, he would be very unlucky to be caught by a random search getting on or off the ferry.

But he couldn't tell Maisie any of that – not yet, at least.

His footsteps took him past Strickland's second-hand warehouse. It would be helpful, he thought, to find a pretext to carry out a search of the premises. He had mentioned it to Inspector Barden, and the Special Branch man had agreed.

He walked on, wondering if Stephen Cooper had really needed Strickland as a fence of the artefacts. Or had Cooper drawn June's pa into his plan as a way of keeping him onside, so Strickland didn't kick up a fuss about Cooper taking advantage of his daughter?

Jack sighed. His own connection to the Strickland family might turn out to be another reason for Maisie Cooper to resent him, not respect or like him.

What had Florence said: '*You're jealous of the life she's been living.*'

Was he jealous? Certainly, it seemed very exciting, compared to the narrow frame of his own existence in this parochial county town. Was it any wonder Maisie wanted to get back to France just as soon as she possibly could?

'Damn it,' he said to himself as he trudged away, his shoulders hunched, his face set.

TWENTY-FOUR

The mysterious brown-paper parcel was on the kitchen table, alongside the posy in its decimalisation mug and the scrunched-up poem. Maisie stood at the sink, rinsing out her handkerchief.

The tears had lasted much longer than she expected, sitting on Stephen's untidy eiderdown. She had finally been pulled out of her misery by finding a bra under his pillow and that set her thinking about June and, who knew, perhaps several other women on that very same bed. June had been certain that Stephen had someone else 'on the side' and had wrongly assumed it was Maisie. But just because June was mistaken about Maisie didn't mean there wasn't someone else, another face yet to emerge from the crowd.

At the front of the Aga was a shiny chrome rail, perfect for hanging the handkerchief to dry. She draped it carefully, then repositioned her candle on the table and – despite her promise to Nigel Bacon – she undid the string that held the brown-paper parcel closed. It came apart easily.

The contents were exactly what she had suspected. Pornographic magazines, seven of them. She leafed through the first with a kind of academic interest. Dozens of photographs of more or less beautiful women, trying their best not to reveal the disappointment behind their eyes.

She wrapped the package up again and tied the string nice and tight, as if it had never been opened, not even by Stephen. She didn't want to have to discuss the contents with Nigel

Bacon, or for him to have the faintest suspicion that she knew what they were.

Still, she thought, it was another small mystery solved.

But could it have something to do with Stephen's death, some kind of blackmail situation, perhaps? That didn't seem likely. Was Nigel Bacon the sort of man whose reputation was fundamental to his sense of self-worth or his business dealings? Pornography was legal, after all, if distasteful.

Maisie smoothed out the thick writing paper that had wrapped the posy, regretting the impulse that had made her screw it up into a ball. She read over the six lines, took her diary out of her handbag and held it at an angle to the candle flame, comparing the extract to the copy she had made of the entire thing. It brought to mind something she had learnt at school that the poet W H Auden had once said: 'No good poem is not better read aloud.'

So that was what she did, speaking the words with deliberation in the warm atmosphere of the quiet kitchen.

> *The secret things of the grave are there,*
> *Where all but this frame must surely be,*
> *Though the fine-wrought eye and the wondrous ear*
> *No longer will live to hear or to see*
> *All that is great and all that is strange*
> *In the boundless realm of unending change.*

Yes, she thought, when she had finished. Deceptively simple. And what was the key idea? The 'secret things' that 'no one will live to hear or see'.

Then she heard tyres on the gravel of the drive and hurried to open the front door for Mr Chitty.

***

As it turned out, Mr Chitty was not alone. Nicholas, the boy that Maisie kept seeing with him – at the wake in the pub and in his shop – was in the small van's passenger seat, sitting very upright and alert, like a friendly whippet. Mr Chitty got out and greeted her politely.

'A brisk evening, Miss Cooper. I hope you enjoyed your cycle?'

'It was invigorating. I liked it very much. And it made such a difference to be independent.'

'I'm glad. Now, how is our Gazelle Champion? Indoors, is it?'

'Follow me.'

She had brought it back out into the hall. Mr Chitty looked it over by the light of his torch and pronounced himself satisfied.

'I cleaned it with warm water,' Maisie told him. 'It was a little muddy.'

'That is to be expected.' He kept his torch beam low so as not to dazzle her and waved a vague hand towards the van. 'My grandson Nicholas will oil the moving parts back at the shop.'

'The tyres are a little soft.'

'Yes, there ought to be a pump attached to the frame. Have you seen one?'

'I can go and have a look.'

'Never mind. Wait for the light of morning or the end of the power cut,' said Mr Chitty with a placid smile that revealed his very even false teeth.

'Do the lights go out at the same time every evening?' she asked.

'I'm afraid they do. Drop the pump in when you are next in town. I imagine you will be speaking to Maurice Ryan?' Maisie frowned. Was he trying to find something out? 'Forgive me. I don't mean to pry,' he said meekly. 'Chichester is a small town. I think we all know too much about one another's business.'

Maisie forgot her flash of suspicion and remembered how kind he had been.

'Thank you,' she told him. 'I really do appreciate your understanding and I feel I must apologise for my brother's behaviour.'

'You are not,' said Chitty, in the tone people use for quotations, 'your brother's keeper.' Then there was an odd pause and he looked flustered. 'Yes, but not, I mean to say, that there is any . . . I will be on my way. Nicholas and I will be on our way.'

He picked up the lightweight racing bike and Maisie felt a pang that she had not thought to ask him to adjust the saddle and let her keep the Gazelle Champion, instead of the rather stolid Raleigh Chiltern. No, it would still have been too big and, without trousers, it would be impossible to ride a men's frame without causing an affront to public decency.

She followed him outside and watched him open the rear doors of the van. The boy ran round to help, draping the bike with a rough blanket and guiding the front wheel into the space.

'Thank you very much, miss,' Nicholas said politely.

'Do come in and see us if you have any trouble,' said Mr Chitty. 'My grandson will be pleased to help you as he is off school for half-term. And do forgive my indiscretion.'

Maisie frowned. What did he mean, 'indiscretion'?

'You've been very kind,' she insisted.

He started the engine and pulled away, nosing carefully out onto the main road. She supposed they were local, too. She ought to have asked.

What indiscretion was Mr Chitty referring to? Did that mean that there might be another connection with Stephen as well as the fact that he owed Mr Chitty money? Could there be another motive there, despite Mr Chitty's gentle manner?

Back indoors, she locked the front door on the inside and returned to the kitchen. There were five keys on her bunch, including the spare one from the kitchen door that she herself had added. She knew that another was for the gate into Nigel Bacon's garden, but apparently that was never locked. She supposed the small brick-built outhouse would need one. She hadn't yet had time to inspect it in daylight.

Front door, back door, garden gate, outhouse. That left a fifth key that she couldn't identify.

Was it important?

The unidentified key was made of tarnished brass, only about two inches long with a narrow shank and a very simple bit, cut with a single groove. The round 'handle' part was shaped like a decorative bow. It looked like it might open a cupboard or a chest.

On a whim, she took her candle back upstairs to Stephen's untidy room where there were bedside cabinets either side of the narrow double bed, but neither was locked and they contained only underwear, socks, books and a half-empty bottle of cheap whisky. Next to the window was a two-over-three chest of drawers, with keyholes about the right size, but it didn't fit. In any case, the five drawers were unlocked, stuffed with an extraordinary selection of mixed clothing, men's and women's, even children's – presumably from a previous tenant. She decided to look through it in the morning when she had better light.

Then she found what she was looking for. At the foot of the enormous wardrobe, beneath the hanging rail of suits and shirts, the jumpers and towels piled up below, was a drawer. If you didn't know it was there, it would be easy to overlook. It had a curved front and a keyhole of precisely the right size, protected by a small brass escutcheon. The mechanism moved with a soft but unmistakable 'click'. She pulled the drawer open towards her.

At first, she thought it was merely somewhere to tidy away bed linen. There was a pile of thick cotton sheets, several pillowcases and three or four itchy woollen blankets. At the left-hand end, though, something caught her eye. Tightly folded upon itself was a small eiderdown with a jolly pattern of brightly coloured triangles, circles and squares, suitable for a child's bedroom.

She unfolded it and discovered, wrapped within, a notebook – a school exercise book with soft covers and lined pages. It felt thin, as if some of the leaves had been torn out.

Maisie opened it and had the odd impression that something had gone wrong with her eyes. Of course, the light was poor from just one candle, but around a dozen pages had been largely filled with a flowing script that she could make nothing of. She angled the page to the flame, trying to see more clearly what was written.

The text ran from right to left, looping strokes modified with diacritical marks indicating vowels. Here and there were numbers that she could recognise; otherwise, it was incomprehensible.

She had never learnt to read Arabic.

TWENTY-FIVE

A little later, Maisie was sitting at the kitchen table once more, assembling her thoughts. She wondered about going back to her idea of making a list – of the people she had met and the questions she wanted to ask them. There were also a few people she had not yet met but she had heard mentioned – Derek Fieldhouse of Framlington Manor, the farmer and landowner, for example. Also, there was the shadowy presence of Stephen's alleged second mistress.

She opened her diary to write it all down but became distracted by the poem she had copied out into its pages. She touched the petals of the wild flowers. Despite now being in water, the poor things looked much the worse for wear. Her eyes went back to Stephen's impenetrable notebook. Wasn't that now her strongest, most substantial clue? Her brother had hidden it, after all.

But what to do? Where to start?

The odd phrase Mr Chitty had used came back to her, the one that had made him flustered.

'*You are not your brother's keeper.*'

Then she remembered the source of the phrase, transporting her back to a whiff of incense and interminable childhood boredom, wearing uncomfortable clothes on a hard church pew, listening to the meanderings of a shapeless sermon on the nature of evil and the blessed bounty of forgiveness.

Yes, that was it. The near-quotation came from a passage in the Bible, when God asked Cain if he knew where Abel, his brother, might be found. The Lord already knew, of course, that Cain had murdered Abel and, Maisie supposed, anticipated Cain's prevaricating reply: '*I do not know. Am I my brother's keeper?*'

No wonder Mr Chitty had suddenly seemed so flustered. What a thing to say to someone whose brother had been murdered.

Maisie felt sorry that she had begun to dislike him for his mild inquisitiveness. He was a kindly old man who took an interest in the people around him, that was all. It wasn't his fault that she had such a strong reaction to anything that seemed like prying. He wasn't to know it was the reason she had left England, cutting virtually all ties with her previous life, starting again with a pristine clean slate.

The truth was, ever since their parents' deaths in one of the last ever London 'pea-souper' fogs, Maisie had protected her privacy with an almost fierce determination. She knew herself well enough to understand that this was a reaction to becoming, for the worst of reasons, the centre of attention, the recipient of a surfeit of cloying sympathy. All the kindly requests to be allowed to help, to comfort and condole, had made for an intolerable burden for a young woman who wanted nothing more than to be left alone with her grief.

So she had fled across the Channel to start again and left her brother alone with his dark thoughts, and look how that had turned out.

'Never mind all that now,' she told herself, her voice surprisingly loud in the quiet kitchen.

She returned her attention Stephen's notebook.

'Now, here's a puzzle . . .'

Maisie spoke reasonable Spanish and German as well as her fluent French. Her natural curiosity had led her to take an interest in the basic structure of Arabic, seeing it regularly in the calligraphic decoration on the walls of the

Paris mosque, a popular visit for the wealthy Middle Eastern tourists whom it was sometimes her job to entertain. She knew that Arabic words were often written with only their consonants, the vowels being understood from context. But Stephen had used the optional vowel marks above and below his text. Maisie had an idea that the one that appeared as a little loop was called 'dhamma', but she couldn't remember what the others were or what any of them sounded like. In any case, this meagre theoretical knowledge was no help in deciphering what her brother had written.

She turned the pages, searching for the numbers she had noticed. Some of them were accompanied by pound signs and dollar signs and indicated quite large sums – six, seven or even eight digits. Then, at last, alongside a set of numerals in a different format, she found a word she recognised.

Reading from right to left, the word was made up of four consonants, m, h, m and d – مُحَمَّد. It was 'Mohammed', the name of the Prophet, 'peace be upon him', as she had learnt to add. The digits alongside had a recognisable English format, beginning 01.

It was a London telephone number.

Maisie tapped her fingers on the table. Had there been a telephone to hand, she would have dialled the number straight away and asked to speak to 'Mohammed', but, of course, she couldn't.

She thought back. Inspector Barden had asked about Stephen's Arabic contacts, hadn't he? In reality, she knew very well the name of Stephen's friend, Mohammed As-Sabah, though she had only met him once, back when she was still in school. On leave from the army, Stephen had taken her to the Horse of the Year Show at Haringey, a wonderful festival of show-jumping, and Mohammed had been there. Thinking back, she thought he was perhaps buying horseflesh but, being still a schoolgirl, she had felt sidelined as the young men chatted and she sat disregarded on her hard plastic seat, watching the competition.

Why had she held the information back from the police? Because she resented their unexplained inquiries, angry that she hadn't been told the direction of their investigation.

She looked closely at the tight cursive script, looking for Mohammed's family name, As-Sabah.

How would 'As-Sabah' be written? She wasn't sure. But then, if there was no family name, if there was just 'Mohammed', then it must be the telephone number of a friend, surely? And would Stephen have more than one Arab friend called Mohammed?

Well, of course, he might have. It would be like having more than one friend called Jack or James or Charlotte or Kate. Not so much a coincidence as very likely.

Looked at another way, if there was a connection with oil and diplomacy and international trade, wasn't Mohammed a potential suspect in Stephen's murder? How might she find out if he had been in touch with her brother?

Well, by confronting him somehow.

Maisie looked at the time. It was almost six o'clock and, early though it was, she felt a deep yearning for her bed. She was still a little stiff from the overnight boat train from Paris, sitting almost upright in a railway carriage that smelt of dust and old cigarettes. Then, bobbing across the Channel, giddy with nausea, in a passenger ferry that was too small to remain stable on the waves. Then, a brutish, slam-door British Rail train, much worse than the French service, up to London Victoria in the damp, cold dawn – followed by yet another, rattling out through Surrey, down past Arundel Castle and the sodden water meadows to the south.

And, of course, that wasn't all. Everything that had happened since that moment had been exhausting: three nights at the grimy Bedford Hotel; the organisation of the coffin and cremation; finding Church Lodge empty, unfriendly and cold; the long hours of nothing to do until, finally . . .

No, nothing was final. She was a long way from anything final.

She yawned. Yes, she was very tired, but she was sure she would not sleep. There was too much information racing round in her head, fragments of knowledge chasing one another like greyhounds. She decided to walk to the Fox-in-Flight and make a call from the payphone.

TWENTY-SIX

Her handkerchief had dried so Maisie took it from the rail of the Aga, folded it small and slipped it inside her handbag. She put on her mackintosh and went out into the darkness of the night, carefully locking up behind her. The power cut was still in progress and the street lamps were unlit, the rhododendron borders huge lumps of black looming shadow.

She paused on the threshold, wondering why it was she still couldn't shake the impression that she was being observed.

Then a couple of cars went past, driving close together, one after the other, their headlamps momentarily sweeping across the untidy gravel drive, and broke the spell.

She walked quickly the hundred yards to the pub. The long public bar was warm and quiet, with a fire at one end. Hanging above the counter, evenly spaced, were three hurricane lamps, illuminating the optics, the bottles and the glasses with a warm glow. There were only seven or eight people sitting at the low tables and one older man at the bar, playing backgammon on his own.

Maisie asked the publican the whereabouts of the phone and he led her to a hooded half-cubicle next to the toilet door.

Despite the fact that no one was paying her the slightest attention, she felt exposed and hesitated before dialling. She had copied the number into her diary to avoid carrying Stephen's notebook around in full view. The habit of secrecy, she reflected, was becoming more and more pronounced.

She put a coin in the slot and spun the rotary dial, hearing the familiar clicking sound as the movement was translated by the mechanism into a sequence of numbers. After a moment's pause, it rang and, quite quickly, someone answered.

'Mohammed As-Sabah.'

'Good evening, I'm not sure you will remember me, but my name is Maisie, Maisie Cooper. I am Stephen Cooper's sister.'

'What a pleasant surprise. I do remember you,' came the smooth reply.

'I'm sorry to call you out of the blue.'

'Yes?'

'I'm not sure where to start.'

Mohammed's affable tone sharpened. 'Has something happened?'

'Yes, I'm afraid so—'

'Is it Stephen?' he asked quickly.

'It is. I wonder if I might be able to speak to you about—'

'Would you mind if we didn't speak on the phone,' he interrupted.

'I beg your pardon?'

'In person is always better, don't you think?'

'It was just—'

'I will come to you. Not this evening. It is too late. I can travel tomorrow. How would that be? Where should I come to?'

'Church Lodge, Framlington.'

'The village where you were brought up? Good, I will see you at Church Lodge.'

'Yes, but—'

Maisie was again interrupted, this time by the pips indicating that her money was running out. She looked in her handbag for more change but had no appropriate coins. When the pips stopped, he spoke quickly, clearly anxious to use the last few seconds before it cut off.

'Shall we say midday? No, that is not possible. I have an early meeting myself in the City. Perhaps two o'clock or two-thirty? Yes, two-thirty. I will ask my driver to—'

The connection was broken and Maisie was left staring at the receiver, uncertain if she should be reassured or frightened. She drifted over to the bar, wondering what exactly she had done. Mohammed had not sounded pleased.

Had he been shifty, in fact, evasive? Had she just made an appointment to meet a murderer? And how did he know Framlington?

Maisie leant on the polished counter where so many people had leant before, drinking their 'swift half' at lunchtime before returning to the fields to work, or lounging of an evening, arguing about politics or sport or religion. 'People' meant mostly men, of course. That was the same the whole world over, wasn't it? From pole to pole, the communities of regulars lounging in drinking establishments were always mostly men.

'What can I get you?'

It was the publican, Gerald Gleeson, wiping his hands on a tea towel branded with the insignia of Harvey's, the local brewery.

'I meant to come in and thank you for your hard work at the reception.'

'People seemed to enjoy it,' he replied, complacently. 'Now, the bill. Just to let you know, it's already in the post just to make it official.'

Of course, thought Maisie, the local publican would know the place was just rented and would want payment as soon as he could get it.

'Now,' he said, eyeing her as if he could judge her tastes from looking into her face, 'how about a nice port and lemon?'

Maisie could think of nothing worse.

'Vodka and tonic, please. A single. Do you have any lime?'

'Lime cordial?'

'No, thank you. Just a slice of lemon.'

'There, I knew it would be lemon,' he told her, and went off to prepare her drink.

Maisie watched him. She would like to have a good long chat with Gerald Gleeson at some point, when he wasn't busy in the bar or distracted by customers. She was certain Gerald would know Stephen at least as well as Maurice Ryan or Nigel Bacon. Alcohol was a great loosener of tongues. Where did lonely men go to talk, after all, when there was no one to talk to at home?

Why did she think Stephen was lonely?

It was just a feeling, something to do with his call out of the blue.

Then she wondered if Stephen might have told Gleeson something to turn the publican into an enemy. Perhaps, also, he had heard Stephen's phone call to Paris?

Gleeson put the vodka and tonic on the beer mat in front of her, raised the hatch and went to stoke the fire, shaking a few knobs of coal from the scuttle into the hearth, momentarily dousing the flames. Maisie sipped her drink, watching the smoke turn a darker grey, then seeing the heat slowly working its way through the additional fuel until tongues of blue flame began snaking out.

She checked her watch. It was just before six-thirty and the pub was starting to get busy. All but two of the low tables were in use. Someone had put a coin in the discreet jukebox and requested 'I'd Like to Teach the World to Sing' by The New Seekers. Several men had brought their wives, touchingly formal in their best blouses and lightweight cardigans, coats folded in their laps. But the population was still more than three-quarters men.

At that moment, June Strickland came bustling in. Maisie saw Gleeson go up to her, a look of exasperation on his face. He gave her his Harvey's tea towel and turned his back, trudging sulkily away towards the stairs.

Going up to his private quarters, Maisie thought. *He's been waiting for her, so he can go and have a sit-down and she's late. And, by the look on his face, it isn't the first time.*

June was warmly greeted by several of the men, in particular the earthy old soul perched on his bar stool playing his solitary game of backgammon. Maisie saw June respond, chatting to him girlishly, invitingly. He put a hand on her backside and she squirmed away, laughing what sounded to Maisie as a horribly false giggle, but no one else seemed to think so. Everyone else was having a wonderful, bucolic time. Only Maisie was out of sync.

The jukebox began playing George Harrison's 'My Sweet Lord' as June came round to the hatch at the end of the bar and did an enormous double take.

'Hello, June,' said Maisie. 'How are you?'

'What are you doing here?' said June, astonished.

'I came in to make a phone call,' said Maisie. 'Now, I'm having a drink.'

'On your own?'

'Yes, that's all right, isn't it?' asked Maisie, crossly. 'It's legal for a woman to have a drink on her own?'

'No, that's not what I'm asking,' said June quietly, almost whispering. 'I mean you're on your own?'

Maisie realised June wanted to speak to her privately.

'You have something you want to tell me?'

June nodded but was distracted by someone calling for a refill.

'Let me just get everyone sorted,' she said, urgently. 'Stay here.'

TWENTY-SEVEN

Maisie sipped her vodka and tonic and watched as June dispensed drinks and charm. It took a good fifteen minutes as more or less everyone needed to refresh their glasses. The men who had come out with their wives all trooped up to the bar, one after the other, each making the most of their interaction. June was pouting and flirtatious. The wives sat in silent disapproval until their husbands returned, gratified, sure they had shown themselves to be roguish men of the world, but with a faint air of disappointment because their moment had passed.

As Maisie watched, she began to ponder if June might be capable of murder. Had she been with Stephen, in his bed, might she have been capable of asphyxiating him and dragging his body to the pool – using Nigel Bacon's wheelbarrow, perhaps – believing she would inherit Church Lodge?

It seemed unlikely, but it also seemed unlikely that she should think she was married on the strength of a bogus handwritten Gothic certificate.

Finally, everyone was settled and June brought Maisie a second drink.

'I don't think I want another.'

'Don't worry. It's on the house.'

'That isn't what I meant . . .' Maisie began, then stopped, reminding herself not to become defensive. 'Never mind.'

'There's no need to look so serious,' hissed June.

'I beg your pardon?'

'You'll be making people stare. Just talk normal, like we're friendly with one another.'

Maisie did her best, relaxing her shoulders and putting on a smile. 'Yes, of course.'

June was again dragged away and, as she drew the ale from the pump, Maisie noticed she was still wearing the gaudy ring on her wedding finger – a cheap, sterling-silver setting with a cut-glass bead, pretending to be a diamond. Maisie wondered if Stephen had bought it to serve as a prop in their bogus marriage. From Woolworths, perhaps, like the exercise book?

June sidled back to the hatch. 'I need to ask you something, quickly, before someone else comes.'

'Go ahead.'

'Jack Wingard dropped me off tonight instead of my pa, and he wants me to do something and I don't know if I should. That's why I was late.'

It took Maisie a moment to realise Jack Wingard must be Sergeant Wingard. June gave another little incongruous giggle for the benefit of the patrons, to disguise the seriousness of what she was saying.

'How do you know Sergeant Wingard?'

'He used to teach me to read,' said June, surprisingly.

'When was that?'

'It doesn't matter. He wants me to squeal. I don't know what to do.'

'He wants you to give evidence against someone?' said Maisie, wondering if this was her first real clue.

'Shush, there's no need to say it out loud,' hissed June. 'I want to know what you think, if I ought to. Jack just kept asking me and asking me and . . . And then there's the other thing,' she said, twisting her ring. 'If they find it's all stolen, then I won't get my rights, will I?'

June was frowning, finding it harder to keep up the pretence of normal conversation. Maisie took a moment to digest the idea that she could no longer reject the theory that Stephen had stolen the valuables from the cathedral crypt.

'We should talk about this somewhere else,' she said.

The older man, perched on a bar stool playing backgammon on his own, tapped his glass on the counter.

'Another one in here, June, when you're ready.'

'In a minute, Bert.' She gave Maisie a meaningful look. 'And I was there, of course.'

'What do you mean, "there"?'

'In his house. He got up early to go and have a swim in old Nigel Bacon's pool and he never came back.'

'You were upstairs in his bed when he was murdered?'

'I was. My pa was going to collect me soon after Steve left to go swimming.'

'That early?'

'It wasn't that early. And Steve said he had things to do after so there was no point me stopping.'

'But he didn't come back.'

'No,' she sniffed. 'So I went back to sleep and then, later, there was an ambulance and all the rest of it and they asked me to identify him. It was horrible.'

June wiped her eye with the sleeve of her men's cardigan, gave Maisie a bright, brittle smile then bustled away to oblige Bert at the bar. Once the pint was poured and paid for, she returned to Maisie with a packet of Golden Wonder crisps.

'Open them. We'll pretend you ordered them,' said June. 'Old Gerald Gleeson's told me often enough it's my job to talk to the blokes, not the women.'

Maisie did as she was told, opening the bag, finding the little packet of salt and sprinkling it.

'Why don't we meet in private?' she suggested.

'There's something else as well,' said June, 'about the grass.'

'I beg your pardon?'

'I told you, I was there,' as if that explained it. 'So was my pa.'

Maisie wasn't following. She couldn't see how the information was more important today than it had been when

June lit the Aga in the cold kitchen. Or had June not known at that point whether to trust her?

'Perhaps your father can bring you to Church Lodge in the morning?' she said.

June shook her head. 'No, that's not a good idea.'

'Well, can I come and find you in Chichester?'

'On the bus?'

'I have a bicycle. It can be any time you like,' Maisie said earnestly. 'I think this could be very important.'

'Listen—'

She stopped abruptly as the front door swung open with a damp gust of air. It was Nigel Bacon. He looked round the long room, nodding and smiling, and was greeted by three or four of the patrons. He approached the bar, tapping on the counter and calling out 'Service' with a grin. Maisie hoped he wouldn't notice them too quickly.

'God, it's him,' whispered June. 'No, it has to be soon and private. Come into town, later, to the Bell, after closing.'

'The Bell? In Chichester, tonight?'

'Near the shop. Next to Somerstown estate. The theatre pub.'

'Yes, I know where it is. You mean ten-thirty?'

June indicated the patrons of the bar.

'If Pa doesn't come in, one of them will give me a lift. There's always at least one wants to put his hand on my knee when he's changing gear.'

June's expression was so world-weary and miserable that Maisie didn't know how to reply. She was an odd combination. Though Stephen had been able to trick her, she was undeceived in the ways of the world.

Then Nigel saw them and beamed. 'Aha.'

'Tonight,' said June under her breath, looking at Maisie from under her eyelashes. 'You'll come?'

'So,' boomed Nigel, 'two lovely ladies. Now, what do you have in common to talk about, I wonder?'

Maisie watched as a quick sequence of emotions played out on Nigel's ruddy features. First, confected amusement, then self-doubt, then embarrassment as he realised that the thing that united the 'two lovely ladies' was grief.

'I came in to make a phone call and June was kind enough to pass the time of day with me,' said Maisie. 'I was about to leave.'

'Not on my account, I hope,' said Nigel, with a faint echo of his former exuberance. 'I wouldn't want to be the ghost at the feast . . .'

Maisie felt almost sorry for him. Again, she watched his face sort of crumple as he realised that, speaking of ghosts, he had made another *faux pas*. She folded over the top of her unfinished bag of crisps and put it in her handbag.

'Goodnight. I'm sure we will all meet again soon,' she said, holding June's gaze. It was all she could think of to indicate that she intended to keep the appointment. 'Goodbye.'

She wove through the saloon bar, turning left and right through the low tables and chairs. People watched her as, she supposed, was normal when a stranger enlivens the dull routine of a weekday evening in the village pub. And, in a way, she regretted leaving. The Fox-in-Flight, surely, had never seemed so homely, with a candle in a jam jar on every table and three paraffin lamps over the bar.

She went outside. The evening was quite mild. She looked up at the sky. Cloudy, no stars. She hoped it wouldn't come on to rain.

She thought now it must be true that Stephen had been responsible for the cathedral robbery. How would he have attempted to turn the proceeds into cash? Through a local second-hand dealer, perhaps? June's awful father, for example? And had they then fallen out? What was the phrase?

'There's no honour among thieves.'

She paused at the gate to Church Lodge, contemplating the looming shadows, hearing the disquieting rustling in the undergrowth. She flinched, wondering if Nigel Bacon might be a peeping Tom as well as a devotee of cheap pornography. She walked quickly up the drive and let herself in with a hand that shook slightly, grateful to close the heavy door behind her.

Would she do it, though? Would she cycle into Chichester at ten-thirty on a Thursday evening to meet June in a dark side street under cover of darkness?

Of course she would.

TWENTY-EIGHT

Maisie had been out for less than an hour and it was still lovely and warm in the kitchen at Church Lodge. She decided she ought to try and have a catnap. She put a few knobs of coke in the firebox and, with regret, left its friendly glow and took her candle upstairs.

The first floor was cold. She put the candle on the bedside table in the spare room, leaving it lit, not intending to sleep for long. She lay down and turned on her side, wriggling to find a comfortable position on the lumpy feather mattress, still wearing all her clothes. She pulled the eiderdown over her shoulder and, in an effort to still her mind, tried to focus her imagination on something commonplace – her favourite shopping street, rue Saint-Antoine, visualising the *crèmerie*, the *boucherie*, the *pâtisserie* and the *traiteur*. She began to drift off.

Then, annoyingly, she realised she might well sleep right through her appointment.

She got up and opened her suitcase, looking for her travel alarm clock, a reliable little thing that folded away inside a hard square case with rounded corners and a brass clasp. When the case was opened, the face of the clock could be propped up to form a triangle, pert and cheerful, gently ticking away the seconds.

She set the alarm for nine o'clock, licked her fingers and pinched out her candle, then lay back down.

Time passed and her mind whirred. She found she was too hot. She pushed back the eiderdown and turned onto her other shoulder, reversing her pillow. Soon, she was too cold. She sat up and leant her shoulders against the head-board.

Useless.

The room was very dark. She groped for her handbag and took out the salted crisps, eating them one at a time, savouring the salt on her tongue. The inside of the bag was slick with cooking oil. When they were all gone, she licked her fingers and wiped her hands on her handkerchief. Then she sighed.

Yes, useless. She couldn't now lie down, not with her gullet awash with greasy fried potato.

The illuminated dial of her travel alarm showed seven-thirty on the dot. She wondered what her friends were doing just then in Paris. Not yet at dinner, that was certain. Aperitifs, probably, at the local brasserie, then on to an economical restaurant serving what was, in France, everyday cuisine, but would be thought exceptionally fancy in England. Sophie would be there, probably trying to line up a date for Maisie when she returned – that nice man with a thin blond moustache from the newspaper, for example. What was his name? Etienne Jacques.

She thought about work. She had taken a week's paid leave, thinking that would easily be enough. It was owed to her, after all. She hadn't taken a proper holiday for six months and that had only been a long weekend, wine tasting in the Champagne region, partly as research for her job. Soon, though, she saw that she would have to call her fearsome boss, Madame de Rosette, and request an unpaid extension to her absence. It was not a conversation she was looking forward to, setting aside the expense of the international call.

Maisie got up and opened the door to the landing, over-looking the chequerboard hallway. By coincidence, at just that moment, outside the double-height windows, the orange street lamps flickered on and steadied. The power cut had ended.

She went downstairs to the kitchen and put on the electric light. The bare bulb was harsh and dazzling. She made a cup of black tea and sat down at the table. There was Stephen's notebook, the posy in the decimalisation mug, the poem, the package of pornographic magazines. She took her diary out of her handbag and placed it alongside, contemplating the oddly assorted relics.

Relics of what, she wondered?

Why, of a life lived in parallel to her own, but on different tracks. Maisie and Stephen had each gone their own way, either side of a range of hills that separated them, only now and then catching a glimpse of one another's progress, seldom together, sharing the same destination, apart from the brief unhappy period just after their parents had died.

She tapped her fingers, a brisk tattoo on the rustic table.

'Stop feeling sorry for yourself,' she told the silence.

Easier said than done.

Maisie poured away her rather bitter tea and, instead, half-filled the dimpled pint pot with cold water. The salt on the crisps had left her thirsty. She drank the water down in one. Feeling better, she straightened the bits and pieces on the table as if they were, indeed, relics or museum pieces on display.

What to do next?

She opened Stephen's notebook in the middle where it would most easily lie flat. She slid the ballpoint pen out of the little loop on the side of her dairy and wrote a heading: 'What I know.'

She paused, feeling oddly self-conscious, and found herself thinking about Sergeant Wingard. She supposed he did this sort of thing all the time, making a written record of facts associated with a case. She thought of Inspector Barden with his slicked-down hair and Detective Constable Hands with his acne. They must do the same. Or perhaps Barden asked the questions and Hands wrote up the answers, laboriously picking out the letters with two fingers at an ancient, police-issue typewriter in some dingy corner of Scotland Yard.

Was Scotland Yard dingy? She really had no idea.

Her mind was wandering. She pursed her lips and began.

The first thing she wrote was a list of names, leaving several line spaces between each, simply all the people she had met. Then she began adding notes on their relationships to Stephen, to one another and to her.

Mr Strickland, (first name?), second-hand dealer, warehouse on the edge of Somerstown estate, Chichester. Fell out with Stephen over cathedral theft?

June Strickland, believes herself Stephen's lawful wife. Can that be true? Who else knows this? Capable of violence? Knows something – what?

Sergeant Wingard, investigating Stephen's murder, friendly with June, resented Stephen. Unforthcoming, rude.

She frowned. Was that entirely true? She added some more notes.

Allowed me to read initial report. Resents my questions? Definitely resents the Special Brach investigation. Why?

She drew an arrow between Wingard and June and wrote along it: *Friends?*

What sort of friends, she wondered?

She wrote down the names of Barden and Hands, then added, on a different line, with a question mark: '*Mohammed As-Sabah?*' She wrote '*OIL*' in capital letters in a circle on its own.

Surely, for Special Branch, that was the connection? And money, of course. Perhaps, when Mohammed turned up at Church Lodge tomorrow, she would find out. She made a mental note not to forget that she should be here at two-thirty. For her own protection, perhaps she should tell someone else Mohammed was coming, since she didn't really know the man or what he was capable of – maybe Gerald Gleeson?

Without really thinking about it, she found herself writing '*Fox-in-Flight*', then surrounding the word with a tiny sketch of the public house, adding the smaller shape of the forge next door. That reminded her to add, on the facing page, the name of Jon Wilkes (*deaf and nosy*), Reverend Millns (*uncharitable smoker*), Gerald Gleeson (*bullies June*) and the shadowy presence of Derek Fieldhouse to whom Stephen owed money, perhaps a lot of money.

Enough to incite Fieldhouse to murderous revenge? He was another person she needed to speak to.

Laying it all out like this, she realised that she and June were surrounded by men – men she had no real idea if she could trust. She added Maurice Ryan and his secretary, Miss Clement, with the query '*married?*'

Shouldn't there be another woman, though, the 'bit on the side' June had talked about? She drew a question mark and the words '*Second Woman*'.

Could the sleek Charity Clement be that person? And would that have made Maurice Ryan into Stephen's enemy if he knew of his wife's extramarital affair? Obviously, yes, if it were true. But Maurice Ryan had also been helpful, meeting her from the train, giving her the name of the investigating officer. But then, if Ryan were guilty, wasn't that precisely what he would feel obliged to do?

She took some time over Nigel Bacon, writing up a whole paragraph of tiny notes and queries regarding the pornographic magazines, the gate in the wall, his swimming pool, his competitive attitude to June. She was about to write down the word '*pals*' when she hesitated. Was he the sort of man she would expect Stephen to be pals with?

No, she decided, not unless there was something that Stephen wanted from Nigel, something Stephen did not have.

What might that have been? What was Stephen perennially short of?

Money, obviously.

She wrote down the two words '*City Finance*'. That was, according to the police report, Nigel's occupation. She underlined them twice.

Who was left? She let her mind wander, searching for anything and anyone she had missed.

Oh yes, there were two more women, the shop ladies who claimed to have liked Stephen very much, one hearty and smiley, Beatrice, and the other more intense with her tight grey ponytail. Then she squeezed in the unseen Mrs Fieldhouse and the elderly Casemores, plus the unknown person who had mown the lawn. In a corner she wrote '*Chichester Observer*' and '*Crypt*'. She drew a line connecting those two things to Inspector Barden.

She found she had entirely covered the double page. From a simple list, it had grown into a kind of map of relationships and motivations. She turned the exercise book sideways and wrote Stephen's name in block capitals along the crease between the two leaves, then drew a circle around it.

Whatever else she discovered, everything must come back to him.

Maisie began to think about timings. At the moment of Stephen's death, June was in his bed. June's pa was somewhere on his way with his truck to pick her up. Nigel was next door, obviously, but said he hadn't seen Stephen that morning. The other villagers were all within a few hundred yards.

Was there anyone at all who wouldn't have had the opportunity – given a certain amount of daring, luck and physical strength – to asphyxiate him?

She frowned. That was important, the physical strength required to subdue quite a big man. A little run to seed, granted, but with the reflexes of a natural athlete.

Why, though? That was the key. Who was there among this list of miscellaneous strangers who had been angry or jealous or vindictive enough to want to kill him?

Satisfied with her notes, Maisie stood up, feeling a certain stiffness in her neck. She counted out a few deep breaths like she and Sophie did on Saturday mornings in their apartment on the Place des Vosges, Maisie following her flatmate's impressively flexible body in a sequence of yoga poses.

She drank another half-pint of fresh water at the sink and went upstairs to look at the two-over-three chest of drawers in Stephen's room, the one stuffed with a random selection of clothing. Very glad the electric light was working, she sorted through, laying things out on the bed then folding them neatly when she found they weren't suitable, returning them to the drawers.

Eventually, she found what she was hoping for – a pair of trousers that looked like they would fit, cream flannels, probably cricket whites for a boy of fifteen or sixteen.

She took off her skirt and pulled them up. They were perfect, stylish even, with a plain leather belt already in the loops. Coco Chanel – the stylish French fashion designer and entrepreneur who had died the previous winter at the age of eighty-something – would definitely have approved.

Further rummaging produced an Arran jumper that reminded Maisie of Nigel Bacon. She put it on over her blouse and cardigan. Dressed like that, she would be warm enough for the chilly February evening.

She laid her skirt under a corner of the mattress to press and went back downstairs. She put the long strap of her handbag across her chest – a habitual defence against Parisian pickpockets – and wheeled her Raleigh Chiltern outside, locking the door behind her. The weather, happily, was dry.

She put on the cycle clips Mr Chitty had left in the basket, folding her borrowed trousers carefully round her ankles, then the windproof gloves. The combination lock was in the basket. She was ready.

Feeling like an adventurer, she clicked the dynamo into place on her rear tyre and pushed the bike across the gravel. Once she had reached the smooth tarmac at the corner of Church Lane, she pushed off, feeling properly independent, in control of her own destiny.

This is simply marvellous, she thought, then she wished there was something made of wood that she could touch, so as not to jinx it.

But there wasn't. Just the chilly evening air, slightly damp, but with no hint of rain, and the road that unfurled like a dark destiny in front of her.

IV

WRATH

TWENTY-NINE

Maisie swept along, turning the pedals easily with the breeze at her back, and was overtaken by only four or five vehicles, also heading into town. She was dazzled by twice that number, however, going the other way, out into the countryside. She supposed they were village dwellers returning to their rural homes from town-centre restaurants, pubs and clubs.

Which organisations might meet in Chichester on a Thursday evening? The Freemasons? The Rotary? Perhaps an amateur drama group?

Although she enjoyed the exercise, the wind still stung her face and ears. She was glad when, after five miles of invigorating pedalling, she was finally able to dismount a hundred yards before Strickland's second-hand warehouse, just by the left turn she needed. She leant her bike against a phone box. She was still a little early so she put the palms of her gloved hands over her ears to warm them up. The outskirts of the city seemed very quiet.

Had June understood her attempt to tell her she would keep her appointment? What time would she have finished work at the Fox-in-Flight? Had she already prevailed on one of her 'followers' for a lift? Maisie knew that Gerald Gleeson always came back downstairs when the news came on at nine. How late would he then stay open? The village clientele were likely early risers and therefore early to bed as well. But that didn't actually matter. June would be free to go before then. Maybe she had been travelling in one of the cars that overtook Maisie on her way into town.

Then Maisie wondered why June had been so keen to keep their arrangement from Nigel Bacon. Because he would insist on driving her into Chichester, taking advantage of the proximity to grope her knee?

Maisie checked her watch by the light that spilled from the red phone box. It was ten-twenty.

Strickland's warehouse was quiet and dark, so she got back on her bike and went past, pedalling slowly through the Somerstown estate, a small enclave of awful 1960s houses, wood-clad maisonettes with built-under garages. She emerged onto Lavant Road, near a wooden bus shelter. On the opposite side were the playing fields and the lights of the extraordinary Chichester Festival Theatre, like a hexagonal spaceship.

Two men were coming towards her – an older chap with grey hair and paint on his overalls and a blond youth, possibly leaving late from the theatre workshop. They crossed the road and made for the Bell, a small square pub with windows on two sides, but it looked like the publican had shut up early, before the legally prescribed 'last orders' at half past ten. Maisie could imagine the tea towels draped soberly over the beer pumps, the shutters closed until the following midday.

The older man in the painty overalls banged on the door and a voice came from inside, telling them to be on their way. He called back a cheerful insult and he and his younger companion walked away towards the city centre.

Maisie stood still for a minute, wondering what to do. June was nowhere in sight. There was little chance of her emerging from the Bell, but this was the place she had mentioned. So where was she?

A local Dunnaways taxi went past, taking a fare north, out of town. As the sound of its tyres on the tarmac faded, Maisie felt the oppressive silence close in upon her. The air was still. She could even hear someone running, pounding away, then some more footsteps, clip-cloppy heels and an uneven tread, like someone in high shoes, stumbling or walking with a stick.

Then, there she was, June Strickland, appearing out of nowhere, limping towards her.

Maisie was about to speak, to ask what June needed to tell her late at night on this cold deserted corner, when she noticed a dark stain covering the side of her face, her brassy blond hair stuck to it. The zipper of one of her boots was almost completely undone, the white plastic flapping round her calf. She stumbled and fell to her knees, not more than fifteen feet away, her eyes vague and unfocused, looking blearily at Maisie, and reaching out with her hands like a sinner asking for absolution. Her mouth moved but no sound came.

All at once, Maisie realised that she had been so shocked that she had frozen. She let her bike fall and rushed ahead, just in time to take the weight of June against her shoulder as she tipped forwards. By the light of the street lamp, Maisie saw the dark stain rubbing off on her borrowed Arran jumper.

Blood.

Lots of blood. Too much blood.

In her career in hotels and as a Paris tour guide, Maisie had received useful training in first aid. She put June gently on her side, pulled off the Arran jumper and made a pillow of it for her head. She thought she heard June speak and leant in close, putting her ear to her lips.

Yes, June was trying to say something but it was impossible to make out what it was.

Maisie looked around. She felt horribly exposed, kneeling on the pavement in borrowed trousers, meeting with June in the middle of the night, seeing the blood oozing from a wide gash just above her hairline. She felt a first tingling of panic in her throat, a desire to shout for help but, at the same time, a desire to run.

What reason could she give for being here? Nothing plausible. Nothing that would sound like this was an innocent rendezvous.

June made another murmur and, this time, there seemed a little more energy behind the words. Maisie leant in close once more.

'What is it, June?' she said softly. 'What are you trying to say?'

The sound came again, a vague whisper, indistinct. June didn't seem to be in control. She had simply to wait for her next breath before trying to articulate as the air left her lungs . . .

But articulate what?

Maisie discovered that she herself had forgotten to breathe. She took a great wheezing lungful of air, her knees beginning to complain about the hard ground. The faint words came again. This time, she thought she could work out what they were.

'Albert Close.'

At least, that was what Maisie thought she heard. She looked round, trying to find a street sign.

Was this side street Albert Close? Was that it? Or was that where she needed to go?

June reached up her left hand, waving it vaguely at nothing, catching the big silver-and-glass ring in Maisie's short curly hair.

'Try and tell me again, June.'

June's eyes closed and her face relaxed as she lost consciousness, the weight of her left hand hanging inert. Maisie tried to untangle the ring and found it impossible. She gasped as she tugged it free, taking a chunk of her hair with it, then she held her cold fingers against June's lips, hoping she would feel the intermittent warmth of her breath.

Yes, perhaps. A little.

Maisie tried to assert her logical mind.

An ambulance. That was what was needed. But how to summon one? Should she bang on the doors of the Bell, disturbing the landlord for a second time?

No, it would be quicker to shoot over to the phone box on St Paul's Road.

But could she leave poor June alone on the cold pavement? Yes, she had to.

She picked up her bike and stood on the pedals, rushing away through the ticky-tacky maisonettes. When she reached the phone box, she found someone using it. No, not using it. A drunk, standing inside the cubicle, about to undo his flies and urinate.

Maisie jumped off her bike, flung it aside, swung the heavy door open and took hold of the drunk's shoulder, pulling him out. He staggered away, groping at his trousers. She snatched up the receiver and dialled nine-nine-nine, her breath coming in short, sharp gasps.

The answer was almost immediate, asking which service she required.

Maisie took a moment to steady herself, then spoke nineteen to the dozen, hoping she was making sense.

'There's been an accident outside the Bell, the pub, the one at the bottom of Lavant Road, in Chichester, near the theatre. A woman is hurt. She's on the pavement, on the ground. Her name is June Strickland. She's bleeding, badly. Come quickly.'

The operator began asking for her name and further details, but Maisie found she didn't have the patience to reply.

'I have to go back to her,' she blurted.

She put the phone down and cycled back through the quiet estate. June was still there, of course, illuminated by the orange street lamps. Maisie touched her cold fingers to June's neck and wrist and could find no pulse. She put her cold cheek close to June's lips and could feel no warm breath.

Was she dead?

Maisie rolled June onto her back and began chest compressions, but all they did was cause a few bubbles of bloodied saliva to dribble out of June's pale lips and slide down her cheek.

'Oh, God,' said Maisie aloud.

She heard a siren, faint with distance, calling out into the night. Was it a police car or an ambulance? Then the noise stopped because, of course, in this quiet provincial city, nothing much happened and there was no traffic to speak of and no one needed warning of their approach.

It would be on her in minutes, seconds even. What would she say when they arrived? That she had made an appointment to meet June to discuss her brother's murder and now she had witnessed . . .

Panic began to overwhelm her again. She knew she wasn't thinking straight. She knew she ought to stay and explain herself, that she should trust that she had nothing to fear from the truth. But she was overtired and overwrought, assailed by questions and suspicions on all sides.

Like a spectator to her own life, she saw herself stand up and stagger away, ready to run, ready to hide. Though her logical mind screamed at her to stay, something pushed her to get back on her bike and pedal wildly away into the night.

THIRTY

Maisie didn't go far, just a few steps, then paused, leaning against the damp timber of the bus stop, no more than five or six seconds, just enough for her mind to become still, her breathing to become regular. At the same time, the events of the last few minutes replayed in her imagination in a sequence of snapshots: June's hair matted with blood; making a pillow with an Arran jumper; manhandling a drunk out of a phone box; staggering away in distress.

Maisie forced herself back to June's side. Her face was slack and lifeless. Should she restart the chest compressions?

Too late? Pointless, perhaps?

She did so all the same.

The ambulance swung round the corner and came to a hurried halt – a converted Bedford van with bulbous fenders and shiny chrome headlamps. Two men climbed out of the high cab. One went round to the back while the other, a heavily built man in his fifties, came and knelt down next to Maisie.

'Carry on doing what you're doing,' he said brusquely.

He put two fingers to June's neck, feeling for a pulse. He took a stethoscope from a pocket in his jacket and listened for breath sounds.

'Is she alive?' said Maisie.

'Okay, now stop what you're doing.'

Maisie lifted her hands away as if scalded, holding them out in front of her. The ambulanceman listened, then felt again at June's neck and wrist. His colleague brought an intubation kit.

'Has she been given mouth-to-mouth?'

'No,' said Maisie. 'Should I have done that?'

Without answering, the second paramedic began preparing June for intubation, tipping her head back, straightening the pathway between her mouth and her trachea.

'Pulse?' he asked his colleague. The other man shook his head. 'You get the stretcher?'

The first ambulanceman stood up.

Maisie felt frustrated. Why was he moving so slowly? She wanted to jump up and push him out of the way, shove him aside, fetch the stretcher herself and pick June up with her bare hands. She could do it. She felt detached, alienated, but incredibly strong, capable of anything, as long as she didn't have to think, as long as no one asked her why she was there and why she had wanted to run.

She did none of these things. She was still frozen, holding her hands out in front of her, not daring to speak, not daring to move, feeling the cold of the pavement seeping through her borrowed trousers into her knees, hoping that whatever she had done wrong, whatever mistakes she had made, would not make things any worse.

The first paramedic brought the stretcher and the second squeezed the air bag, pushing air into June's lungs. Did that mean she was all right now, that she was alive? Did her face have more colour?

A patrol car pulled up behind the ambulance – a white Ford Zephyr with a red stripe down the side and a boxy 'Police' light on the roof. Maisie's eyes went from June, to the paramedics, to the officer climbing out of the vehicle. As June was lifted onto the stretcher, Maisie stood up and stumbled.

'Miss Cooper?' said Sergeant Wingard.

Quickly, he moved towards her and gently took her arm. Maisie felt like she was on a carousel, that she kept getting glimpses of her surroundings, but could not piece them together into a whole.

'I don't know what happened,' she said, quickly. 'I was here and then she came, and she was going down and she was bleeding . . .'

He held out a hand for Maisie to stop talking, made sure that she wasn't about to collapse, then bent down. She watched him touch June's shoulder then her cheek. There was an expression of deep pity on his face, but also a sense of impotence or failure. Maisie had the fanciful idea that he had expected something like this.

But was it a fanciful idea?

The second paramedic continued pumping the bag.

'St Richard's?' Wingard asked.

'Yep,' one of the ambulancemen replied, the fat one, the one who had repeatedly checked June's pulse. Then he added something in a low voice that Maisie couldn't hear.

'One moment,' said Wingard, taking June's limp hand.

'We've checked for a pulse,' said the first paramedic.

'Be quiet, for God's sake,' said Wingard.

Masie was struck by the controlled fury in his voice. Then, in complete contrast, very gently, he removed the ring from June's wedding finger and put it in a pocket of his uniform.

Maisie felt her stomach lurch. There would be hairs from her own head caught in the setting.

'All right,' said Wingard.

The paramedics carried June away and slid the stretcher into the back of their ambulance. Wingard stood up, his shoulders hunched, his face closed off and set. Then there was a noise of doors slamming and the paramedics came back round. Maisie wondered why neither of them was riding in the back with their patient.

Was it because June was no longer a patient, just a thing, a cargo to transport?

THIRTY-ONE

The paramedics climbed up into the high cab of the converted Bedford van and started the engine. Maisie watched them go, the driver struggling to make a three-point turn, then pulling away in the direction of the hospital.

'It was June,' said Maisie, turning suddenly to Sergeant Wingard, feeling the words come of their own accord. 'No, you saw,' she corrected herself. 'You knew. The emergency service must have told you. I'm sorry, I should have said something. I didn't know it was you at first. I know you were close to her.'

She thought about Wingard's criticism of Stephen and that June had told her that he had taught her to read.

'You don't know anything,' he said quietly.

'No,' said Maisie. 'I don't. I don't understand. I'm sorry, but I . . .' Maisie put a hand to her brow.

Wingard seemed to realise that she was on the point of falling again. His entire demeanour changed. 'Let me help you.'

He took her arm and led her to the shallow wooden bench in the bus shelter. He made her lean forward with her head between her knees, looming in front of her.

'I'm all right,' she told him.

'Just stay down for a moment.'

She did as she was asked, breathing deeply, recovering her equilibrium. She tried to ignore the slideshow of horror that was flickering behind her eyes. Eventually, it passed.

She sat up and saw that he had fully composed his features, reasserting his professionalism. He sat down next to her.

'Tell me what you saw, please, what you did.'

Maisie took a deep breath.

'I came to meet her. She asked to meet me. I saw her in the Fox-in-Flight and she asked if I would meet her after closing, here, in Chichester.'

'Go on.'

'So, I came.'

'How did you get here?'

'I have a bicycle. It's over there,' she added, as if that explained something very important. She waved a hand to where she had let it fall. 'You see?'

Wingard went to fetch it. Maisie watched him. He moved easily. In a way, he remined her of Stephen – lithe, athletic. Was that why she had the growing impression that she recognised him? Unlike her brother, though, Wingard hadn't run to seed. He picked the bike up with one hand, carrying it away from his body so as not to sully his uniform. He leant it against the end of the bus shelter and sat back down. She realised she found his presence reassuring.

Maisie glanced over to where June had lain.

'That's my jumper,' she said quietly.

'You should put it back on. You'll get cold. You're probably in shock.' He moved towards it, reaching out a hand to pick it up.

Maisie stopped him. 'I can't. That's her blood.'

His face taut, Wingard gently unfolded the jumper, taking care only to touch the very edges. She watched him examine it. Then he came back and draped it over the bench between them. Maisie shivered. He wasn't trying to intimidate her, was he?

'Can you tell me, Miss Cooper,' he said, with an obvious effort at self-control, 'the sequence of events, from the beginning?'

The adrenaline was draining out of her body, leaving her vulnerable. Her teeth began to chatter.

'No, I don't think I can,' she told him.

She felt herself shudder, like an old dog, quivering and unsteady.

'Wait here,' he told her.

Wingard went to his patrol car, taking the bloodstained jumper with him. He came back with what looked like a packet of sweets.

'What's that?' said Maisie.

'Dextrosol. They're usually for diabetics but they sell them in Sidney Bastow's, the chemist. Pure glucose, very good for shock. They will help.'

He put two rectangular tablets in the palm of her hand and went back to the car. Maisie placed one of the glucose tablets on her tongue. It tasted of orange – at least, it tasted of a synthetic imitation of orange. Wingard came back with a blanket and draped it over her shoulders. She began to feel a little better.

'I will call the station and get someone to come and pick up your bike. You will need to accompany me and make a statement.'

'What about June?'

She saw his face become taut once more. What was the emotion that he was trying to repress? Pity? Anger? Love?

'They know what they are doing,' he said, evenly. 'She is being cared for.'

A look passed between them and Maisie wondered if either of them really believed June might still be alive. Then an odd change came over his features – pained but also wary. Maisie remembered that June had called him by his first name, that she and Wingard were friends. Could they also have been lovers?

'Can you stand?' he asked.

Without wating for her to reply, he helped her to her feet and led her to the Zephyr. He opened the rear door and she got in, treading on a corner of her blanket and stumbling, feeling stupid and clumsy. She put out a hand to prevent him from shutting her in.

'Someone might steal my bike,' she said. 'Could we bring it?'

'My colleagues won't be long.'

'But Mr Chitty loaned it to me, I mean he rented it to me. I couldn't bear it if it was taken, I really couldn't.'

Wingard shook his head. 'I'm sorry, there isn't room.'

'I would be so grateful if you could just put it in the boot and tie it down or something and bring it with us to the police station.'

'It will be fine. It will only be fifteen minutes.'

'Please.'

'There's no need—'

'I have been back in Chichester since Saturday,' she interrupted angrily, almost shouting. 'It's now Thursday. My brother, who I was coming to see, died just before I got here. And there is a Special Branch investigation into whatever he has been doing that has nothing to do with me but, somehow, I am expected to know about it and to be able to answer a whole lot of questions. And then, I discover, he didn't just die, he was murdered and everyone I meet claims to be his friend or his wife, for God's sake, and the one person in all this who has helped me, who has shown me any humanity, is old Mr Chitty from the bike shop. And I know that you must be very distressed about June but, please, just do as I ask and put the thing in the damn boot.'

Maisie stopped, feeling she had probably gone too far. Then she was surprised to see a look of sympathy on Sergeant Wingard's handsome face. Realising she was still holding the second Dextrosol tablet, she put it in her mouth.

'I am glad you're beginning to feel better,' he told her, offering her a rare smile.

'I am,' she conceded.

'And I hope, in the fullness of time, that you will agree that I too attempted to show you a little humanity.'

'I'm sorry. I didn't mean to—'

'Never mind.'

He fetched the bike and lifted it into the boot, leaving the lid open, then got in the driver's seat and pulled away, driving very cautiously through the darkened streets. Maisie sat in the back, thinking how cruel it was for June to have been so brutally attacked. What reason could there be? What harm could she have possibly done to anybody? But then came another thought. What did June know that someone had decided mustn't be shared?

Maisie watched the buildings slide past, a quiet provincial city where everyone was in bed, asleep, apart from an emergency room doctor, a couple of paramedics and a few representatives of the forces of law and order.

And perhaps, she thought, a murderer.

THIRTY-TWO

Wingard took Maisie to the same interview room in which he had allowed her to read the initial report into Stephen's death. Inevitably, he offered her sweet tea and biscuits, custard creams rather than Bourbons. She forced herself to drink and eat, feeling a lack of fresh vitamins in her diet, wishing she had bought more than one nice green Granny Smith apple earlier that day.

Was it still 'earlier that day'? She glanced up at the clock. Eleven-forty-five. So, yes, but only just.

She told Wingard about her visit to the pub, leaving out her phone call to Mohammed, but describing June's arrival and her cryptic invitation to meet.

'And she seemed wary of Nigel Bacon?'

'Wary of being overheard generally, I think, but definitely not welcoming his attention.'

As Wingard gently probed, making formal notes on an official pre-printed form, Maisie realised there was something she was holding back. The fact that June had told her that Wingard wanted her to turn informer. '*He wants me to squeal,*' she'd said. Squeal about what? She didn't know. Was it something to do with Stephen? Or was it about her father?

They pressed on, through the events between Maisie's early drink at the Fox-in-Flight and cycling into Chichester. A guarded expression came into Wingard's eyes.

'No one can vouch for you?'

She was annoyed that he didn't take her word on trust.

'Obviously not.'

163

He consulted his notes. 'Between six-thirty and nine-thirty, then, you were alone at Church Lodge. What about on arrival in Chichester?'

She got distracted, remembering the episode with the drunk in the phone box. He pressed her for a detailed description but, when she was unable to provide one, he said: 'But that was after you found June, when you called the emergency services?'

'Yes.'

'Can we go back a little? Tell me about when June appeared. How soon did you realise that she was injured?'

Maisie did her best, hating every moment. 'It felt like a long time. I was frozen, you know, in shock, but it can only have been a few seconds.'

'And then?'

'She was on her knees. I suppose that's how I grasped the seriousness of the situation. I stopped her from falling and got her blood on my jumper.' Maisie swallowed, feeling nauseated by the memory. 'Not my jumper, actually. I found it in a chest of drawers at Church Lodge . . .'

He led her into sharing some more details and she gave them, as best she could. Thankfully, he didn't need her to describe the injury just above June's hairline.

'Did she speak, at all?'

'She tried to. I couldn't hear.'

'Nothing at all?'

Maisie racked her memory. What had June said?

'It was as if there were words on her breath, you know what I mean? It was . . .' Maisie frowned. 'I'm sorry. I can't remember. There's kind of a blank.' It was an odd sensation. Maisie was almost certain there was something there, a fragment of memory to be retrieved from the aftermath of shock, but she couldn't find it. 'Is that normal?'

'If anything comes back to you, please tell me straight away.'

'I will.'

'Straight away,' he insisted. 'It could be very important.'

'I realise that,' said Maisie. 'But I have no telephone.'

'Go to the pub, to a neighbour. Do you know any of the neighbours?'

'Nigel Bacon.'

'Not him,' said Wingard without leaving her time to ask why. 'Anyone else?'

'The Casemores who live in one of the cottages on the main road?'

'Yes, they'll be fine.'

He tapped his pencil on his pre-printed form. Was he going to ask her to sign it then send her home?

'Is that all?' she asked.

'One more thing, if you wouldn't mind.' His eyes unfocused and she could see that he was unhappy with what he had to say. 'You say you think she was dead before the ambulance arrived?'

Maisie felt ashamed.

'I'm not sure. I had a moment of panic. I've never really seen death. In the Women's Royal Army Corps, we were logistics, supply. I suppose my life has been a sheltered one. It was frightening, to be unable to help, to believe that whatever I did might be the wrong thing.'

'I see,' he said, a deep sympathy in his eyes.

'But you believe me?'

'Of course, I believe you, Miss Cooper.'

He looked almost hurt. She couldn't bear to tell him that she had given up for ten seconds and fought the desire to run away.

His pen scratched its way across the official police form, then he asked her to read the statement through. She did so, impressed by the way he had managed to put down all the events in chronological order, despite her elliptical narrative.

He told her: 'I'm afraid I must ask you, officially, if you are satisfied that it is a true account of what you have told me? If so, please sign it. I will organise someone to give you a lift home. And . . .' He hesitated. 'Thank you for trying to help poor Junie.'

He passed her his pen and left her. As she scrawled her signature, Maisie felt a pang of disappointment. She realised that the process of sharing had been therapeutic. She would have liked to continue the conversation in a less formal context – for example, in his patrol car on the ten-minute journey out to Framlington. When he came back, she tried to catch his eye.

'I want to tell you how sorry I am. I know a little of how Stephen behaved towards your friend and—'

'Forgive me, Miss Cooper. Duty calls. I'm needed elsewhere. I'm sure we will speak again.'

'Yes,' said Maisie, disappointed. 'I understand.'

She walked ahead of him, through to the front lobby, and sat on an uncomfortable bench for five minutes, awaiting her ride. She felt herself becoming drowsy with fatigue and the aftermath of emotion. Then someone touched her shoulder.

'Your taxi is here,' said Wingard. 'It's a Dunnaways black cab. There will be plenty of room for your bike.'

'Thank you,' said Maisie, vaguely.

Wingard left with a nod, back down the flickering-neon corridor, leaving her to navigate the steps outside on her own. The taxi driver had already got her bicycle on board and was in the front seat with the engine running. She supposed it was his last fare before he went home to bed. She got in behind and shut the door.

'Church Lodge, please,' she said.

'I know,' said the driver.

They set off. The houses went past, then the trees, then the tight S-bend through the village of East Bitling where a few street lamps were still alight, then a mile of straight road through open fields. It was a relief when they finally turned in onto the unweeded gravel drive.

'Thank you,' Maisie murmured.

She got out and the taxi driver left her to manoeuvre the bike on her own. She leant the saddle against her hip and looked in her handbag for money.

'It's paid for,' said the driver.

'Oh, thank you,' she repeated.

There was an awkward moment's pause while he waited for a tip and she was too tired to realise, then he sighed and pulled away.

Maisie wheeled her bicycle to the front door, unlocked it with the heavy iron key and stepped inside. She locked up, left the bike in the hall and climbed the stairs to the lumpy feather mattress in the unloved spare room.

She undressed, crawled beneath the covers and fell asleep, oblivious at last.

THIRTY-THREE

Back in Chichester, Jack returned to his desk. He had paper-work to complete.

He took a cardboard file from his in-tray, opening it across his blotter. It contained the ongoing investigation into the robbery from the cathedral – at least, up to the point where Inspector Barden of Special Branch had been brought in to take over. It was good of Barden to admit that his services were not really required. Both Special Branch and Chichester police had agreed to tread carefully until the valuable relics had been recovered.

He turned the pages – the official forms, the scene-of-crime report, the statement given by the curator. There was a set of glossy photographs. By chance, the sixteenth-century monks' representation of 'wrath' was on top – an image of a bear on a rampage through the crowded streets of a medieval village while, in every shambling dwelling and on every corner, naked human beings fought and tortured one another. In the top right corner was a Latin phrase in a gothic script.

Jack had paid attention in Latin classes at school and more or less understood what it meant. To make sure, he had found it in his grandmother's dictionary of quotations and made a note. It was from Thomas Aquinas: 'A passion of the sensitive appetite is good in so far as it is regulated by reason, whereas it is evil if it set the order of reason aside.'

He put the robbery file back in the in-tray. He was tired. It was after midnight and he was supposed to be back on duty in just a few hours. His best option was sleep, but he knew sleep would not come.

He rang St Richard's Hospital and asked to be put through to admissions. The phone rang for a long time before someone picked up. He gave his name and rank and asked, without any real hope, if June Strickland had been taken to the intensive care unit or to one of the wards. Might they have been able to revive her?

'No, Sergeant. She was declared dead on arrival by the receiving physician.'

'Thank you.'

He put the phone down with an icy pang of guilt. Was it his fault? Was June dead because he had pushed her to stand up for herself and . . .

And what?

To make it possible for him to put Strickland on trial for the physical and mental abuse of his own daughter.

Jack took the gaudy ring from his pocket – the ring that Stephen had stolen from the cathedral crypt and given to June, helping to convince her that they were married. Jack had tried to persuade her not to wear it, but she wouldn't listen. Now it made no difference. She was dead and could no longer be pursued as an accessory.

He stood up. At the end of the interview room corridor was a rudimentary gym with a set of dumb-bells and a punching bag hanging from the ceiling. He took off his jacket and shirt and put on a pair of leather gym gloves to protect his knuckles.

Then he took out his rage on the innocent leather bag.

THIRTY-FOUR

Maisie woke after nine o'clock on Friday morning. It took a moment or two to realise that she felt entirely rested. No nightmares had haunted her dreams.

Perhaps, she thought, there might be a delayed reaction later on.

If she was honest, she felt ashamed of how she had reacted to last night's circumstances. Hadn't she made a fool of herself – and in more ways than one? It wasn't just the panic and the desire to flee, but also how desperately she had needed Wingard's sympathy.

She sat up and stretched. Should she have confronted Wingard with the fact that she knew he was trying to persuade June to turn informant? No, of course not. Suddenly, she thought she understood his reticence. She realised that he knew very well what he had said to June in the car outside the Fox-in-Flight, that he had put her under pressure. And that meant, as clearly as night follows day, that he must be worrying that her death was his fault.

Maisie got out of bed, groping with her bare feet for Stephen's slippers.

Was that all true, or was she weaving her own melodrama out of a set of unconnected . . .

She stopped, realising that there was a fundamental question she had never asked. *Had* June actually been murdered? Mightn't she have been hit by a car or injured in some freak occurrence, like a tile falling from a roof, for example? Why was it that she hadn't thought beyond murder?

Because of Stephen, of course. Otherwise, what were the odds of two unconnected deaths taking place in backwaters like Chichester and Framlington?

She went to the chilly bathroom and brushed her teeth, dabbing the wet bristles of her toothbrush into a jar of pink Eucryl tooth powder. Her face in the mirror was red and creased, her eyes vague. If anything, she had had too much sleep. She pulled on yesterday's clothes and went downstairs.

In the kitchen she decided she couldn't face another day beginning with a dismal cup of unsweetened, unwhitened tea. She splashed some cold water on her cheeks at the enormous sink, trying to freshen her features, pushing her damp fingers through her curls, checking the borrowed flannels had no blood on them and would do for a quick trip to the village shop. She would look the part of a country lady, as if she had been out already, weeding the begonias or whatever one did in a February garden.

She shuddered. Deep beneath her diaphragm and repressed in the very back of her mind were sinister imprints of the previous night's events, stalking her imagination. She determined to ignore them.

She wondered if there was a launderette somewhere in the village or if she should buy some soap powder and do her things by hand. But where would she dry them? Oh yes, there was a wooden drying rack in the kitchen ceiling that could be lowered on a pulley. That would do nicely.

She went outside, slipping her feet into a pair of wellington boots that were kept upside down with two other pairs on a wooden rack by the front door. She crunched across the gravel and out onto Church Lane. Everything was slick with overnight rain, but a pale sun was doing its best to dry out the pavements and the verges.

She walked along the main road to the village shop, a red-brick building with a tall gable at the front, its facias painted mustard-yellow. A labourer emerged, the man she had seen playing solitary backgammon at the bar the previous evening. He carried a pouch of Old Holborn rolling tobacco and some Job cigarette papers.

'Nice morning,' said Maisie briskly, not wanting to reveal her true emotion.

'Well, there 'tis,' he replied, nodding.

Maisie smiled, remembering the ubiquitous Sussex phrase from her childhood.

When was it appropriate to say 'there 'tis'?

At any time.

What did it mean?

Whatever the speaker wanted it to mean.

She pushed open the door and was transported back in time, almost to her own childhood, certainly to the years just before her parents' death. There were jars of boiled sweets behind the counter, just as there had been when she was small. There was a marble cold shelf with an enormous rotary slicer for cooked ham and beef. On the floor were heavy hessian sacks of muddy root vegetables – potatoes, swedes and turnips – as if they had only recently been pulled from the ground.

She wandered through the shelves, noticing that they were well stocked with all kinds of things that Stephen had loved, which would have baffled her French friends: Bird's custard, Angel Delight, Fray Bentos pies and, of course, dehydrated Vesta ready meals.

'Hello, my dear,' came a voice from behind her.

Maisie turned round. It was one of the two women who ran the place, the one with a severe grey ponytail whose business partner claimed to be firm friends with Stephen.

'Good morning,' said Maisie.

'How are you?' asked the woman.

'Very well, thank you,' said Maisie, feeling anything but.

The woman looked at her keenly, but not unkindly. 'Are you really, though?'

Maisie hesitated, surprised by the intensity of the woman's gaze. She looked much younger, now she was no longer wearing her outdated funeral clothes – not an 'old maid' at all.

'Yes, bearing up,' she said.

'My name is Alicia Knight. It must be a very difficult time.' She left a pause. 'I heard the news.'

Somehow, without having to say so out loud, Maisie knew that the 'news' was that June was dead.

'How did you hear?' she murmured.

'We get up very early for deliveries, milk and so forth. The men who drive the vans. It's a kind of bush telegraph.'

'I see,' Maisie replied.

'Poor June. I believe she really loved Stephen. She was what might have been called simple in my day. She couldn't really read, despite Jack Wingard's best efforts. Of course, it's Beatrice who is truly local. She knows everything and everyone inside out and she's closer to your age.'

Maisie frowned, feeling she was missing something connected to the information Maurice Ryan had given her.

'I felt very sorry for June and ashamed of my brother . . .' Maisie began.

The shop woman nodded, sympathetically. 'You must still feel under an enormous amount of pressure. It is so difficult, isn't it, not knowing? Nothing is more tiring than ignorance.'

This was not what Maisie had expected when she breezed into the village shop. She had been intending to simply buy a few essentials – a jar of instant coffee, a pint of milk and so on – and go back to Church Lodge for a breakfast of bread and cheese and caffeine.

The other woman – Beatrice – came bustling over to join them, wearing dungarees over a flannel shirt and carrying a heavy hessian sack of carrots on her shoulder. She seemed to do so effortlessly, though it must have weighed at least forty pounds.

'Maisie Cooper.' Beatrice smiled. 'Do you remember me from school?'

'I don't think I do?'

'No reason why you should. We were in juniors and Sunday school together, but you were older.'

'I'm not sure . . .'

'It's not important,' the second woman reassured her, 'but it's a blessing you came in. Alicia and I were saying we would like to talk to you properly, you know, about your brother. And now, with this other business, well . . . Please say you will?'

Beatrice left the thought hanging, her eyes bright and her expression generous and open. Alicia, the older of the two, was still looking at Maisie with an almost hypnotic gaze. Maisie found herself nodding.

'Yes, I think I would like that.'

'Excellent.' The younger woman grinned. 'Come at two. We shut for half an hour for a sit-down and lunch.' She casually transferred the heavy sack of carrots to her hip. 'The village finds it annoying whenever we close, but they only have to remember and plan ahead, don't they?'

'I suppose so.'

'And it is only for half an hour,' said Alicia. 'Beatrice and I have been working since six.'

'Yes, I see. Two o'clock,' said Maisie, remembering Mohammed's impending visit. 'I have someone coming at two-thirty but yes, thank you, I will.'

'Now,' said Alicia, 'I'm sure you came in for something?'

Maisie managed to complete her purchases without any further unexpected confidences and left the shop with an up-to-date copy of the *Chichester Observer* dated Wednesday 16 February 1972, a jar of Maxwell House, a packet of soft brown baking sugar, half a pound of best butter and a bottle of gold-top milk.

'Everyone knows gold top is the best. Why would you buy anything else?' Alicia insisted, shaking her head in disbelief. 'Life is short. Surely people should understand that?'

'Life is for living,' agreed Maisie.

Alicia was behind the counter. Beatrice was ripping the string seal from the top of her bag of carrots. Maisie looked from one to the other, realising with surprise that her words hadn't created any embarrassment. They all smiled – a little triangle of agreement. Maisie was struck by the healthy contrast with Nigel Bacon who had been mortified when his saloon-bar banter touched, albeit accidentally, upon death. Likewise, Mr Chitty, with his *faux pas* about Cain and Abel and Maisie not being her brother's keeper.

'Now, don't forget,' said Alicia. 'We'll be expecting you.'

'We would like to explain ourselves,' added Beatrice, surprisingly.

Further conversation was prevented by the arrival of another customer. Maisie left them and spoke to no one else on the brief walk home.

Thirty-Five

Back in the kitchen at Church Lodge, Maisie savoured her coffee. The Maxwell House 'instant powdered blend' was dreadful, of course, but with plenty of brown baking sugar and fresh creamy milk, it made a reasonable imitation of her habitual Parisian *café crème*.

She drank it sitting on a tea towel on the back doorstep, looking out at the stark orchard garden where even the shadow of her awful memories couldn't entirely undermine a growing sense of well-being. She felt almost as though last night's surge of adrenaline was still in her muscles, that she could do anything, confront anyone.

She made a second cup of rich coffee, drank it quickly, fetched the keys from her handbag and headed out onto the lawn, the clumps of cut grass clinging to her borrowed wellingtons. There was the brick-built outhouse, the bare branches of the trees casting skeletal shadows over the shabby door. Perhaps it would contain fruit and vegetables put away at harvest to be eaten out of season, potatoes in a heap and trays of apples in twists of newspaper.

The key fitted and turned easily, showing that the out-house was in regular use. The door was a little stiff – no, not stiff, something was obstructing it on the other side. She put her shoulder to it and it opened.

She sprang back as a disgusting cloud of flies came surging out, all round her face. She ran three or four steps to get away, bending over, batting her hands in the air, not wanting to take a breath with the awful buzzing round her nose and ears.

No, please, she thought, don't let there be a body, a corpse, a rotting corpse, please.

The flies dispersed and she stood up straight, still tense with apprehension. Tentatively, she took a couple of steps towards the outhouse. The morning sun shone in though the open doorway, illuminating a heap of potatoes, just as she had imagined, piled up in a back corner, some of them scattered across the dirt floor, stopping the door from swinging easily open. But that wasn't the source of the flies. They were not feasting on vegetables. They were laying their vile eggs in meat – putrid, rotting meat – two carcasses, perhaps pheasants, hanging from a rafter.

Maisie knew all about hanging game in order for the flavour to mature and for the meat to become tender, but she had never confronted animals left too long. The poor beasts' feathers were crawling with maggots.

Could she just leave them? How about leaving the door open so that crows or magpies could pick over the bones? Or could she ask the gardener who came to mow the lawn to do something? But he had recently been. He probably wouldn't be back for a while.

In the end, the alternatives all seemed worse than simply relocking the outhouse door and forgetting about it. After all, she'd soon be out on her ear and it would become the landlord's problem.

She went indoors and had to wash her hands, even though she had touched nothing but the handle. She carefully dried them then sat down at the table to look through the local paper for new information about the robbery from the cathedral crypt.

The first few pages of the *Observer* were all planning decisions and arguments about new roads, with the theft relegated to the inside. Interestingly, though, the journalist speculated that the criminal had hidden in one of the tall cupboards in the robing room in the south transept before the cathedral was locked up, then had gone about their nefarious business overnight, leaving the building with their booty the following morning, unnoticed among the modest congregation of the early mass. The 'effraction' hadn't come to light until later that morning. Only easily portable items had been taken, concealed within a shopping bag or a rucksack, perhaps. Most of the pieces had greater historical than financial value, but not all. There was a black-and-white illustration of the most important loss, the one which the Special Branch officers had been most interested in – a sixteenth-century devotional book of prayers and sermons around the theme of the seven deadly sins and the seven holy virtues.

Maisie pushed the paper away. Time was moving on. How long did she have, in fact?

It was just after ten by the kitchen clock. Her two o'clock appointment with Alicia and Beatrice fitted in very well, given she needed to be back at Church Lodge at two-thirty, in time to greet Mohammed. In the meantime, it would be a great mistake to sit and brood.

Maisie washed up her coffee things and went back outside, crunching down the gravel drive. The rubber boots were, luckily, a perfect fit and she didn't have to watch out for puddles. She thought about how carefully she dressed for work in Paris, the effort she was obliged to make to appear *soignée*, 'turned out', like a horse, for heaven's sake. She wondered how on earth she put up with it.

It was still a pleasant day. She hesitated at the gateway, wondering where to begin. Just then, a shiny MG Midget sports car in British racing green slowed and drew up alongside her. The roof was down and she was greeted by the driver, a squat man in very smart tweeds, a crisp white shirt and what looked like a regimental tie.

'Miss Cooper? Do you have a moment?'

She was struck by a sense of driving energy and intrigued by the fact that he knew her name.

'How can I help you?'

He climbed out and she saw that he was only a little over five foot in height, but emanated an aura of vigour and life. He slammed the door, waving a cardboard document wallet by way of greeting. He had a look of determination in his wide-open eyes. Maisie began to worry that this tweedy, barrel-shaped man might turn out to be another of Stephen's creditors.

'Well, this is a pleasant surprise. Your brother told me so much about you and, let me assure you . . .' He paused, looking her up and down. 'First impressions do not disappoint.'

Maisie felt herself cringe slightly. She wasn't a fan of heavy-handed 'gallantry'. He held out a hand for her to shake and she took it.

'I'm sorry,' she said. 'I'm not sure we've met or been introduced.'

To her surprise, he turned her hand palm down and raised it towards his lips. For an awful moment, she thought he was going to kiss the back of her wrist but, thankfully, he stopped and executed a kind of restrained bow instead.

'Derek Fieldhouse, farmer, property manager, all round good egg.' He let go of her hand. 'And, if you don't mind me saying so, your brother's best friend. Well, hereabouts. We had . . .' He waved his document wallet at everything and nothing. 'We had such a lot in common – the army, of course, an appreciation of fine things, horses, hunting, a love of Sussex and, in particular, this beautiful corner of the world. Also, might I say, a sense of honour and duty. People don't know what loyalty is any more. He was one in a million. I was very sorry to hear of his death. Stroke, was it? Or heart attack?'

Maisie found herself smiling. Here was someone who, to her relief, thought the world of her brother, but who also hadn't yet heard that he had been murdered. She felt herself warming to this pocket battleship of a man.

'That's lovely to hear,' she said. 'I didn't see you at the church?'

'I was very, very sorry not to be at the service. Busy, busy. No rest for the wicked, eh?' He shook his head with regret. 'There will be a cremation, I suppose? Perhaps I might come and pay my respects, as long as it isn't a private affair?'

'It's tomorrow at eleven, at the crematorium in Chichester. Of course, you would be welcome.' Maisie made a quick decision. 'I wonder, might I drop in and speak to you?'

'Delighted. I would be delighted. Do come. I would say "come now" but I have to drop off some papers . . .' He gestured towards the village shop with his document wallet. 'Trust me, I can tell you some stories,' he said with a laugh.

'You're in Framlington Manor, aren't you?'

'Yes, we call it the "manor"—' Fieldhouse grinned '—but it's nothing but an old farmhouse that's got above itself.'

Maisie felt herself smiling. After the stress and upset of the previous evening, it would be a pleasure to talk to someone else who truly liked her brother. Yes, Mohammed was one of Stephen's oldest friends, but his cautiousness on the phone had given her an inkling that, when he arrived later, he would bring only new reasons to despair of Stephen's behaviour.

'Are you free today? What time would suit?' she asked. 'You're Stephen's landlord, aren't you?'

'Common mistake, but no.' He considered for a moment. 'Just after one?'

'That's ideal. I was just about to go for a walk, while the sun's out.'

'Come to the kitchen door,' he said, glancing towards the shop as if his mind was already on his next task. 'We don't stand on ceremony.'

On a whim, Maisie asked him: 'I thought I might have a look at the livery stables. Jon Wilkes, the blacksmith, mentioned them.'

For a second he looked taken aback then, just as quickly, his bonhomie returned. 'Do, yes. You'll find old Bert struggling a bit. He's been under the weather.' Fieldhouse slapped a palm against his bald head. 'Oh, but Stephen told me what a fine horsewoman you are. Better than he was, that was his judgement, which is saying something. Why don't you have a hack up and down the gallops?'

'Oh,' said Maisie, delighted. 'I would love to do that.'

'Splendid. Bert will sort you out.'

'I don't have a hard hat.'

'Will you need one? You're dressed for it otherwise.'

He looked her up and down again. It was true. The flannel trousers were as good as jodhpurs and the wellingtons were close-fitting like riding boots.

'You really don't mind? I don't want to be making work for your man?'

'No, of course not. If you've been in the pub, you'll have seen him propping up the bar, playing backgammon against himself. He always wins!' he added, and laughed at his own joke.

Maisie nodded. She had seen him early that morning, too.

'Well,' she said, 'if you're sure.'

'You'll be helping.' Fieldhouse was actually walking away now, calling back to her over his shoulder, making for the village shop. 'The horses need exercise and there's never enough time in the day. Isn't that right?'

Maisie supposed it was because he would see her later that he didn't say goodbye.

THIRTY-SIX

Maisie now had three appointments for later on – Derek Field-house, then the shop ladies, then Mohammed – and an excellent way of passing the time until then. The stables were easy to find. She simply followed the road to the edge of the village, past the car repair shop with two National petrol pumps run by the Davies family, then a little way up Stook Lane.

The yard was a large open area of concrete hardstanding, strewn with straw and surrounded by loose boxes. Beyond, she could see a lovely long gallop covered with lush, dark-green grass. It ran gently uphill for about a thousand yards, dead straight, right up to the treeline.

'Old Bert' emerged from one of the stables, pulling a hand-cart full of straw and horse manure. He dragged it over to the grass verge where a tall heap of dung was quietly steaming.

'Good morning. Mucking out?' said Maisie.

'That's where 'tis,' he said.

Maisie hesitated. Was this a good idea? Yes, it would be a kind of antidote to last night's upset. But would she be imposing?

'I just met Mr Fieldhouse. He said I might have a ride. Do you mind?' She smiled. 'I won't if I'm in the way. I'm Maisie Cooper, by the way.'

'I'm right pleased to meet you proper.' He rubbed the back of his dirty hand across his runny nose. 'He bought me a drink a few times. Your brother, I mean. I ate my fill at your wake, too. What a terrible shame.'

'Thank you,' said Maisie.

'Can you ride, though, anything like your brother could?'

'He came down here regularly?'

'Many a time.' He laughed and added, with a cheeky grin: 'When he was out on horseback, he couldn't get into any more trouble, could he?' He saw Maisie was a little taken aback. 'No, don't mind me. Take people as you find them, that's what I say. He was what he was and there was a sight more good in him than bad.'

Maisie smiled at this generous summing-up and had to bite her tongue so as not to answer: 'That's where 'tis.'

'Thank you. I appreciate that.'

'Anyway, I'll be grateful to you. I been under the weather and I'm behind. Didn't get out of bed for two days.'

'I'm sorry you've been unwell. Only if you're sure,' said Maisie.

He showed her the tack room and found her a hard hat, a saddle and bridle. He told her the chestnut mare might suit and that she would find her 'spry'. Maisie assumed that meant energetic.

The mare was only thirteen hands. Maisie was sure that she could mount her unaided, but he helped her by making a cup of his two hands for her boot. She swung her leg over, twitched the reins and they clip-clopped out of the concrete yard and onto the grass. The mare knew where she was going and immediately accelerated into a trot that Maisie allowed to stretch into a canter. On the right-hand side, a spiny hawthorn hedge raced by. As soon as Maisie felt that the two of them were moving to the same rhythm, she squeezed her knees and encouraged the mare into a gallop. The horse lengthened her stride and they were away, pummelling the turf. Maisie felt a thrill of recognition and longing.

How I've missed this, she thought, as the upset and trauma faded from the front of her mind.

As the top of the gallop approached, with a feeling of disappointment, Maisie sat back a little, encouraging the mare to decelerate.

Yes, she thought, *'spry' is a good word for this lively, light-footed animal.*

Twice, the mare almost stumbled on the downhill slope, so she took it easy, returning to the yard at a trot. She jumped off at the gate and led the mare back to her loose box.

'That was wonderful,' she told him.

'Nice seat, Miss Cooper.' He nodded.

'Thank you,' said Maisie, smiling. In any other context, his remark would be considered extremely forward. 'I never ride at home.'

'In France, would that be? Your brother did say.'

'In Paris, yes,' she told him, feeling a little guilty at the idea Stephen had talked about her while he had seldom been in her thoughts.

'How would you feel about your brother's horse?'

'Surely Stephen couldn't afford a horse in livery?'

'No, not he, but I call it his. It's the grey, the one he liked to ride. Belongs to that Nigel Bacon, but he chose too big for himself, did old Nige, too strong. He's afeared.'

'Should I be frightened, too?' she asked.

'Not if you know what you're doing and I reckon you do. Come see.'

He led her to a loose box in which a lovely grey horse stood bored and unresponsive. Maisie made an encouraging sound in her cheeks and held out a hand. The stallion looked up and moved slowly towards her.

'Here,' said Bert, and he gave her a handful of cobnuts from the pocket of his coat.

Maisie let the horse eat them from the palm of her hand, the warm, sensitive lips just grazing her skin.

'He's lovely.' She thought back to something Jon Wilkes had told her. 'Is it true Nigel mistreats him?'

'Not him, no,' said Bert and Maisie wondered precisely what that meant. Before she could ask, he went on: 'How about you take him out? I'm only a little bloke. You can see he's too big for me.'

It was true. He was only five-foot-two to Maisie's five-foot-eight.

'I would love to.'

He helped her transfer the saddle and bridle from the mare, lengthening the girth, and gave her a boost once more. This time she was grateful for his assistance. The grey was sixteen hands, at least.

The experience of riding Nigel's stallion was completely different. If the mare was spry, the stallion was – what was the word? – explosive. So much so that, at first, Maisie was taken aback at the power and bounce beneath her saddle. Quickly though she realised that the horse was well broken and, for a sympathetic rider, extremely responsive. She thrilled at the feeling of almost-racehorse speed as four mighty pounding hooves ate up the turf, driving the thousand yards uphill to the top of the gallop in no time. She turned and they trotted three-quarters of the way back down before Maisie swung his head round for a second surge, urging the horse on, galloping right up to the fringe of the woods where the soft ground became scrubby underfoot.

They paused and Maisie let the stallion dip his head and snatch a few mouthfuls of soft green grass. There was a temporary sign on a gate that led into the woods: '*Forestry Commission – work in progress – no bridleway.*' Beyond the gate was a deeply rutted lane under the trees, the mud churned up either side of a ridge of chalk and flint. A little further up she could see a stack of cut timber, twelve-foot lengths of tree trunk left to season in the shadows.

The horse pulled and she let it follow the choicest grass. She looked down at the village, the smoke rising from two dozen chimneys, the ugly concrete of Church Lodge, the mellow brick and flint of Framlington Manor. Further away, on the horizon, she could just make out the silver line of the sea.

Exhilarated and, if truth be told, rather pleased with herself, free of all her troubles for just a while, Maisie encouraged the stallion into a trot down the gallops, leaning back to prevent him from picking up too much speed. In the yard, she put the saddle and bridle away in the tack room and slipped a canvas head collar on him so she could keep him still. She spent a happy twenty minutes rubbing him down before thanking Derek Fieldhouse's labouring man a final time.

'No, it's you who've done me the favour. I'm behind, see?' He nodded and gave her a look that seemed to say that there was more he could tell her if only she asked the right question. 'I'm sorry about your brother, though.'

'People who like horses,' said Maisie, 'like people who like horses.'

'That's where 'tis.'

'You were in the pub yesterday, weren't you?' she enquired. 'At the bar?'

'Most evenings.'

'Do you happen to know who gave June a lift into Chichester last night after her shift?'

'Ah, yes,' he said. 'I heard about June. There's a great pity, too.'

Maisie remembered seeing him coming out of the village shop with his tobacco. No doubt that was where he had learnt of June's death. She began to worry that Beatrice and Alicia were simply nosy gossips.

'Did you see who ran her home?' she insisted.

'From the Fox? It's usually old man Strickland comes for her.'

'But you didn't see?'

'I did not.'

'You don't remember what time she left, do you?' she asked, hopefully.

'Well, Gerald Gleeson always comes back downstairs when the news comes on his old telly round nine o'clock. But maybe just after because old Gerald told her she owed him a half an hour for being late.'

That would mean June was in Chichester just under an hour before the time of her pre-arranged meeting with Maisie. What had she done in between?

'Did she talk to anyone else?'

'She talked to near enough everyone, did June. She was that friendly,' he added with, Maisie thought, a kind of connoisseur's appreciation of sympathetic barmaids everywhere.

'And before, who else was there? Any other neighbours?'

'The Casemores with their sherries.' He nodded. 'One dry, one medium. Then there was Nigel Bacon, mild-and-bitter. But you saw him. That was before you left. Mr Chitty from the bicycles had a half of stout and dominos by the fire with Fieldhouse's farm team, you know, two lagers and a shandy.'

Maisie wasn't interested in people who weren't closely connected to Stephen, but she was impressed at his remembrance of details.

'Did Mr Fieldhouse himself come in?'

'Yes, he likes to, most weekday evenings.'

'On his own?'

'Who might he be with? Daphne, his missus? Not a chance of that,' he said, as if Maisie wasn't thinking straight. Then he laughed a rather unkind laugh. 'He comes with his dog, instead.'

'Derek Fieldhouse must have come after I'd left,' she said, almost to herself.

'Just after,' he agreed.

'Anyone else?'

'Beatrice from the shop came over, someone said, with sausages for Gerald for next day's lunch.'

'The younger one, Alicia's friend?'

'That's it.'

'But you didn't see her?'

'I weren't there all the time. There's skittles in the back room and I went through to make up a four.' He smiled at the memory. 'Knocked them skittles silly, we did.'

Wondering about what the shop ladies might have to say to her, she asked: 'What do you think of her? Beatrice, I mean?'

'Nice woman. Born and bred, you know?'

'But you can't be sure if she actually came in or not, I mean actually inside the pub, or if she might have spoken to June. In fact, any one of these people might have talked to June or even given her a lift.'

'It wasn't her pa?'

'I don't know,' said Maisie, frustrated. 'Do you?'

'No, that's where 'tis. I can't be sure.'

THIRTY-SEVEN

Physically, Maisie felt as fit as a flea, pleasurably tingling with the unaccustomed exercise. Mentally and emotionally, she felt adrift. Everything she learnt – about Stephen's life and his relationships with everyone else in the village – seemed to make the pattern of his life harder to understand.

She returned to Church Lodge to wash and change. She couldn't pay social calls smelling of sweat and horseflesh.

She dressed in the last clean clothes from her small suitcase. If she was to remain decent, she really would have to scrub things by hand or find a launderette. Perhaps tomorrow morning in Chichester? Or even later this afternoon, depending on what happened with Mohammed? At the same time, she could revisit the library and consult a few back issues of the local newspaper. How many might they hold? At least a month, surely?

Thinking about the library, she wondered if she might find copies of the national papers, the *Times* for example. If they didn't have physical editions, they would probably have it in on microfiche. It was, after all, the 'paper of record'. Didn't every major library provide it as part of their reference collection? She wanted to know more about Kuwait and oil. And she wanted to meet the lover of poetry who had given her what she thought was her first and most important clue.

Perhaps she already had – but how would she know?

She laced up her outdoor shoes and crunched out across the gravel. Between Church Lane and the village shop was a row of four low cottages, their window frames and door frames all painted the same mustard-yellow colour, indicating they belonged to the same landlord. The Casemores were in their tiny front garden, Mr Casemore wielding the pruning secateurs, Mrs Casemore directing him.

'There, just above the side shoot.'

'Like this?'

'A little higher.'

'Like this?'

'A little more. That's it. You know I would do it myself if I could?'

'I know, dear.'

Maisie bustled past, taking care not to catch their eye, noticing once more the enlarged knuckles and twisted joints of Mrs Casemore's arthritic hands. She felt pleased with herself, glad that her eyes hadn't simply skated over the old couple without taking in any details. Then she shook her head. What was she playing at, thinking herself a detective?

Well, the police wouldn't share their thinking or their conclusions, so what choice did she have?

At the village shop, a small truck was delivering bags of firewood. The younger woman, Beatrice, was stacking them beneath a corrugated-iron shelter beside the front door. Maisie watched her stretch to ease her back and wipe her brow. She saw Maisie and gave a cheerful wave. Maisie nodded, smiled and strode on, crossing over to the forecourt of the Fox-in-Flight.

It was empty of cars, but Gerald Gleeson was out with a yard broom, sweeping a few leaves into a corner and stuffing them into an empty potato sack.

'That's a never-ending job, isn't it?'

He looked up at the trees. 'There'll be new ones coming in soon.'

'Let's hope so,' said Maisie.

Next door to the pub, Jon Wilkes was outside his forge attending to a skewbald pony wearing a head collar held by Mr Chitty's grandson, Nicholas. The boy looked very thin and frail alongside the muscular horse and the heavily built blacksmith.

'Good morning to you both,' she called out.

'And to you, Miss Cooper,' Jon replied, lifting one of the horse hooves, checking its iron shoe. 'Lovely day. All right, are we?'

'Yes. You, too, I hope.'

'Hello,' said Nicholas, smiling politely.

She walked on, thinking about what a pleasant place Framlington might have been, under other circumstances.

Beyond the forge was a turning up into the Downs, a narrow road that soon wound away between deep hedgerows towards the valley villages of Harden and Bunting. Framlington Manor was on the corner, a lovely Georgian house of brick and flint, surrounded by a six-foot wall. Maisie hesitated, looking up the side road, an unhappy frown creasing her features.

The truth was, she was haunted.

Just a little way up this country road, on the left-hand side, was the village overspill, a council estate of eighteen narrow houses where she and Stephen had been brought up in almost-poverty. It was a place whose good memories – and there were many – had been obliterated by the shock of their parents' deaths.

Maisie never wanted to see it again. She felt awkward just being in the vicinity of the tatty green where Stephen had taught her to weave daisy chains and ride a bike without stabilisers and choose the best conkers and light fires with pieces of flint and dry grass.

Why had she allowed the warmth of those memories to fade over the years?

Because, she now acknowledged, she had allowed grief at her parents' deaths to become unwholesome rage and, for fear of turning her anger outwards, she had fled.

★★★

191

Derek Fieldhouse had told her to come to the kitchen so she went in through a narrow pedestrian gate in the six-foot brick wall and found herself at the side of the house, in a beautiful kitchen garden. Where Nigel Bacon's had been sterile and over-formal, the Fieldhouses' plot was a delight. Everywhere she looked, edible and aromatic plants merged into one another, even now in late winter, full of promise for spring. There were even some stone planters with geraniums, planted out early and covered with glass cloches to protect them from frost.

The top half of the stable-style kitchen door was open. As Maisie approached, a beautiful red cocker spaniel jumped up, straining to put its paws on the rail.

'Well, hello there,' Maisie told the dog. 'Aren't you handsome.'

'One does one's poor best,' called Derek Fieldhouse, jokily misunderstanding. 'Come in, now, come in.'

Maisie stepped over the threshold. 'Thank you, Mr Fieldhouse.'

'And please call me Derek, not Mr Fieldhouse,' he insisted. 'I'm a simple chap. I went to school with my ploughmen. My father didn't want me getting ideas above my station. I'm not going to stand on ceremony now, am I? But you went to the posh school, isn't that right?'

'I suppose,' said Maisie.

It really was annoying how often people brought that up.

'Enjoy it?' he asked. 'You don't look like you did.'

'Actually,' she told him, impressed by his perceptiveness, 'I regret it, in a way.'

'People make assumptions, do they?' asked Derek, sympathetically.

'They do,' said Maisie, glad to say out loud something that had been bothering her on and off since she arrived. 'First of all, that you come from wealth, which was absolutely not the case for Stephen or for me. We were just lucky that an aunt with nothing else to spend her money on remembered us. Then, second, people decide that you think you're better than everyone, better than those who didn't have the same advantages. But don't we all know people who turned out very well from unhappy circumstances and people who, despite their coddling, ended up . . .'

She stopped, getting rather close to expressing what she really thought of how Stephen had turned out. Derek seemed on the same wavelength.

'That's exactly what I thought you might say. Good God, it's easier to fail than to succeed. And it's easier to take the short cut than go the hard way. Not everyone learns that early enough.'

'Do you mean my brother? I'm under no illusions. You can speak your mind.'

'Always do,' he assured her. 'Now, listen, didn't I tell you he and I were close? Yes, he did some silly things, but I honestly believe he'd seen the light.'

'What silly things?' she asked, not wanting to interrupt his train of thought with her own ideas.

'I suppose you know about June?' Maisie was about to share her shock at the young woman's death, but it was clear that wasn't what Derek was referring to. 'Stephen didn't like the fact that people thought of him as a, what's the word, a cad, a seducer?'

'That sounds about right.'

'That's exactly it. He wanted to put them straight. That's why he decided to marry her. He was turning a new page.'

Maisie wondered how much Derek actually knew.

'I see. Go on.'

He surprised her with another change of heart. 'I suppose he decided he was doing the right thing. I couldn't agree.'

'Because?' she encouraged.

'What did they really have in common, apart from you-know-what? Did she like riding or shooting or any of that? Of course not. Then the silly fool decided to go the whole hog, private, but candles and incense.'

'Is that what he told you?'

'It certainly is. I told you we were pals.'

'He didn't.'

He looked shocked. 'I beg your pardon?'

'He cooked up a kind of sham marriage certificate and completely took her in,' said Maisie, wearily.

Derek Fieldhouse looked astonished. 'He never did?'

'I'm afraid so.'

'Well, I'll be damned. When was this?'

'Maybe ten days ago. She showed me but I didn't make a note of the date.'

'And she believed him, without a vicar or a registrar or anything?'

'He persuaded her that his "contacts" meant that he didn't need one.'

'I'm sorry to hear that,' said Derek, slowly. 'Still, what the heart wants, the heart wants.'

Maisie dropped her gaze, wondering if June's awful father could have known about the cathedral theft and been black-mailing Stephen to 'make an honest woman' of his daughter?

'Or not the heart exactly,' said Derek, with a ponderous wink.

Maisie did not want to discuss Stephen's sex life, so she changed the subject and told Derek that June was dead, per-haps from an accident, perhaps something else.

He nodded. 'One of the lads on the plough team told me just before you got here. Isn't it awful?'

'Can you think of—'

'A reason?' Derek gave her a straight look. 'A likely candi-date? So, you lean towards not-an-accident then?'

'Perhaps we shouldn't speculate,' said Maisie, wanting to take back control of the conversation. What did she actually know about Derek Fieldhouse, after all? 'I so much enjoyed my gallop, by the way. Thank you for giving me permission.'

'My man gave you a hand?'

'Yes, thank you.'

'Talk much, did he?' asked Derek, frowning.

'A little,' said Maisie. Then, because she thought perhaps Derek was fishing to find out if the stable hand had been welcoming and helpful, she added: 'We had a good chat.'

'Did you?' said Derek, as if it was an important piece of information. Then his expression once again became avuncular. 'Which one did you take?'

'I went out twice, first a chestnut mare, then Nigel Bacon's grey stallion.'

'That bastard,' said Derek and Maisie was taken aback by the sudden bad language. Seeing Maisie's reaction, he explained. 'The horse, not dear old Nige. Excuse me, won't you? That grey has been nothing but trouble.'

'It has?'

'Nige doesn't dare ride it and, of course, it gets more and more bad-tempered. And the stable lad can't. He's too old and, not to put too fine a point on it, too short.' Derek laughed. 'As am I, though I tried . . .'

Maisie smiled again, thinking of the old farmhand as a 'lad'.

'One other thing,' she said, finally arriving at the main reason for her visit. 'Sergeant Wingard suggested you could help me regarding who owns Church Lodge. You said it isn't you?'

'Common misapprehension. It's owned by a family company, answerable to shareholders, not to me. My wife's in charge.'

'I wonder, could I speak to your wife?'

'She's in her own rooms. She has someone come in to help her in the mornings, you know. It takes a while.'

He said it as if Maisie would know what sort of help that entailed. Accountancy, perhaps? Or beauty therapies? In any case, the conversation seemed to be becoming less friendly and she didn't want to outstay her welcome. She might need to talk to Derek again at some point.

'Good heavens,' said Maisie, glancing at her watch. 'Is that the time?' It was nearly ten to two. 'I must be at the shop.'

'They close in a minute, you know.'

'I'm going round for a chat.'

'Are you? What about?' For just a second, Derek's face grew hard, business-like, his eyes frankly inquisitive. Just as quickly, he softened his features. 'Listen to me. That's none of my business. Off you trot. Come back again, won't you.'

'Or perhaps I'll see you in the Fox-in-Flight one evening?'

She saw his eyes begin to wander. His mind was moving on.

'Perhaps. Busy man, you know.' He opened the two halves of the stable door and the spaniel ran outside with her, tangling itself round her ankles. 'Heel!' shouted Derek angrily and the dog slunk back inside, clearly frightened of physical punishment.

'Thank you again,' said Maisie, feeling less kindly disposed towards its owner.

'Jolly good, jolly good,' he replied, without meeting her eyes.

She remembered what Maurice Ryan had told her about a substantial payment to Stephen from a limited company back in September the previous year.

'Oh, that company you mentioned, the one that owns the village properties, what's it called?'

'Fieldhouse Holdings,' he answered, tersely. 'Be seeing you.'

He shut the stable-style kitchen door on her, first the bottom half, then the top, leaving her alone in the well-kept kitchen garden, feeling none the wiser.

THIRTY-EIGHT

Maisie was disappointed. She had hoped to find that Derek Fieldhouse's property company was BFI Ltd. That would have solved the mystery of the large payment into Stephen's bank account – far too much though for doing odd jobs like mending a garden wall.

As she retraced her steps, past the forge and the pub towards the shop, she was considering the alternative reason why Stephen might have cooked up a bogus marriage certificate. The idea popped into her mind unbidden.

June had told Maisie that it was because, otherwise, she had decided to deny him sex. Derek Fieldhouse believed the same thing.

'*The heart wants what the heart wants,*' he had said. '*Or not the heart exactly.*'

Derek had also put forward the idea that Stephen might have been more deeply attached to June than perhaps people gave him credit for.

But what if June had been able to deploy another argument? She considered again whether Stephen had needed June's father in order to turn the proceeds of the cathedral robbery into cash. Could June have used that as a way of pressuring Stephen into marriage?

Maisie was so absorbed in her thoughts that, without knowing how she got there, she found that she had reached the front door of the shop. Alicia was just about to close.

'Come in, dear Miss Cooper. I'm so glad you decided to take up our offer. Quickly now,' she said jokingly. 'Before another customer arrives.'

Maisie slipped inside. Alicia shut the door, turned the cardboard sign over to 'Closed' and shot the bolt. Maisie followed her behind the counter and into the rear of the shop, through a rather spartan room in which a small quantity of dry goods was stored. On the table beneath the window was a calculating machine and two large ledgers. On an undershelf, Maisie could see a wire tray of paperwork, receipts, invoices and the like. Either side of the window were shelves supporting a dozen foolscap box-folders.

'My own private hell, Miss Cooper,' said Alicia, gesturing towards the paperwork.

'Maisie, please. In what way?'

'It is I who struggle with the accounts,' she replied.

Maisie didn't mind paperwork, but she agreed, politely. 'Oh, I see. Boring for you.'

They went through the office to a corridor off which Maisie glimpsed two bedrooms, both doors ajar. On the door to the left was painted a letter 'A'; on the door to the right a letter 'B'. At the end of the corridor was the living room, beautifully laid out to get the best from windows that faced south and west, with two comfortable armchairs and a lowish leather sofa.

'What a lovely room. Is this a bungalow?'

'Yes,' said Alicia. 'You don't notice from the front because the shop feels somehow imposing with its high gable. Have a seat, won't you? Bea will only be a moment.'

Maisie was beginning to feel she was imposing. 'I'm interrupting, aren't I?'

'Not at all. Look, I'll prove it.' Rather like a conjuror, Alicia whisked three napkins from the coffee table and revealed three generous plates of sandwiches. 'Ham and mustard. Will that do?'

'Marvellous,' said Maisie, only now realising how hungry she was. 'I've been riding and I think I'd forgotten that it isn't just the horse that works hard.'

'Let's start, then.'

Alicia sat down on the sofa and took a bite out of one of her sandwiches. She pushed a plate towards Maisie who chose a wonderfully soft armchair and began to eat with relish.

'Oh, delicious,' she said, covering her mouth with her hand. 'Is this the same ham you serve from the slicer on the counter?'

'Only the best.' Alicia smiled. 'Now, we only heard the most basic of facts about poor June. Do you know any more?'

Maisie didn't want to bring June's death back into the front of her mind. 'Not really, no.'

Beatrice entered the room, her hair wet and her face shining. She was wearing an old-fashioned summer dress with a narrow waist and a loud floral print. She threw herself down in the other armchair. 'Sorry I'm late. I was not presentable. I had to bathe.'

'You were a little sticky,' said Alicia.

'Wasn't I? All those logs!' Beatrice put almost an entire sandwich in her mouth and said something inarticulate. She held up a hand, chewed and swallowed. 'Sorry again. Ravenous,' she explained. 'So, what are we going to talk about?'

'We're going to explain ourselves,' said Alicia, with a meaningful look towards her friend.

'That's what you said earlier,' said Maisie. 'I wasn't sure what you meant.'

'Oh, yes,' said Beatrice. 'Our behaviour at the church.'

'And the reception,' said Alicia.

'Yes,' said Beatrice. 'And the reception. You see, from the outside, it must have looked rather odd.'

★★★

As the two friends talked, Maisie reflected on just how easy it is to be taken in by first impressions. She didn't say so out loud, but she felt an uncomfortable flush of shame at the assumption she had made in the churchyard that the shop ladies were simply nosy busybodies.

'First things first, Bea,' said Alicia. 'You finish your sandwiches. I'm ahead of you.' She turned to Maisie. 'Now, let me begin with something quite straightforward. We liked your brother. He didn't fool us. We knew exactly what we were dealing with, but we liked him. He had a remarkable . . . *joie de vivre*.'

Maisie smiled. 'Yes, I suppose he did.'

'But he wasn't what you might call . . .' Alicia hesitated.

Maisie thought she was waiting for permission. 'I think I know what you are going to say.'

'What you might call honest,' said Beatrice brutally, through a mouthful of bread and ham. 'By the way, this butter is very good.'

'It's from the new supplier,' said Alicia. 'It's more expensive but, I agree, it's better.'

'How much more expensive?' said Beatrice.

'I don't remember.'

'But you've increased the price to the customers?'

'Not yet.'

'We're selling it at the same price as before?'

Alicia looked guilty. 'Yes.'

'So, we're making no money on it at all?'

'Bea, do you think Miss Cooper has come round to listen to us discussing the price of butter?'

'No,' said Beatrice, smiling wearily. 'Carry on.'

She put another sandwich in her mouth and leant back. Alicia resumed.

'So, yes, "undeceived" as the poet says. We liked him and we felt, I mean we were worried . . .'

'We didn't want it to go off like a wet firework,' interrupted Beatrice. 'We promised ourselves we'd make the church service and the wake go with a swing, just for the fondness of our memories of him.'

'And we overdid it, perhaps?' wondered Alicia.

'Well,' said Maisie, evasively.

'We could see you weren't comfortable,' said Beatrice. 'You almost snubbed us.'

'I'm sorry. I really didn't know who anyone was at that point.'

'It couldn't matter less,' said Beatrice. 'We just wanted to do him justice and try and get everyone to celebrate him. Do you understand?'

'But what did Stephen do to make you like him so?' asked Maisie.

'Didn't you know?' said Alicia. 'Wasn't it in his papers?'

'What papers?'

'You must have seen his papers,' said Beatrice.

'From his solicitor, Maurice Ryan,' said Alicia.

'You aren't mentioned.' Maisie frowned. 'At least, as far as I could see. There are just outstanding bills and demands for payment.'

'That's precisely where you should have found us,' said Alicia.

Maisie's heart sank. She felt a new emotion for her wastrel brother – anger that he had left her such a disastrous mess to clear up.

'Is it more debts?'

'No,' said Beatrice surprisingly. She turned to her friend. 'Alicia, isn't that just like him?'

'It is,' Alicia replied. 'Generous to a fault.'

'Generous?' repeated Maisie incredulously. This was not a word she'd heard used about her brother since she'd arrived in Framlington.

'It was when we were in trouble here in the shop,' explained Beatrice.

'What was?'

'He staked us,' said Alicia.

'As they say in the movies,' Beatrice added.

'He did what?'

Beatrice brushed the crumbs from her fingers onto her plate. 'He lent us money.'

V

GREED

THIRTY-NINE

Extraordinary as it was, once this fundamental aspect of their relationship with Stephen was out of the bag, Maisie was able to pull together the competing strands of Alicia and Beatrice's conversation. She let them finish, then tried to sum up.

'You had a cash-flow crisis and Stephen made you a loan.'

'Yes, he said it would stop him from spending it and, as we paid him back, it would give him an income that he would have to make an effort to stick to.'

Maisie thought about Derek Fieldhouse and his assertion that Stephen was trying to change.

'And this was last September?'

'Yes, it was,' said Alicia, surprised. 'How did you know?'

'You've seen his bank statements, haven't you?' said Beatrice.

'Maurice Ryan showed them to me. He drew out a large sum in cash. And since that moment,' Maisie went on, 'you've made monthly payments to Stephen's account. You are "B Otterway".'

'Guilty,' said Beatrice, happily.

'It's silly,' said Maisie, 'but now I say it out loud, I remember you. We called you "Otter" in school. You were only little and what my mother called a "proper little madam".'

'Still am,' said Beatrice, complacently. 'You know, the school is still there? It hasn't been abolished or merged or anything. And, did you also know, June Strickland also went

205

there when her family still lived down the bottom of Church Lane, just before the vicarage? She was the same number of years younger than me as you were older.'

Making her twenty-six, thought Maisie. On first meeting, she had guessed about that.

'Village life,' said Alicia, tightening the elastic band round her ponytail. 'Tendrils everywhere.'

'Anyway,' said Maisie, trying to get the conversation back on track. 'You'd like to know if I am going to insist that you honour your debt.'

'Maisie,' said Beatrice, 'I'm speaking to you as a friend because your brother was a friend. We're not, frankly, very good at running a village shop. I mean, we love it here and the customers like us and we've improved.'

'We're much better than when we started out,' said Alicia.

'Slightly better,' contradicted Beatrice. 'Slightly less incompetent, as you can tell from the farrago about the better butter. "Better butter." That's a tongue twister.' She got up and went to a lovely bureau under the west window. 'Now, there's this.'

She came back and sat down, pushing the plates aside. She slapped a cardboard document wallet down on the coffee table. Maisie recognised it. She had seen it that morning, being waved by Derek Fieldhouse. Beatrice pulled out an official letter, demanding '*Payment of Arrears*'.

'He owns the shop as well as Church Lodge?' said Maisie.

'Yes, and the cottages at the top of Church Lane and the stables and I don't know how many other properties. He always claims it isn't his business, that he's simply the messenger boy for Fieldhouse Holdings, that he answers to his shareholders, but we know better. The shareholders are him and his wife. I got on to Companies House to find out. You can't keep it secret unless you register in Jersey or in the Bahamas or something. Anyway, he wants more money or he wants us out but he just doesn't like to admit what a grasping bastard he is.'

'Beatrice!' scolded Alicia.

'Yes, well, he is,' replied Beatrice. 'Quite literally, possibly. I remember his father and he's not a jot like him.'

'That's enough,' Alicia insisted.

Beatrice changed tack. 'Maisie, if we hadn't had Alicia's mother's old clothes to wear, we wouldn't have been able to afford anything new to dress in mourning. We did laugh when we looked in the mirror. We're not greedy people. We're happy to make do. They do say women eventually become their mothers, don't they? Anyway, as regards honouring your debt, that's easy. We can't.'

'It's true,' said Alicia sadly. 'We're very sorry. We simply can't.'

There was a pause as Maisie took this in. She had found out the answer to one or two minor questions – the identity of B Otterway, what Stephen did with the money from BFI Ltd – but she didn't really feel any further along.

At that precise moment, they were interrupted by a distant knocking – a customer politely tapping on the shop door – and Maisie realised that it must be two-thirty and she was about to be late to meet Mohammed. They wished one another goodbye at the door and Maisie promised to take full account of all they had said. She would come back and speak to them soon.

'Oh, and would you do me a favour?' she asked. 'Could you possibly let people know, for any who might be interested, the cremation will be held tomorrow at eleven o'clock?'

'Of course,' said Alicia.

'We'll make sure everyone is aware,' said Beatrice.

Once outside, Maisie's first thought was that the two women made a rather wonderful pair of characters and not at all what she had expected to find. She paused to look in through the window, watching them attend to their first after-lunch customer. Alicia set about slicing some ham and Beatrice had a felt-tip pen in her hand to change the price of the butter.

Shouldn't the shop be a little gold mine with its captive audience of local inhabitants?

This question was followed by a new and less generous thought.

If Alicia and Beatrice were financially incompetent, in fear of eviction by Derek Fieldhouse and in debt to a man who was murdered, had the police given any thought to that?

★★★

Maisie hurried back to Church Lodge and unlocked the front door, checking her watch. It was just after half past two. She ran through to the kitchen, found a few sticks of kindling in the basket, laid them in a wigwam with three or four twists of newspaper and lit the Aga. The kindling burned up quickly, then the wigwam collapsed into a tidy heap of embers. She added some lumps of coke from the scuttle with her fingers, then washed her hands at the sink.

The more she thought about it, the more likely Alicia and Beatrice seemed as suspects. Both were plausible candidates to be Stephen's 'other woman' and his murder would be the cleanest way to avoid repaying their substantial debt. Plus, June might well have known something about them and needed, in her turn, to be silenced.

She dried her hands, realising that she was rather excited to be seeing Mohammed. How old had she been when they met at the Horse of the Year Show? It must have been 1953 or 1954, with Stephen already enlisted and her still in school. Was he really a member of the Kuwaiti royal family or was that just something Stephen had said to impress his teenage sister?

While she was waiting, she opened Stephen's exercise book and looked at her map of all the things she had learnt – the human relationships and the financial connections. She spent a minute or two adding some more details from her conversations at the stables, from talking to Derek Fieldhouse and from the unexpected revelations at the shop. Where she had written 'Second Woman', she drew an arrow towards Alicia and Beatrice as well as Mrs Fieldhouse.

What was her first name? The elderly stable lad had told her when she had asked if Mrs Fieldhouse had come into the Fox-in-Flight with her husband after Maisie had left. She remembered because of the odd way he had phrased his answer.

'*Daphne, his missus? Not a chance of that.*'

She should have asked why it was so preposterous that Mrs Fieldhouse would have come to the pub with her husband. Was it because they were on bad terms? And were they on bad terms because Stephen was having an affair with Daphne and because Derek Fieldhouse knew and resented it? And wasn't that a motive for murder, especially if you were an energetic pocket battleship of a man?

No, that wasn't fair. Derek Fieldhouse wasn't precisely Maisie's cup of tea but she had no reason to think he was a monster.

Oh, except for his voracious pursuit of money. And, of course, if Stephen had cuckolded him . . .

Maisie remembered the Casemores' conversation, overheard at the reception in the Fox-in-Flight, gently arguing about replacing the stair carpet. Mrs Casemore had said that it ought to be at the charge of the landlord. What had Mr Casemore replied?

'*I don't think that's a fight we are likely to win.*'

And the cottage was painted, like many others, with the regulation mustard-yellow on all the door and window frames, meaning it was part of Fieldhouse Holdings of which Derek and Daphne Fieldhouse were sole shareholders.

Maisie added a couple more notes to the increasingly dense sprawl across the centre pages of Stephen's notebook, then she spotted a second interesting connection between Derek's wife and one of her other items. It was, perhaps, a little remote, but she drew a dotted line from 'Second Woman' and 'Mrs Fieldhouse' to the posy and poem. In the little bunch of wild flowers, what had been the most important bloom?

Daphne.

Had Daphne Fieldhouse left Stephen a posy comprised mostly of *Daphne odorata*?

Maisie sat back on the hard kitchen chair. Was she becoming fanciful? This wasn't a murder-mystery play, after all, or a riddle in which hidden connections were obscured by wordplay. It was real life. Then again, people did odd things when they had secrets they were obliged to conceal.

No, on refection she didn't think she was being fanciful in the slightest. How else was Stephen's lover – if indeed she was his lover – supposed to leave her own personal tribute? If they were having an illicit affair, she couldn't express her sorrow at his loss openly; it would have to be concealed.

Maisie followed her train of thought a little further. If Derek Fieldhouse had been cuckolded by Stephen, wasn't it likely that he, Derek, would attempt to cover up any suspicion of guilt of Stephen's murder by claiming to be Stephen's 'best friend hereabouts'? Even if the Daphne connection was meaningless, that was worth pursuing.

Another idea popped into her head, like a bubble bursting at the surface of water. What had Alicia said that had also rung a faint bell in her imagination?

'*So, yes, "undeceived" as the poet says.*'

Maisie hesitantly drew a dotted line connecting the posy and poem with the village shop. If Alicia was a lover of poetry, was she also a candidate for an affair? What about Beatrice? Her hearty vigour seemed much more likely. Then again . . .

Maisie had no reason to assume the relationship between Alicia and Beatrice was a romantic one. If it were, it would be normal, she supposed, to have separate bedrooms, to avoid the whiff of scandal. But they could just as easily be platonic friends with no interest or opportunity for finding themselves husbands. Weren't they of an age that corresponded with the imbalance in male and female populations after the Second World War? If four hundred thousand British men died in the conflict, the vast majority of them of marriageable age, that meant four hundred thousand women would very likely be obliged to go without marriage. In France it was, if anything, worse. Although the number of 'military deaths' was lower, 'civilian deaths' from the Nazi occupation were far higher.

No, they were too young for that.

She closed the exercise book and held it between thumb and forefinger. As she had noticed before, wasn't it a little thin? Where were the pages Stephen had pulled out of the middle? Had he used them for some secret purpose? Were they somewhere in the house, waiting to be found, the key to all the mysteries?

The local newspaper was still open at page five, the follow-up report on the cathedral robbery. She thought about the devotional book and then the seven deadly sins and how they each might constitute a motive for murder – greed first among them. But hadn't Stephen been trying to live within his means, using the shop as a kind of investment, generating a modest regular income?

Maisie heard a crunch of tyres on gravel.

'At last.'

She put the notebook back in the drawer and went out to meet Mohammed's car. It turned out to be a long black saloon, considerably bigger than her and Sophie's Paris living room. Above the Bentley insignia in the centre of the bonnet was a short staff and a flag, a black trapezoid on the 'hoist' side opposite three horizontal bars of colour – green, white and red. A uniformed chauffeur got out and walked round to the rear door, opening it almost silently.

Good heavens, thought Maisie. *Perhaps he is royal, after all.*

There was a brief pause, then Mohammed As-Sabah climbed out, dressed for the City in a beautifully cut pinstripe suit. He glanced around, sniffed the country air, looked at Maisie and said: 'Little Miss Cooper, you are a picture. I'm so sorry I'm late. My meeting ran on and on. Where is the old scoundrel? Is he hiding?'

FORTY

A little while later Mohammed and Maisie were sitting at the kitchen table in Church Lodge.

'Dead?' said Mohammed, rubbing his chin. 'I can't believe it. And murdered?'

All jollity and facetiousness had fallen away. She had given him the bare bones of what had happened, from the moment her flatmate Sophie gave her Stephen's unexpected message.

'Yes, murdered. It seems there is no doubt.'

'I am appalled,' said Mohammed quietly. 'And it seems so unlikely.'

'I know,' she said, realising that, for once, she was the one who knew, who had the awful news to break.

'That he should have spent so many years in the army and then, to meet his death in a . . .' He searched for the right words. 'In this rather idyllic English village.'

'It does seem very unfair,' said Maisie.

'And how are you?' he asked kindly. 'This must be quite terrible.'

'It has been, but it's finally beginning to sink in. I've become . . .' She hesitated. How honest should she be, she wondered? 'I'm not sure how to explain.'

'Please try,' he said encouragingly.

Maisie supposed she could be frank. Mohammed was one of Stephen's oldest friends and he did appear to be a good listener.

'I've become . . . interested,' she told him.

'Yes?'

'In what happened and why it happened.'

'I see.'

'And because everyone I talk to seems to be hiding something.'

Mohammed laughed. 'It's easy to think that,' he said. 'What do the English say? "Just because you're paranoid, it doesn't mean they're not all out to get you." Is that it?'

'No, not that.' Maisie shook her head, frowning. She didn't want him to make jokes. 'I mean everyone seems wary, although they try to appear frank and earnest and claim to have been his friend.'

'Human behaviour is endlessly fascinating,' said Mohammed, with an air of indulgence, 'and the extremes of human behaviour must always be compelling.'

'But is it extreme?' Maisie insisted. 'I mean, murder is, of course, an extreme act, but isn't it often for the most mundane of reasons? Sordid, even – someone known to the victim, someone who owes them money or the other way round, or sexual jealousy, or spite. It's mostly about greed, isn't it, wanting more?' Maisie tapped her fingers on the rough kitchen table. 'I'm making it sound like I'm enjoying this, but I absolutely am not.'

'No, of course. I quite see.'

Mohammed looked at his watch. It was a huge chunky thing with multiple dials so that he could, she supposed, know the time in all the most important cities of the world. It looked rather cumbersome on his narrow wrist.

'Forgive me. I am not impatient, but I mustn't leave too late. I apologise for the Bentley. I prefer not to travel ostentatiously but, in the end, I had no choice but to take an embassy car.'

Mohammed was not a big man but she could see he was powerful. It was obvious from his suit and his cufflinks and his tiepin but, most of all, from his bearing, his easy self-assurance.

'So, it's true. You are important, a veritable VIP?' asked Maisie. 'Stephen always said that you were. I never knew whether to believe him.'

'The Kuwaiti royal family has many branches, most with the same or similar names.'

'Really?'

'Are there not hundreds of Johnsons?' He smiled. 'Is not every one of them, in theory, a son of John? It isn't so different.'

Maisie hesitated. She dearly wanted someone to trust, someone to whom she could properly unburden herself. Stephen's notebook was in the utensil drawer of the kitchen table. Maisie realised her fingers were resting on the handle. She had to make an effort not to take it out and show it to him. But, before she did that, she needed to turn the conversation to Inspector Barden's line of inquiry.

'Would you like a cup of tea?'

'I would, please. Black with brown sugar.'

Perfect, thought Maisie. That I can manage.

She set about making it, wondering how to proceed with her next topic of conversation.

'You know he had a Qur'an?' she told him. 'It's on the shelf over there.'

Mohammed turned towards the dresser but didn't get the book down. 'How interesting,' he said politely.

'I understand you were doing business with Stephen, something to do with oil? Can you tell me anything about a company called BFI Limited?'

There was a brief pause, as if Mohammed was listening for a sound in the distance, a sound that unsettled him. 'Why would you ask that?' he wondered aloud.

'It came up, with the police – oil, I mean.'

'How did it come up?'

Maisie told him about the conversation with Inspector Barden and Detective Constable Hands. He listened intently.

She gave him his black tea and sat down. 'And then they had to go back to London. On the train.' She smiled brightly before adding, 'They weren't riding in a Bentley.'

He paid no attention to her attempt at humour. 'That is interesting.'

'Isn't it?'

'But, if you are correct in your recollections, at no point did they suggest themselves that there was a connection with oil, or with Kuwait?'

Maisie was taken aback. Hadn't they? She ran through the conversation once more in her mind, realising her mistake.

'I suppose not. I sort of assumed . . .' She stopped, not knowing what to say.

How could she have been so stupid? It was she who had first mentioned oil. Barden hadn't refused the idea and, out of that, she had invented a whole backstory with Stephen and Mohammed in cahoots to pull off some huge deal.

'I thought perhaps you might be working together?' she said helplessly.

'Why might that be?'

'Because of your friendship, his Arabic skills?'

'Why would that be important?'

'Well, for diplomacy and communication, I suppose. And, of course, he had strong connections with the Protectorate.'

'And you imagine being an officer in the ousted British occupying forces would count in his favour?' he asked mildly.

'No, perhaps not, looked at in that light.'

'And his excellent Arabic – I grant you, a very unusual accomplishment for a westerner – do you imagine that there aren't enough Kuwaitis capable of expressing themselves adequately in the Queen's English, on their own behalf?'

He spoke with no particular emphasis but he was succeeding in making Maisie feel extremely small.

'I'm sorry. Of course, you are right.'

216

'Perhaps it is not important,' said Mohammed. 'I know nothing of BFI Limited, by the way. Perhaps that too is nothing.' He looked at her with his head on one side. 'They will return, these Special Branch officers, Inspector Barden and Detective Constable Hands?'

'They said they would. The local police resent their presence. I know that in any case,' said Maisie, trying to give at least an impression of basic competence, of having thought things through. 'They didn't seem particularly focused on any one aspect.'

'They wouldn't. To admit their focus would be to give up an advantage.'

'Oh,' said Maisie.

Mohammed fingered his tie. She noticed that the tiepin was decorated with a tiny enamel version of the flag that flew from the bonnet of the Bentley, a black trapezoid and three coloured bars: green, white and red.

'I should leave you in peace,' he said, unexpectedly.

'So soon?'

'I am expected for a dinner at the Foreign Office this evening.'

'Good heavens.'

He looked her in the eye and she felt that she was being subjected to some kind of test.

'Is there any other reason why you should think Stephen was in business with me? Some paperwork, for example? How did you know what number to call?'

She took her fingers off the handle of the utensil drawer.

'I made a note of it from his diary,' she lied.

'Could I see it?'

'I'm afraid not.' He raised an eyebrow. She smiled apologetically. 'I was allowed to look at it at the police station. They still have his papers for evidence or whatever they do. Perhaps I shouldn't have called you at all?'

'No, no,' he murmured, 'you did the right thing. Once you had set the hare running, it was only fair to warn me.'

He looked down and stroked the palm of his hand along his thigh, smoothing a wrinkle in the pure wool of his expensive suit. Maisie thought that it was probably a habitual gesture that he used to control his emotions.

Because, despite his self-control, it was absolutely clear to her that she had made him extremely angry.

FORTY-ONE

Maisie wasn't certain where she had gone wrong.

'Have I done something very stupid, Mohammed?' she asked.

'This is what I feared,' he told her. 'This is why I prevented you from saying too much on the phone. One never can tell who is listening.'

'Listening to your private calls? Surely not?'

'Who knows?' he said quietly. 'I will do my best to prevent this situation from becoming more complicated, but now I must leave.'

'I'm sorry,' Maisie repeated. 'I didn't know that I was saying the wrong thing.' He stood up. She did the same. 'The cremation will be on Saturday at eleven, tomorrow, if you are able – if you wish to pay your respects.'

'Thank you,' he said coolly, without committing himself. 'You see, Maisie, in this metaphor, where you have set the hare running, I am the hare, not the hunter. You have given Barden and his man a reason to take an interest in me, for Special Branch to take an interest in me. This is unfortunate. To coin a phrase, in my position, one must be whiter than white.'

He smiled slightly, as if the expression amused him, but the smile was completely without warmth.

'You mean as a foreigner.'

'Yes.' He raised his chin. 'But the world is changing. Do you read the papers, Maisie?'

'Of course I do,' she told him.

'The world is changing,' he repeated. 'For many years there has been a First World and a Third World and very little in between. We are entering the "age of oil". This year, maybe next year – you'll see.' He looked round to make sure he was leaving nothing behind. 'Now, it has been a pleasure. We must meet again.'

He held out his hand. She took it and they shook. Maisie felt like she was being dismissed from the presence of some grandee who would, the moment his back was turned, forget her.

'What has Stephen done?' she asked. 'Is this why he's dead? Is it something to do with you, or with oil, or with the Arab world, or . . . ? I don't know.'

Mohammed didn't reply straight away. He let go of her hand and looked out of the window.

'You see the bare branches of the trees? They are nothing to do with the spring, but they will become the spring.'

'What does that mean?'

'I have had no contact with Stephen for seven years.'

'Since 1965. What happened then?'

'We fell out.'

'Oh,' said Maisie. 'Can you tell me why?'

'He was greedy and tried to take advantage of our friendship.'

'But in what way?'

'I would rather not say.'

'Because it reflects badly on him?' Maisie gave a sad smile. 'Don't worry. I have no illusions.'

'No,' said Mohammed softly. 'Because I don't want you to know.'

He had once more succeeded in making Maisie feel stupid, but she couldn't help herself from explaining the obvious inference.

'Because, if I don't know, I can't tell anyone.'

He nodded. 'You are an intelligent woman. I am very sorry for Stephen's death. He was a complicated man. Would you agree, he never recovered from your parents' accident?'

'I do think it had an impact.'

'If I were you,' he said carefully, 'I would keep my cards close to my chest.'

'I will,' she said.

'But, if anything happens, I would be grateful to be informed. You have my number.'

'Yes.'

He sighed. 'I have annoyed you. You have annoyed me. This is an unhappy meeting, an unhappy *retrouvailles*.' He pronounced the French word for 'reunion' perfectly. 'Perhaps, one day, when all this is behind us, you can show me Paris?'

The words sounded like a kind of apology and the suggestion was a surprise.

'Perhaps,' she said uncertainly.

'And you will explain to me your reticence. There is something you have not told me. Isn't that so?'

Maisie wondered if he was simply fishing or if she had somehow given herself away.

She forced herself not to look down at the utensil drawer and turned the question back at him.

'Mohammed, is there nothing else you can share? It isn't fair to leave me in the dark. You know everything I know,' she finished, weakly.

'Do I?' he said, doubtfully. 'You are unusual for a westerner. You pronounce my name correctly, aspirating the "h" and distinguishing the double "m" as two sounds. Why is that?'

'I suppose I pay attention.'

'Of course.'

He smiled and nodded – or was it meant as a small bow? She followed him to the front door expecting him to turn and say something else but he went straight outside. The chauffeur got out and opened the door of the Bentley. She watched Mohammed get inside. The chauffeur closed the heavy door and the car pulled away without him meeting her gaze.

***

Maisie went back indoors, shut the door behind her and stood, becalmed, in the chequerboard hallway, her eyes on nothing. She had hoped that, in Mohammed, she would finally find an ally. As it turned out, she had simply succeeded in making a new enemy.

'Enemies and friends,' she murmured, aloud.

It was true what she had told Mohammed. Lots of people kept telling her how much they had liked Stephen. Jon Wilkes was the first, at the reception. *I should pop in and speak to him properly*, she thought. Then there was June, of course. Then Nigel Bacon, obviously. He said he was Stephen's 'pal'. Then the old boy at the stables who shared his love of horses. Then the shop ladies, Alicia and Beatrice, with their financial debt alongside an obvious fondness. And Derek Fieldhouse who claimed to be his 'best friend hereabouts'. Even Mohammed hadn't entirely disavowed his old comrade.

And yet, one of these 'pals' had murdered him, hadn't they? How could that be? What was she missing?

What about Maurice Ryan and Miss Clement? Maisie rather liked her – the bright clothes, the self-possession. Would Stephen have 'liked' her too? She had told Maisie, uninvited, that Stephen was 'an interesting client'. Wasn't Miss Clement still a strong candidate for 'Second Woman'?

Well, yes, at least until she had spoken to Daphne Fieldhouse who remained, she wasn't sure why, her prime candidate.

Oh, but the affection for Stephen was not universal. Sergeant Wingard had called Stephen a 'wretch'. That, at least, was categoric. And June's father, Mr Strickland, who had made an inarticulate noise in his throat and mentioned his name with contempt.

Maisie sighed. It had already been a long day. What was the time? A little after three? Good heavens, half past, already.

Outside the tall windows the sky was darkening. What would all those people be doing right now? It was a Friday afternoon. Most of them would be working, others making tea and reading the paper.

And what should she be doing?

She thought about the evening, just beginning to come into focus ahead of her. What time could she reasonably go to bed? Nine? Half past eight, even? And, from now till then, what use would she be? What more could be learnt from sitting and thinking and fretting?

She returned to the kitchen and drank a glass of water. It did her good. She looked in her handbag for the keys then sort of weighed them in the palm of her hand, contemplating her deadline. Between today and tomorrow, Saturday at 'close of play', she would have to 'make alternative arrangements' before returning to Paris. But the police investigation into both deaths, surely, would prevent her leaving? Could she not prevail on Derek Fieldhouse to give her a few days' grace?

Unlikely. She thought she knew what he would say if she asked: *'It's nothing to do with me. It's the shareholders.'*

But she also knew that would be a lie. Beatrice Otterway had got in touch with Companies House and found out for sure that the only shareholders were Derek and Daphne.

Maisie wondered how Beatrice had gone about it. That might be a way of getting to the bottom of the mysterious BFI Ltd mentioned in Stephen's bank account.

More and more, she wanted to speak to Daphne Fieldhouse. Might she be the weak link in her husband's voracious exploitation of the village? If so, how would Maisie get access to her alone? Perhaps while Derek was in the pub?

She recalled what Bert had said when she asked if Fieldhouse had come into the Fox-in-Flight with his wife: '*Not a chance of that.*'

There was also Reverend Millns' remark at the reception: '*You wouldn't expect to see her in the graveyard, would you? Very difficult.*'

Neither comment seemed to make much sense, unless of course it was 'difficult' socially because Daphne Fieldhouse had been Stephen's mistress. But, if that were so, wouldn't someone have told her?

Maisie remained unconvinced but, if it wasn't that, what was she missing?

FORTY-TWO

Maisie made up her mind to visit Framlington Manor later that evening and try to speak to Daphne Fieldhouse while her husband Derek was in the Fox-in-Flight. If he followed the same schedule as the previous evening – and Bert had suggested he was a person of habit – that ought to be possible. The best way to be sure, of course, would be for her to be in the Fox-in-Flight already, waiting for Derek to come in. That way, even if he only stayed for one drink, she would have a chance of nipping out and catching Mrs Fieldhouse in private.

But what was Maisie going to ask her?

Well, even if the police didn't detain her in England, she felt a duty to solve not just Stephen's murder but also June's, and to do this she would need an extension at Church Lodge. Second, she would try and find out if there was any way she could mitigate Derek's behaviour as a landlord and find ways to make Fieldhouse Holdings' tenants' lives a little easier, in particular that sweet old couple, the Casemores. Maybe also the ladies in the shop? Maisie felt grateful for the friendliness many of the villagers had shown her, determined to do what she could to help – and perhaps compensate, at least in part, for all of Stephen's upset and disappointment.

No, that wasn't fair. He had made the shop ladies a loan.

Yes, but where had the money come from in the first place? That was the worry. What exactly was BFI Ltd? What could those letters mean?

Just for a second, gazing at the darkening kitchen window, an image of June came into Maisie's mind, the first time she saw her, at the front door of Church Lodge, slightly distorted by the semi-obscured glass. Then, like a nightmare, the memory transformed itself and the image was of June bleeding and dying, calling out soundlessly for help.

Maisie stepped back from the sink and shook herself.

No, she thought, it would do nobody any good – least of all herself – if she sat about brooding. The best thing to do was to follow up some of her other ideas. If she could find out more detail of the robbery, maybe that would lead her to understand the bigger picture?

***

Half an hour later, Maisie got off her bike outside the public library in the centre of Chichester. For the first time she had to lock it up. She slotted the front wheel into the rack, alongside several children's bikes, presumably kids studying in the library after school. No, it was half-term. Maybe their parents were at work and they were marking time, unable to go home alone.

She was back in her wellington boots and flannel trousers. She had brushed the knees and they had come up reasonably clean. In the chest-of-drawers she had found another jumper, this one in Air Force blue with cotton shoulder protectors sewn over the close-knit wool.

She went inside, hesitating, wishing she could go and sit in some quiet corner of the stacks to read. Wouldn't it be wonderful to escape into fiction, to retreat from the world as she had many times as a child in this very building? That made her think about the extract from Shelley. Was it really a clue or was it something that might be shared innocently? She

226

knew it by heart having read it many times. She could even visualise the swirly handwriting.

> The secret things of the grave are there,
> Where all but this frame must surely be,
> Though the fine-wrought eye and the wondrous ear
> No longer will live to hear or to see
> All that is great and all that is strange
> In the boundless realm of unending change.

Was it about taking secrets to the grave, as she had decided, or was it actually about murder? No, not really. The imagery was gothic, but that didn't mean . . .

Maisie was worried that she had assumed the poem was directly related to Stephen's death – his murder in fact – by a kind of confirmation bias. It fitted the pattern only once you decided what the pattern was. Taken on its own, couldn't it be an innocent tribute, something about how Stephen was a better man than he appeared, that his faults would be forgotten after he was gone?

Or could it, in some way, have been a kind of posthumous threat?

She didn't want to make the same mistake she had made with the oil connection, adding two and two together to make five. What the poem was actually trying to say might simply be that we can never know precisely what our fellow humans are thinking and feeling.

She went upstairs to the reference section and spent twenty minutes with old copies of the local paper, but she didn't learn anything new. As she had seen in the copy bought from the village shop, the *Chichester Observer* was mostly a platform for local arguments. Plus advertising, of course.

Maisie did find some information on Kuwait and oil. With the help of a librarian, she was able to consult back issues of the *Economist* and discovered that the oil producers of the Middle East had come together, determined to set their own prices – hence the energy crisis being felt to greater or lesser degrees all across the First World. It was the root cause of the power cuts in the UK, the *Economist* argued, because the coal miners had decided to go on strike in order to take advantage of the extra pressure on government from this new oil price cartel.

All of this was very interesting, but Maisie wasn't sure it fitted into the pattern of Stephen's life. She put the *Economist* aside. The more she thought about it, the more she believed that her most tangible evidence was the sudden large payment into Stephen's bank account back in September last year and there was no reason to think that had anything to do with oil or diplomacy or the Arab world. In any case, Mohammed had explained to her how foolish that idea was. In fact, he was seriously annoyed at being involved.

Might that have been his way of deflecting her, though? She had taken his anger and frustration at face value, but couldn't that be a pretence, just like Derek claiming to be Stephen's 'best friend hereabouts' could?

She asked the librarian if it would be possible to research BFI Ltd. She provided two avenues. The first was to write to Companies House, as Beatrice Otterway had done with Fieldhouse Holdings. The second was to employ a financial consultant, probably someone in the City of London, who could research the question for her. In either case it would take time.

The librarian glanced up at the clock. It was getting on for five.

'Perhaps you could make one or two phone calls,' she suggested, 'but it's rather late for office hours. I imagine you will have to wait until Monday.'

'Yes, of course,' said Maisie. 'Thank you.'

She wanted to try and call Companies House but didn't want to use a payphone so she left the library and went straight to Maurice Ryan's office. Miss Clement was just approaching from the direction of the Market Cross. She had a small packet of post in her hands.

'Good evening, I wonder if I might have a word with Mr Ryan?'

'Hello, Miss Cooper. He's with a client, I'm afraid. I don't expect him back to the office this afternoon.'

'Oh.' Maisie took a punt. 'Did you know my brother at all well? Personally, I mean, as opposed to just in relation to his business affairs?'

'Yes,' said Miss Clement, carefully.

'Do you think I might ask you one or two questions?'

Miss Clement seemed to catch the gravity in Maisie's tone.

'What's happened?'

'I'm sorry. I hope this doesn't come as a shock. June Strickland is dead.'

'How awful,' said Miss Clement, clearly appalled. 'How did it happen?'

Maisie wondered how much she could reasonably share. The police investigation was, after all, ongoing.

'She was struck,' she said, leaving the details vague.

'By a car?'

'It's possible.'

'By someone?' said Miss Clement, wide-eyed.

'I fear that may be so.' She paused. 'I wonder,' said Maisie, 'could I prevail on you to make a phone call?'

'Of course. I've just been to the Market Cross to collect post from the other professional offices. I must date-stamp its arrival. Would you like to come in?'

'If you don't mind.' Maisie followed Miss Clement inside. 'Might you have the number for Companies House?'

'Of course. We often need to contact them. But they won't be open now. They close at four.'

'Oh,' said Maisie, disappointed.

She sat down on the same hard chair as before to think, doing her best not to lean her head against the stains of hair oil on the wall. Miss Clement opened and date-stamped her post, placing each letter in a separate page of what Maisie knew in French as a '*parapheur*', an A4 filing book made of sheets of blotting paper for correspondence awaiting perusal or signature. She didn't know what it was called in English.

'Is there something else,' Charity said perceptively, without looking up from her task, 'that you want to ask me?'

Maisie took a breath. Was she being overly presumptuous? No, she had a right, didn't she?

'How well did you know my brother?'

'Quite well,' said Miss Clement, 'but not as well as he would have liked.'

FORTY-THREE

Maisie was intrigued. 'What does that mean?'

'Stephen was what people call "keen on the ladies",' said Miss Clement.

Maisie was reminded of remarks she had heard from Derek and from Nigel.

'I know.'

'For a while he was keen on me,' Miss Clement continued.

'But you rebuffed him.'

'I don't think it made him happy,' said Miss Clement, 'his attempts to "play the field".' She used the English idiom carefully, as if she had practised it in private. 'He wasn't a happy man, you know?'

'I am beginning to see, but then there are other people who think he was just living his life, doing his best.'

'I can't agree,' said Miss Clement.

'You are very categoric.'

'We met as outsiders, he and I.'

Maisie considered this. 'How was he an outsider? He was from here.'

'But he had been away so long and his experiences . . . It is difficult for a soldier to come home. He had seen so much and then . . .' She waved a hand, taking in all of Chichester, the cathedral, the traditions, the oppressive conservatism, the small-town gossip. 'Surely you can imagine. You live a cosmopolitan life in Paris. How would it be for you?'

Actually, quite pleasant, thought Maisie, but it might also, perhaps, feel like a kind of failure. 'How did you come to live here?' she asked.

'I married Maurice in London,' said Miss Clement, confirming Maisie's guess. 'He was just qualifying and he had the opportunity to purchase this business from a retiring solicitor. I came with him.'

'Did Mr Ryan know about Stephen's—'

'His attempts to woo me?' interrupted Miss Clement, with a smile. 'No. Maurice is very single-minded, focused entirely on retirement.'

'But he can't be more than fifty years old?'

'No, but he has a plan. He will build up the business and sell it and we will move to Guadeloupe – that is where my family is from – where the cost of living is much lower. He says it is possible in two or three years. He says England is depressing.'

'But he seems, well, so established here . . .' Maisie stopped. She had, of course, only encountered his 'professional' self. She smiled at Miss Clement. 'Well, good luck.'

'I don't want to go. I know no one in Guadeloupe. My family are all in Brixton, in south London. I don't want to go to the other side of the world and be a stranger there having been a stranger here.'

'I understand,' said Maisie.

She hadn't been keen about returning to her own childhood home; why should Miss Clement?

'In another life,' Miss Clement said judiciously, 'I might have paid more attention to your brother, but that would have been a mistake in this tiny provincial city where everyone knows one another's business. Maurice is not an exciting husband, but he is doing well. He's out on the golf course now – or he was before it got dark – extending his network. The "great and the good", you know. He's very proficient at that. Maurice is a competent lawyer but a brilliant salesman.'

'Forgive me, but these offices . . .' Maisie looked round the rather austere room with its sun-damaged prints. 'Do they inspire confidence?'

'We seldom receive people here. Maurice's clients are not the kind who travel for professional help. Professional help comes to them.'

'Yes, I see that.' She thought for a moment. 'Miss Clement . . .' she began.

'You can call me Charity.'

'Thank you, Charity. Is there anything you can tell me that, perhaps, I don't know? Are there any questions I ought to have asked?'

'My first thought would be the robbery from the cathedral crypt,' said Charity without hesitation.

Maisie's eyes widened. 'It would? How do you know?'

'I don't "know". But Stephen mentioned it to me. It was at a reception in the assembly rooms. I think he was a little drunk. He regretted it as soon as the words were out of his mouth. I thought I should mention it in my turn.'

'That he intended to carry out—' Maisie began.

'No, no,' Charity interrupted, 'it was nothing as clear as that or I should have told the police. He just claimed that someone had told him the theft would be easy.'

'When was this?'

'A few weeks ago.'

'Before it happened.'

'Oh, yes, well before.'

'Do you think he did it?'

Charity Clement seemed to make an effort to picture the crime. 'It is possible. Like I said, he was an outsider. You could easily imagine him losing sight of right and wrong. That happens, you know, when people find themselves too alone.'

Maisie thought about all the odd decisions Stephen appeared to have made, casting about for direction and purpose. Above all, she wished she had been home to take Stephen's call, to hear his voice. When her attention returned to the room, Charity was tidying her desk, straightening her blotter and her phone.

'I wonder,' asked Maisie, 'could I possibly make a call? I really would be very grateful.'

'Be my guest. It's nine for an outside line.'

Maisie picked up the receiver and dialled, willing her flat-mate to pick up. It was an hour later in Paris. When Sophie answered, Maisie felt awkward that Charity Clement would overhear, so she spoke quickly in French, probing to know precisely what Stephen had said. After a minute or two, she hung up. She thought she ought to offer Charity Clement a little explanation.

'I was just talking to my flatmate about when I would be back home.'

'I could hear. Your flatmate has a very loud voice.'

'Yes,' said Maisie, smiling. 'That's very true.'

'And, of course, being from Guadeloupe, French is my first language.'

'Obviously, it is,' said Maisie, feeling stupid once more. 'You aren't really Charity Clement, you are "Charité Clément".'

'*Voilà*,' said Charity. 'Anyway, that is interesting, is it not? From what your friend says, Stephen was thinking of moving away from Chichester, coming to stay with you in Paris. You didn't know that?'

'No, I didn't.'

'I wonder what it was – *La goutte d'eau qui a fait déborder la vase.*'

Yes, thought Maisie, the 'drop of water that made the vase overflow' – or, in honest vernacular English, Stephen's final straw.

'Charity, you said he was drunk when he spoke to you about the cathedral. Did he drink to excess?'

'He may have done, though I often felt he was holding himself back, that he knew himself well enough to be aware of temptation and do his best to resist it. And, of course, we remained on good terms, he and I.'

'I'm glad,' said Maisie, gratefully.

Maisie left Charity Clement and went to fetch her bicycle from the rack outside the library. She thought she had been told the truth. Stephen had tried it on but Charity had rebuffed him and they had remained friends, largely because they were both fishes out of water in parochial Chichester. And Stephen had at least some sense that his appetites could lead him into trouble and he had fought them.

Greed was an 'appetite', wasn't it? But at austere Church Lodge, Stephen seemed to have made peace with living frugally.

Masie set off on foot, wheeling her bicycle. In a sense, this was all negative information about things that hadn't happened. The news from her flatmate was different. She supposed that she had sounded impatient, forcing Sophie to search her memory.

'*I told you that he was most insistent, that it was urgent that he should see you.*'

Yes, thought Maisie, you did. But not forcefully enough.

Also, she was now sure she'd had it the wrong way round. Stephen had been ringing not to get her to come to England, but in order to warn her that he was about to turn up on her doorstep in Paris.

Would he have arrived with the proceeds of the robbery from the crypt, on the run from justice and – who knew – an angry and cuckolded Derek Fieldhouse? And, if there was a candidate for the personification of greed, surely it was Derek, fleecing the villagers with his rent rises?

Maisie flicked the dynamo onto the bicycle tyre and cycled north, away from the library and the cathedral. The street lamps had all come on with the dusk and the sky was grey-black, choked with low clouds. On St Paul's Road, she stopped outside Mr Strickland's second-hand shop, his truck parked at an angle on the scrubby land, the heap of rusting scrap metal looming like a strange and complicated machine.

She went closer. There was a scrunched-up newspaper and a few sticks in a large brazier, as if ready to burn something. A little light filtered out round the doorjamb of the shop and, as she came closer, she saw that it was just ajar.

This was an opportunity, wasn't it, to ask a few pointed questions? Maisie felt like she was close to an important discovery. Could Strickland have been the 'drop of water that made the vase overflow'?

She chained her bike to a nearby lamp post and went inside.

FORTY-FOUR

Although the lights were on, it was very gloomy. The warehouse was about the size of half a tennis court and packed with furniture – wardrobes, sideboards, wall cupboards and dressers of all shapes and sizes. Any items with shelves were covered with crockery and glassware. On the floor in between the bigger pieces was an array of odd incidental items: an elephant's foot umbrella stand with half a dozen walking sticks and canes; a modern swivel chair in puce leather; a telephone table with a black ebony veneer. The whole place felt crowded and oppressive, like a nightmare.

Maisie wondered if she should simply leave. What was to be gained from confronting Mr Strickland?

Well, information obviously. She hadn't planned to stop but, now she was here, it was an opportunity to speak to him privately. She could begin by giving him her condolences. It would be instructive to observe how he behaved in response. She had her suspicions about the relationship between June Strickland and her pa.

She moved along a narrow aisle to where a platoon of rolled-up carpets stood to attention on their ends against a wall. Then she tried another alleyway through the extraordinary parade of redundant furniture, too big for smaller modern homes, too ugly for larger traditional homes.

She doubled back to where she had seen the elephant's foot umbrella stand. She realised she was moving quietly, as if she felt she shouldn't be there. She regretted not knocking loudly on the front door and announcing her presence.

What reason could she give? Well, it was only natural that she might come and pay her respects.

Behind the elephant's foot was a hallstand with a diamond-shaped mirror inlaid at head height, designed for people to check their hats and ties on their way out of doors. Maisie caught a glimpse of movement and half turned. Mr Strickland was approaching her at speed with something in his hands – something wooden, cocked over his shoulder, ready to strike.

Quick as a flash, not stopping to think, she reached into the umbrella stand and whisked out a gnarled oak walking stick. She was just in time, raising it above her head to parry and stepping to the side. The pickaxe handle crashed into the hallstand, breaking the diamond-shaped mirror, sending shards of glass in all directions.

Maisie flicked the heavy walking stick sideways and caught Strickland hard on his right wrist. He cried out and his grip loosened. Before he could react any further, Maisie used her fencing skills to strike him twice, very quickly, on the right ear. He cowered away. She pushed the end of the rustic walking stick, with all her weight behind it, abruptly into his diaphragm.

He dropped the pickaxe handle and fell back on his backside.

'Stop, stop,' he cried out. 'I thought you were a burglar. I was only defending myself. A man has the right to defend himself, doesn't he?'

'You knew it was me,' said Maisie. She felt surprisingly calm. For the moment, she had the upper hand.

'No, no,' he wailed. 'I don't see so well.'

'You could see fine driving your truck the other day.'

'Where are my glasses? Have you broken them?' He pawed at the floor around where he sat. 'I'm like a mole without them.'

'You weren't wearing any glasses – not now or in your truck.'

'Well, that explains it, doesn't it? How could I be expected to see who it was?'

'Don't be ridiculous.'

'You've broken my wrist.' He held out a limp hand. 'That's what you've done.'

'Have you got a phone in here? I'm going to ring the police station.'

'No, don't do that. They've got a down on me. They're always trying to pin something on me and I'm just a poor old man trying to make a living.'

Despite the poor light, Maisie could see his eyes were shifty, unable to look at her, unable to stay still. She remembered Charity's information that someone had told Stephen how easy the cathedral theft would be.

'What do you know about the robbery from the crypt?'

'What?'

'You heard me.'

'Nothing.'

'What does it have to do with Stephen?'

'I don't have to talk to you. I'm going to have you for GBH.'

'It was your idea, wasn't it?'

'Wouldn't you like to know?'

'Yes, that's why I'm asking you. Did Stephen arrange for you to sell it on?'

'I've got nothing to be ashamed of.'

'Do you have the stolen jewellery on the premises? Is that why you're frightened of the police?'

'They'll plant it. They'll plant something. That's what they'll do. They've got it in for me.'

His eyes flicked away and Maisie realised that it was the pickaxe handle lying on the floor by the damaged hallstand that he couldn't keep his gaze away from for more than a few seconds. Despite the dim lighting, there was a noticeable stain on the wood, a kind of brown smear. It reminded her of the drying blood on her borrowed Arran jumper.

She had a horrible thought. Was that the weapon with which he struck June?

'Stand up,' she instructed him.

'I can't. You've broken something.' He held out his limp hand again. 'And I'm not breathing proper.' He began to gasp.

'You aren't seriously injured in any way.'

'I am,' he panted. 'I can feel my lungs filling up with fluid from where you stabbed me.'

'Don't be ridiculous. Nobody stabbed you.'

'You did,' he said, making it sound like a challenge. 'Call the rozzers, then. I don't care. I'll tell them what you done on private property to a man doing no more than defending himself and his stuff.'

Maisie watched him, weighing up his situation, then realising that he had forgotten to keep pretending to be breathless and hurt. He began making short, sharp inhalations in quite a convincing imitation of someone having a panic attack. Meanwhile, Maisie waited, watching his eyes, dark and calculating, shadowed by the tall furniture and the weak lighting, flicking now and then towards the pickaxe handle. The guilt on his face was much more than simple robbery and fencing stolen goods.

Maisie thought about what June had told her, the incomplete story of Wingard attempting to persuade her to give evidence against someone. She was sure, now, that it had little to do with Stephen or with Strickland being the fence for the stolen jewellery, but something altogether more unpleasant. It was her own father's abusive behaviour the police officer was targeting.

'That's how you killed her, isn't it?' she said.

'I don't know what you're talking about. Killed who? Why would I hurt a soul? I'm a poor old man trying to—'

'You killed your own daughter. Perhaps didn't mean to, but you hit her with that pickaxe handle and she died. Because she'd decided to denounce you to the police.'

'You don't know what you're talking about.'

'You hit her and she staggered out through the Somerstown estate, bleeding. Has Sergeant Wingard come to question you?'

'He's the worst. He's the one always trying to get me, ever since he was a kid. And what have I ever done? Just gone about my business, keeping myself to myself, no trouble for no one.'

'I know what happened,' said Maisie. 'I can see it written all over your dirty face.'

The pretence at victimhood completely evaporated and he became still. His expression was awful, a kind of leer, as if there was something in this situation that excited him. Maisie readied herself for him to go back on the attack. She took care to stay just out of reach with her wrist cocked so that, at the slightest trouble, she would strike him again with the gnarled oak walking stick.

At that moment, the lights went out.

Of course, thought Maisie. The regular early-evening power cut.

The gloom was total. She heard Strickland struggle to his feet and lashed out with the walking stick, not necessarily in order to strike him but to make him keep his distance. It didn't connect but she heard him shuffle away, then there was silence.

Maisie felt herself at a disadvantage. This was Strickland's lair, a place he knew well, somewhere he could almost certainly navigate in the dark, whereas she . . .

There was an almost indiscernible movement of darkness on darkness, low down. He was on all fours, trying to locate the pickaxe handle by touch.

Maisie was torn. Should she try and get it herself, or should she take advantage of his preoccupation and flee?

She decided on the second, edging backwards, her left hand trailing along the tall, dark furniture, the oak walking stick held out in front of her, like a rearguard. She now knew what the murder weapon was and she believed that Sergeant Wingard knew what the motive for murder was.

A car went past outside, its headlamps slicing through the darkness, just a shaft of illumination where the double doors had been left ajar. It was enough to see Strickland, kneeling in the dust, his dirty, deeply lined face angled up towards her, his left hand on the pickaxe handle, his right held against his chest.

Perhaps I did damage his wrist, thought Maisie. Good.

She turned and ran outside. The best she could do now was to call the police and summon them to help her.

It was very dark because the sky was choked with cloud. The phone box on the far side of the road was empty. She placed her call and gave the information – where she was and the nature of the emergency. Once again, she had no time to give her own name because Strickland had emerged onto the scrubby bit of land between the warehouse and the road. From the windows of the nearest house, a warm yellow glow of candles or paraffin lamps just made him visible. He carried the pickaxe handle in his left hand, still cradling his right by his sternum.

Maisie hung up the phone, stepped outside and prepared to defend herself.

Instead of coming for her he made for the brazier in its pool of ash, over by the scrap heap. He thrust the pickaxe handle into the paper and kindling and fumbled in his pockets, reaching round to his right-hand side with his left hand, surprisingly deft. A second later, he had his cigarette lighter out. He flipped it open and summoned a flame.

He touched it to the paper.

Maisie felt a sudden surge of anger and determination. This horrible man, who had groped her as she got out of his truck, in this very spot, was about to burn the principal evidence against him in the murder of his daughter.

She ran straight for him across the road. In the darkness, she slightly stumbled against the kerb and he dodged away. Luckily the oak walking stick saved her from falling. Strickland scurried towards the door of the warehouse.

'Don't you hit me again. By God, I'll make you pay for it.'

But Maisie was no longer interested in Strickland himself. As the flames from the burning paper licked upwards, she gave the brazier a kick to the top rim. It toppled over and the contents spewed out over the ground. She used the toe of her wellington boot to kick the pickaxe handle away from the burning paper. Luckily, the kindling had not yet caught.

Strickland shouted an oath and made for his truck, climbing up into the cab and slamming the door. There was complicated noise of ignition and crunching gears, then he pulled away, swinging out and accelerating with a rapid chug of the diesel engine away from the city towards the darkened hills.

Maisie's handbag on its long strap was across her chest. She took out her handkerchief and used it to cover her hand as she picked up the pickaxe handle and carried it away to the far side of the road. She felt calm, quite unlike the aftermath of poor June's death.

She propped the pickaxe handle against the phone box and stood quietly, waiting for the police to come.

FORTY-FIVE

The first officers Maisie spoke to, 'at the scene' as they put it, were unknown to her. They took a short statement then drove her away to the stark interview room at the police station down by the canal. It turned out Sergeant Wingard was not on duty.

She waited twenty minutes before, finally, Police Constable Goodbody – a sullen young man with a narrow, ferrety face and a habit of cracking his knuckles – came to take her statement. He made her plod through the sequence of events, one thing at a time.

'None of this is important.'

'Let me do my job, Miss Cooper.'

'What you need to do is get in touch with Sergeant Wingard.'

'A man's entitled to his evening off, isn't he?'

'Have you left someone at Strickland's warehouse?'

'You mean his old shop, miss?'

'Yes, obviously.'

'You're telling us how to do our duty now, are you?'

'And you have the pickaxe handle?'

'That's not for you to worry about.'

'Don't tell me what is and what isn't for me to worry about,' fumed Maisie. 'He attacked me with it and I believe it is the weapon that killed his daughter.'

'You don't look so bad for a little woman attacked with a pickaxe handle.'

'What?'

He cracked the knuckles on his right hand. 'We only have your word for it, don't we? Did anyone else see this so-called attack?'

'It was in the warehouse, in the shop. How would anyone else have seen?'

He cracked the knuckles on his left hand. 'What about outside, when you say he chased you into the street? Was anyone around for that little escapade?'

Maisie stood up angrily, pushing the uncomfortable plastic chair away with the backs of her knees. The ferrety constable looked frightened and cowered back. She was about to launch into a violent tirade when the door opened and Sergeant Wingard stepped into the room, looking like he had just come from a formal dinner, very smart in a lounge suit and clean white nylon shirt.

'Good evening, Miss Cooper.'

'Do you have the pickaxe handle?' she snapped at him. 'Is it being examined?'

'Barry?' said Wingard, gesturing to his colleague. 'I heard you from the corridor. Would you like to answer Miss Cooper, now?'

'Well, obviously we do,' said the ferrety constable.

'And is anyone investigating Strickland's warehouse?' she demanded.

'Barry?' prompted Wingard.

'It's being searched,' the constable replied, sullenly.

'And,' said Wingard, 'you searched Church Lodge a week or so ago, Barry, didn't you?'

'After the discovery of the body,' he said shortly. 'Nothing to report.'

'Good, that's all clear,' said Wingard. He turned to Maisie with just the shadow of a wink. 'So, you can see, Miss Cooper, that we are on top of our investigations.'

'And Strickland himself?' Maisie insisted.

Wingard frowned. 'Barry, why don't you go and make us a couple of cups of tea.'

The constable stood up, tugging on the hem of his uniform jacket. He left the room without speaking. Wingard shut the door behind him.

'Well?' she demanded.

'Strickland's disappeared,' he said, uncomfortably.

'That's marvellous,' sighed Maisie, slowly retaking her seat.

'We'll find him. He took his truck. He'll have parked up out of sight somewhere – an old barn, up a lane in some woods. There's a couple of places we have in mind. Perhaps I'll send Barry. He doesn't seem fulfilled in his work.'

He was trying to be light-hearted, but Maisie didn't play along. She was finding it difficult to concentrate. She was thinking about the conflict in the warehouse, how extraordinary it was that her fencing skills should have come back to save her in the moment of crisis. She hadn't held a sword for years.

'Where were you just now,' she asked, 'out of interest?'

'I was busy with the preparations for the Rotary Club poetry evening, Miss Cooper,' he explained. 'We give awards to children in different age groups. I would have been back here sooner but I went to Strickland's myself to visit the scene when someone came to fetch me.'

'Right,' said Maisie, frowning, feeling slightly dizzy. She took a deep breath. Was all this never going to end? 'I see.'

'Are you all right?' he said. 'You look a little grey.'

'It's nothing,' said Maisie, returning to the present. She looked up, realising the room was lit by electric light. 'Is the power cut over?'

'Not yet, but we have a generator.'

She looked at him more closely. His pleasingly regular features and darkish complexion were becoming familiar. No, not familiar. It was something else.

'Yes?'

'You look different out of uniform and . . .' She stopped. What was it, on the fringe of memory?

'That's very common,' he said. 'No one looks at a policeman. They just see the uniform and they are frightened or reassured, depending on circumstances.'

He sat down opposite her and Maisie said with a smile: 'I don't need another cup of tea, thank you.'

'That's all right. It was the easiest way to get Barry out of the room. If he brings you one, I wouldn't advise you to drink it.'

'Why not?'

Wingard raised an eyebrow. 'Let's just say it might not contain only tea.'

'He deserved what I said. He was a condescending pig.'

'Yes, that was always going to be true. People are who they are.'

Maisie didn't reply. She sat for a moment, feeling the tension ebb away from the room, from her muscles. Something was different between them, but she wasn't sure yet what it was. Perhaps it was Wingard? Yes, his manner had changed. He was less evasive, more forthcoming, more willing to meet her gaze with his soft dark eyes.

'You grew up in the village,' he reminded her. 'Do you remember June from back then?'

'Yes, but . . . Please, I'm so sorry about June. I know she meant a lot to you.' Again, there was a memory she couldn't quite capture. 'You attended Westbrook College, like me?'

'I did – the boys section.'

'I'm sorry. I have rather incomplete memories of that time, then going straight into the Women's Royal Army Corps after school and my whole life . . .' She stopped, very close to knowing what it was she wanted to remember. 'There was rationing and Latin and—'

'I understand,' said Wingard, kindly.

'In fact, how did you . . . I don't mean to be rude, but how was it that you were there?'

'You wonder how I, a poor boy brought up by his grandma on her pension in a tiny bungalow at the top of Parklands Road, could have attended the posh school?'

'On a scholarship,' she said, remembering. 'Stephen and I were paid for by an aunt.'

'You lived in the council houses up behind Framlington Manor. When you left school, you were never seen again,' he said quietly.

'That's right,' said Maisie, wishing she could picture him back then. 'You didn't go on to university or anything like that?'

'No, nothing like that.'

'Can I ask you why?'

'Because of the poor old granny.' He laughed. It was a lovely wholesome sound. 'That's not fair. She's not a "poor old" anything.'

'But you look after her?'

'I still live there in the same tiny bungalow.'

Maisie hesitated, thinking again about him taking the ring from June's finger. Why had he done that?

'You weren't once engaged to June, were you?'

Wingard laughed again, but this time it was a sad kind of humour, full of regret for an important mistake that someone had made. That he had made, perhaps? For the first time, though, it was as if he had allowed Maisie to see him without his policeman's mask.

'I'm sorry. Was that a rude question?'

'No, I was never engaged to little Junie. I felt sorry for her.'

'Why do you call her that?'

'There were three of us scholarship kids and we were expected to give back. We were sent out into the village

primary schools to do reading with the slower children. I
ended up in Framlington where June was struggling. I was
fifteen. She must have been seven, perhaps.'

'Struggling to read.'

'Yes,' said Wingard.

The door opened and the ferrety constable brought in two
cups of tea in chipped stoneware cups and saucers.

'That's your one,' he said meaningfully to Wingard, without looking at Maisie.

Once he had gone and the door was closed, Wingard put the
cups to one side then paused, as if putting his ideas in order.
Maisie watched him. His face reflected his memories – dismay
and helplessness. She had a sudden insight, confirming her
own suspicions about June's relationship with her father.

'You realised back then that her father was a menace,' she
guessed.

'A "tyrant indoors",' said Wingard, as if he was quoting
somebody. 'That's what my grandma called him. It's shocking, isn't it, how the older generation allowed a man to be
king and judge and executioner in his own home? Whatever
he did, however cruel and unreasonable, it was his business
and nobody else's.'

'No one ever said anything?'

'I did.'

'Good for you.' She frowned. 'But you were just a child.'

'I told the vicar.'

'The vicar of Framlington?'

'Yes.'

'The current vicar?'

'No, the previous one, Canon Dander. Soon after, he
moved on to Bunting, you know, up along in the Downs?'

'And . . . ?'

Wingard shook his head. 'He made the Stricklands move
out of their house on Church Lane, but that was all. Canon

Dander washed his hands of Strickland, made sure that whatever was happening was no longer happening on his patch, but took it no further.'

'And what did you do then?'

'Nothing.'

The word sounded very empty and final in the sparse interview room.

'But you'd done something. You'd tried,' she said gently.

'Yes, I had.' He sighed. 'And I got the Westbrook College staff to send me to Parklands School instead for the extra reading, so I could keep an eye on Junie in her new place, as far as I could, I mean, with me just a kid.' He sighed. 'I think that was what first made me want to become a police officer.'

'You had a desire to "protect and serve".'

'That's the American police, Miss Cooper. You've been watching too many films.'

They shared a smile and there was a pause, freighted by something unsaid. His hand was on the table. She wanted to reach out and take it in her own.

'How awful,' said Maisie.

'Yes, Miss Cooper.'

'Please call me Maisie.'

'If you wish.'

He didn't offer his own first name. Then, somehow, his mood changed and he was no longer interested in memories. He was once again brisk and efficient, briefing her on what he had discovered.

'I examined the pickaxe handle just before I came in to speak to you. You may have noticed the dry blood caught in the grain of the wood. He probably tried to wash it under the tap but that's not such an easy thing to do well. The handle end is quite shiny from repeated use and therefore there are fingerprints visible to the naked eye. If we can show that only he used it and it turns out to be June's blood, I believe we will be able to bring a prosecution for the murder of his daughter.'

'But you don't know where he has gone?'

Wingard shook his head. 'No.'

'Should I be worried?' asked Maisie.

'You should lock all your doors and windows. Lock yourself into your bedroom, if you can. Have a telephone by the bed.'

'I don't have a telephone.'

'No, I'm sorry. I knew that.'

'Is there such a thing as police protection?' He didn't answer straight away and Maisie felt an odd frisson in the stark interview room, as if she was engaged in some kind of strange flirtation, rather than a discussion of how she might be kept safe from a murderer. She decided to try and get an answer to another of her many questions. 'Were you angry with Stephen because you thought he was taking advantage of June?'

'He was.'

'June told me the story. She came to Church Lodge. She was cross and upset because she hadn't been invited to the church. I told her I had no idea who she was. I thought everyone in the village knew but, of course, the Stricklands lived in Chichester. I invited her in and she began at the beginning and . . . Well, let's just say that between June and my brother the appreciation was mutual.'

'Perhaps,' said Wingard. 'But then he tricked her with that bogus marriage certificate.'

'I know,' Maisie sighed. 'That does seem cruel.'

'It was damn cruel,' said Wingard, his face hard. 'I couldn't tell her, though. It made her so happy.'

'I can't believe it,' said Maisie. 'It just wasn't Stephen's character. He might have been weak or sly, but not cruel.'

Maisie dropped her gaze, not through embarrassment, but because she was thinking about something else. She could feel Wingard's eyes on her, waiting to see if she had anything to add.

'Perhaps we should—' he began.

'You tried to persuade June to make an official accusation, a sworn statement, against her father.'

'How do you know that?' said Wingard, for the first time looking surprised, knocked off balance.

'She told me. Last night, you gave her a lift to the Fox-in-Flight for work and, just before she went in, you tried to persuade her to . . . Now, I can't remember exactly what she said. Something slangy like "squeal". And she wanted to ask me about it, woman to woman, I suppose, because I had taken the trouble to listen to her story without judging her.'

Maisie remembered again her first meeting with June, in the kitchen at Church Lodge and then in Strickland's truck, on the way into Chichester. She'd had a sense that the relationship between June and her pa was an unwholesome one. It would inevitably become more dangerous if Strickland knew that June was thinking of making a complaint against him. Maisie could imagine June going too far and threatening him with denunciation, not thinking what the consequences might be.

Maisie told Wingard her idea. He listened without comment.

'Anyway, that's why, later that evening, I came into town to speak to her. And, of course, I'm sure you've worked out that I was worried that Stephen had something to do with the robbery at the cathedral and that maybe it was June's father who was supposed to sell on the goods. And you know that's why I was there, at the side of the road, outside the Bell, when she came staggering round the corner. And she must have told her father what she intended, that she was going to do it, that she was going to give you what you asked for, an actionable accusation, and so he . . .'

Maisie stopped, looking up into Wingard's eyes. The clock on the wall ticked away the seconds, but she didn't hear it. All of a sudden, she was seventeen and back in the school hall at Westbrook College. A nice-looking boy with blond hair and a willowy physique, singing in a sweet tenor voice one of the songs in the school play.

And she was standing opposite.

Then, to her surprise, another memory came back to her, complete in every detail, like a technicolour film of her own past. She found herself blushing as she remembered a school leaving party and a doctored punch laced with illicit alcohol, served by the other sixth-formers, and a moment of adolescent connection ending up with kissing Jack Wingard very thoroughly behind the cricket pavilion.

The next day she had gone away on summer holiday with her family in the New Forest. At the end of that she had enlisted and she had never spoken to him again until . . .

Well, until he had been called upon to investigate her brother's criminality and murder.

'Oh, Jack. I'm so sorry.'

He didn't seem to notice the change in her tone, the use of his first name, caught up in his own guilt and regret.

'Yes, that's right. All those years, I wanted to make him pay. And instead . . .' He sat back, looking utterly defeated. 'It's my fault she's dead.'

VI

GLUTTONY

FORTY-SIX

Jack offered to drive Maisie back to Framlington. They pulled away in silence, Maisie in the front alongside him. He surprised her by stopping briefly at Strickland's warehouse.

'People always want more than they need, more than they deserve,' he said, unexpectedly.

She waited for him to elaborate but he got out and went to speak to the scene-of-crime team. Meanwhile Maisie didn't know what to do for the best.

Should she tell him that she had remembered their kiss? Wouldn't that simply embarrass him? And what right did she have to go raking up the long-dead past? Wasn't it all complicated enough already?

He got back in, started the engine and drove on. Maisie stayed silent, finding it impossible to escape from her memories. She glanced across at his handsome profile, the firm line of his jaw, his dark hair just touching his ears, his eyes concentrating on the road ahead. How changed he was – so much a man, so little like the slender blond teenager he had once been.

Her heart sank. The past meant nothing. Less than nothing. It was, in fact, a hindrance. He had made it quite clear that she was nothing more than an unfortunate complication in his investigation.

Eventually, he swung the Ford Zephyr into the drive at Church Lodge and parked parallel to the front door, seeming to emerge from his own reverie.

'I agree with your deductions about who attacked June and why. On the other matter, the team has searched Strickland's warehouse without finding the valuables stolen from the cathedral.'

'No jewellery, no devotional book?'

'Nothing.'

'Perhaps he's already passed them on?'

He turned off the engine and the lights. It was very dark. The power cut was still in force and the street lamps were all off. Maisie wondered if she should worry about Strickland being out there somewhere, cradling his injured hand, looking for some new weapon with which to come at her. She thought about the disturbing rustling sounds she had twice heard in the undergrowth and peered out through the blackened window glass, barely able to make out the outline of the house. Could that have been Strickland prowling about, looking for the valuables?

'You saw me remove the ring from June's hand?' said Jack, unexpectedly.

'Before the ambulance took her away?'

'Yes,' he said, very quietly.

'That's why I wondered if you'd been engaged to her, but obviously that didn't make sense.'

'I see why you might have misunderstood.' Jack gave her one of his rare smiles. It made Maisie feel warm and reassured. For a second, she felt like reaching out a hand and touching his face, then he surprised her. 'It was from the robbery, of course.'

'But it's so ugly, so . . .' She tried to remember the word she had used in her head, describing it to herself. 'So gaudy – a bit of old glass and sterling silver.'

'Don't worry.' He smiled. 'Your sense of value is not entirely undermined. The stone is only semi-precious and the metal, as you say, is base, but it has tremendous historical significance.'

'From what period?'

'Tudor, like the book. Stephen presented it to her.' Jack gave her a look. 'They were your hairs, weren't they, caught in the setting?'

'Yes, they were. She caught her hand in my hair,' said Maisie. Then she thought she saw that he had been trying to avoid another complication, too. 'You knew it was one of the stolen items and you knew Stephen must have given it to June.'

'Yes.'

'But you believed she truly loved Stephen and hoped that maybe he might get her away from her awful father. And you didn't want her to be seen as an accessory, even after death.'

'That's right.'

Maisie pondered for a moment.

'Surely Stephen would have told her not to wear it in public?'

'He did,' said Jack. 'But, when he died, she couldn't help herself and I couldn't do anything because the important thing was always retrieving the book and the jewels.'

'She mentioned something about that when we first met, something like: "He gave me a ring but I don't know if I should show you." I suppose, later, she couldn't help herself. It was her way of saying—'

'That she was his true wife. Actually, though—'

'It was just how Stephen took advantage of her,' acknowledged Maisie, sadly.

'It was.'

There was a pause, a moment of stillness, and Maisie thought about how they had suddenly become close, finishing one another's sentences, completing one another's thoughts. Should she ask him if Stephen's death and June's were connected? But he seemed to believe that June's murder was the inevitable and sorry conclusion of a story that had been developing since June was a little girl.

'I thought wearing the ring was almost a good sign,' he told her, 'a sort of self-assertion. That was why I spoke to her once more, in the car outside the Fox-in-Flight, about testifying against her father, but obviously I didn't want to have to arrest her for handling stolen goods.'

'It was definitely Stephen, then?'

'Oh yes.'

'You have proof?'

'I had June's word – and, of course, the fact of the ring he gave her.'

Maisie thought about the long charitable relationship between Jack – as both a boy and a man – and poor victimised June Strickland. She could see how it might have become a kind of mission, almost a chivalric quest to see her delivered from harm, her enemy vanquished.

But had Jack loved June, perhaps, and so been moved to violence against the man who, apart from her father, had most cruelly deceived her? It seemed he was capable of concealing evidence, of turning a blind eye where it suited him. Might he also stoop to . . .

Could Jack have murdered Stephen?

Maisie bit her lip. Where was the danger, now? Was it Strickland or was it Jack? Or was it someone else altogether?

No, that was ridiculous. Jack was now the closest thing she had to an ally.

Another idea popped into her head. Might Jack have left the charming wild-flower posy and the poem as a kind of veiled insult?

'You said you were busy preparing for a poetry award at the Rotary. Is that right?'

'Yes, a committee meeting, that's all. The event isn't for a couple of weeks.'

'Are you interested in poetry?'

'Why do you ask?'

Maisie considered mentioning the verse from Shelley to gauge his reaction, but she was beginning to feel the pressure of time because of the plan she had made in her head to speak to Daphne Fieldhouse while her husband Derek was in the pub. This might be her last chance – a weekday evening. The next day he might have a different routine and, in any case, she would soon be on her way.

'It was just something someone said.'

Jack waited but, when she said nothing more, he sat up straighter, seeming to come to a decision.

'I'll come back later this evening, if I may, just to make sure you're all right.'

'Come back here?'

'Yes, if you wish.'

'Please do but, right now, would you mind dropping me at the pub?'

He glanced at his watch. She could just see the fluorescent dial. It was six-thirty.

'Are you sure?'

'There's something I must do, something I've been planning and, if I don't, I'm not sure when I'll get the chance.'

'What, precisely?'

'Oh, it's just a conversation I need to have.'

'Miss Cooper, you're not investigating your brother's murder, are you?'

'Call me Maisie, please. And no, of course not,' she said quickly.

'I will call you Maisie if you call me Jack.'

Maisie felt a surge of pleasure but covered it with words. 'I will. Thank you. But there's someone I must talk to about another matter. Stephen's affairs are quite difficult to disentangle,' she improvised, though it was not entirely untrue.

'I see.'

It was impossible in the darkness to see if he believed her. He turned the key in the ignition, reversed and then pulled forward, out of the drive and just a hundred yards down the road to the pub.

'Thank you,' said Maisie.

'How long will you be?' he asked her.

'I don't know. Perhaps an hour or two?'

'I'll go and check one or two of those possible hiding places. I'll be back . . .' He checked his watch again. 'No later than nine, in any case.'

'That's perfect.' She got out of the car but, before closing the door, she told him: 'Stephen wasn't a seven-stone weakling. There's the question of the physical strength required to subdue him, to suffocate him and drop him in the pool. It would need a strong man, someone of your size, at least. Have you considered that?'

'Yes, Maisie, I have.'

Because they were parked on the forecourt of the pub, there was a little more light cast by the many small flames inside the windows. There was an odd look on his face, one she couldn't quite read, almost as if he had hoped all along that this would happen, that they would become a kind of team.

But they weren't a team, thought Maisie.

Could they become one?

Perhaps, but certainly not yet.

She smiled briskly, shut the car door and turned away. She felt a tinge of regret as she heard him drive off, but also a lingering doubt.

FORTY-SEVEN

The view through the windows of the Fox-in-Flight was quite as charming as it had been the previous evening, though Maisie thought the atmosphere a little more sombre. The bottles and the glasses and the optics were illuminated by the glow of three hurricane lamps. Candles were on every table, their flames elongated by their jam-jar holders. Maisie had an idea the patrons might, as a consequence of poor June's death, be overindulging, like in a moralistic painting by Bruegel.

No, if she was contemplating a tableau of 'gluttony', there was no need to summon an old master. No need, in fact, to look further than the valuable sixteenth-century book and other items Stephen had stolen.

Why had he taken them? Money, she supposed. For what purpose? To clear his debts?

If the goods weren't in Strickland's warehouse, could they be somewhere in Church Lodge? Where hadn't she looked? Barry Goodbody had searched the place, but the police constable was barely competent and she didn't think that was strong evidence that they weren't actually there. She'd found the hidden notebook, after all, without too much trouble.

Inside the pub, Derek Fieldhouse was at the bar, tightly packed in his tweed suit, being talked at by Nigel Bacon, energetic and wiry in his Arran jumper. No, not talked at, exactly. Hissed at. It was clear, even from a distance, that Nigel was leaning in far too close to Fieldhouse's ear. Was it for privacy? In any case, it was clear that Derek was not enjoying Nigel's conversation.

Was Nigel trying to get Fieldhouse Holdings involved in some kind of scheme? They were both men of finance and Derek had spoken of Bacon as a friend, calling him 'old Nige' . . .

Then, just for a second, Maisie remembered herself at the hatch and June's urgent voice, trying to give the appearance of normal conversation. She realised there was something she had forgotten, June's second reason for wanting to talk to her.

'*There's something else as well,*' June had said, '*about the grass.*'

What had she meant by that?

June had followed up by talking about her 'pa' being there. Was that it? Did June think her pa murdered Stephen? Or did she mean that someone else was there, busy in the garden, and might have seen?

Through the window, Maisie saw Gerald Gleeson come out from behind the bar in his grey flannels and put a couple of logs on the fire. He seemed very serious and moved slowly, exchanging a word or two with his patrons, looking round wistfully as if confirming June's unhappy absence.

Maisie shivered, feeling unsettled from all the shocks. She sat down on the bench below the window, thinking about the bogus wedding certificate. There was no point arguing. Stephen had been, in Jack's word, a 'wretch'. What was more, he had left her, Maisie, nothing but trouble and debts.

And since then?

Violence, firstly with June's death and then with Strickland's clumsy attack. Then knowing – at least thinking that she knew – that a father had killed his daughter and that he would almost certainly try to get his revenge on Maisie for her accusations and for saving the incriminating murder weapon from his brazier.

Maisie once more felt that urgent desire to be elsewhere, to walk away, to go home to Paris and pretend none of this had happened. She could be sitting on a bench on the Place des Vosges, right now, talking to her languid, foppish neighbour, knowing it would soon be spring.

What was the point in trying to salvage Stephen's reputation? He was dead. No one cared. He would be forgotten by the people of Framlington in a month or two, a week even. None of it was her business. She wasn't obliged to try and fix it.

Maisie shook her head. No, that wasn't true.

All the upset and adrenaline, the fight or flight, was making her cynical. A reasonable reaction, she thought, but that wasn't the person she wanted to become. It wasn't just death, it was murder. She wanted to find out what really happened and, in that way, reassert the happy memories of their unspoilt childhood – loving parents, building castles from straw bales in the fields, harvesting blackberries from the hedgerows, stirring the gravy for Sunday lunch while her mother drank her glass of sweet sherry and put the joint aside to rest.

With renewed determination, Maisie got up off the bench and crossed the side road that led out into deeper countryside. How inky-dark it must be up in the Downs, she thought.

She found the side gate of Framlington Manor almost by touch and went through into the charming kitchen garden. There was a flickering light burning inside the kitchen, but the curtains were closed and it did little to help her find the path. She brushed up against a curry plant and smelt its distinctive fragrance, then stumbled into some obstruction, perhaps one of the stone geranium planters covered with a glass cloche. Finally, she placed her hand flat on the stable door, preparing to knock, hoping it wouldn't send up a volley of barking from the excitable cocker spaniel.

No, the dog would be at the pub with Derek. At least, that's what Bert had suggested.

Maisie tapped on the damp wooden panel and waited. There was no answer, no sound. She knocked again. The quiet stretched out.

She began to feel unnerved, wondering what might be going on inside the manor, if something had happened to Daphne Fieldhouse? What had Reverend Millns meant about it being difficult for her to come to the church? Bert seemed to think it preposterous that she might visit the pub of an evening. Why had no one seen her? Was it because she was dead and no one knew? Were they all in league and only she – the stranger, the outsider – was in the dark?

Maisie stepped away from the door, her breaths coming quickly. She was making herself frightened, not just with the nature of the ludicrous ideas that were marching through her imagination, but also by the fact that they were spiralling out of control, building on themselves, becoming more and more detached from reality. She had a flashback to the panic she had felt when she briefly fled from June last night, daubed in blood.

She stepped down off the step and turned, banging her shin on another planter, crying out. She crouched down and rubbed her leg, like an animal trying to make itself small and invisible, mentally berating herself.

Why hadn't she simply gone inside Church Lodge with Jack and laid her cards on the table? What if Strickland had followed them out here to Framlington and was waiting for her to be alone in some quiet, dark corner?

Somewhere like the Fieldhouses' secluded kitchen garden?

There was a sound from the front of the house, a creak, like a big door being opened on reluctant hinges. Maisie shuddered.

For heaven's sake, she tried to tell herself, *it's just a door.*

'Hello? Is someone there?' someone called.

It was a voice without colour, without charm. A woman's voice.

Maisie felt a huge surge of relief.

'Just a minute,' Maisie called back, making her way round to the front door.

'Who are you? What do you want?' the woman asked.

FORTY-EIGHT

Ten minutes later, Maisie was sitting on a leather ottoman by an open fire in the drawing room of Framlington Manor. The power cut was still in progress and the only light came from the huge blaze in the enormous metal fire basket, set in the middle of a monumental stone hearth, surrounded by lovely thick beech logs. Opposite her was Daphne Fieldhouse, a woman with an unhappy face and dark eyes beneath grey brows. Her hair was dyed an unbecoming ash blond. She wore green velvet trousers and a matching thin jacket.

It had been an odd first meeting. Maisie had followed the sound of Daphne's voice to the front door and Daphne hadn't wanted to let her in. Maisie had explained that she was Stephen's sister and, after a short pause, Daphne had relented and wanly invited Maisie through to the 'lounge'. There had then followed, from Daphne, several disorientating minutes of vague monologue, beginning with a short appreciation of Stephen's charm before a longer, more critical passage about his behaviour. She expressed admiration for his background as soldier and sportsman, but told Maisie that he should have been ashamed at what he had subsequently done with his life. Each time Daphne took a breath, she speared a cube of pink Turkish delight dusted with icing sugar from a wooden box on her lap and greedily ate it.

'Would you like a piece?' she finally asked.

'No, thank you,' said Maisie.

After a while, Daphne's monotonous assassination of Stephen's actions merged into a broader critique of the village and all the characters it contained – their slack attitudes to business, their dilatory engagement with social and parish affairs, their disregard for economic development, the incompetence of the church in administering its residential property, the general insipidity of the vicar.

Maisie listened with a polite smile frozen on her face, hoping she was managing to conceal her dismay. Behind her glazed eyes she was reconfiguring several assumptions.

The reason Daphne Fieldhouse hadn't attended the church or visited the reception at the pub might have been explained, either by Bert or by the Reverend Millns, but they both must have assumed that she knew. It wasn't to do with social embarrassment or the possibility that Stephen had had an affair with her. It was because of the awkwardness of the terrain – the bumpy ground and gravel paths at the church, the narrow doorways and the narrow porch and awkward steps up and down at the pub.

It was because Daphne Fieldhouse was confined to a wheelchair.

Maisie remembered what Derek Fieldhouse had said when she asked if she could speak to his wife. She hadn't understood it at the time.

'*She has someone come in to help her in the mornings, you know. It takes a while.*'

It must be a nurse, Maisie thought. Someone to help her get up and bathe and get dressed.

The monotonous voice went on and on. The connections and clues that Maisie had imagined dissolved in the flow. However dissipated Stephen had become, Maisie decided, he would not have entertained an affair with this unhappy woman.

Also, it seemed very unlikely that Daphne Fieldhouse was interested in wild flowers or poetry. Had she had something to say, she would not have used Shelley's verse to hint at it, but would have spoken her own thoughts aloud, indifferent to the consequences.

And there was no way that she was the weak link in Fieldhouse Holdings' management of its property portfolio, either. In fact, it seemed more likely that Daphne was the 'tyrant indoors' in this context, while Derek was the public face, the man whose superficial affability was commanded to smooth over their rapacious exploitation.

When, finally, Daphne had talked herself out, Maisie decided it was her duty to at least try and make an appeal on her own behalf and in favour of Alicia and Beatrice and the elderly couple, the Casemores.

'So, you are the power behind the throne,' Maisie began, inadvertently quoting Reverend Millns.

'You've met my husband, I see.'

'I have,' said Maisie, not quite following.

'Then you understand.'

Maisie realised that Daphne meant that she, Maisie, had met Derek and judged him wanting, as Daphne had. She forced herself to smile.

'I wanted to talk to you about Church Lodge. I understand that you own the property?'

'We do. I do. It's all the same. The company structure is advantageous for tax reasons. It's my money, not Derek's.'

'Right. Can you tell me, did Stephen owe you money, at his death?'

'He did.'

'Can I ask you how much?'

'It doesn't matter,' said Daphne, surprisingly. 'I've written it off. That, too, has certain tax advantages. Once you have money, it's child's play to make more. Did you know that? Anyway, he was an entertaining man. He took trouble . . .' The drab voice trailed off. 'At least, at first.'

It was odd to listen to her. Each thing Daphne said was imbued with a kind of certainty, almost dogmatic, yet the delivery was washed out and unemphatic. Maisie watched her eat the last cube of Turkish delight and toss the empty box onto the fire.

'Can I ask how, exactly, Stephen "took trouble"?' Maisie asked. 'It would be a comfort to me, given the mess he made of some other aspects of his life.'

'He was entertaining. He made me laugh. That's all.'

'What about?'

'Small things – things he and I found amusing.'

'For example?'

'The way the postman always tries to find out what one's letters are about. Have you met him?'

'No, not yet.'

'The way the vicar previews his sermons in general conversation, like an actor selling that weekend's upcoming performance. The way the labouring classes respect their "betters" to our faces, but mock us behind our backs. The strange motivation that caused Nigel Bacon to spend money I'm not sure he really has on that mighty grey stallion that so frightens him.'

It all sounded very bitter and acerbic, rather than 'entertaining', but Maisie wanted to continue to draw her out.

'I can imagine Stephen telling those stories with great amusement.'

'The way my husband thinks himself an emperor,' Daphne went on, 'a little Napoleon, spending my money, managing my property, when he is no more than a jumped-up corporal.'

'I see,' said Maisie, remembering how she herself had thought of him as a pocket battleship. 'Is your husband not gifted for business?'

'I tell him what to do. I believe that he is, at the very least, capable of following instructions.'

Daphne's voice had grown so faint that Maisie had to lean forward to make it out. She felt frustrated, weary of Daphne's arrogance. Could it be a façade behind which she was hiding?

'You know he was murdered?' Maisie asked, abruptly, hoping to provoke a reaction. 'Stephen, I mean.'

Daphne Fieldhouse nodded. 'Derek came home full of it. He told me some woman had broken it to him.' She stopped and a vague light came into her eyes. 'Oh, that must have been you.'

'Yes,' said Maisie. 'I was surprised he didn't already know. It was common knowledge in the village by that point.'

'Yes, that would be surprising. He loves gossip.'

Maisie waited for her to say more, but she shivered and lunged forward in her wheelchair, grabbing a log from the pile and tossing it onto the flames.

'If I have correctly understood,' said Maisie, 'you are what one might call the brains behind Fieldhouse Holdings. You set the objectives of the business and so forth.'

Daphne took her weight on the arms of her wheelchair and sat herself up straighter. Maisie recognised that she had found something with which to engage the woman's attention.

'I do, indeed.'

'So, it is to you I must appeal if I am to stay on for a few days more in Church Lodge.'

'Not possible.'

'Not possible?'

'No. And you'll need to clear out Stephen's things or Bert can bag them up for charity. I understand the previous tenants left clothes upstairs, though obviously I haven't been up there myself.'

Maisie waited, but Daphne clearly didn't feel any need or responsibility to elaborate. In reality, there was very little of Stephen's that she wanted. Perhaps the pint pot, the Qur'an and one or two other tokens to remember him by. Maybe Alicia and Beatrice could help? Might they have room to store them?

'And the position of the village shop. That also is . . .' Maisie wondered what to say. She didn't know the details. 'I suppose they are in arrears?'

'I will be doing them a favour in evicting them. They will not be able to dig themselves any further into their pit of debt.'

'I see. And the very worn stair carpet at the Casemores' cottage?'

'The what?'

'They happened to mention it,' said Maisie, innocently.

'They are at liberty to replace it.'

Maisie's irritation was growing. She decided to try and fight back.

'Isn't it rather the responsibility of the landlord? In fact, were one of them to have an accident, tripping on a frayed edge, for example, wouldn't that leave you open to a claim for damages?'

Daphne didn't reply. Maisie could see that she had hit home. The woman was calculating the likelihood of the accident, the difficulty of proving liability, the cost of the repair. Whatever conclusion she came to, she kept it to herself.

'What do you want, Miss Cooper?' said Daphne. 'Are you like your brother, initially diverting, then scratching around like a hungry hen for financial support, for investment?'

This, thought Maisie, *was important*.

'Is that what Stephen did?'

'What do you think?' asked Daphne.

'I am prepared to believe he might have.'

'Oh, trust me, he did. He came to me with his little exercise book with his pages of notes of so-called meetings with "the Kuwaiti oil minister", with his "good friend Mohammed" who was, apparently, "a prince of the blood". Do you think I believed in any of that?'

The question gave Maisie a kind of flashback to her conversation with Inspector Barden after the wake. He had asked something similar, hadn't he?

No, Maisie remembered, he hadn't. It was she who had brought it up. But what did it mean in relation to Daphne?

'Do you read Arabic, Mrs Fieldhouse?'

'Of course I don't. But I read people. It is a skill you, too, might learn, if you were forced to observe life, as I am, instead of being able fully to take part. What I have, I hold.'

Daphne wasn't looking at her. Her eyes were directed towards the flames, and it was impossible to read what she was thinking.

Maisie stood up. She wanted to think things through and was concerned that, in this unhappy conversation, she might go too far, provoked by Daphne's voracious appetite for gain without consideration or sympathy.

'Thank you for your time. I am grateful to have had the opportunity to know a little more about my brother's time in the village.'

'I believe you both grew up hereabouts,' Daphne breathed. 'Yet you were not often in touch with one another?'

'Not often. We went our own ways—'

'It pained him, you know?'

There was no vagueness or diffidence now in Daphne Fieldhouse's voice. She had deliberately sought a way of hurting Maisie's feelings. Maisie did her best not to reveal that Daphne had scored a hit and retorted, without troubling to hide the acid on her tongue: 'I wish you a pleasant evening with your thoughts.'

The sly combat between the two women might have accelerated or intensified, but the front door was suddenly opened and, out of sight of the fierce fire and the gloomy room, Derek Fieldhouse came stomping in on a waft of cold air.

'You're late,' called Daphne.

'Yes, I'm bloody late,' shouted Derek from the hall. 'I'm seven minutes bloody late, all right?'

FORTY-NINE

The clock on the mantelpiece in the Fieldhouses' 'lounge' said the time was seven-thirty-seven, so Maisie supposed she knew the time of Derek's curfew and that she had just witnessed the depressing everyday tenor of the Fieldhouses' marital relations. She heard Derek's footsteps climbing the stairs as the cocker spaniel came skittering in across the polished floorboards to turn in circles on the hearthrug before finally settling itself in front of the fire.

'My Napoleon is returned from his campaigns,' said Daphne. 'One can only hope he has refrained from using his own initiative.'

'Does Derek have no other business interests?' she asked. 'Outside of Fieldhouse Holdings?'

'Why do you ask?'

'Oh, no real reason,' Maisie lied. 'I was just looking at some of Stephen's papers and there were some payments, some receipts, things that I couldn't identify.'

There was a rather deadly pause. Daphne's mouth narrowed to a taut line.

'Derek is not allowed to play with anyone's toys but mine,' she said and Maisie was shocked at how venomous she sounded.

Maisie left Framlington Manor without speaking to Derek Fieldhouse. As she closed the front door, she heard Daphne shouting up the stairs for him.

She thought about what Beatrice had said, suggesting that Derek didn't look a bit like his father, that he was illegitimate.

Was that important? Then she thought about the fact that, when she and Stephen were little, being brought up in a narrow, two-up two-down house on the council estate just on the edge of the village, the Fieldhouse family had owned Framlington Manor. How was it that Daphne hadn't changed her name upon marriage?

She gave herself a little shake, picking her way through the kitchen garden to the gate in the six-foot wall, feeling sullied by her encounter. She thought about what Jack had said, as they sat in the dark in his car outside Church Lodge.

'*People always want more than they need, more than they deserve.*'

It was a form of gluttony peculiar to the rich, she thought, to those already blessed with more than they could spend, who owned more than they could reasonably enjoy.

Why was 'sufficient' never 'enough'?

Maisie found herself outside the forge, beside a pile of horseshoes, all rusted together, woven into one another in circles, the whole stack standing almost eight feet tall. How many years of work did that represent?

Smoke crept out around the frame of the ill-fitting door. On the lintel above was a horseshoe, nailed open end up, a symbol of good luck. Between the pile of old horseshoes and the door was a mighty anvil, the handle of a heavy hammer pushed into its square hardy hole.

She pushed open the door to the forge. There was Jon Wilkes, working late, his heap of coals glowing and two hurricane lamps in the ceiling, illuminating the sooty workshop with a surprisingly bright light.

'Come in, then,' he told her. 'Don't stand out in the cold. I've seen you trotting back and forth. I reckon you've spoken to more or less everyone you can. Is that right?'

'Thank you.'

Jon's foot was on the bellows mechanism. He pumped it steadily. Maisie shut the ill-fitting door behind her, looking round at the timber walls. They were covered with tools – hoes and scythes, saws, bits and pieces of farm machinery that she couldn't identify. On the workbench, though, were some smaller items.

'Do you make jewellery?' she asked him.

'Happen I do.'

'Can I see?'

'You can take a look. It's not too hot for me, but for hands that aren't used to it . . .' He held out his callused fingers for her to inspect. 'You might scorch.'

Maisie touched one of the pieces with the end of her forefinger. It was too warm to handle but she flipped it over. It was a small bird, woven beautifully from strands of some silvery, sooty metal.

'It's lovely.'

'It's nothing yet. It's all smuts. Polish her up and we'll see what I've got.'

'Do you sell your pieces?'

'Who'd want to buy my old rubbish?'

'You just make things for your own pleasure?' The thought made her smile.

'I do.'

She turned the bird over again. 'If I had any money, I'd buy it.'

'Would you now?'

'I absolutely would.' Jon carried on pumping his bellows with his heavy right boot. Maisie wondered if she had said the wrong thing. 'Perhaps that's not what you want?'

'If I sold them, it wouldn't just be for pleasure any more, would it?' he said. 'It would be for money.'

'That's true,' Maisie agreed and wondered what else to ask. 'That was Mr Chitty's grandson here with you, wasn't it, the other day?'

'Young Nicholas Chitty. Good lad. Half-term, looking for a job to earn tuppence.'

Maisie smiled. 'Tuppence doesn't go far these days, Jon.'

'No, it doesn't.'

His foot kept pumping the bellows. Maisie found it oddly soporific. It would be pleasant, she thought, for life to go on, day after day, accompanied by the pulse of the forge. Unexpectedly, he spoke up without her asking a question.

'In fact, your brother saw I could do with a bit more now and then. Asked me if I could do some work for him on some jewellery.'

'He did?' said Maisie.

'Oh, yes.' Jon gave her a meaningful look.

Maisie frowned. What was he getting at? He looked very serious. She wondered if she ought to be frightened. No one knew where she was, in Jon's rustic forge, surrounded by potential weapons. But she felt no fear.

No, Jon was trying to tell her something. Or, rather, he was trying to get her to make a connection but he was inhibited by the rural tradition of not speaking out of turn, not speaking ill of the dead. Finally, it came to her.

'He wanted to know if you would alter some jewellery for him.'

'That's where 'tis.'

'But you turned him down.'

'Oh, yes.'

'Did he show it to you?'

'He wanted to. I told him I'd have no part of it.'

'Why was that?'

The rhythmic pumping of the bellows continued. Maisie realised he wasn't going to say it out loud, that it was the jewellery stolen from the cathedral crypt and Stephen wanted him to remake it so it would be easier to sell on.

'Have you told anyone else about this?' she asked.

'Not my business to.'

'Who would have done the selling on? Strickland?'

'I don't know anything about that.'

'But there's something else, isn't there, Jon? Can't you just come out with it?'

Jon pursed his lips. 'I don't know where I stand, do I? I don't want Jack Wingard round here asking me questions. I can't afford to have people talk.'

'How about I promise I won't tell Sergeant Wingard. Would that do?'

'Cross your heart?' said Jon unexpectedly.

'Cross my heart,' said Maisie and found herself making the appropriate playground gesture.

'Well,' said Jon, 'here's where 'tis. Old Bert Close was taken poorly and whenever that happened Fieldhouse would ask young Nicholas to do the orchard lawn at Church Lodge. Though he's small, he's a demon for anything mechanical, that boy.'

'The Chitty family are local then?'

'Up to those council houses you and your parents were in, but just before, on the other side.'

As always, Maisie felt conflicted thinking about her old family home.

'Is that important?'

'Perhaps it is, perhaps it isn't.'

'I'm sorry, Jon, but this really doesn't mean anything to me.'

'Well, you haven't let me finish, have you?' he said, with a hurt look.

'All right. Go on.'

'Like I said, Fieldhouse wanted young Nicholas to do the lawn with the ride-on mower because of old Bert being poorly and the lad was excited to get the chance to drive it round under the trees. Then Fieldhouse didn't want him to do it after all.'

'And?'

'I went past there the other day, didn't I, and I looked in your gate. It were done, weren't it?'

'Yes, it was . . .'

Maisie's mind was trying to recreate the timeline of events on the morning of Stephen's murder. She remembered the clumps of cut lawn round her feet and the fact that June, too, had mentioned the grass.

'Well, then,' said Jon, as if everything had become clear.

'Well, then?' she encouraged.

He nodded, his foot steadily pumping the bellows, the coals breathing in and out.

'It's about who was there and who wasn't. If I were you, I'd think on't.'

Maisie tried to get Jon to speculate but with no success and, in the end, she gave up. It was clearly not in his nature. She was reminded of Inspector Barden.

'*I can't discuss suspicions, only facts.*'

'Thanks for talking to me, Jon,' she said. 'Who else should I ask about this?'

'I don't rightly know,' said the blacksmith.

Before she left, between the rakes and the hoes and scythes on the timber walls, she was surprised to see a framed verse.

'Malcolm Casemore did that for me in return for a good turn,' said Jon, 'three years back. It's a poem.'

'Why, it's a limerick,' she said.

'He's a clever one, is Malcolm Casemore. You'd never guess to look at him. He was famous once, they say. Now he's just an old man who doesn't own his own four walls.'

Extraordinary how poetry keeps cropping up, Maisie thought.

There were five lines, written out by hand in a lovely, swirly copperplate script. Around the words were little drawings of farm implements, surprised horses, smoke and flames. At the foot of the page was an anvil and a hammer, its wooden handle pushed into the square socket, the hardy hole.

'Did Mr Casemore draw the pictures, too?'

'That was his missus. She did them, before her arthritis got so bad.'

> *There once was a farrier called Jon*
> *Who glided through life like a swan,*
> *With his anvil and hammers,*
> *His fires and clamours,*
> *The soul of the burg Fram-ling-ton.*

'It's charming.'

'Folks seem to like it.'

Maisie looked closely at the signature. It was difficult to make out in the flickering of the hurricane lamp. Was it 'Harry Mallon'? It definitely didn't say 'Casemore'.

FIFTY

Sergeant Jack Wingard was in his police car, driving a tour of likely hiding places, looking for June's father. First, he had tried the lanes around Dell Quay and Apuldram, including the damp foreshore by the boat pound where Strickland sometimes worked, cleaning molluscs from the hulls and applying anti-foul coating, when the second-hand business was poor. Then he had driven to two separate smallholdings, each of which was owned and run by old Sussex families, each one known to the police for repeatedly sailing close to the wind. Because Jack was seen as a local man, too – albeit one who wore the blue uniform of the Sussex constabulary – he was welcomed cordially but no one had seen Old Man Strickland or could help in any way.

Did they know about June's death?

Yes, they did. It was a bad business: 'But there 'tis.'

For want of a better idea, Jack drove back out through Framlington, into the valleys between the soft green hills. As he made his way towards Harden and Bunting, he slowed at each gateway into the fields. Finally, he came to the gravel car park at the foot of Bunting Down and pulled over, leaving the engine running.

Above the car park was a lane, rutted with chalk and flint, leading up into the woods. He couldn't go any further in the Zephyr because the ride was too low and the stones could damage the sump, but Strickland might easily pick his way under the trees in his truck and park up for the night in complete solitude.

Briefly, Jack thought about taking a walk up through the beech trees, but he was still wearing his best shoes and suit from the Rotary meeting. And there were scores of other tracks. The likelihood of Strickland choosing this one among so many was slim.

Jack realised he was hungry, that he'd had nothing substantial since his grandmother's shepherd's pie at lunchtime. He turned the Zephyr round and retraced the few hundred yards to the Bunting village pub, the Dancing Hare.

Because he didn't want conversation, he went round the back and knocked at the kitchen door. The publican – a tall, thin man who habitually overindulged at his own bar – gave him a cheese and pickle sandwich in about twelve inches of French bread. Sitting at the side of the road, doggedly working his way through his stodgy snack, Jack's thoughts returned to Maisie.

Why had their brief teenage kiss proved such an indelible memory? Because she was special. What would it be like to come home from a long day and find her waiting, pleased to see him, glad to know the details of his day? Wonderful. How much would he enjoy learning about all of her thoughts and aspirations? What would it be like to hold her in his arms, to kiss her once more as a man?

It would be a kind of dream.

He looked down at the remains of his sandwich. He had barely eaten half of it but, already, he had no more appetite.

He got out of the car and tossed the remains over the hedge into the ditch, then he paused.

Why had Maisie seemed so interested in poetry? That had been a surprise, but he had been too focused on his grief at June's death to follow it up.

The answer was, he thought, that she was – as he had suggested – conducting her own investigation. Poetry was, in some way he didn't understand, a clue.

But, if she was thinking about clues, might she go so far as to forget herself and wander into danger?

He got back into the car and started the engine, annoyed with Maisie and with himself. He checked the time, remembering he had promised to return at nine o'clock. Might he go back sooner?

No, that would only annoy her. And he had other places he needed to check, where Strickland might be holed up.

He struck the steering wheel with the heel of his hand and, with a rare curse, put the car in gear.

FIFTY-ONE

It was very dark outside and Maisie's first thought was to go home and lock herself in to wait for Jack to return and tell her if he had found Strickland. She walked past the village shop and smiled vaguely at the memory of Alicia and Beatrice's lovely sandwiches and friendly conversation.

Then she frowned. They, too, were strangers, however charming. She would do well to remember that and not take what they told her at face value – Alicia's intense gaze, Beatrice gobbling and talking through the crumbs. And they owed Stephen money – they owed her money, come to that, though they apparently couldn't pay it. And she still couldn't know for certain that there wasn't something else – a sexual or romantic relationship between Stephen and either, or both, of the women. Though Beatrice seemed more Stephen's type than Alicia, out of the two of them.

A little further along the road, Maisie saw there was a warm light on in the Casemores' cottage and the door was ajar. She soon saw why. A small grey cat was in the tiny front garden, studiously investigating the wild-flower borders. On the threshold stood Mrs Casemore, urging the animal on.

'Do your business, Shadow, then you can come back indoors.'

Maisie decided to take advantage of the opportunity. 'That's a lovely name for a grey cat,' said Maisie.

Mrs Casemore squinted at her in the darkness.

'Why, it's Miss Cooper. We've been meaning to write you a note, then we forgot. Didn't we, Malcolm?'

'What's that?' came a voice from inside the tiny cottage.

'Come in. Will you have sherry? We are very fond of sherry. We have medium and dry.' She looked doubtful. 'But perhaps you would prefer Cinzano?' she asked, as if suggesting something unfathomably strange. 'We don't have any Cinzano.'

'I would love a glass of sherry,' said Maisie, truthfully.

'I am glad. Go in, go in. I must wait for Shadow to . . . Well, you know. We prefer not to have a kitty tray.'

Maisie opened the rickety wooden gate and Mrs Casemore stepped aside for her to go indoors. The lintel was very low and Maisie almost felt the need to duck her head. Inside, there was no hall, just a staircase with a threadbare carpet running up one side of a front room furnished with pale wooden pieces she recognised as the peak of modernism back in the 1930s. There was even a hexagonal metal clock on the wall, very at odds with the low ceilings, exposed rafters and small-paned windows.

Malcolm Casemore stood up politely and held out a hand. She took it.

'This is an unexpected pleasure,' he said. 'Medium or dry?'

'Dry, please.'

'Ah good. Me too.' He turned away to a lowish sideboard where two bottles stood on a silver tray with two schooner glasses. He poured both. 'Will you, Hilly?' he called.

'No, thank you. I've already had mine.'

Malcolm Casemore gave Maisie her glass.

'They say it worsens Hilary's arthritis, that she must not overindulge. Do you think that's true?'

'I'm afraid I have no idea.'

'No, foolish question. Why should you? Cheers, however.'

'Cheers.'

They chinked glasses and sipped their drinks. The sherry was extremely dry, almost acidic, but unquestionably delicious.

'We have it from Purchase's, the wine merchant in Chichester. They get it direct from Spain. It's our only extravagance.'

'Superb,' said Maisie enthusiastically. 'What a treat.'

Malcolm invited her to sit down and, as she did, Hilary Casemore came back inside, shutting the door and pulling across a heavy velvet curtain to prevent a draught. There was a tiny fire burning in the grate and Maisie thought it was probably more than enough to keep the whole cottage warm.

'You know the village well?' said Maisie, just to move the conversation on.

'Oh yes. Very well,' said Malcolm. 'Though we moved in after you moved away.'

A question came back into Maisie's mind. 'There's something I was wondering, perhaps you can tell me. There were Fieldhouses at Framlington Manor when I was a girl and there still are now, even after marriage. Do you know why that is?'

'Pure coincidence, I believe. Derek Fieldhouse was a distant cousin – so distant there was no issue of consanguinity – but his name also was Fieldhouse.'

'I see.' Maisie chalked that query off her mental checklist. 'So, how long exactly have you lived here?'

'How long is long?' interrupted Malcolm with a twinkle.

'Don't start getting poetic,' said Hilary. 'We've been in the village eight years last Christmas, and very happy, too.'

'Oh, poetry,' said Maisie. 'That reminds me, Mr Casemore. I saw your limerick on the wall of the forge.'

'Not my limerick. Our limerick,' said Malcolm, warmly looking over to his wife.

'You wrote it together?'

'We wrote it together,' said Hilary. 'We are "Hilary Malcolm". That's our pen name, our pseudonym. We write together.'

She said it as if it ought to mean something to Maisie and, in truth, it did, but only something very vague and distant.

'Of course,' said Maisie. 'That's why the signature on the limerick didn't say "Casemore". I thought it was "Harry Mallon".'

'Hm, "Harry Mallon". Not such a bad name,' said Malcolm, 'but I prefer our *nom de plume*.'

'Me too.' Hilary beamed.

'Hilary did the little drawings,' Malcolm went on, 'and I did the copperplate. Did I overdo it, do you think? Was it too . . . ?'

'Swirly?' asked Maisie.

'Yes, exactly. Too swirly?'

Maisie didn't answer. She thought she had made another connection. Swirly handwriting.

'Are you all right, dear?' asked Hilary, sensing her guest's uneasiness.

'What are the flowers in your front garden?' Maisie asked tentatively.

'Oh, wild flowers, really. Self-seeding, no trouble. Apart from the two clematis round the door. They need no end of pruning.'

'Yes, I saw you doing that the other day. But the wild-flower borders? Are they daphne and cyclamen and . . . ?'

'And snowdrops. Yes.'

'I think,' said Malcolm, slowly, 'that Miss Cooper has penetrated our subterfuge, Hilly.'

'Yes, Malcolm,' Hilary responded, a little abashed.

'I hope you don't mind,' said her husband. 'We are poor people. We made our own modest posy and hoped that the accompanying verse would express more fully our regard for your brother than mere show.'

'Lilies are very dear,' said Hilary.

'As are chrysanthemums,' said Malcolm, shaking his head.

Pleased with this discovery, Maisie pressed them. 'I'm sorry, but I have to ask. Would you mind? Your posy, what did you mean by it?'

'By what?' asked Malcolm.

'She means the lines on the paper round the posy. That's right, isn't it, the verse from Shelley?' asked Hilary.

'Yes,' said Maisie, inwardly congratulating herself for having tracked down the quotation independently.

'That isn't a very good question to ask a poet, my dear,' said Malcolm. 'If there was a better way of saying what we meant, we would have used it. Or written our own verse.'

'So, you meant exactly what the lines said?' asked Maisie.

'That's right,' they replied together.

'That there is nothing left at the end,' continued Hilary. 'That all of our secrets go with us into the grave so those we leave behind should hesitate to judge.'

Maisie suddenly knew why the name 'Hilary Malcolm' rang a bell.

'You were in Spain, in the Civil War. You wrote protest verse. You were very well thought of, anthologised with W H Auden.'

'Yes,' they both said at once, obviously delighted to meet someone aware of their work.

'We met in Spain,' explained Hilary.

'We fell in love on the battlefield,' said Malcolm.

The idea of these two gentle old souls falling in love beneath artillery fire was so incongruous and touching that Maisie laughed. 'What an extraordinary story.'

'Thirty-six years ago,' said Malcolm.

He held out a hand to his wife. She placed her twisted fingers in his.

'You have no idea how boring a war can be,' said Hilary.

'The waiting,' Malcolm explained.

'The great gaps in time.'

'Then the awful clamours.'

'You do love that word,' said Hilary, smiling to her husband. 'I do.'

'You used it in Jon's limerick,' said Maisie. 'It went "His anvil and hammers, his fires and clamours".'

'Yes, you have to pronounce "fires" as two syllables,' said Hilary.

'That is legitimate, I think,' said Malcolm.

'Is he actually the "soul" of the village?' asked Maisie.

'Well,' said Malcolm, with an apologetic smile, 'one is allowed a little poetic licence.'

'He did us a very great favour three years ago and we wanted to thank him for it,' said Hilary. 'He managed to fix our hot water heater, making a part that Fieldhouse's plumber couldn't find.'

Maisie wondered if Fieldhouse's plumber had tried very hard.

'I could show you some of our first editions?' said Malcolm.

He clearly wanted very much to fetch the appropriate volumes. Maisie smiled and agreed, feeling she shouldn't disappoint them but also pleased to be there, sitting back in her narrow Thirties armchair and allowing them to talk.

They had a lot to say – about the nature of poetic expression and the 'soul of man', about the challenges of writing as a couple under a single pseudonym, about making a living in a world that saw no reason to remunerate 'the bard'.

'I became a teacher, of course,' said Malcolm. 'Doing so, I became one of those people who attempts to inculcate a love of words in recalcitrant youth. If successful, those youths will go on to be poets and, finding no other means of keeping their fires lit and bread on the table, will also fall back upon education, creating a new cycle of impoverished wordsmiths whose pleasures must be taken in the act of creation, not through material reward.'

'And so on, *in perpetuum, ad infinitum*,' said Hilary.

'But,' said Maisie, bringing them back to the point, 'you didn't have any special message with the Shelley. You just meant that once we're dead and gone – or perhaps even during our lifetimes – we all deserve a little sympathy and understanding.' She paused. 'That Stephen needed understanding.'

'We all deserve,' Hilary began, 'for others to take the trouble to . . .'

'To know where one is coming from,' interrupted Malcolm and looked pleased with his surprisingly modern phrase.

'The idea of taking secrets to the grave,' said Maisie, 'had nothing do with his murder?'

'Good heavens, no,' said Hilary. 'Had we any information regarding that, we would have spoken to the police.'

'Indeed, we would,' said her husband.

They both smiled and their words reminded her of Charity Clement saying something similar.

'Of course,' said Maisie.

Another glass of sherry was poured and snacks offered. Maisie accepted both with a feeling of frustration. She had hoped from the very beginning that discovering who sent the posy and poem would be the key to the mystery of Stephen's death. She had believed that, if she could just find out who had slipped the humble wild flowers in among the more formal tributes, she would have the answer to the question of who had killed her complicated, charming, disappointing brother.

It took a little while before she could respectfully leave the Casemores' cottage, fortified with two delicious sausage rolls baked by Malcolm himself. She also learnt that Stephen had made a habit of coming in to them on odd Sundays, bringing with him a brace of pheasant or partridge that he had shot and hung up to mature.

'In that way, the meat becomes tender,' Hilary explained.

Maisie knew all about rotting meat. Hadn't she come across the carcasses of two miserable dead creatures in the outhouse at Church Lodge, putrid, crawling with maggots and blowflies?

'The flavour develops, too,' said Malcolm. 'It isn't to everyone's taste.'

'Gamey,' said Hilary with a smile. 'We liked it – I mean Malcolm and I and your brother.'

Yes, it turned out that Stephen and the Casemores were friends and, as the old couple talked, relating the stories they and Stephen had shared – of love and war and travel – Maisie's heart sank. Here, yet again, was an example of people who had been true friends to her brother. True in the sense that they knew him, knew all of him, and accepted the good with the bad, the rough with the smooth. And they were, to adapt Jack's phrase, people who didn't always want more than they needed or any more than they deserved.

And what had she done?

She had fled abroad, leaving Stephen to his contradictions and demons, his challenges and deceptions.

'Are you all right, my dear?' asked Hilary for a second time.

'I think, perhaps, I'm a little too hot.'

'We do keep the cottage nice and warm. It's age you know.'

'After sixty, one feels the cold dreadfully,' said Malcolm, completing his wife's thought.

VII

PRIDE

FIFTY-TWO

As she left the Casemores' stuffy cottage, Maisie found herself reflecting on the question raised by the conundrum of the cut grass and the disagreement over time. Nigel Bacon maintained that Stephen was habitually a late riser. But, on that fateful morning, both he and June had told her that Stephen intended to get up early to make a start on his new fitness regime, trying to take more exercise because he wanted to 'get back in shape'. That was corroborated by Derek Fieldhouse's assertion that Stephen was trying to turn over a new leaf.

Once Stephen had left, June had stayed in bed. Had she gone back to sleep? It was too late to ask her now. Later, Nigel Bacon had called the police when he saw Stephen's body in the pool. What time was that? She thought the report said nine-thirty. She would have to check.

Maisie realised she was standing in the road at the top of Church Lane, a picture of indecision. The street lamps were back on and the eeriness of the village in darkness was quite dissipated. She could see in through the gate of Church Lodge and Jack's car was not there.

How long had she been? An hour and a half, perhaps, with Daphne Fieldhouse, then Jon Wilkes, then the Casemores. She checked her watch. Yes, just a little after eight.

It was tempting to go inside and light a fire but she did, genuinely, feel rather overheated from the Casemores' airless living room and the excellent sherry. She wandered along the main road, past the Davies family's shabby petrol station with its two dirty National-branded pumps. It didn't look like much of a business. She wondered if they were managing to make ends meet.

She walked on, thinking about how poverty was rather a theme of Framlington.

No, that wasn't quite true. There was poverty – the Casemores, the blacksmith Jon Wilkes' money trouble, Alicia and Beatrice's failing shop, Stephen's debts – but there was also wealth, in particular the Fieldhouses and Nigel Bacon.

Did she know that for sure? She supposed Nigel was rich. He certainly gave that impression. But then, to a certain extent, so had Stephen.

No, of course he was. He had to be wealthy if he could run to a heated outdoor swimming pool in winter. But why was his formal garden looking so ragged? And then there was what Daphne had said: '*The strange motivation that caused Nigel Bacon to spend money I'm not sure he really has on that mighty grey stallion that so frightens him.*'

Thinking about Nigel reminded her of the Casemores' story of sharing Stephen's fondness for game birds. Nigel had two shotguns in a locked cupboard on the first floor that Stephen was in the habit of borrowing.

She tried to imagine her brother dressed up in rural finery on official shoots with teams of beaters and enthusiastic gun dogs. That was one of her own treasured memories of time spent with Stephen, employed as teenagers for a few shillings as beaters themselves, stomping through the summer and autumn undergrowth, smelling the tang of the wet bracken, seeing the panicked birds flying up like fireworks from their hiding places.

Then she realised it wasn't a happy set of ideas at all. Here was another black mark on Stephen's report. Surely, pheasant and partridge were not in season. Stephen was a poacher, alongside everything else.

By the light of the last village street lamp, she stopped. It was a pleasant evening, though chilly, and she told herself she wouldn't stay out too long. She wanted to be fresh in the morning for the cremation. And she wanted to be back at Church Lodge at nine for Jack. She ought to admit that she had remembered their adolescent kiss.

How would he respond? It was hard to tell. The confusion of personal feelings with his professional responsibilities made everything so hard . . .

To her surprise, she found herself imagining taking his handsome face in her hands and touching her lips to his. What would it feel like? What would his lips taste like?

She heard a faint sound, comforting and familiar, not far away, the vibration of a horse's soft mouth, then a faint whinny, perhaps the mare calling to the stallion or the other way around.

She took the small turn up Stook Lane and stepped into the concrete yard. There it was again, the characteristic noise of a horse sighing and whinnying and scraping at the hard ground. It came from the stallion's loose box.

Maisie went over to the half-door and looked in. The powerful grey horse paid her no attention, walking in agitated circles, rucking up the bed of straw then scattering the heaps. Its ears were back and, now and then, it tossed its head as if to drive away flies. But there were no flies. It was simply unhappy, cooped up indoors. Jon had told her that Nigel mistreated the horse but Bert had told her: '*No, not him.*'

Could he have meant Derek? How had Derek referred to the stallion?

'*That bastard.*'

Maybe, Maisie thought, *it was both of them*?

She went and fetched some cobnuts from the sack in the tack room. She filled both pockets of her trousers so that she had plenty, then reached over the half-door and undid the latch, stepping into the loose box, making what she hoped was a comforting 'tchuk-tchuk' noise in her cheeks.

The stallion slowed, looked towards her then veered away with a dangerous little kick of its hindquarters. The space suddenly felt very small for the two of them.

'All right, now,' Maisie crooned.

She held out her flat palm, hoping the horse would recognise her scent and know her as a friend. The horse caught the odour of the cobnuts and approached her, moving quickly.

She stepped back against the stable door, apprehensive of the horse's momentum, holding her hand stretched out in front to keep a little distance from the heavily muscled animal. But he stopped in good time and hoovered them up from her flat hand with his thick but sensitive lips. She put her left hand in her other pocket and gave him some more, patting his neck with her right palm, speaking softly.

'That's it, there's a good man. That's it, I know.'

The stallion was still wearing the canvas head collar she had put on him after her gallop. There was a lunge rein – a straight run of woven rope – hanging on a hook on the wall of the stable, standing out white against the dark timber. She attached it to the head collar and led the stallion outside.

The horse was immediately happier. Its ears became pricked and it accepted her lead, walking wide circles around the yard. Maisie wondered if she could get a saddle and bridle on him to give him a proper run – she had been given permission, after all – but decided it was too dark. Perhaps, she thought, she had done the horse a disfavour by taking him up on the gallops earlier, showing him what he was missing, making him even more miserable with spending his days a prisoner in the loose box.

As they made their slow circuit of the yard, the iron hooves clattering, Maisie became aware of another sound, indistinct at first. Then it came to her what it was, drifting over the hedges in the night – a diesel engine in low gear, coming down the lane. She hoped its lights wouldn't distract or spook the stallion, but there were no lights, just the ominous chug-chug-chug of the motor in the darkness.

Maisie had a premonition of danger. She took the stallion to the gateway onto the gallops and looped the lunge rein loosely round the post. There was grass growing at the foot and the horse dipped its head to crop it. Maisie walked away to where the concrete of the yard joined the gravelly lane. She could just make out the top of the cab above the hedgerow, a dirty white roof reflecting a little light from the last street lamp.

Strickland's truck.

So that was where he had been hiding, up in the Forestry Commission woods at the top of the gallops.

Just then, the truck emerged from a bend in the hedges. Maisie wished she had stepped back into the yard, out of sight, but it was too late. Strickland slammed on his headlamps and Maisie was dazzled, turning away and shielding her eyes. She heard him hit his accelerator. The engine note changed from a chug-chug-chug to a whine.

He was coming for her.

At first, she retreated towards the stables, thinking she could lock herself in, but the doors were only half-height and, in any case, she would then be trapped. If Strickland drove right up to the stable door, he could imprison her with nowhere to go. And who knew what weapon he might be carrying this time?

Could he even have a shotgun?

The truck slewed into the concrete yard and Maisie ran up to the other end, to the gateway to the gallops, slipping the lunge rein clear of the post. Adrenaline gave her the spring to launch herself onto the stallion's back, her stomach across his spine, then she swung her right leg round to assume a sitting position. The thought came into her mind that she was doing something very foolish, mounting a sixteen-hand horse, bare-back in the darkness of the night.

But what choice did she have?

Strickland was reversing in order to make a three-point turn and come after her. Maisie coiled up the lunge rein and took a firm hold. It was attached to the right-hand side of the head collar and, if she wasn't careful, it would pull the horse in circles. She wound her left hand into his mane and urged him out onto the gallops.

Surely Strickland wouldn't follow her there?

He did, though. As Maisie and the stallion trotted up the soft hill, the truck, with its lights blazing, nosed out of the yard, its wheels spinning in the muddy patch at the bottom of the slope. Then it began to pick up speed.

Maisie had nowhere to go but up – up the grassy slope towards the dead end and the Forestry Commission woods. The stallion's trot became a canter. Strickland started blasting on his horn, trying to spook Maisie's mount, the noise harsh and incongruous in the quiet countryside. The stallion didn't like it, rearing and tossing his head.

Maisie struggled to balance the pressure between her two hands, one holding far too many loops of straight rope, the other slipping on the greasy mane, the harsh strands of horsehair cutting into her fingers. Despite her pulling back, the horse picked up speed.

Strickland was getting closer and Maisie didn't feel she could dare gallop, but then she had no choice. The stallion whinnied and kicked and, fully aware of their pursuer, lengthened his stride. There was nothing Maisie could do to restrain him. Her left hand was slipping. The truck with its blaring horn and high-pitched engine was almost upon them. Then she lost her grip entirely on the mane and her unbalanced right hand tugged the horse's head sharply to the right.

'Woah-woah,' shouted Maisie stupidly, but it was too late and she had, in any case, no control. The stallion took three long strides sideways across the gallop and launched itself at the hawthorn hedge, leaving Strickland and his truck on the other side. For a second, they were airborne and Maisie prayed that the landing area would be level, that they wouldn't somersault, with half a ton of horseflesh rolling over her pinned form.

FIFTY-THREE

The stallion's hooves hit the ground. Maisie was thrown forward and she found herself winded, lying along his neck with her left arm wrapped round beneath. But she managed to keep her seat and the horse, seemingly aware that it was now safe, decelerated to a gentle canter, then a trot, and Maisie was able painfully, gasping for breath, to properly regain her balance.

The horse slowed to a walk, found an area of pasture that was well grassed, and dipped its head to eat.

Maisie jumped down and let the stallion crop the grass. At the bottom of the hill, on the long straight road from East Bitling, a couple of vehicles went past. Despite her breathlessness, Maisie was seized by a desire to run down to the road, to charge out and appeal to them to stop, to ask for help, but they were too far away and travelling too fast.

In any case, Strickland's truck was long gone. He had killed his headlamps and reversed back down the gallops and fled, out through the yard.

Maisie waited for her heart rate to return to normal, allowing the horse to eat its fill. Then she walked the stallion down to the road and found a gate that wasn't padlocked, just held closed with a loop of binder twine. She led the horse through and they made their way along the verge. She returned him to his loose box in the yard and emptied her pockets of cobnuts.

'Thank you, thank you,' she breathed, leaning her face against his long cheek as he nuzzled her palm. For a fanciful moment, she felt a deep connection to Stephen. Hadn't his favourite horse just saved her from . . .

Well, murder.

She removed the lunge rein and hung it up, then left the stallion, apparently much happier, standing still as a table but at a slight angle, his right shoulder leaning against the timber wall. She closed the half-door and brushed herself down. She felt bruised from the heavy landing, being thrown forward onto his bony neck, but she had done herself no serious damage. Her left hand was raw from gripping the wiry mane but no blood had been drawn.

She stood quite still and listened. Would Strickland come back for her? On foot, even?

She decided not. If she heard the truck, she would run for home. Otherwise, she thought she was safe, for now.

The walk back to Church Lodge took just a few minutes and, when she got there, she was conflicted to see the white Zephyr parked outside the front door. She felt lost and angry at the sudden idea that Jack's might have been one of the two cars she had seen go by towards the village, when she had been desperate and seized by an urge to cry out for help, alone and bruised and . . .

Then, all at once, he was out of his car and striding towards her. 'What happened? Where have you been?'

It was like the moment in the stable when the stallion had suddenly turned and come at her, except that Jack did not stop.

She expected him to stop, to keep a certain distance, professional and social, but he didn't. He kept coming. If anything, his stride lengthened and, then, he was in front of her and had wrapped his arms around her, holding her close to him, as if she was something precious that he thought he had lost and now had found.

***

A little later they were in the kitchen and the Aga was lit. Maisie was on one side of the rustic table and he was on the other. He had apologised for his suddenly intimate behaviour outside and Maisie was left with the impression that, on reflection, he thoroughly regretted it.

What did she feel herself?

A new sense of loss that it appeared that they were obliged to reinstate their previous distance.

With his professional manner returned, Maisie mirrored his formality and gave him as lucid an account as she could of all she had done since they parted earlier that evening. It took her a good twenty minutes: first, the conversations with Daphne Fieldhouse, Jon Wilkes and the Casemores; then, the need for fresh air and the visit to the stables; next, the sudden eruption of Strickland's truck chugging unlit down the lane; finally, the mad chase up the gallops and the escape across the hawthorn hedge.

'You must be an exceptional horsewoman,' said Jack.

'It was basically an accident that we got away. I didn't mean to tug right. The stallion did the rest.'

'All the same,' he said, his eyes averted.

There was an awkward silence and Maisie found that she was determined not to break it. What would be the point? He had closed in on himself, curled himself up like an armadillo, all scales or armour or whatever it was, determined to keep his true self hidden. She found it extremely annoying and not a little rude. In the end, though, the pause went on so long that she couldn't help herself.

'What have you and your merry men discovered?' she asked flippantly. 'Anything of interest?'

He looked up. She was astonished to discover an expression of deep sadness in his eyes, clearly visible in the harsh light of the bare kitchen bulb.

'It would be better for me to leave,' he told her, standing up abruptly, pushing his kitchen chair over behind him with the back of his knees. He bent and righted it. 'I'm sorry. I behaved very foolishly. Don't forget to lock every door.'

He left the kitchen and Maisie was so surprised by the swiftness of his departure and the depth of his emotion that she hesitated before following. When she did emerge from the gloomy corridor beneath the stairs, the front door was closing behind him. She ran forward and reopened it, standing irresolute on the threshold.

What did she want to say? She wasn't sure.

The headlamps were on and the car was pulling away. He was already leaving.

'Jack,' she called pointlessly. 'Wait.'

As the Ford Zephyr disappeared out into Church Lane, she had a flashback to the moment earlier that evening when she had wondered if, motivated by Stephen's deceit of June, Jack had blown a fuse and killed her brother.

No, that was ridiculous.

But, if it wasn't that, what was the emotion that she had seen on his face?

Could it be for her?

And, if it was, what would that mean?

***

Because she sat for a while in the lonely kitchen after he left, Maisie became stiff, more and more aware of the bruising from the mad ride and the dangerous jump across the hawthorn hedge. She decided the only solution was a bath and sleep.

She checked all the doors and windows and took her handbag with the bunch of keys inside it upstairs to her room. She found some fresh rough towels at the foot of Stephen's wardrobe and took them to the bathroom. It was unnecessarily large, presumably a converted bedroom, and the iron roll-top tub stood in the centre of the room in glorious isolation on claw feet.

She turned on the taps and found about an inch of Radox bath liquid in a bottle on the windowsill – June's surely, not Stephen's. She unscrewed the cap and tipped it into the water, just where the flow hit the surface. It smelt of synthetic roses and foamed up beautifully, like a bubble bath in a film.

There was no lock on the bathroom door as such, but the mechanism included a metal latch that could be pushed to the side to prevent the handle from turning. She did so, then moved a low, wicker bathroom chair from over by the window and wedged it beneath the handle. If Stephen had given June a key to Church Lodge, Strickland might now have it.

Maisie let her dirty clothes fall on the painted floorboards and lowered herself gently into the water. It took her a minute or so because it was almost too hot. Once she was submerged, her body began to relax and her mind took over, spinning and freewheeling, like a kaleidoscope shifting and turning, fragments of light, fragments of information. Every pattern had value but only one would explain everything she had discovered.

She tried to be methodical, to work through the clues she had collected, to assess them and connect them and discard them until she had the only pattern that could accommodate all the facts, all the opinions, all the claims and counter-claims, the links, the consistent testimony and the contradictions.

Unfortunately, she found that she was too tired. After a while, in a kind of drowsy daydream, she saw her brother in a vague vision, running away, but calling her to come after him.

Finally, she dragged herself from the cooling bath water, exhausted and none the wiser.

FIFTY-FOUR

Maisie woke the next morning with a sense that something had shifted. Late the previous evening, she had dragged herself from the tepid bath, dried herself on Stephen's rough towels, and gone to sleep. Her bedroom door had a similar lock mechanism to the bathroom so she felt secure. She had again used the wicker bathroom chair as additional security, wedging it under the handle.

What was it that had shifted? Had she been granted some kind of revelation in her sleep? There was something that she knew she ought to be thinking about. What was it?

Oh yes. Sergeant Wingard. Jack Wingard and his unexpected embrace – how natural and comforting it had felt—

She sat up with a start.

The cremation, it was today.

She got out of bed and searched her small suitcase. She had nothing left respectable enough to wear. All her clothes needed washing. She remembered the skirt she had put beneath the mattress to press in the absence of an iron and pulled it out. It had a single firm crease on one hip where she had accidentally folded it over but it would do. She would not be dressed correctly in mourning but everyone would know the reason why. She hadn't travelled from Paris in the expectation of Stephen's death.

She paused, remembering an image that had come to her just as she was falling asleep in the cooling bath water last night.

Stephen running away.

Yes, the more she thought about it, the more it seemed natural and in character that Stephen had intended to do a flit and disappear across the Channel, leaving his mistakes behind.

She went to the window and pulled back the blanket that Stephen had nailed up over the frame. It was raining, lightly but steadily.

'Oh no,' she said aloud.

How would she get to Chichester? She couldn't cycle in the rain in a narrow skirt and the filthy borrowed cricket whites were definitely not acceptable for the chapel of remembrance.

Feeling rather self-conscious, not to say apprehensive, she moved the chair away from the bedroom door and flicked the little catch to one side, quietly turning the handle. It reminded her of her first meeting with Nigel Bacon when he rattled the kitchen doorknob. She realised she had barely seen him since that day. Was he keeping his distance? She had expected him to be a persistent nuisance.

She opened the door and looked out onto the landing. It was quiet and gloomy. Beyond the balustrade she could see the rain running down the double-height hall windows. The wind was from the south-west, blowing the weather against the front of the house.

She went next door to Stephen's room and looked through the chest of drawers for suitable clothes left behind by the previous tenant. She found what looked like a girl's school shirt that would fit. Though she was tall, she was slim. Over the top of that she could wear one of her two cardigans. She had a waterproof mackintosh but that didn't solve the problem of how to get into town in the rain.

Then she remembered. She didn't even have the bicycle. She had left it outside Strickland's second-hand warehouse, chained to a lamp post. Then, when Jack had given her a lift home, she had found herself so involved, so caught up in the unexpected emotion of remembering him from school that she hadn't asked him to pick it up for her.

She checked her watch, squinting at the tiny box indicating the date, 19 February. It was already nine-twenty. The cremation would begin at eleven.

Good heavens, she thought.

How long had she slept? Almost ten hours, surely.

Still, she had time to catch the ten-past-ten bus. It ran on a Saturday, just as it did every weekday. The trouble was, the crematorium was on the outskirts of Chichester. She would have to make peace with the fact that she would arrive bedraggled, having walked a mile or so from the town centre in the drizzle.

She applied a little lipstick and brushed her hair. Reasonably satisfied with her appearance, she went downstairs to the kitchen and made herself two cups of coffee, one after another, using the Maxwell House instant and the gold-top milk. Somehow, today, it didn't resemble a proper *café crème* at all.

She thought about her flat on the Place des Vosges and her Paris friends. She hoped they were missing her as, she realised, she was so dearly missing them. She supposed she would have to ask Jack for permission to leave. What would he say? That he wanted her to stay, not just because of the investigations, but for him? There was a rap on the front door and she went to answer, wondering – hoping? – if it might be his face she saw.

It was the postman, a very loud man, his face red from being out in the chilly rain. He handed her three letters, their addresses smudged from the drizzle.

'Looks like bills,' he said, 'and one foreign.'

Maisie was reminded of what Daphne Fieldhouse had told her, something that Daphne and Stephen used to laugh about.

311

'*The postman always tries to find out what one's letters are about.*'

'Thank you,' said Maisie.

'Don't open them till Monday, that's my advice with bills,' he said with a grin, but without any indication that he was about to go on his way.

Two were, indeed, bills, indicated by their return addresses, one from the Fox-in-Flight – to 'make it official' as Gerald Gleeson had said – and one from the undertaker. The third had followed her from Paris. It was thicker, containing some other correspondence, forwarded by her flatmate.

That was kind of Sophie, making sure that she didn't lose track of her real life. Maisie decided she would save it for later to cheer herself up after the cremation.

'I must get on,' she said. 'Good morning.'

He just stood there and Maisie was beginning to think that she would have to snub him and go back inside when a long black bonnet surmounted with a colourful flag of black, green, white and red came nosing through the gateway onto the unweeded gravel of the drive.

The postman gave a low whistle. 'Well, I never did. Would you look at that?'

★★★

Maisie found it very difficult to get rid of the postman for the simple reason that he very definitely didn't want to leave. For a professional gossip, it was all too mouth-wateringly fascinating. The Bentley with its exciting occupants was followed by a Dunnaways cab, out of which emerged Inspector Barden and Detective Constable Hands, the very picture of constabulary duty. They hung back. Maisie heard the inspector instructing his cabbie to wait, but he didn't approach. Mohammed stayed in his car.

'Thank you for my letters,' said Maisie firmly to the post-man. 'I need to speak to these gentlemen.'

'Quite a party,' he said.

'I'm sure you need to be on your way.'

'Are they police, then?' asked the postman with a quizzical look on his face.

Maisie could see that he had no shame, that he honestly believed that whatever happened on his postal round was his business, that it was natural that he should take an interest. She felt herself becoming angry and allowed a little of her emotion to be heard in her voice.

'That's enough, now. I'm sure you've lots to do. Goodbye.'

He held her gaze for a moment then, perhaps, saw some-thing in her eyes that he didn't want to argue with and left. Once he was gone, the chauffeur got out of the Bentley and opened the rear door for Mohammed to get out.

'Good morning, Maisie,' he said.

'I don't have long,' she told him. 'I have to get the bus into Chichester. It's Stephen's cremation today.'

Saying it out loud made her feel cold inside.

'I remember,' replied Mohammed. 'I will accompany you, if you wish. I mean, we will drive you.' Maisie wasn't sure she wanted a lift, but he went on. 'Inspector Barden will not attend. His business will not take long.'

'You know one another,' she said, surprised.

'No, Miss Cooper,' said Barden, approaching. 'But we have become acquainted. Do you have just a couple of min-utes? Might we come inside?'

Maisie was sheltered under the porch but the three men in their raincoats and turned-up collars were not.

'Of course,' she said.

They went into the hall and she, Mohammed and the inspector sat down on the chairs Detective Constable Hands had brought through from the dining room the other evening. Hands went and stood at the foot of the stairs.

Maisie had a flashback to their cross-purposes interview. It felt like ages ago. A week? A month? Maisie had to count back the days to be sure. Wednesday, after the reception. And now it was Saturday and, if she had her way, she would go straight from the crematorium, up to London, to Victoria station, and buy herself a ticket for the overnight boat train to Paris. She had nowhere else to go, after all.

She glanced at the post in her hand. No, she would have to deal with one or two outstanding details before leaving Framlington.

Or would she? Couldn't she simply write to Gerald Gleeson and the undertaker when she had funds?

She realised Barden had been speaking for some time.

'So, you see, this part of our investigation was based on a misunderstanding.'

'I'm sorry, I was thinking of something else. What did you say?'

'I, too, should apologise,' said Mohammed. 'I was unnecessarily abrupt. It was natural you should think of me from Stephen's diary, wasn't it?'

It took Maisie a moment to remember the lie she had told Mohammed, that she had found his name and telephone number in Stephen's diary among his effects at the police station.

'What exactly are you apologising for?' she said generally, not sure who she was asking.

'The Bishop of Chichester requested the assistance of Special Branch in the case of the robbery from the crypt,' said Inspector Barden. 'The bishop sits in the House of Lords. What the bishop requests, he gets, if you follow me, whether or not it is indicated.'

Maisie began to see the reason behind the double investigation. 'Go on.'

'I didn't have a chance to talk with Sergeant Wingard on the day of the church service but I have since, on the telephone. He was naturally put out when we were called in for no reason on a business that he was already on top of. Jack Wingard is a good man. I can't see why he hasn't been promoted further than he has. The facts are quite clear and are in the process of being elucidated by the local force.'

'Except the jewels and the precious book have not been recovered,' said Maisie, thinking about the fact that Jack was aware that June was in possession of one of the rings.

'Well, that's true, but they will be. A watch is being kept. Perhaps there will be a further search of these premises. It may be something was missed. I hope that won't be inconvenient to you.'

'And no one seems any closer to uncovering Stephen's murderer. Am I right? But perhaps I will already be gone,' said Maisie, 'if I am allowed.'

'That will be a matter for Sergeant Wingard,' said Barden.

'We are digressing,' said Mohammed. 'Time is rushing on. The bottom line is this. You, Maisie, made a quite innocent connection between my name in Stephen's diary and the presence of Special Branch. Inspector Barden came to see me and explained the case. I was able to reassure him. I have had no contact with your poor brother for a number of years.'

'Yes,' said Maisie, 'but you didn't tell me why.'

Mohammed glanced at the two policemen, Barden by the fireplace, Hands at the foot of the stairs.

'I have already shared the reasons with these gentlemen. It does not reflect well on him.'

'On Stephen?' asked Maisie. 'Not much does. I would still like to know.'

'Very well. He took, as the phrase goes, "my name in vain" and tried to run a kind of scam in which his association or friendship with me could be parleyed into a deal in which he would be rewarded for introducing certain investors to Kuwaiti oil producers.'

He paused and Maisie supposed he was refraining from going into detail to spare her. He was unaware that she knew that Stephen had tried the exact same scam on Daphne Fieldhouse.

'To cut a long story short,' Maisie said, emphatically, 'Stephen traded on your friendship to mount a fraud. More recently, here in Framlington, in addition to carrying out the robbery from the cathedral, he tried to do the same thing.'

Mohammed did not look surprised. What else did he know, Maisie wondered?

Inspector Barden stood up.

'Well, your brother's other activities aren't for us.'

'To sum up again,' said Maisie, once more feeling a fool now she had all the facts, 'on the day of the church commemoration, you weren't here in connection with Stephen's murder at all.'

'Only insofar as he was suspected of the robbery,' said the inspector.

'Nor, as I surmised, for international organised crime or oil.'

'No, Miss Cooper, nothing so glamorous,' Barden assured her. 'Special Branch has enough on its plate and is only too happy to leave the recovery of the valuables in the hands of the local force who know the terrain. Like I said, they're a good bunch of lads and will doubtless soon accomplish this and . . .' he gave a wry grin '. . . give the bishop satisfaction.'

She showed the officers out into the rain and they climbed back into their cab and drove away. She checked her watch. The bus would be through in a little while. If she delayed much further, she would end up with no choice but to accept Mohammed's offer of a lift.

She wondered if he would then stay for the service. She wasn't sure whether she wanted him to or not.

FIFTY-FIVE

Maisie went to the kitchen for a glass of water and Mohammed followed her. She filled the dimpled mug and drank at
the sink, looking out of the dirty window at the rain. She
could feel his presence behind her. She appreciated the fact
that he said nothing, that he was waiting for her to speak.

She put her two bills on the table and, wanting some
comforting connection from home, opened the letter from
Paris. The contents made her gasp aloud. There was a short
note on a scrap of office paper from Sophie but, more
importantly, an envelope addressed to her in her brother's
handwriting.

'Would you excuse me?'

She went out into the hall and stood beneath the double-
height windows. The letter was written on two double pages,
clearly pulled from the middle of Stephen's exercise book,
eight sides. It was a kind of confession and, also, an appeal
for help. As she scanned the carefully shaped words, her
doubts and uncertainties fell away and she knew exactly
what must have happened.

But, if she knew 'what', did she also know 'who' and 'why'?
Probably.

Did she know 'how'?

Almost.

She came to a decision, putting the letter away in her handbag and walking quickly back to the kitchen. Mohammed
had been waiting patiently.

'I must show you something,' she said.

'Before you do, I insist on apologising formally,' said Mohammed. 'I was concerned that the involvement of Special Branch would become a diplomatic issue but that is all over.'

'I understand.'

'Also – and perhaps this will help make amends – I have information for you.'

'You do?'

'Yesterday afternoon, I asked a man I know, a useful man, to make inquiries about your BFI Limited.'

Maisie was reminded of the librarian's advice the previous afternoon to contact a financial consultant in the City of London.

'Go on?'

Instead of answering, Mohammed took a letter of his own from an inside pocket of his beautifully cut suit. Maisie noticed that he had chosen something plain rather than the pinstripe he had worn the other day. His black tie was unadorned, without the enamel Kuwaiti tiepin.

So, he is definitely intending to stay for the service, she thought.

'This is my man's answer. You will see.'

Maisie took the envelope and slid out a single sheet of expensive laid notepaper. She thought she knew what it would tell her. She hoped she wasn't wrong. If she was, she would have to start again, fumbling in the dark.

She unfolded the sheet of paper, read the names and breathed a long sigh.

'No accounts have been presented, obviously,' said Mohammed. 'The company's formation is too recent. There is very little to it, simply the shareholders and the date of incorporation, September last year.'

'Yes,' said Maisie, breathing a sigh of relief at her suspicions being confirmed.

'You are not surprised, I see,' said Mohammed.

'No,' said Maisie. 'I am not.' Maisie put the letter down on the table with the others. 'Now I must also show you something. We have time. It will only take a few minutes.'

She opened the utensil drawer and brought out Stephen's notebook with its ten or twelve pages of Arabic script, the first few copiously filled, then several more sparsely covered. She passed it across the table. Mohammed didn't touch it.

'What is this?'

'Stephen's notebook. I found it concealed in a wardrobe.'

'And it is of interest to me because . . . ?'

'I didn't find your telephone number in his diary at the police station. I found your name and number in here. I'm sorry I didn't trust you enough to show you the other day. I wasn't sure then what I had done to make you so angry. I see that now.'

He shook his head. 'It is over.'

'Please, open it.'

Mohammed reached for the exercise book and lifted the cover revealing the first page. He became very still and said something that Maisie didn't catch.

'What was that?'

'*Iqra*,' he said quietly.

'What does that mean?'

'It means "read". It is the first word of the Qur'an, the recommendation to study and reflect. It is fundamental to our faith.'

'I don't understand.'

'Didn't you say you had a copy here on the shelf?'

He turned to the dresser and found it. He put it on the table and opened it the right way up for her to read, if only she understood Arabic. So doing, he said something under his breath that Maisie couldn't follow, presumably some devotional phrase to show respect for the holy book. He

320

turned the exercise book round as well, so the two texts were alongside one another.

'Here, you see?'

He pointed with a beautifully kept hand to the first words of the Qur'an and the first words of Stephen's notes. In the printed sacred text and on the soft lined page of the cheap exercise book she saw the same letters.

اِقْرَأ .

'That is . . . what did you say?'

'*Iqra*,' he repeated.

'Meaning "read"?'

'That's correct, the command of the prophet, peace be upon him, to receive and study the word of Allah, may his blessings be upon you. It is a sacrilege, what your brother did here.'

Maisie looked closely at Mohammed's face. He seemed sad rather than angry. She repeated his own question back at him.

'This doesn't surprise you?'

'It does not.'

Maisie needed to say out loud what she thought he meant.

'So, he copied out verses of the Qur'an as a kind of prop, to give the impression of doing business in Arabic, of having access to Arab diplomats and businessmen, certain that the people he was trying to dupe would be unaware of the subterfuge.'

'That's right.'

Maisie thought of Daphne Fieldhouse. She hadn't been taken in. What had she said?

'*He came to me with his little exercise book with his pages of notes of so-called meetings with "the Kuwaiti oil minister", with his "good friend Mohammed" who was, apparently, "a prince of the blood". Do you think I believed in any of that?*'

'So,' said Maisie, 'he thought he just needed lots of . . .'

Mohammed completed her sentence with a sad smile. 'He needed lots of what I suppose some English people might call "funny-looking" writing.'

Maisie found herself trying to keep all the new information straight in her head.

'And he did something like this when you fell out seven years ago?' she repeated.

'Yes.' Mohammed closed the exercise book and put the Qur'an back on the shelf, repeating the same devotional phrase. 'Indeed, he pretended to have converted.'

'Oh.' Maisie once more felt ashamed of her brother.

'I trusted him. I found it shocking when his lie was revealed. Our friendship could never fully recover. Then, when you called, I thought perhaps it was time to put the past behind us, to rekindle some of our old warmth.'

The pause stretched out, each absorbed in memories of the man whose mortal remains they were about to burn to ashes.

'We must go,' said Maisie, returning to the present. 'I would be grateful for a lift. But would you please come back here with me after the service? I think I know everything now.'

'Why do you need me? You can't simply tell the police and be done with it?'

Maisie thought of her unfinished business with Jack Wingard, the fact that much of what she had worked out was supposition, not fact.

'No, I have to confront them.'

'You say "them"?'

'All of them.'

'All right. It is Saturday. I have no planned meetings. For my people, also, it is the weekend.'

They went outside and Maisie carefully locked up. She didn't want to say any more and he did not pressure her.

She found herself deeply grateful for his tact. She noticed a figure in a rain cape, standing by the gateway to Church Lodge. For a second, she was frightened by a terrifying flashback to the previous evening and her escape on horseback across the fields, thinking it might be Strickland come back to get her. But, then, the figure turned and she recognised the nasty ferrety face of Police Constable Goodbody.

'What's going on?' she asked.

'The sergeant asked me to watch the house,' he said without meeting her eye. The policeman obviously bore a grudge from their interaction at the station. 'While you're out.'

'Did he? Why?'

'I'm sure I couldn't say,' he said rudely. 'You should try not to keep sticking your nose in, if you want my opinion.'

'What is your name, Officer?' asked Mohammed.

The policeman hesitated then obviously found no plausible reason to refuse. 'Constable Goodbody.'

'I will be in touch with your superiors regarding your tone,' said Mohammed, with no discernible change from his normal urbanity. 'Do you understand?'

'I don't know what you mean,' said Goodbody, looking flustered.

'You will,' said Mohammed.

The chauffeur opened the door and Maisie got in. Mohammed went round to the far side and took the front passenger seat. They pulled out into Church Lane and turned right, heading out of the village.

'Oh, could we stop here?' said Maisie suddenly. She had seen the Casemores, looking bedraggled and unhappy at the side of the road, carrying a canvas shopping bag. 'Could we give them a lift, please? They are a lovely old couple and I think they may have missed the bus.'

'Of course,' said Mohammed.

The Casemores were delighted to be riding in the Bentley and filled the journey from Framlington to the crematorium with inconsequential chatter. Maisie said little. She was wondering if Jack would be at the service and if she would be able to speak to him privately and get him to see things her way.

She hoped so. She felt strong, certain of her facts, confident of her assumptions.

But would he agree?

FIFTY-SIX

Jack was back in uniform but still at home, ready for Stephen's cremation, a cup of tea on the table in the small square kitchen. He checked his watch and then looked out of the window at the bare sticks of the wisteria on wires round the frame. Ten o'clock.

His grandmother, Florence, came through from the living room where she had been laying in a fire for later, in anticipation of sunset. Her hands were smudged with soot and she carried a galvanised bucket of yesterday's wood ash. He looked at her blankly and she asked him what he thought he was up to.

'Nothing.'

'Run along and put these ashes on the compost, then.'

He smiled. 'Of course.'

He went out into the garden, feeling the dampness in the air. It would soon come on to rain, dragged in from the Channel on the south-west wind. In Framlington, there might already be drizzle.

He tipped out the bucket of ash and went back indoors. Florence was standing waiting for him, one hand leaning on the small kitchen table.

'So, you've still not spoken? No better?'

'No,' he told her. 'Worse.'

In a few words, he described what had happened when he had embraced Maisie and held her tight to his chest like a drowning man clinging to the wreckage of his boat.

'Good.' Florence smiled at her grandson kindly. 'At last.'

'No,' said Jack. 'Not good.'

He explained the stilted official conversation that had ensued.

'You are a proper fool,' she told him.

'I know.'

'It's pride, that's what it is.'

He sighed. Was it pride? 'Perhaps.'

'Why shouldn't she have gone away from school and lived her own life, Jack? That was years ago. She barely knew you and was little more than a child.'

'She was seventeen. We both were.'

'A child,' Florence insisted. 'And the poor thing lost her parents a few years after.'

'Seven years after. She was out of the army and working in a hotel or something in the West Country.'

'But you hadn't seen one another. And you've not told her, now she's back, how you're pining?'

'I don't know if she's even truly remembered me. I thought perhaps there was a moment . . .'

'If the same thing had happened to you,' said Florence, clearly still thinking about Maisie's bereavement, 'wouldn't you want to go away and start a new life?'

'I know,' said Jack. He stood up and smiled at her. 'But I didn't go away. I stopped where I was with an annoying old lady who always thinks she knows best.'

They both laughed.

'Well,' said Florence, 'now she's back and it's a chance of happiness you're wasting if you don't make things plain between you.'

'It isn't as simple as that,' said Jack, grudgingly.

'Is that right?'

'Yes.'

'Why on earth won't you just tell her how you feel?'

Jack pondered for a moment. Had Maisie recognised him? In the end, he wasn't sure it made any difference.

'Because she's made it pretty clear she doesn't want me to.'

FIFTY-SEVEN

On arrival at the crematorium, Maisie wondered at first if she shouldn't confront everyone in the chapel. There they would all be, conveniently in one place, except for Strickland of course. She wondered if the police had made any headway in locating him.

Maisie stood at the back, a little to the side, with Mohammed. It was a smallish chapel, able to accommodate a congregation of forty, maybe, at a squeeze.

There would be nowhere near that number.

'Why are we not taking our seats?' asked Mohammed.

'I want to watch them as they come in first,' said Maisie.

Maisie had seen Daphne Fieldhouse arrive in a converted van with a ramp at the back to give access for her wheelchair, just as she, Mohammed and the Casemores were getting out of the Bentley. Daphne's husband Derek manoeuvred his wife to the front row of the chapel, partly blocking the aisle between the pews, then sat next to her on the left-hand side. The Casemores chose the second row beside Alicia and Beatrice who had arrived earlier, presumably on the bus the Casemores had missed, once more dressed in Alicia's mother's hand-me-downs. Opposite them, in the second pew on the right, were Gerald from the pub, Jon from the forge and Bert from the stables, making up a sort of 'village chorus'. Behind them, to her surprise, were Mr Chitty and his grandson, Nicholas. Nigel Bacon arrived, walked down to the front, looked as though he wanted to sit with the Fieldhouses, then changed his mind and walked back to sit behind everyone else.

Just before eleven, Reverend Millns arrived, all bustle and officiousness, like a businessman on his way to one more meeting among many in his busy schedule. Maisie rather hated him for it. He joined the Fieldhouses at the front. Finally, Maurice Ryan and Charity Clement entered and sat at the very back, opposite Nigel Bacon, as if they wanted to make a quick getaway when the service was over. The only other person missing was June Strickland who had wanted to be here to say goodbye to Stephen. It was painful to think how brutally she had been prevented.

'Shall I sit with you?' Mohammed asked.

'You won't mind joining in?'

'I will sit when you sit, stand when you stand. If I know the hymns, I will sing them.'

He said all this with such gravity that Maisie smiled.

'How is it we haven't met more often?' she asked him.

He smiled, too. 'You know the answer to that.'

She realised that he was referring to his estrangement from Stephen. She hoped Mohammed regretted it, at least a little, as she regretted her own distance – physical and emotional – from her brother.

'Of course.'

'But that needn't always be the case,' he added.

'Do you ever travel to Paris?' she asked.

'Not often, no, to my regret. But I have the freedom to organise my own calendar. Perhaps you would be able to show me aspects of the city that most tourists miss?'

'I would love to,' said Maisie.

They stood for a moment, smiling at one another, their minds focused on the future, not the dismal present.

Jack slipped in at the back, removing his policeman's helmet. 'Good morning, Miss Cooper.'

So, Maisie thought, he has gone back to ostentatious formality. Then she noticed the warmth in his eyes and realised it was just because they were in public and he was on duty.

She followed his lead. 'Good morning, Sergeant Wingard. Thank you for coming.'

'Are you all right, Maisie?' Mohammed asked her.

'I'm fine.'

'You seem a little flushed,' said Mohammed. 'You should sit down.'

There was a shuffling in the doorway. They all glanced round. The pall-bearers were ready but hesitating, seeing that Maisie had not yet taken her seat.

Jack raised an eyebrow. 'I haven't had the pleasure . . . ?'

Maisie introduced him to Mohammed. Jack clearly wanted to ask who Mohammed was and what he was doing there, but good manners prevented him.

'The front right-hand pew has been kept for you,' said Mohammed. 'I will go on ahead.'

He left them and Maisie took advantage of a moment in *tête-à-tête* to quickly ask: 'Jack, can you direct everyone back to Church Lodge afterwards? Can you insist that they all come, even Daphne Fieldhouse?'

'Why should I do that?' he asked doubtfully.

'It's complicated.' She frowned.

'Maisie, what's happened? What have you done? Is it Strickland again?'

'No, I haven't seen him. Nothing's happened. I mean, I've been thinking and . . .' She took the plunge. 'I think I know what happened. Well, I believe I do and . . .'

She realised that several members of the congregation were looking round, trying to hear what she was saying. Jack moved slightly to shield her from their eyes. The pall-bearers were still waiting. She took a deep breath, then suddenly found herself telling him that she couldn't cope with another night away from home, that she needed to get away.

'I'm going back to Paris tonight. I mean, I have to be out of Church Lodge today, by what Maurice Ryan calls "close-of-play", so I'm going to get the Victoria service to London and then the overnight boat train.'

'I see,' said Jack, a look of disappointment on his face.

'But can you, please, being a policeman, can you get them all together? Then it will be over and I can . . .' She felt suddenly very small, even though she was not much shorter than him. 'I would so like it to be over and done with before I go.'

Jack's expression transitioned from disappointed to hurt. 'Being a policeman?'

'Well, you have authority,' she said weakly.

Eventually he sighed and nodded. 'I will request their presence.'

'Including Maurice Ryan and Charity Clement? One of them would be coming for the keys later anyway. Can you insist?'

'I can request.'

'Please, Jack.'

She held his gaze and knew that she was blushing once more, as Mohammed had noticed earlier. Was this the moment to tell him that she remembered their kiss? If she did, would she discover that it meant nothing to him? At least, nothing like what it now seemed to mean to her?

'I will do my best,' he told her.

To Maisie's surprise, Jack walked down to the front with her. When she took her seat on the central aisle, with Mohammed to her right, he went and stood to one side, watching the congregation. At some signal she did not notice, the organist began to play and the service began.

The music was 'For Those in Peril on the Sea', a hymn she and the undertaker had chosen. She thought it suited the daring, enterprising aspects of Stephen's character and the undertaker had told her that it 'embodied the appropriate mood of regret'.

The organist only played two verses, by which time the pall-bearers had placed the coffin at the front of the room on the mechanical rollers that would transport it into the oven. Reverend Millns got up, automatically fingered his unfortunate moustache, then began the service with 'a few words of remembrance of our dear friend'.

Maisie tried to switch off. She felt weak and unhappy – light-headed having drunk two cups of strong coffee on an empty stomach. At least, as strong as it was possible to mix the Maxwell House instant.

When they all rose for the second hymn and everyone joined in, she stayed in her seat, her eyes in her lap. Next to her, Mohammed stood and sang the words in a pleasant baritone. Because he was a tenor, she could just hear Jack, carrying above Mohammed's deeper voice, from over to one side.

> '*The day thou gavest Lord, is ended;*
> *The darkness falls at Thy behest;*
> *To Thee our morning hymns ascended,*
> *Thy praise shall sanctify our rest.*'

Maisie didn't want to cry but, of course, everything about the occasion was designed to make her cry. She wished she had been a better sister, that Stephen had been a better brother, a better person. She wished that their parents were still alive, pottering about like the Casemores, enjoying a well-earned retirement. She wished that the world wasn't at the mercy of rapacious landlords like Daphne Fieldhouse, that people who already had a lot could be satisfied and not always want more. That people could be proud of who they were, rather than proud of what they possessed.

FIFTY-EIGHT

The rest of Stephen's cremation service passed in a blur. Masie remained seated throughout. It was only twenty minutes, in any case. As she finally stood, she noticed Jack had gone to wait by the doors, speaking to each mourner in turn. Some looked surprised, others vexed, others indifferent, but she could tell that he was successful in imposing his authority.

'I need to speak to Sergeant Wingard,' she told Mohammed. 'I'll go back in his car.'

'I am worried about you, Maisie. Forgive me, but you have a bad colour. I don't mean to impose, but can't you focus instead on us meeting in the Tuileries Garden in a few weeks, when all this . . .' He waved a hand. 'When you will have let all this go.'

Maisie smiled. 'No, I can't, not yet. I won't be able to let it all go unless I can get everything out into the open. And it has to be today. I won't get another chance.'

'Then today it must be,' he said gravely. 'Come. I will catch up with your amusing friends the Casemores before they totter off for the bus.'

'And can you accommodate the shop ladies, Alicia and Beatrice?' Maisie pointed them out.

'Of course.'

He strode out of the chapel, exchanging a few words with Jack. She followed. The rain had stopped and the sky was trying to clear. Jack put a hand on her arm. It felt entirely natural that he should do so.

'I need you to tell me what you are thinking,' he told her. 'Come in my car.'

'Thank you, I was intending to. I really am grateful for your trust.'

'Quickly, though,' said Jack. 'I don't want them to get there before us. And you will only have ten minutes to give me your version of events as we drive.'

Maisie got into Jack's Ford Zephyr and they pulled away, leading the procession out of the car park, the other mourners allowing them to go first out of respect. Maisie immediately began talking, trying to keep all her thoughts in order by telling the story as she had learnt it, including her misapprehensions and the dead ends, Mohammed's full name and his role in the past and the present, finally ending up at the only coherent pattern that, she believed, took account of every fact.

'There's no chance of a prosecution without a confession or some new and incontrovertible evidence,' said Jack, frowning, as they entered the village.

'But nothing else fits,' said Maisie.

'It may not be enough.'

'That's all I have. Don't you believe me?'

Jack paused, looking directly into her eyes. After a moment he simply told her: 'Yes, Maisie. Of course I believe you.'

***

As they pulled into the untidy gravel drive of Church Lodge, Maisie felt reassured – buoyed, even. It was a huge relief to feel she had Jack's wholehearted support.

She got out of the car, strode up to the front door and unlocked it. She intended to go inside and set out more chairs in a large circle on the chequerboard tiles of the hallway for everyone to sit, but there was a loud rumpus coming from round the side of the house, shouts and running feet.

Suddenly, an unkempt man came skittering across the gravel. He had a plastic fertiliser bag grasped in his left hand and a filthy bandage around his right.

Strickland.

He was swiftly followed by the police constable, finding it difficult to grab his prey because his arms were caught beneath his rain cape.

Goodbody.

Maisie jumped down off the front steps in front of Strickland and raised her forearm, locking out her shoulder at the level of his chin. In his panic to escape from the policeman, he ran straight into her, the point of her elbow catching him on the jaw. He fell back with a cry and lay stunned.

The fertiliser bag described a lazy loop in the air, then landed, scattering its contents over the shingle and weeds: seven or eight rings, two bracelets, three shiny metal plates, a golden chalice and finally, a small illuminated book bound in gilt-decorated leather.

Maisie glanced at Jack with a smile. He grinned in reply.

'Sergeant Wingard,' she said, 'how's that for "new and incontrovertible evidence"?'

FIFTY-NINE

The first thing to come to light, once everyone was assembled in the large open hallway with a fire burning in the massive stone hearth, was where Stephen had hidden the remaining artefacts from the cathedral crypt. The fact that they hadn't turned up sooner was due – and Maisie felt slightly guilty that she took great pleasure in this fact – to Constable Barry Goodbody's incompetence and squeamishness.

Jack sent everyone but Maisie, Strickland and Goodbody indoors while he collected up the precious items and wrapped them carefully in the blanket he kept in the boot of the Zephyr. Then they all trooped round to look at the outhouse.

The lock was smashed. A big lump of flint lay discarded on the lawn. The cloud of flies was swarming in and out of the broken door. They kept their distance and Strickland denied breaking in.

'You can't prove it—' he began.

Jack interrupted to give him the official warning.

'I'm not saying nothing,' Strickland replied, but he couldn't help himself. 'These are too tight.' He showed Maisie the handcuffs on his thin wrists. 'You don't want me trussed up, do you? You know I didn't mean anything. It was just a mistake.'

He seemed to genuinely believe he could elicit her sympathy. She supposed it was natural that an abuser would feel themselves justified in whatever they did, even the most appalling of actions.

'It was a mistake when you attacked me in your shop, was it?'

'I never.'

'When you chased me up the gallops in your truck?'

'What's that?' said Goodbody, suddenly interested.

'Shut up, Barry,' said Jack. 'No, in fact, Constable, go ahead. It's your turn to speak. Tell me exactly how it is that you missed the stolen goods from the cathedral when you searched Church Lodge?'

'What do you mean?'

'Strickland seems to have found them easily enough,' said Jack. 'I hope you're proud of yourself,' he added witheringly.

'But he probably knew they was there, didn't he?' complained Constable Goodbody.

'You should have left no stone unturned, Barry.'

'How did you know?' Maisie asked Strickland.

'I didn't, did I, then I thought about it and it came to me,' Strickland replied. 'If June saw Steve messing about in the old outhouse and put two and two together and told her old pa, like she ought to, I'd have found them sooner.'

'Told you to avoid a beating,' said Maisie.

Strickland made a hurt face. 'Now, that's not fair – and a man's got a right to bring his own children up how he sees fit, hasn't he?'

Maisie saw Jack clench his fists and worried he might do something he would regret.

'You've been a terrible father, you know that?' she said quickly.

There was a slight pause, then Jack seemed to have himself under control.

'But you, Barry,' said Jack, 'you didn't find the goods when it was your job to search the premises, not just in the context of the robbery, but also for the murder investigation.'

'I didn't go in,' said Goodbody. 'I mean, I opened the door and there was the maggots and it was that rank—'

'Didn't you notice that the pile of spuds had been disturbed?' interrupted Jack. 'Didn't that make you think to check, to root around a bit?'

'No.'

'Why the hell not?'

'I was sick, wasn't I,' said Goodbody loudly, his nasty little face screwing up in shame and frustration. 'It made me puke, those poor birds hanging by their feet and the blood and the flies. God, I'm going to puke again if you make me think about it.'

'All right,' said Jack. 'Take Strickland indoors and tell everyone we'll be in shortly.'

'Yes, sir,' said Constable Barry Goodbody, attempting to reassert a little of his professional dignity. He took hold of Strickland under the arm. 'Come on, then.'

'This is brutality,' said Strickland. 'I've got witnesses.'

They disappeared into Church Lodge and Maisie and Jack were left alone. Jack took the ring Stephen had given June from the pocket of his uniform jacket and put it in the boot of his car with the other treasures.

'About what I was saying, about leaving tonight,' she began. 'I just wanted to—'

'Never mind that now, Maisie,' he interrupted, and she thought it cost him something to do so. 'We can't keep them all indefinitely. Strickland being here might be to our advantage. I suggest you tell your story, more or less as you told it to me in the car. I know you'll do it brilliantly. Let's see if we can flush out something in the way of more evidence.'

There it was at last, thought Maisie. They were finally a team.

'Thank you, Jack.'

For second, she thought he was about to kiss her, but then they both noticed Nigel Bacon's inquisitive face in the window by the front door and silently followed Strickland and Goodbody inside.

SIXTY

There was a very peculiar atmosphere in the chequerboard hallway of Church Lodge, Framlington. More chairs had been brought in from the dining room and kitchen, and it was like some kind of private theatrical performance, set up almost 'in the round', with Maisie standing in front of the fire to complete the circle. Mohammed had fetched her some water, choosing a rather dainty little wine glass instead of the dimpled pint pot that she preferred.

She drank it down, looking at the assembled faces: Alicia Knight and Beatrice Otterway, Jon Wilkes, Gerald Gleeson, Bert Close, Hilary and Malcolm Casemore, Daphne and Derek Fieldhouse, Nigel Bacon, Maurice Ryan, Charity Clement, Mr Chitty and his grandson Nicholas.

She put the empty glass on the mantelpiece and somehow the action brought quiet.

'As some of you know, this all began for me when Stephen rang my flat in Paris and left a message about wanting to see me urgently. That was ten days ago, now. I thought, at the time, that he was asking me to travel quickly to England but, later, I discovered that he was warning me that he would soon be turning up on my Paris doorstep.'

'How's that?' said Maurice Ryan.

'The message her flatmate left her was incomplete,' said Charity Clement. 'I told you. Maisie rang back from our offices.'

'Oh, yes.'

'Thank you, Miss Clement. Now, Mr Ryan, if I may?' said Maisie.

'Yes, by all means.'

'You were very kind and met me at the station. Could you tell everyone how you knew to be there?'

'Well, Stephen left you our number so you could get in touch. You called with your arrival time. I assumed that Stephen knew you were on your way.'

'You didn't think to confirm with him?'

'I didn't, no,' said Ryan, spreading his expressive hands in apology. 'Sorry.'

'Stephen could have borrowed my car and fetched Miss Cooper himself,' said Nigel Bacon. 'We were pals.'

'At that point, Mr Ryan,' said Maisie, ignoring Nigel, 'last Saturday morning, you didn't know he was dead?'

'I did not,' said Ryan.

Maisie looked round the room. 'Mr Ryan gave me a lift to Framlington but we were denied entry. I put up at the Bedford Hotel in Chichester for three nights and got on with organising the village commemoration and the wake and the cremation. Finally, I was given the keys to Church Lodge. I thought at that point Stephen had had a heart attack or a catastrophic stroke, but I soon learnt differently.'

'Isn't Miss Cooper wonderful,' said Daphne Fieldhouse to no one in particular.

Maisie pressed on. 'After the wake on Wednesday – that's three days ago – I began to hear more details of Stephen's life and found he was apparently in reasonable health and not a likely stroke victim and that it was unlikely to be a heart attack if the pool was heated. In fact, the more I learnt, the less I understood, so I tried to focus on facts, such as the exact time of death.'

'About nine-thirty,' said Jack, 'as far as can be ascertained from the medical evidence.'

'And my evidence,' piped up Nigel Bacon, apparently proud of his involvement. 'I actually saw him. It was my pool. Is anyone thinking of that?'

'Don't interrupt, Nige,' said Derek Fieldhouse. 'Let the professionals get on with it. Or, as it may be, Miss Cooper.'

He gave Maisie a quizzical look which she did her best to ignore.

'I was in a bit of a daze and I apologise if any of you found me odd or rude or inattentive.'

'Quite understandable,' said Alicia.

'Oh, not at all,' said the Casemores, both at once.

Maisie ploughed on. 'There was so much to organise and I didn't know which way was up. Then I met June and she broke the news to me that she believed herself married to my brother.'

Just for clarity, Maisie explained the sequence of events surrounding the sham marriage certificate.

'Silly little bint,' started Strickland bitterly, then seemed to think better of it. 'No, you won't get me to say nothing.'

'You know, Strickland,' said Jack, 'that we have clear fingerprints on the pickaxe handle that Miss Cooper saved from your brazier. Yours and no one else's.'

Alicia and Beatrice both put their hands over their mouths. The Casemores said something inaudible. Gerald, Jon and Bert looked frankly interested. Maurice Ryan and Charity Clement did not react, seeming to assume a kind of professional detachment. Mr Chitty whispered something reassuring in his grandson's ear.

'So what, Mr Sergeant-bloody-Wingard?' roared Strickland.

'And June's blood on the other end, the heavy end.' Jack's voice wasn't quite steady. 'And the shape of the timber corresponds precisely to the wound.'

Maisie wondered if this was a good idea after all. Jack had allowed her to use shock tactics, but she was now worried that Jack would find it too much, thinking about poor June, and lose his temper and ruin everything. She moved a little to her right, into Strickland's eyeline, and went on the attack.

'Why did you kill her? Was it because she was finally going to make a complaint about your violence over so many years? Or was it because she insisted on wearing the ring Stephen gave her, the one from the cathedral loot that you egged him on to steal, that you hoped to steal from him in your turn?'

'I don't know what you're talking about.'

'Yes, but I do.'

'How do you know?' said Strickland guiltily.

'Because he told me,' said Maisie truthfully, though no one but she knew how.

'No, he didn't,' said Strickland, his eyes widening. 'He couldn't have done.'

'Why not?'

'Because he's dead.'

'So, you don't deny it?'

'Stop it. You're confusing me.'

'Then let's leave that for a moment,' said Maisie. 'Why don't you tell us all what you were doing when Constable Goodbody interrupted you just now?'

He didn't reply straight away. Maisie saw there was a dark bruise beginning to come through on his unshaven chin, the result of the impact of her elbow. Was there also dry blood on his forehead from rubbing up against one of the disgusting hanging pheasants?

'I was looking for some spuds, wasn't I?' Strickland lied. 'He used to let me have a few, your brother. Then I found that old fertiliser bag and I didn't know what was in it and just picked it up for no reason. And then this one . . .' He pointed at Goodbody who was guarding the front door. 'He laid me out.'

'No, he didn't,' said Nigel Bacon. 'I was watching from the hall window. That was Miss Cooper's work.'

He laughed noisily and looked around as if everyone else was going to join in, but no one did.

'But,' said Maisie, 'none of that really matters, does it, because you killed your daughter and you're going to go to prison for the rest of your life.'

'Or he could be hanged,' said Derek Fieldhouse. 'Capital punishment for a capital crime.'

'They don't hang no more,' said Strickland, then Maisie saw a look she recognised come into his eyes, an expression of calculation and cunning. 'Couldn't it have been an accident, though? Accidents happen, don't they?'

He glanced round the room, round the circle of strained or baffled faces. Who was he looking for, Maisie wondered? Who was it that he thought he had a hold over? Or was it something else? Did he have something he thought he could trade with the police for leniency in sentencing?

'I'm not sure we've managed to keep this chronological after all, have we,' said Daphne Fieldhouse's colourless voice. 'I'm tired. Take me home, Derek.'

'Yes, Daphne,' Derek replied.

Was Derek also keen to get away, Maisie wondered?

'Not yet,' said Jack quietly.

There was an authority to Jack's voice that impressed and reassured Maisie. His simple words were followed by a silence in which everyone appeared to take stock. Then Malcolm Casemore surprised her by raising his hand.

'I'm sorry, I am not certain of the protocol, as it were, but once a teacher, always a teacher, I suppose, and . . .' He raised his hand higher. 'Might I speak. Would this be a suitable moment?'

'Don't waffle, Malcolm,' said his wife, brusquely.

'No, Hilly.' He glanced at Maisie and then Jack. 'It is with regret that I must add to the . . . I mean, I am sorry, Miss Cooper, to have to . . .' He lost his thread and turned to his wife. 'You have the bag?'

'Of course I have the bag.' She passed it to him with her twisted hands.

'Maisie, your brother was a friend of ours,' said Malcolm, 'as I told you. He gave us a gift. Had we known what we now know, we would not have accepted it.'

Maisie remembered being served sherry in their tiny living room and thought she knew what was coming.

'When was this?' asked Maisie.

'It was just a couple of days before he died.'

'Before he was murdered,' said Strickland, his eyes furtively darting round the room. 'Let's not forget that.'

Maisie wished she could see for sure who he was targeting.

'We should never have—' Malcolm Casemore began.

Hilary Casemore stood up. 'I believe, given what we have today learnt, that it must be a part of the robbery from the crypt. We are accessories after the fact. That is, I believe, the phrase. We are prepared for whatever punishment the law deems fit.'

Malcolm Casemore stood up too and pulled a shiny silver tray out of the canvas shopping bag. Maisie recognised it as the one on which the two bottles of sherry had stood, one medium and one dry, in the Casemores' tiny living room.

'Put it back in the bag,' said Jack.

'But we wish to return it?' said Malcolm.

'Don't change your grip. Just drop it back in the bag and pass it to me.'

Malcolm Casemore did as he was told. Jack took the bag and put it down beneath his chair.

'Fingerprints,' said Strickland pointlessly. 'You don't fool me.'

'No one's trying to trick you,' said Maisie. 'We're only interested in the truth.'

'Miss Cooper,' asked Jack, 'will you need Mr and Mrs Casemore for anything further?'

Maisie thought about it. On reflection, there was no need to talk about the wild-flower posy and the poem. That had turned out to be a red herring – and a well-intentioned tribute of a kind to her brother.

'No,' said Maisie. 'I have nothing more to ask them.'

Jack nodded and addressed the two elderly poets. 'I will come and take your statement later or, perhaps, tomorrow morning,' he told them.

'We will be ready,' they said simultaneously.

'I doubt there will be a prosecution,' he told them gravely.

'No?' Hilary brightened.

'No clamour?' said Malcolm with a weak smile.

'No, sir. No clamour.'

'Thank you, Sergeant,' said Hilary.

They left and everyone watched them go.

'Must we stay, though,' drawled Daphne Fieldhouse. 'Can one be held indefinitely, like this?'

'Shouldn't we let Miss Cooper continue?' said Mohammed, to everyone's surprise. 'Surely, Segreant Wingard, hers is the story we have been assembled to hear?'

Maisie frowned. The more confusion and cross-talk there was, the better she liked it. Someone was much likelier, then, to give themselves away. She could see in Jack's face that he thought the same.

'And who are you?' asked Daphne, as if noticing Mohammed for the first time.

'That's a good idea, Mr As-Sabah,' said Jack pleasantly. 'Miss Cooper, the floor is yours once more.'

Maisie took a moment to collect her thoughts then picked up her narrative from the moment of digression.

SIXTY-ONE

'I don't think we need to review all the events around poor June's death,' said Maisie. 'But I have to mention a couple of things I learnt from her. Firstly, on the day of his death, Stephen rose early, in part to begin his new fitness regime, but for other reasons as well.'

'I've got something to say,' said Bert unexpectedly and Gerald Gleeson and Jon Wilkes seemed to shrink away from him on either side, as if he was somehow contaminated.

'Go on,' said Maisie.

'If it was the day for mowing, and it was, your brother often went out, to the stables or the shop or wherever, because the noise got on his nerves. But I wasn't mowing that day because I was poorly.'

'That's what I told you, Miss Cooper,' said Jon.

'That's where 'tis,' insisted Bert.

But the blacksmith hadn't finished. 'All right, Bert, hold your horses. Young Nicholas was up for being sent. I told Miss Cooper that, too.'

Young Nicholas shrank back into his chair, looking very frightened and small.

'But my grandson wasn't required,' said Mr Chitty, putting a protective arm around the boy's narrow shoulders. 'Isn't that right, Mr Fieldhouse?'

'True enough. I took a fancy to do it myself.' Derek patted his stomach. 'I need the exercise, just like Stephen did.'

'Well, that's cleared that up,' said Maisie with a smile, but knowing how crucial the information would prove. 'Sergeant

Wingard, I don't think we need keep Mr Chitty and his grandson any longer?'

'No, perhaps not.'

'Perhaps you are not aware, Sergeant Wingard,' said Mr Chitty, punctiliously, 'that the late Mr Cooper owed my business money for the loan of a Gazelle Champion racing bike? I wouldn't like to conceal the fact.'

'The police,' said Jack very seriously, 'do not consider that a plausible motive for murder.'

'I appreciate your consideration, Sergeant, and Miss Cooper,' said Chitty. 'What do you say, Nicholas?'

'Thank you for having me,' said the boy, in a small, well-trained voice.

Again, all of those left behind watched them leave and the tension rose another notch. It was obvious, wasn't it, that the murderer was still in the room? Once the door had closed behind them, Gerald Gleeson piped up.

'What about us then,' he said, indicating himself, Jon and Bert. 'What are we here for still?'

That remains to be seen, thought Maisie, but she told him something different.

'There are one or two questions we think you will be able to answer.'

'Fair enough,' said Jon.

'All right,' said Bert then added, inevitably, 'if that's where 'tis.'

Maisie addressed Maurice Ryan and Charity Clement. 'I hope you have time, too, if you wouldn't mind?'

'Yes, of course,' said Ryan. 'Anything to help the police.'

'Thank you. There is still, for example, the unresolved gap in time between when Stephen left June in bed upstairs and when he was seen by Nigel, drowned in the swimming pool.'

'Not drowned,' said Jack. 'Murdered by asphyxiation and then pushed into the water.'

'Yes,' said Maisie. 'Murdered by asphyxiation and dumped in the water.'

She let the idea hang in the air.

'Is that it?' asked Daphne Fieldhouse. 'Are we done?'

'Then I thought to myself,' said Maisie, ignoring her, 'that there were lots of things that didn't quite add up and, because of the man he was, lots of reasons for someone to want him dead.'

'You could say the same of all of us, surely?' said Derek with a man-of-the-world grin.

'Could you?' asked Strickland.

'None of us is perfect,' Derek insisted.

Maisie looked methodically round the room, taking in each of them in turn.

'It could be a person with an underdeveloped sense of right and wrong. Or a person under pressure themselves. Or a person with an inflated ego, puffed up with pride, who couldn't bear to be crossed. Or someone with money worries that Stephen's death would alleviate. There were so many reasons.'

'Too many for me,' said Daphne.

Maisie picked out Alicia and Beatrice in their oddly assorted, old-fashioned mourning attire. 'The shop was in trouble and Stephen had lent you money. Yes, you were just about managing to make payments, but I thought about it and did some simple maths. It was going to take you years to pay him back at the rate you were going. How much nicer it would be if he could simply die and disappear and your debt could be forgotten?'

'But we liked your brother,' said Alicia plaintively.

'We did, Maisie,' said Beatrice. 'You know we did.'

'Yes, that's what everyone kept telling me, how much they liked him. And, yet,' Maisie insisted, 'he ended up dead.'

'This is so unfair,' said Beatrice.

Maisie picked out Nigel Bacon. 'You resented his success with June. How much did that hurt your pride?'

'You overstate the case,' he argued.

Maisie pointed at Derek Fieldhouse. 'He entertained your wife and she clearly found him much more congenial company than you.'

'I say, that's a bit rich.'

'She heard you,' said Daphne to her husband, 'when you came stomping in the other day. This is becoming more interesting, at last. No one has any secrets from the inquisitive Miss Cooper, it seems.'

Maisie went on. 'And you, Mrs Fieldhouse, Stephen let you down by trying to trick you into unwise investments.'

'What investments?' asked Nigel, suddenly.

Daphne ignored him, giving her answer to Maisie. 'But even if that were a motive for murder, you don't think I, trapped in this wheelchair, could have overpowered him, do you?'

'On your first point, I'm not sure I have ever met someone so utterly focused on cold hard cash as you are, Mrs Fieldhouse.'

'Is that so?'

'On your second point, no, I don't think you could have overpowered him – at least, not on your own.'

'And you know very well,' said Daphne, 'that I saw through his taradiddle, that I turned him down.'

'Turned him down how?' said Derek Fieldhouse.

Daphne paid no attention. 'You remember, Miss Cooper, I told you how he came to me with his ridiculous stories of Kuwaiti oil ministers and royal princes. Believe me, only a fool would have been convinced.'

'What did you say?' said Nigel Bacon.

'Shut up, Nigel,' said Derek. 'This is nothing to do with you.'

'Or is it?' said Maisie.

This time the silence took on a completely different quality, then someone moved. Was it because they were preparing to make a break for it? Maisie thought Jack had the same idea and he once more spoke with the quiet voice of authority.

'Stay quite still, if you please, all of you.'

Maisie looked round. Who hadn't yet spoken? No one. It was time for the final push. With a feeling of revulsion, she turned back to Strickland. In a sense, she needed his co-operation.

'There were two further reasons why Stephen got up early. One was in order to write me a letter. It gives a clear account of some of the things Stephen was thinking about in the hours before his death.'

'Do you have this letter?' asked Derek Fieldhouse, looking very focused. 'Out of interest,' he added.

'The letter travelled to Paris, arriving just after I had left, then back again to England, forwarded by my flatmate. I read it for the first time this morning. It is here in my handbag.'

'Good,' said Derek. 'That's very useful.'

'The second reason for his early start,' Maisie continued, 'was that he had arranged to meet someone.'

'And who was that?' asked Nigel. He looked across at Fieldhouse. 'And, Derek, just hold back from telling me to shut up this time, would you?'

Maisie held the pause for as long as she could. 'June's father.'

'What?' cried Strickland.

'Yes, you.'

'What are you talking about? I never touched him.'

'His letter tells me the whole story, the robbery from the crypt, the idea that you could fence the pieces, then his change of heart and the fact that he arranged to meet you.'

'Prove it,' said Strickland.

'It tells me he wanted to warn you that he was going away, but that if you ever touched June again with your filthy hands, he would see you brought to justice.'

'What's that got to do with anything?'

'It means you were there,' said Nigel. 'That's what it means.'

'It gives you a very powerful motive,' said Derek.

'Why are you getting involved, Derek?' asked Daphne, an odd look on her face. 'Why are you so keen to keep chipping in?'

'But how would I have done him,' said Strickland, 'big bloke that he was and me just a poor old man with nothing to look forward to but the grave?'

'Yes,' agreed Maisie, surprising him. 'That's a good question. There's no way you could have overpowered him. And he was smothered, not beaten or knocked insensible. That would take strength, the ability to immobilise him as he lost consciousness. So, if it wasn't you, who was it?'

Strickland looked furtive once more.

'I don't know what to say. I don't know what serves me best.' He turned to Jack. 'Is there let-offs for those what helps?'

'What did you say?' said Jack, looking disgusted.

'Is there let-offs? Like, if I told you how Steve hid in the cathedral at closing time and slipped out in the morning mass next day.'

Maisie saw Jack take a moment to compose himself before replying.

'If you have something useful to say, I will make sure that the judge knows it. I can't say fairer than that.'

'Doesn't sound that fair to me.'

'It's the best I can do. I can't make deals.'

Maisie reached into her handbag for the letter Mohammed had given her earlier, from his 'useful man'.

'Is that it?' asked Derek. 'Is that poor old Stephen's letter?'

'No, this is something else.' Maisie held the letter out to Strickland. 'Can you read this?'

'Can I read?' said Strickland. 'Course I can read.'

'Have a look at the names.'

Strickland peered at the paper and whistled and nodded.

'That's right,' he said, without explaining to everyone else. 'You know who I saw.'

'Yes,' said Maisie. 'I know.'

She turned and looked at Nigel Bacon.

'What arrogance to call the company after yourself.' She turned to Derek Fieldhouse. 'And you, too. Your own initials. Of course, in Stephen's bank account, it just appeared as BFI Limited. But, thanks to Beatrice, I found out that it isn't difficult to know who is behind the facade of a limited company. My friend, Mr As-Sabah, had a financial consultant look into it. Would you like to see, Mrs Fieldhouse?' She held the letter out to Daphne. 'Would you care to read what it says?'

Daphne took the paper in her thin fingers. 'BFI Limited,' she read aloud. 'Bacon Fieldhouse Investments, directors, Nigel Bacon and Derek Fieldhouse.'

'That's right,' said Strickland. He pointed a dirty finger first at one then the other. 'I'll come across. That's who I saw that morning.' He turned back to Jack. 'Remember, you promised to tell the judge.'

'Be quiet,' said Jack.

'What do you think of that, Mrs Fieldhouse?' asked Maisie.

Daphne Fieldhouse looked at her husband.

'What is this, Derek?' she asked venomously. 'Have you been playing with someone else's toys? I thought you said Nigel was on his beam ends.'

'Shut up, Daphne,' said Derek. 'For God's sake, just shut up.'

'Or was it my money you threw away?'

'You were both so keen,' said Maisie harshly, 'desperate even, weren't you, good old Nigel Bacon, good old Derek Fieldhouse, to convince me that you were his "pals", his "best friend hereabouts". Weren't you?'

'I honestly was, though,' said Derek.

Maisie was almost impressed at how good an actor he seemed while Nigel simply gaped.

'Stephen convinced you, didn't he,' continued Maisie, 'that you were on to a sure thing, that he would get you in on the ground floor of the new Middle Eastern oil cartel and he persuaded you to make a down payment last September. And that's why you, Derek, have been trying to foreclose left and right, have been skimping on repairs, because you've overspent the money your wife allows you to run her business. Her business, not yours, the one you married into. And you, Nigel, how has the London stock market crisis affected your income? Not for the better, I imagine.'

Nigel looked rather green.

'Everyone's taken a hit,' he said, his gaze unable to settle.

'I have requested a report into Mr Bacon's affairs, Sergeant Wingard,' said Mohammed, 'if that might be of interest.'

'Thank you, Mr As-Sabah.'

'It's the striking miners and the damn oil crisis,' said Nigel. 'It's pure greed, that's what it is. And it's getting worse.' He pointed at Mohammed. 'It's all thanks to your lot. When will you be satisfied?' He looked round the room. 'What right do they have to hold the world to ransom?'

Mohammed didn't answer. Maisie went back on the attack.

'So, the two of you leapt at Stephen's plan. Except the contact with the well-placed diplomats and the "prince of the blood" didn't materialise.'

'What do you think of all this, Mr As-Sabah?' interrupted Daphne. 'I suppose you were the one true thread on which Stephen embroidered his fantasy?'

Mohammed put his head on one side, as if making a careful judgement. 'It takes a very stupid mind to think it possible that a modern nation might possibly do business in such a way.'

'I agree.' Daphne wheeled her wheelchair away from her husband so that she could turn to face him. 'A very stupid mind indeed.'

Maisie pressed on, determined not to lose momentum.

'Nigel, Derek, when you both saw Stephen that morning, coming from his goodbye chat with June's father – though you didn't know that was where he had been – you had got to the point where you felt, both of you, that you had to challenge him on it. Nearly five months had passed from the September payment and nothing material had transpired. You planned it, didn't you? Derek, you made sure that no one else would be there, neither Bert nor young Nicholas, to mow the lawn and be a witness. And I'm sure it was you, Nigel, who had the brilliant idea of attacking him when he walked through for his morning swim, when he came to start his new regime, getting himself back into shape.'

'This is preposterous,' said Nigel.

'I imagine you both, just beyond the gate in the garden wall, Bacon and Fieldhouse, directors of BFI Limited, egging one another on, in a private space that isn't overlooked by a single neighbour, when he was wearing just his swimming trunks and his dressing gown, more or less defenceless. Then, knowing Stephen as I do, I can imagine him refusing to take your threats seriously, goading and belittling, making the two of you more and more mad that he had so easily duped the pair of you. And then, just as he was getting ready to slip into the water, one of you got his arms round him to stop him struggling – I expect that was Derek – while the other, Nigel, took hold of his dressing gown and wrapped it round his mouth and nose. And the two of you squeezed and you squeezed until he was no longer moving and he was dead.'

'Ridiculous,' shouted Nigel, his eyes swivelling, left and right.

'Don't believe her, Daphne,' pleaded Derek.

'My money, Derek,' said his wife, coldly. 'Throwing away my money.'

Maisie had to steel herself to go on. Describing what she believed had happened was extremely painful.

'But there was a witness. You didn't know that, did you? June's father was still there. He had hung around after Stephen gave him his ultimatum, watching and waiting, wondering where the loot from the cathedral robbery might have been hidden. And he saw you through the gate between the gardens. He saw everything, as you choked the life out of my brother by the side of your pool!'

'It was Derek,' shouted Nigel. 'Not me. He was the one who wrapped the dressing gown round his head.'

'You stupid fool,' shouted Derek. 'What's wrong with you?'

'I tried to stop him,' shouted Nigel.

'No, you never,' said Strickland in a horrible high voice and then laughed. 'I saw what you done. June never did, but I did. I was peeping through the gate. I'd have made you pay for my silence if I'd had time.'

Derek Fieldhouse leapt from his chair. His hands were round Nigel Bacon's throat before Wingard could move. Nigel's chair tipped over backwards and the two of them went sprawling. Then Derek jumped up, backing away towards the perimeter of the circle, looking like he was about to run when a single blow from Jon Wilkes's meaty fist sent him stumbling to the floor.

'I didn't mean to do it, Daphne,' Derek wailed, his nose bleeding. 'It was Nigel's fault. It was Nigel's idea.'

'Damn it, Derek,' shouted Nigel.

They traded insults and accusations. Jon Wilkes sat himself on Derek's chest. Jack had Bacon pinned as well, but he didn't interrupt their shouting. Maisie knew that he was allowing them to wail and argue, incriminating one another.

The faces of Maurice Ryan and Charity Clement were calm. She thought they understood their role – professional fair witnesses, primed to remember what was said and commit it to signed statements later on. Gerald Gleeson and Bert Close watched from the front door alongside Barry Goodbody, their eyes wide.

***

Maisie turned away and rested her forearm on the mantelpiece. She could feel the slight tenderness of the bruise coming through from the impact with Strickland's chin. She found herself retreating into her imagination, an alternate timeline in which she had been at home in Paris to receive Stephen's message, then at home to greet him a couple of days later with his travel suitcase and a bag of stolen jewellery and precious historical artefacts.

What would she have told him?

To go home and face the music?

To keep walking, not to involve her?

Or would she have let him in and tried to help him turn his ill-gotten gains into hard cash?

No, not that, not the third option. But the first two?

She was glad, on reflection, that she had never had to face that dilemma.

EPILOGUE

After Derek Fieldhouse's attack on Nigel Bacon, Gerald Gleeson was allowed to leave and call for two police vans from the phone at his pub. Then he came back and the whole party was relocated to the police station in Chichester.

It took the rest of the afternoon for each and every witness to the implosion of Fieldhouse and Bacon's murder conspiracy to be taken into separate interview rooms where they gave complete statements of all that they knew, all they had seen and all they had heard. They were then sent home or, in the cases of Gerald, Jon and Bert, to the Fox-in-Flight to – no doubt – share the gossip as widely as they knew how. Meanwhile, Fieldhouse, Bacon and Strickland were incarcerated in separate cells in the police station basement.

Finally, Mohammed's Bentley and Jack's Ford Zephyr processed back out of town, through the trees, through the S-bends at East Bitling and through the arable fields to Church Lodge, Framlington.

Maisie rode with Jack, but they barely spoke. Waiting on the doorstep, shivering under the porch, was Malcolm Casemore, full of unnecessary apology about the silver plate.

Wingard reassured the old man. 'You didn't know where it came from, sir.'

'No, we didn't.'

Malcolm left, reiterating his gratitude, but not without offering them two of his delicious home-made sausage rolls. They went indoors and, to everyone's surprise, found a note on the doormat from Daphne Fieldhouse.

'*Stay until the end of next week, if you wish to. DF.*'

The three of them went to sit in the kitchen. Maisie and Wingard shared the sausage rolls while Mohammed watched, unwilling to consume pork.

It was seven o'clock in the evening. The power was off again and the room was lit with two candles and the light from the bluish flames of the coke in the firebox of the Aga. They had left the door open to encourage it to burn up quickly. The clearing sky had turned the weather very cold.

'How did you know?' asked Mohammed.

'You don't have to talk about it any more if you don't want to,' said Jack kindly.

'You knew more than you said out loud, though, didn't you?' persisted Mohammed. 'Otherwise, how could you have been so sure on so little evidence?'

'I spoke to everybody,' said Maisie. 'They told me everything I needed to know, though they weren't aware they were doing it.'

'Yes,' said Jack. 'A guilty person will always find it impossible to keep silent the thing they are always thinking about, the thing they are trying to conceal.'

'That's true,' said Maisie. 'I'm sure it is, but I'm not talking about people who were guilty. I'm talking about bystanders, people who were close, but not involved. Like the story of the poem and the posy of wild flowers.'

They both looked baffled. She told them how she had been misled by that 'clue' and how she had finally tracked down what it meant.

'Remarkable,' said Mohammed.

Maisie put a hand over her mouth. 'Oh, Jack, I've remembered what she said.'

'What who said?'

'What June said.'

Jack seemed to shrink into himself. 'Go on.'

'I'm sorry, Jack, I know these are terrible memories.'

'It's all right,' he encouraged. 'What did she say?'

'Well, it was outside the Bell, on the cold pavement, and it was very faint. I thought she said "Albert Close" and I looked around for a road sign.'

Jack looked Maisie in the eye and read her thoughts. 'She didn't say "Albert Close", she said "Bert Close".'

'Exactly. But Bert didn't know what it was that was so important, or he would have made the connection himself,' Maisie continued. 'June was there, remember, up in Stephen's room. She knew that Bert was ill and couldn't do the mowing but someone did, someone who had to be there at the precise moment Stephen was killed. Not her pa but someone else, either a witness or – more likely – a murderer.'

'Derek Fieldhouse,' said Mohammed.

'But it wasn't conclusive. That was a problem all along. I kept finding so much negative evidence, too many people all in the same place all at once. You heard what Strickland said. He was just waiting to get his hands on the cathedral artefacts before turning his mind to blackmailing Derek and Nigel.'

'When did it all become clear, Maisie?' said Mohammed. 'Was there a sudden epiphany, a moment of revelation? I really am very impressed.'

'Well, that was Bert again,' said Maisie. 'I was at the stables and I was thinking about the fact that Jon Wilkes said Nigel mistreated his stallion. It's a lovely grey horse, over sixteen hands. I owe it everything.'

'I don't understand,' said Mohammed, who had not heard the story of the dramatic chase up the gallops. 'You owe a horse everything?'

'Never mind,' said Maisie. 'I'll tell you later. So, Jon said it was Nigel who mistreated the horse but Bert gave me the impression it was Derek, so I thought to myself: "Maybe it was both of them?" And that led on to—'

'You wondered if, in the same way they might both be responsible for the cruelty to the stallion,' said Jack, once again completing her thought, 'could they both be responsible for the murder?'

'Exactly. It gave me the idea that those two very proud but inadequate men were in league with one another.'

'Was that really enough?' asked Mohammed. 'I mean, the two things were unconnected.'

'They were, but I was so immersed in the life of the village by then that it seemed meaningful to me. And, actually, it did connect to the very first clue out of all the clues, the first thing someone said to me that honestly didn't make sense.'

'Go on,' said Jack encouragingly.

'Well,' she said, 'it was this. Eventually, everyone in the village knew that Stephen had been murdered. But, when I told Derek, he pretended it was news. I just asked myself what possible reason there could be for someone to pretend that they were not aware of a man being murdered – a man who lived in a house owned by the family investment company he ran on behalf of his wife – and the only thing I could come up with was that he wanted to distance himself from the knowledge out of guilt.'

★★★

Maisie decided she needed a few minutes to herself. It took her a while, but she finally persuaded the two men to go together to the pub where she would soon join them.

'As long as you don't mind being in the presence of alcohol, Mohammed?' Maisie asked.

'I will try not to be tempted,' he replied with a wry smile. 'Perhaps there will be something *halal* that I can eat.'

'The chips are superb,' said Jack. 'Cooked in beef fat.'

'Chips it will be,' said Mohammed.

Once they had left, the kitchen seemed much bigger. Maisie looked up at the ceiling, letting the tension of the day's events leave her body. There was the wooden drying rack on its ropes and pulleys. She still hadn't done any laundry.

Never mind. Tomorrow was Sunday. She would perhaps go to the early service at eight o'clock, as a kind of goodbye, visit her parents' grave in the churchyard, then spend the rest of the morning bent over the sink. It would do her good, she thought – a couple of hours of mindless physical activity. That made her think of the bike, still chained to a street lamp outside Strickland's shop. She hoped it was all right. She didn't want to disappoint kind Mr Chitty.

She pulled one of the candles closer and opened Stephen's letter. She had only read it once with Mohammed waiting in the kitchen, impatient to be on their way to the crematorium. It was, of course, written on the pages torn from the centre of his exercise book.

Dearest Maisie,

Well, you won't be surprised to hear that I am writing to you because I am in trouble. I'm sorry I've waited until now to be in touch and I don't doubt you would be correct in thinking badly of me.

I could go on with the apologies but it's more useful to come to the facts. Bear with me. There's a lot to tell.

You, of course, have an infallible memory so I won't insult you by asking if you remember old Mohammed As-Sabah . . .

The next two pages of Stephen's neat handwriting told a story Maisie already knew – of his friendships, his generosity to some, his deceit of others.

Obviously, I'm ashamed of my behaviour towards poor June, in particular. There's a local copper who has a very poor opinion of me, I think because he has an attachment to her himself. Or could it be something else?

Well, actually, yes, it could and thereby, as they say, hangs another tale . . .

The next section of the letter was the story of the robbery from the cathedral crypt. It told her exactly how it was done, but she already knew most of that. An enterprising journalist had pieced the story together and published it in the local paper.

She turned the page.

The devotional book is a lovely thing, a compendium of sins and virtues. You probably think the former are more appropriate to this tale of mine than the latter. That has been true in the past – but I hope for not much longer.

It is my intention – though you will find this hard to believe, I don't doubt, and good on you for being, despite your untrustworthy relative, as straight as a die yourself – to turn over a new leaf. I made up the bogus marriage lines to make June happy, nothing else.

Maisie thought, uncharitably, that it was actually in order to get June to continue to have sex with him. That was, after all, what June had told her when they first met.

Now, I've broken it to June that I'm going away. To soften the blow, I've told her that there's someone else I love and left her the choicest ring as a sop to her pride.

Of course, thought Maisie. That was why June had been so certain there was 'another woman'.

This is a pure fiction. I'm not sure I am capable of love.

Maisie had to stop reading for a moment as she took in the bleak sadness of what her brother was telling her from beyond the grave.

But a man needs something on which to build. I hope that foundation might be you.

If I turned up on your doorstep in Paris, would you send me away?

You would have every right. I would be 'a man on the run' as they say in the adventure novels, with my ill-gotten booty to turn into hard cash. I was thinking one of those dark-fronted antique shops on the rue du Paradis?

But have no fear. I would not impose on you for long. My next step would be to disappear for a second time. I was thinking of Casablanca. That would be the right combination of seediness and specious glamour, don't you think? A metaphor for my existence, perhaps!

Maisie smiled. Derek Fieldhouse had, incredibly, been right. Stephen had been trying to start afresh. But he was not equipped for it. He spoke like a child, as if the past was simply dust one could shake off one's shoes.

So, that's my question. Answer quickly, won't you? I don't have a phone. You could leave a message at the Fox-in-Flight or with Maurice Ryan and the delicious Charity, but I may have to skedaddle before I get it. If that is the case and our next contact is a surprise to you, in person on your doorstep in the Place des Vosges, then I dare hope you will welcome me with open arms.

And also, perhaps, with an indulgent – though disapproving – smile?

Anyway, be sure that I have always loved you, dear Maisie, however far apart we might have grown, whatever my silence or my actions might have suggested.

With deepest affection from your disappointing brother,
Stephen

Maisie folded the letter and put it away, fetched her mackintosh and went outside, locking the heavy front door behind her. She heard the innocent rustling of nocturnal animals in the rhododendrons and strode out onto the main road through the village, past the Casemores' cottage and Alicia and Beatrice's village shop. She crossed the road and paused outside the pub, looking in through the smoky windows at Jack and Mohammed, chatting and sharing a basket of chips by the light of a candle in a jam jar. Just then, Jack turned his head and saw her, his face softening, half rising from his chair.

With a rush of pleasure, she pushed open the door and went inside.

THE END

ACKNOWLEDGEMENTS

Thanks are due to Luigi Bonomi who told me I could do this, then helped (in every way) to make it happen; to my early readers Alison Bonomi, Benjamin Graham, Anthony Horowitz and Flora Rees; to my supremely gifted editor Beth Wickington and all the team at Hodder & Stoughton; and, finally, to the booksellers, festival co-ordinators, podcasters and others whose dedication and enthusiasm are so essential to a flourishing book industry.

And, of course, to the person from whom I learnt to write books - the best and only Kate Mosse.

Read on for a sneak peek
at Maisie's next sleuthing
adventure in *Murder at Bunting
Manor*, coming this November.

PROLOGUE

It was a crisp autumn day on the cusp of winter, November 5th, 1971. In a village hidden in a fold of the Sussex Downs, preparations for Guy Fawkes Night were almost complete, watched by a stranger, a woman dressed in several layers of ill-assorted clothes – almost rags. She had walked to Bunting along the pilgrim way, across the hills.

The bonfire field was beside a lane that led up to an untidy failing farm. For an hour at least – she had no watch – the stranger observed the villagers stacking prunings from overgrown hedges and fallen trees. Then the publican arrived – a little unsteadily – with the 'Guy', a pair of old striped pyjamas crammed with straw. The village shopkeeper brought the head, an upturned paper bag stuffed with newspaper and decorated with black wool for his long stringy hair, the face drawn on with a thick felt-tip pen – dark eyes, heavy brows, an ugly mouth with blacked-out teeth. The stranger watched her sew the head to the pyjama collar with a darning needle. It lolled to one side, grinning foolishly in the failing sun.

Finally, a strongly built woman in a worn wax jacket drove up in a tired Land Rover with an enormous box of fireworks. Her labouring man began setting the rockets in the ground, the Catherine wheels on the fence.

Earlier, a little before 'last orders' for the lunchtime service, the stranger had gone to lurk at the back door of the pub, the Dancing Hare, begging for scraps. A kind young woman with wide-set eyes, clear skin and nervous hands had given her a piece of quiche left over from someone's plate and told her she might come back at evening opening time, at five-thirty, for something else.

The gift had made the stranger feel warm inside. She had eaten it 'out of her hand', as the country people said, standing on the village green, watching a drab couple teaching two smallish boys – one English, one brown-skinned with dark brows – how to wash their tiny car, an off-white Hillman Imp with rust peeking through the paintwork round the wheel arches. Then, the four of them had gone back inside their ugly salmon-pink house, leaving their buckets and sponges and chamois leathers on the front step. The girl from the pub had turned up and was shouted at to 'bring in the things' and 'not make another mess like this morning'.

The stranger's cold feet were sore from her trudge over the hills, so she left the bonfire field and went to sit in the porch of the church, looking out at the gravestones. Then, after a while, looking at nothing at all.

Time passed. Day became dusk, dusk became almost night.

From a smart-looking converted worker's cottage on the far side of the green, a red-faced overweight man, encased in a grey three-piece suit, picked his way through the puddles around the green, a sheaf of music in his hands. Seeing the stranger, he screwed up his piggy face in a sneer of contempt and went inside. Discreetly, she followed him, sitting quietly in a rear pew, almost out of sight beside a pillar, while he practised Christmas hymns at the organ.

Soon she heard footsteps and there was the girl from the pub again, looking reluctant and unhappy.

'At last,' said the red-faced man, heaving himself off the organ stool and lumbering towards her. 'What's this I hear about you not singing the solos at Christmas, Zoe?'

'I'm sorry, Mr Kimmings, I don't want to.'

'Don't want to?' he spat. 'What's that supposed to mean?'

'I'm very sorry,' said the girl.

'You need to learn that life isn't about what you want to do,' he told her. 'It's about doing your damn duty. That's what young people don't understand. I'm surprised you haven't a better sense of your obligations. What are you? An orphan with no family, living off the kindness of Mr and Mrs Beck, off the kindness of the state.'

'Yes, Mr Kimmings.'

'I'll thank you to give me my rank and call me "Commander". Someone should take a slipper to you, you little minx.'

'In school,' said the girl, truculently, 'they tell us it's rude to call people names.'

Quick as a flash, he lurched forward and slapped the girl's face with the flat of his meaty hand. The stranger stood up in her pew. The girl ran towards the door. Just then the vicar – a tall man with a bland unremarkable face – stepped inside, catching her in his arms, clutching her to his chest.

'Now, what's the matter?' he asked, his eyes wide.

The girl pulled away, taking a couple of stumbling steps.

'Stop it. I hate you. I hate you both.'

She sounded like a small, broken child. The stranger wanted to say something to comfort her, but she didn't have time, because she ran away and the two men disappeared into the vestry.

The stranger shuffled outside. A hundred yards away, she could see the girl disappearing into the Dancing Hare. The church bell chimed and a car pulled in – a Triumph Herald. Its occupants came tumbling out, a happy family looking forward to the fireworks but keen to get into the pub nice and early for their quiche or 'fish-in-a-basket' beforehand.

The stranger made her way to the back door and stood in a corner, away from the lighted rear window, through which she could see children with parents who loved them, a wife who respected her husband, a husband devoted to his wife. At least, that was how it seemed.

She wondered if the girl would remember her promise, but soon the door opened and the pale face looked out.

'Are you there?'

'I'm here,' said the stranger, her words only just louder than the breeze.

The girl stepped outside. The slice of quiche was warm in her hands, steam rising in the chilly air.

'If you want, there's room to sit down in the woodshed.'

'No one will be coming out for logs, then?'

'We'll not be needing any more. We shut early to go up to the bonfire and the fireworks. You should stay for the display.'

The girl went back inside and the stranger did as she suggested, perching on a heap of cut beechwood in the log shelter, pulling her rags around her for warmth.

Maybe I will stop on, she thought. *There's no one who'll miss me.*

Once she had finished eating, wiping her oily fingers on her clothes, the stranger crossed the road and took the path through the woods towards the untidy gravel drive of Bunting Manor. From the shadow of the encroaching trees, she paused to peer in through tall leaded windows, seeing the firework woman in the worn wax jacket, opening a trapdoor in the floorboards. She descended to her basement, returning a few moments later with a dusty bottle of wine.

The stranger moved on. At the corner of the building, a cold moon revealed steps that led down to the outside door of the wine cellar, half concealed by overhanging leaves.

That might be useful, thought the stranger, *when I come back.*

ONE

It was ten in the morning on a bright and blue-skied Saturday at the beginning of March, 1972. A week had gone by since Maisie Cooper had solved the puzzle of her brother Stephen's murder. The grief and the loss were still raw. With distressing frequency, memories of all she had seen and learnt came unbidden into her mind, robbing her of sleep, unsettling her days. She was tormented by regret that she hadn't been present enough in Stephen's life to save him from his cruel fate. She felt sickened by all she had discovered about human depravity. She tried to hold on to her sense of satisfaction at having solved the puzzle – the idea that she had, at least, been an agent of justice.

Yes, she had solved the mystery of his murder at a cost of turning her own life upside down.

Feeling rather sluggish, Maisie dressed in the cold bathroom of Church Lodge, brushing her teeth with pink Eucryl tooth powder, running damp fingers through her short curly hair. Downstairs, in the kitchen, she found the Aga was still slightly warm from the previous evening. She had sat up late with Jack Wingard, a sergeant in the Chichester police, talking over old times and, at rather depressing length, the trials that she would soon be obliged to attend.

'You'll be crucial witness,' he had reminded her.

'I know that,' she had replied, more snappishly than she meant. 'Do you think I'll be criticised for interfering in the investigation?'

'I wouldn't be surprised' Jack had replied, sympathetically. 'You may have "invited censure".'

That had made Maisie cross and put a dampener on things, despite both of them trying not to let it. Maisie had tried to lighten the mood with memories of their shared school days. Finally, Jack had left, driving away in his white Zephyr police car, a look of frustrated regret in his lovely warm eyes.

I wonder, thought Maisie, *if we'll ever get past this.*

Maisie stoked the fire box of the Aga with a good shake of coke from the scuttle, leaving the cast-iron door ajar to draw new flame. She felt conflicted, unable to accept Jack's declarations of affection – of love? – but aware that she was deeply drawn to him as well.

She made herself a cup of double-strength instant Maxwell House coffee, improving it with gold-top milk and demerara sugar, and drank it sitting on a tea towel on the back step, looking out at the orchard garden.

She would soon have to leave her late brother's rented home. She had been given a week's dispensation to stay on by the owner, but that was now over. Her open return ticket for the boat train to Paris was in her handbag. If she left that very night, she could wake the next morning at the Gare du Nord and take the *métro* to her shabby apartment under the mansard roof of a building on the Place des Vosges. Then, back to work in her role as a high-class tour guide. Were it not for the preparations for the trial, she might already have left.

Were it not for Jack, too.

Maisie drained her cup and went back inside. The Aga had drawn up nicely and the room was beginning to warm up. On the table was a copy of the local newspaper. On the front page was a drawing of the celebrated Tudor prayer book, stolen from Chichester cathedral crypt and central to her investigation of Stephen's death.

Maisie shut the firebox and set about the task she had allotted herself – cleaning and dusting the large cold house, determined to leave it better than she found it. She worked for almost two hours: Duraglit wadding on the brass door handles; Vim cleaning powder on the porcelain in the bathroom and kitchen; Vigor liquid on the chequerboard hallway floor. As the nearby church clock chimed twelve, still she hadn't attacked the cobwebs high in the double-height ceiling.

She decided to give herself a break and opened the front door. The sky was a limpid blue. Birds were singing in the trees. Last year's fallen leaves, blackened to mulch, smothered the untidy borders, but snowdrops and dwarf narcissi were poking through, like upright green swords. A rabbit came lolloping out from under the evergreen choisya, sniffed the air, looked left and right, then disappeared beneath the dark, waxy leaves of the rhododendron.

'Well, Maisie,' she told herself out loud. 'I think it's time.'

She put on an old quilted anorak she had found hanging in the hall and went outside, walking briskly, crossing the road to the small car park in front of the pub, the Fox-in-Flight. She paused to look in and was surprised to see Maurice Ryan, her late brother's solicitor, sitting in the window with a young woman wearing a rather ratty Afghan coat. They seemed to be discussing something private. The girl kept glancing round the bar to make sure they weren't overheard.

If that's a client, thought Maisie, *I wonder what sort of legal advice she can possibly be seeking.*

She walked on, past the blacksmith's forge then along a right turn leading to an uninspiring red-brick close, a small U-shaped council estate of eighteen cheap houses surrounding a tatty green. A girl of about fourteen years old was sitting on the solitary bench, her left hand gently moving a pram back and forth. Maisie made her way to the last house on the left, apparently identical to all the others but, for her, imbued with special memories.

For the two weeks she had been back in Framlington, Maisie had avoided even looking at her old family home. It was here that she and Stephen had been raised by loving parents. It was here that she had first tasted tobacco and found the taste disgusting and the after-effects depressing. It was here that she had first made herself sick with alcohol – a particularly ripe local apple scrumpy – and her father Eric had sat with her until she had managed to drink a pint of cold water, then let her sink into grateful sleep. It was also here that her mother Irene had taught her and Stephen their first useful words of French, kick-starting their love of languages.

But those loving parents had died a decade before, in a road-traffic accident in one of the last London pea-souper fogs. And now Stephen was gone, too, and she was alone.

What did looking at the house make her feel? Nothing much. It was just a rather mean council house where some unknown new people were pleased or disappointed to live.

A curtain twitched in an upper window and Maisie turned away, not wanting to have to explain herself, trying not to feel disappointed. There was one other place she couldn't fail to find her parents. For the first time in ten years, she would look at Eric and Irene's shared resting place – a memorial she had avoided for the grief it would undoubtedly cause her to feel.

For a minute or two, in the graveyard at the end of the Church Lane, she was frustrated, unable to locate their stone. She felt a kind of panic that it had been removed for some reason, as a kind of punishment.

Why a 'punishment'? Because she had paid it no attention and because the unconscious mind is a harsh judge.

Yes, she had been miles away in the West Country when they had been run over by a London bus. No, their deaths had been nothing but a stupid accident. But they were dead and she was alive. And, now, Stephen was dead as well, burnt to ashes at the dismal Chichester crematorium.

That was the problem. Stephen and Eric and Irene were gone while she still lived. And what was she going to do with her life, with all of its myriad possibilities? What did she want – the hustle and excitement of Paris or the reassurance of rural Sussex?

And Jack.

At last, she found the grave, beyond the yew tree on the southern edge of the graveyard, a modest upright stone in black basalt. She read the confident inscription, the words seeming hollow, though she knew they were well meant.

Eric and Irene Cooper, their love will endure.

It wasn't fair. Why had they been taken? The world was full of people who didn't deserve to live, but Eric and Irene were not among them.

She sighed.

'It's not fair,' she said aloud.

She left the graveyard and trudged back up Church Lane, barely lifting her feet. She saw Maurice Ryan go past in his rather ostentatious bottle-green Rover car, driving back into town. When she turned in at the drive of Church Lodge, she was delighted to find Jack waiting for her, off duty, looking immensely handsome in jodhpurs and tweed hacking jacket. He smiled and she smiled back.

They didn't kiss or even touch one another – there had been just one moment during the investigation into the murder at Church Lodge when he had taken her in his arms, relieved to know she was safe, angry that she had walked into danger – but the next two hours passed in a blur of laughter at the stables and up across the gallops on the Downs, by turns breathless and delighted. When, at last, their horses were tired, they walked them back to the yard and brushed them down in companionable silence, helped by Bert Close, the elderly stable lad.

Once they had finished, Jack asked Maisie what else she had to do, then added, with sadness in his lovely warm eyes: 'Before you leave for Paris?'

'I haven't gone yet,' she told him. 'Oh, and Charity asked me to drop in.'

Charity Clement was wife and assistant to Maurice Ryan, Stephen's solicitor.

'I'll give you a lift. I have a surprise for you, too.'

'You do?'

'It will give you a kind of resolution, I hope,' he told her.

Maisie wondered what it could possibly be.

'Are you sure I'll like it?' she asked.

'I believe you might,' said Jack, in his steady way.

'Then, yes,' said Maisie, lightly. 'I accept your kind offer of a lift.'